The Gathering

The Gathering Dawn

Sally Laity
&
Dianna Crawford

Tyndale House Publishers, Inc.
Wheaton, Illinois

Library of Congress Cataloging-in-Publication Data

Crawford, Dianna, date
   The gathering dawn / Dianna Crawford and Sally Laity.
      p.   cm. — (Freedom's holy light ; v. 1)
   ISBN 0-8423-1303-6
   1. United States—History—Colonial period, ca. 1600-1775—Fiction.
2. Man-woman relationships—United States—Fiction.   3. Young women—
United States—Fiction.   I. Laity, Sally.   II. Title.   III. Series.
PS3553.R27884G38   1994
813'.54—dc20   93-39984

Printed in the United States of America

99 98 97 96 95 94
6   5   4   3   2

For their infinite patience, encouragement,
and tireless support during the writing of this story,
we lovingly dedicate this book to our families.
May the Lord's richest blessings
be always upon them.

The authors gratefully acknowledge the generous assistance provided by:

Philip Bergen, Librarian
The Boston Historical Society
Boston, Massachusetts

Joan Diana, Head Librarian
Pennsylvania State University, Wilkes-Barre Campus
Lehman, Pennsylvania

Vivian Price and Ruth Knox

These people helped us gather necessary period data and maps, shared their extensive knowledge of various settings, and forwarded biographical information on prominent figures who played a part in colonial America's fascinating history. To you we express our sincere appreciation.

Special thanks to fellow writers and friends:

Debbie Bailey
Jeannie Levig
Sue Rich

Philadelphia, 1770

The three-masted *Helen Doone* bumped gently against the wharf, and the dark current of the Delaware River lapped at the pilings and the sides of the ship. Susannah Harrington's heart raced as she felt the deck shudder beneath her feet. Then the ship settled, its motion becoming nearly imperceptible in the water. *At long last, Philadelphia.*

Her hands, gloved in white kid, gripped the cold railing. She watched in fascination as the dock crew wound the vessel's weighty ropes around the mooring posts. The sweet, refreshing breath of April, so unlike the salty ocean wind, whipped a curl across her face. Impatiently she tucked it inside the brim of her bonnet.

Susannah's eyes scanned the vast number of ships moored along the port, darting briefly after the scores of pigeons fluttering between the vessels and warehouses. Her eyes followed the forest of masts up and beyond, to clouds that billowed like huge sails unfurled against the blue sky.

After a moment, she began to take in the sights just beyond the wharf—tall buildings of brick and stone lining the straight broad streets leading into the bustling city. Here and there sunshine glinted off bright church spires, and off in the distance, the land rose on tree-covered hills.

"Oh, it's not at all the way I imagined!" she said, glancing over her shoulder at her gaunt chaperon, the most proper Reverend Luther Selkirk. "Look at all the people, the buildings! I rather expected it would be small. Quiet. Yet it's just the opposite."

"Hmmph," the reverend muttered as he brushed an errant pigeon feather off his immaculate black sleeve. "The place is overrun with thieves and ne'er-do-wells. The sooner you're away from such an unholy atmosphere and safely at Prince-Town, the better."

Despite his remark, Susannah's pulse quickened with anticipation at the thought of setting foot on this new land. *My new home.* Never in her eighteen years had she dreamed she'd leave the picturesque rolling hills of Ashford, England, and travel to a mysterious, faraway world. Eagerly she searched the faces ashore, hoping against hope that Julia had come to meet her. But she knew her best friend's delicate condition would make such a journey quite impractical.

The gangplank crashed down onto the pier, capturing Susannah's attention. She heard the excited chatter of the other passengers at the rail, most of whom were German peasants. They seemed as eager as she to disembark. Crowding forward, they pushed the bundles and crates containing their meager belongings ahead of them.

Out of the corner of her eye, Susannah saw Reverend Selkirk lift his prominent nose and shake his head. She sighed. He was the only person she'd ever met who could find something to criticize in every situation. Seven oppressive weeks in his company had been enough to last a lifetime. Thank heaven she'd soon be free of the haughty man and his overbearing ways. She hoped her composed expression would not betray the relief she felt at the thought.

"Mind you don't get too near those shiftless miscreants while we wait to depart," he continued, pointing a bony finger toward the ragged passengers standing a few yards away. "Indentures." He spat the word. "I find the very thought of selling oneself into servitude most appalling. Akin to selling one's soul."

The memory of her father's kind voice flashed across Susannah's mind. Clearly, poignantly, she recalled him standing before his small flock encouraging them from a favorite passage in Romans: *Be kindly affectioned one to another with brotherly love.* . . . How unlike this austere, black-clad emissary from the bishop of London her father had been! She could never imagine Luther Selkirk ministering with love or humility, traits that had been such a part of her father, the country parson.

Susannah struggled for a moment against the emptiness that filled her heart at the thought of the sudden tragic loss of her parents just weeks before her departure from England. She swallowed hard. Then, after a calming breath, she looked once again at the quiet, unassuming wayfarers, whose language was foreign to her ear. "Perhaps what these good people have left behind is far worse than what lies ahead," she said, sending an understanding smile toward a hollow-cheeked woman with gnarled fingers. "Perhaps they'll obtain land, in time, and start farms of their own."

Selkirk's narrow face contorted with scorn behind his gold-rimmed spectacles. "Nonetheless, Miss Harrington, as the daughter of clergy yourself, you above anyone should remember your proper station and maintain an adequate distance from them. They're dissenters. Members of some *reformed* German church that has broken away from proper religious order. You must not show in any manner whatsoever that you condone their ignorant following of some radical discipline."

Susannah nodded in acquiescence and turned away. If he only knew how eagerly she looked forward to being near the College of New Jersey, among a veritable *den* of reformers and dissenters! The dream that she might in time be included in discussions of the latest theological arguments had stimulated her far more than Julia's promises of endless parties and beaus. She clutched her fur-trimmed pelisse closer against the brisk spring breeze, and her hand felt the excited beating of her heart.

". . . and see you safely on your way." Reverend Selkirk's

voice intruded once again upon her musings. "Your welfare has been my responsibility these weeks at sea. It has been a constant trial, I must say, keeping all those undesirables away from you during the voyage. Thank Providence my task is near its end. But I must insist that you continue to abide by my wishes—as you promised your brother. I should not have to remind you of that."

The mention of Theodore brought a second pang to Susannah's heart, one of homesickness. She pushed her melancholy aside and forced herself to concentrate on the activities ashore. Shouts of warning carried from the busy fairway edging the wharf as wagon drivers threaded their way through the noisy crowds, while tradesmen and street criers hawked their wares in singsong voices. For the first time, Susannah became aware of the redcoated soldiers who seemed to be everywhere, their wigged heads bobbing and turning beneath their high black hats.

"Now, if you will pardon me," her escort said, "I'd best ensure that my luggage is not inadvertently unloaded with your belongings. *Miss Harrington?*"

At his imperious tone Susannah turned toward him, finding his finger but a hair's breadth from her nose.

"Do not attempt to disembark with the rabble. Remain here until I return for you." With that, he hurried toward two crewmen straining with one of Susannah's hefty trunks.

"Yes, Reverend Selkirk. Indeed, Reverend Selkirk," she said with an exaggerated curtsy once he was out of earshot. "Upon my soul! He must consider me a mere child, unable to lift a finger to take care of myself."

"Only if his wig's on backwards, miss. 'Tis no *child* he's worried about."

Susannah spun around and peered upward.

A rawboned sailor with a head full of wild red curls saluted her from the rigging above. The sight of him had grown familiar during her weeks at sea, although he had never before taken the liberty of speaking to her. He swung down, landing with a thud a few feet away, and his blue eyes shone with a friendly twinkle. "Beggin' your pardon, miss. I mean you no harm. Couldn't help overhearin' His Holiness." A broad grin deepened the character lines alongside his mouth as he bowed. "Able Seaman Yancy Curtis, at your service."

Susannah blushed at the sailor's impertinence and tried unsuccessfully to hide a smile. "Thank you, but the good reverend is seeing to my needs. And I'm afraid he found the wearing of a wig at sea most troublesome, except during services."

Yancy's eyes sparkled with mischief. "But it was grateful we were for such small favors, since the man's sorely in need of one."

Forgetting propriety, Susannah giggled.

The seaman chuckled with her, then his glance veered to the side. "Uh-oh . . . the black saint is comin' this way. I'd best be going, before I bring his wrath down upon your head." He raised an eyebrow and nodded. "Welcome to America, lass. She's a proud new land."

Susannah smiled. "Thank you, Mr. Curtis. God be with you."

With a bold wink the sailor sauntered off toward the bow, stuffing his calloused hands into the pockets of his seaman's jacket and whistling a nonsensical tune. A second crewman joined him with a grin, tossing a glance back in Susannah's direction.

Once they were out of sight, she could not suppress a smile of delight. *Oh, Julia, you're right. It's far, far livelier in America.*

Daniel Haynes reined his horse to a stop in front of Parker's Print Shop on Fourth Street and dismounted. With a small bundle clutched tightly in his hand, he glanced both ways before going inside—a precaution now second nature to him. He took the stone steps in one stride and opened the door.

The cheery tinkle of a bell above the door announced his entry, and the pungent odor of printer's ink greeted him as he stepped into an office barely large enough to house two overburdened desks. He removed his hat.

Seth Parker, peering out from the back room, set down an ink roller and grinned around the pipe he held clenched in his teeth. "Well, well. Daniel Haynes. Back from Boston already?" The balding, heavyset man pulled a rag from the pocket of his leather apron and wiped his hands as he approached. "What'd you bring me this time, boy?"

Daniel handed over the parcel with a smile. "A copy of Bowdoin's narrative of the massacre in Boston. And Revere's engraving of it."

"Well done, my boy. Let's have a look." Setting his pipe down among the clutter on his desk, Parker ripped off the package wrapping and surveyed the items. Slowly he nodded as his thumb and forefinger rubbed the stubble on his jaw. "Yes. Yes! Precisely as I'd hoped. These are just the thing to arouse Philadelphia again. It's been getting harder all the time to convince the merchants to continue the boycott of British goods."

"I thought you'd appreciate them. I leave them in good hands, then."

Parker nodded again. "Well, tell me, lad. What's the latest news? The governor up there still willing to let the Commonwealth bring those murderous redcoats to trial?"

"Looks that way. Puritan tempers are running so high he must figure it's the only way to keep a lid on the situation. But nothing short of shipping that bunch of arrogant soldiers back where they belong will bring peace again. Every ship that comes into the bay gets checked by the Royal Navy, and detachments of redcoats patrol the streets like packs of wolves . . . why, you'd think we were the enemy, instead of His Majesty's *loyal* subjects."

"It's not much better here. But at least most of their interference is still limited to the waterfront."

Dan shrugged. "Don't count on it staying down there for long. The king's men are getting bolder all the time." He turned to go. "Well, guess I'll be off. I've a few more *special* deliveries to make before I'm through."

"Wait!" Parker called after him. "Hank couldn't come in to

work today. Could I impose on you to take the wagon to meet the *Helen Doone* in his place? She's docking at this very moment, and I'd like to get started on this right away." He wagged the inflammatory engraving in his hand.

"Sure. Glad to."

"Our two sailor friends, Yancy Curtis and Dunk Hohenleitner, are planning to smuggle in some printing paper in a couple of clothing trunks." His pudgy cheeks dimpled with mirth, and he chuckled. "They'll be dressed as . . . ladies."

Daniel burst into laughter at the thought. "Yancy and Dunk, you say? Wouldn't want to miss the chance of seeing *that* performance." Still grinning broadly, he left by the side door, where Parker's wagon sat ready.

"Come along, Miss Harrington." The reverend's grating voice sounded from just behind her. "Your trunks have been unloaded, and I want to make certain those uncouth customs officials do not disturb the contents. A distasteful, ill-bred lot, they are."

Eagerly Susannah picked up her satchel and followed him down the gangway to the wharf, where a customs agent was rooting through a crudely fashioned chest belonging to one of the German unfortunates.

Standing guard behind the ruthless inspector, several soldiers swung their gazes to Susannah as she approached. None spoke, but their roving eyes and slack-jawed grins gave her such a feeling of uneasiness that, for once, she truly felt the need of her guardian's protection. Stepping closer to him, she looked up to see if the reverend had also noticed the soldiers' unseemly conduct.

He obviously had not. Mouth open, Reverend Selkirk stared with horror at the pillaging hands of the official.

Leaving the foreigner to repack his own pitiful belongings, the agent dismissed him with a nod, then dusted his hands pointedly and walked toward Susannah's trunks.

"My good man." Luther Selkirk raised his eyebrows with disdain. "Surely you cannot subject a young woman of obvious character to such treatment. I can assure you she is above reproach. Kindly permit us to continue on our way without further hindrance."

The odious agent regarded the reverend with a half-smirk. Then, with a quick glance at Susannah, he motioned for her luggage to pass intact.

Following behind Susannah and her escort, workers carried her heavy trunks from the customs area.

"This will do," Selkirk said with a wave of his arm as they reached the edge of the wharf. "You can set them here." Then with a curt nod, he turned to Susannah. "Well, Miss Harrington, I must see you safely to an inn and arrange your further transport. Remain beside your chests while I secure a wagon." Withdrawing his gold watch, he flicked open the lid and peered quickly at it. With a huff, he snapped it shut and tucked it back inside his fob pocket. "I shan't be long."

"Thank you, Reverend," she said with a thin smile. She watched him disappear into the throng milling about on the street. Then, with a final glance toward the *Helen Doone,* she turned her back on the great vessel and her memories of the confining month and fortnight aboard ship.

"Surely, sir," came an oddly shrill voice from the customs area, and she turned curiously. Two rather tall women elegantly dressed in bright French brocades were pleading with the official. "You must agree it's not necessary to open *everyone's* trunks. It would be most distressing to have all our frilly unmentionables soiled by such rough handling."

How curious, Susannah thought. *Besides the reverend and myself, the only passengers I knew of were the German indentures. I'm certain I would have noticed those ladies before now.* Still, there did seem to be something familiar about them . . . but since their backs were to her, she couldn't decide what it was.

The agent's brow was pinched as he eyed them steadily. Then with an impatient wave, he motioned for the workmen to clear the area of their luggage.

Suddenly a scuffle erupted off to one side. "There he is!" shouted a soldier. "That's the one! Stop him!"

Susannah swung around just in time to see a pair of redcoated officers shove a man in ragged clothing roughly to the ground, where they held him down and struck him brutally several times. Horrified, she took several steps backward.

"What happened?" came an angry shout as a crowd of onlookers gathered.

"What did he do?" demanded another voice.

Ignoring the questioning people, the soldiers continued their attack. Two of their comrades kicked the man with their jackboots, drawing a painful cry with each blow.

"There," said one officer, with a final savage thrust. "He won't likely be of a mind to try *that* again. Let's take him in."

Fear and repulsion surged through Susannah. Unable to witness any more of the scene, she turned her head. Her heart pounded in her throat. Was this a sample of life in America— customs agents rifling through one's personal belongings with complete disregard? Soldiers inflicting brutal attacks on passersby?

There had to be a safer place to await Reverend Selkirk's return. Gathering her skirt in one hand, she picked up her small bag and hurriedly made her way along the broad street edging the wharf to where the crowd thinned to a few strolling people. There, still within sight of her trunks, she stopped. She set her satchel at her feet and straightened to keep watch over her things.

The delicious aroma of fresh-baked bread wafted on the air. She breathed in the welcome homey fragrance of a riverfront baking house, which supplied the seagoing vessels. Her stomach growled. In the distance a tower clock chimed three, and Susannah realized it had been hours since she had last eaten.

Suddenly she noticed the approaching staccato sound of hooves striking cobblestone as a horse-drawn wagon pulled up to the wharf and stopped.

The driver, a dark-eyed young man who appeared to be in his mid-twenties, glanced in her direction and studied her with interest as he laid the reins aside. With one hand on the seat, he propelled himself smoothly to the ground, his strong muscles straining against a fitted tan frock coat. He walked around to the front and stood beside the sturdy horse as he peered toward the ship.

With a cautious glance to make sure her escort was nowhere nearby to disapprove, Susannah slid her gaze casually back in the direction of the new arrival.

He nudged the front of his buff three-cornered hat back, displaying softly waving chestnut hair tied into a short queue at the nape of his neck. As he gently stroked the roan's smooth muzzle, he scanned the crowd, and tiny glimmers of light reflected in the brown eyes above his clean-shaven face. There seemed a certain confidence in his bearing, an air of trustworthiness and honesty about him—all of which was made even more notable by the fact that he was one of the most handsome men Susannah had ever seen.

Susannah smiled to herself. If the good Reverend Selkirk could read her thoughts at this moment, she would *never* be rid of him!

Dan returned his gaze to the slender young woman in emerald he had passed a moment ago. He had thought it unusual to see someone so lovely standing alone in the rough dock area and decided she must be waiting for someone.

Then the curved bill of her bonnet lifted to reveal a delicate oval face, and her large wide-set eyes caught his. He smiled to himself as a flush of pink rose to her cheeks. She looked down, and a golden brown curl fell out of place with the movement. He watched her bite her full lower lip, then brush the strand aside with slender gloved fingers. The plume on her hat danced gently in the breeze.

He stared for a long moment, enjoying the bright picture she made against the last dismal grays and browns left behind by winter. *Surely she must have a guardian somewhere,* he mused, idly scanning the milling crowd. Then he shook his head, a slight smile playing across his face. *Ah well, my boy, best keep to your purpose for being here.*

Reluctantly, he forced his attention toward the *Helen Doone.*

Where were Yancy and Dunk anyway? Would he recognize them in women's costumes? But with no trouble at all, he spied them. Grinning, he shook his head and chuckled, then started their way.

Through a veil of lashes, Susannah saw the young man leave his wagon and walk onto the quay. She rose on tiptoe, straining to see just whom he might be meeting. Incredibly, he waved at the two brightly dressed women.

Catching sight of him, the ladies approached his wagon with a strange, exaggerated walk as dockworkers followed toting a pair of heavy trunks.

Susannah tilted her head to one side. Who *were* those women? She studied them for a moment. Then the sight of a wild red curl poking out from beneath one outrageous wig made her catch her breath. *Absurd.* It couldn't be that bold Yancy Curtis—could it? Her eyes narrowed at the other woman. That one looked familiar as well, despite the overabundance of lip rouge and rice powder. Whatever would precipitate such an elaborate charade?

Daniel bowed gallantly, struggling to keep a straight face. With a flourish, he reached out a hand. "Ladies . . . your carriage awaits. Please allow me to assist you."

Yancy Curtis, reaching the wagon, fluttered his lashes dramatically and tittered into a peacock-blue glove. "Why, thank you, young man. You're most kind." With a demure smile at his shipmate, he accepted Daniel's assistance, while the workers heaved the heavy chests into the back. Then as Dan helped Dunk up onto the seat, Yancy reached behind and gave a triumphant pat to one of the trunks.

Susannah's hand flew to her lips. *Smugglers!* She had heard of the problems caused by these Americans with their illegal trafficking on the high seas, bribing officials and smuggling contraband ashore into hidden caves. Such scandalous behavior . . . such lawlessness! She should inform the authorities. . . . Hesitantly, Susannah raised an arm as she tried to spot a customs agent or a soldier near enough to summon. In her search, her gaze swept again to the wagon and locked onto the driver's piercing sable eyes. Something about him made it impossible for her to look away, and she found herself staring.

With the hint of a frown and a desperate expression, he moved his head back and forth ever so slightly in a silent plea.

Susannah felt her resolve falter. Lips pressed together, she studied the young man. He didn't look like a dangerous sort. But . . .

Her heart fluttered in uncertainty.

Then she remembered the savage attack of the soldiers against the ragged man on the wharf only moments before. How could she be the cause of more violence, of yet another frightening scene? After all, she rationalized, the captain surely must have recognized two of his own crew leaving the ship dressed as women. He was, in fact, standing at the bottom of the gangplank. Why, then, had he not turned them in to the soldiers? Was he involved as well? A criminal? He couldn't be. He'd been such an upstanding gentleman during the entire voyage. Perhaps there was something going on that out of necessity must be kept secret.

Lowering her arm, she drew a slow breath and relaxed.

Dan saw the change in her expression and inhaled with relief at the knowledge that she wouldn't betray them. Clucking his tongue, he snapped the reins smartly on the horse's back. The wagon started with a jerk, rumbling across the stone pavement. He thumbed his hat at the young lady and smiled his gratitude as they pulled away.

Yancy nudged him. "Watch out!"

"Oh. Sorry." Dan grimaced, giving a sharp yank on the reins. By inches he missed colliding with a pair of inebriated patrons who had obviously emerged from a disreputable tavern down the street.

Staggering out of the way, one shook a fist at Dan. The other raised the bottle in his hand and bellowed a loud oath as they sauntered at a list toward the dock.

As the wagon neared the corner, Daniel couldn't resist

taking one last look at the emerald maiden. The drunks, he noticed with alarm, were approaching her.

The man with the bottle raised it to his mouth for a gulp, then bowed clumsily.

The young lady stiffened and started to back away, shaking her head as the second man took hold of her arm. Almost stumbling over her satchel, she struggled to pry loose from his grip and free herself.

Dan began turning the horse. "We have to go back."

"What? Are you daft, man?" Yancy tried to grab the reins out of Daniel's hands. "We need to put distance between us and the king's men."

"*Ja,*" agreed Dunk. "We got to hurry."

Dan elbowed the sailor away and motioned toward the dock. "The girl back on the corner. She knew what we were doing, and she kept quiet. Now *she's* in trouble."

Dunk looked over his shoulder toward Susannah and shook his hand. "*Nein.* We must go."

"Look, mate." A note of urgency rose in Yancy's voice. "If it was any other time, understand? We've trouble of our own. Besides, her escort's a puffed-up lordy bishop. He lets nary a man within shoutin' distance of her. He'll be back any second. He'll make short order of them."

"Yeah? Well, there's no one with her now." Tossing the reins at Yancy, Dan jumped from the moving wagon. "I've got to help her."

2

"Please," Susannah said sternly, belying the rising alarm she felt as the two disheveled louts accosted her. "Go away. Leave me alone."

The taller of the two, a bearded and sunken-cheeked man, cocked his head. "D'ya' hear that? The li'l gal said please. Polite, ain't she?" His beady eyes raked over her.

"Purty, too," slurred his chum, leaning closer to her.

Fear constricted Susannah's chest as her nostrils filled with the stench of liquor. She shuddered and took a step backward. Looking past them, she searched frantically, fruitlessly, for Reverend Selkirk.

Shuffling even closer, one reached out a grimy hand and fingered her satin bonnet tie. "An' she shore wears purty clothes."

Panicked, Susannah swatted at the offensive intruder and tried to turn away.

His long bony fingers clamped onto her arm.

She gasped in terror and froze.

The sound of running footsteps barely registered in her mind until she heard a voice, deep and commanding, at her side.

"Let her go!"

Susannah turned and, looking up, met familiar eyes of warm sable.

Daniel dipped his head slightly to Susannah, then shot a

piercing glance to the miscreant who still had hold of her sleeve. With one hand, the young man seized the culprit's shirtfront near the throat and jerked the man upward. "I said, *unhand* her."

With a disgusted grimace, the man suddenly let go.

Susannah nearly lost her balance. She felt a strong arm wrap securely around her shoulders, and unconsciously she swayed against her rescuer. Her eyes darted from him to the vile assailants.

The young man took a protective stance between Susannah and the disreputable tipplers, his gaze never wavering. He tightened his hold. She felt fragile, tucked in his arm. The top of her head barely reached his shoulder.

Scowling, the skinny drunk adjusted his tattered jacket with a filthy hand. "We was just keepin' the li'l lady comp'ny."

"Yeah," his squat crony joined in. "Her bein' by herself, an' all."

"Well, she has company now. Off with you, before I call a couple of lobsterbacks."

The pair exchanged dark looks.

Stiffening defiantly, the gangly one glared at Daniel before peering toward the soldiers lounging outside the customs house. He slumped, his resolve sinking as he assessed the situation.

"Aw, come on, Sam," his partner said with a nudge. "I'm thirsty anyways."

The man's bleary eyes blazed in a last halfhearted challenge. Then, his face twisting into a grimace, he shrugged and turned away.

After the two reeled back toward the tavern they'd just exited, Daniel's attention shifted to the lovely lady beside him. "Are you all right?" he asked softly. He lowered his arm and let her go, feeling a sudden emptiness as she moved away.

With a shaky smile, Susannah nodded up at him.

He was drawn at once into her eyes. Gray-blue, like the summer sky at dusk, something shimmered in their depths that stirred all the yearnings of his soul. For one fleeting second, unfamiliar longings surfaced within him, and he couldn't breathe. Then his gaze fixed on a tiny cleft in her chin. It gave her an appearance of vulnerability.

She bravely straightened her shoulders, and he repressed a smile. "That was a poor welcome to America, miss. This area is far too dangerous for someone like you to remain alone."

"My chaperon merely stepped away to secure a carriage." Even as she spoke she rose to tiptoe and searched the distance, then favored him again with her gaze. "He should return in short order."

Dan inclined his head to one side, enthralled for the first time by the beauty and lilt of her English accent. Her voice was musical, her inflections softer than the hard, clipped cadences uttered by the soldiers. He waited with delight to hear her speak again.

"How ever can I thank you?" she said. "I must say, it was most distressing being accosted by two such unpleasant sorts. I was truly frightened."

"I . . . merely repaid a debt, miss."

"Oh yes." A wry smile spread across her lips. "You were with the two, shall we say, *unusual* ladies in the wagon. I came quite near to summoning the authorities, you know."

He gave a nod. "But you didn't. And it was right that you didn't. That's why I had to help you."

A surprising joy filled Susannah at the warmth in his expression. She found her eyes wanting to linger on the fine planes of his face, a temptation she found most disconcerting. Abashed by it, she quickly looked down, and a loose golden brown curl grazed her cheek. She tried to tuck it away unobtrusively as she moistened her dry lips and observed the coating of dust on the toes of her high-top traveling shoes.

"Will you be settling in Philadelphia, miss?" Susannah looked up at him and gazed curiously at his smile. Was he . . . *hoping?*

"Why, n-no," Susannah stammered, caught in the rich brown of his eyes. "I'm but passing through. On my way to stay with a friend. At Prince-Town," she added. Feeling sudden shame at being so forward, she felt her face flame.

"Princeton," he repeated, a note of disappointment in his voice. "Well, what do you know? I spent some time at the college there myself, studying for the ministry. My duties as postrider on occasion take me through there, so perhaps our paths may cross again." Removing his hat, he clutched it in one hand as he ran his fingers quickly through his hair. "Perhaps by that time I'll be able to arrange a more proper introduction for us. I'm Daniel Haynes, by the way. Might I have the pleasure of asking your name?"

"Upon my soul!" Black cape flaring like raven wings, Luther Selkirk stomped up between them, and his clerical hat blocked Susannah's vision. "If I but leave for the slightest moment, young lady, you wander off, forcing me to search you out. Now I find you boldly conversing with a total stranger despite my warnings regarding the perils of such conduct. It is singularly disgraceful."

"Please, Reverend," she said. "You misunderstand. This young man was kind enough to save me from being accosted by—"

"Oh?" His sparse brows lifted insidiously and almost took flight. "Well, I can see that you require constant watching. Theodore proclaims such deep love for you. But why he ever permitted you to come on your own to this uncivilized colony is a puzzlement to me."

"Excuse me, sir," Dan said. "The young lady was in need of assistance, and I but came to her aid."

"Quite." Lifting his nose, Reverend Selkirk peered over it at Daniel Haynes. "A vulgar territory, this. Perfect for the blasphemous peasants who settle here." Dismissing the young man with a curt nod, the minister turned to Susannah. "I've hired a wagon, at long last, and had your trunks loaded, despite having to deal with a rude driver. Come along, come along."

Pompous oaf, thought Daniel, striding away. *Pity she has to travel with such a stuffed shirt. I should have asked her name sooner. Oh well, . . . a girl that enchanting shouldn't be too hard to find in Princeton.* Unable to resist a final look at the maiden in green, he turned. She graced him with a shy smile as she hurried away. He tipped his hat and turned the corner.

Susannah composed her features once again and accepted Reverend Selkirk's proffered hand as he helped her onto the wagon. The bumpy ride over the cobblestone streets seemed to last forever, especially with her chaperon recanting another endless list of the colony's shortcomings in cadence with the clopping hoofbeats of the horses.

"You must remember your place, Miss Harrington," he continued in a drone. "These uncouth barbarians are swift to seize whatever they can and make off with it. A gently born person such as yourself must refrain from the merest occasion to associate with them."

"Yes, Reverend. I shall be on my guard."

"Once I see to your lodging, I'll arrange the shipping of your trunks." He motioned toward a two-story wooden building they were about to pass. "This is where you will catch the next available coach to Prince-Town. I purposely asked directions to an inn within walking distance of it."

Moments later, the driver stopped in front of a whitewashed brick establishment. The minister climbed down and helped Susannah alight with her satchel.

Susannah noticed a painted sign above the wooden door announcing the name of the inn as the Blue Horn. She followed her escort inside, where candles burned brightly from sconces on the walls of the narrow room, dispelling the indoor gloom.

The reverend rang the small bell on the counter and impatiently checked his pocket watch.

"May I help you?" said a portly, balding man who approached the desk from the other side.

"Yes," Selkirk said. "I'd like to inquire when the next stage departs for Prince-Town. The young lady will require lodging until that time."

"At six tomorrow morning," the man answered. "Promptly."

"Good. Good. I shall pay you, then, in advance." Reverend Selkirk signed the register. Then, from Susannah's traveling monies, which he carried for safekeeping, he withdrew the required fee and handed it to the proprietor. With a hesitant expression, he turned the remainder over to her.

"She will, as well, require breakfast sent to her in her room on the morrow." He counted out several coins from his own funds and laid them on the counter. "This should be sufficient to cover that expense."

"Yes, sir. Thank you, sir." The innkeeper nodded to Susannah. "We trust you will find the accommodations to your liking, miss. Do not hesitate to call if we might be of further service."

She smiled. "Thank you."

The man whacked the bell twice and turned as a young boy appeared. "Take the lady's bags to room 8."

Her chaperon turned to her. "Well, Miss Harrington, once I see to your supper and then escort you to your room, I shall be off. The ship sails with the tide."

Susannah's heart sank, and her appetite vanished. She would have to endure yet another hour in his presence. She emitted a sigh, then nodded in acquiescence as he ushered her to the common room, where other travelers were chatting and visiting among themselves over the evening meal.

Dan hastened toward the Blue Horn in the waning light of late afternoon. This had to be the place where the fetching young woman would be staying to catch the morning stage wagon. He had tried all the others in the vicinity. He bounded up the shallow steps and went inside. Noting the rich emerald cape hanging on a peg just outside the common room, he smiled and plunked his hat on the one next to it. His rapid heartbeat belied the nonchalance he hoped to effect as he strolled into the common room.

The young lass and her traveling companion occupied a

table near the window. When her gray-blue eyes turned his way, Dan managed a look as surprised as hers and waved an offhanded greeting.

"Why, it's Mr. Haynes," he heard her say.

He tipped his head politely as her proper guardian turned a cursory glance in his direction.

"Perhaps he might be of a mind to join us," she continued. "He was so gallant on the quay on my behalf; I should like very much to thank him properly."

The rail-thin man in black lowered his pointed nose just enough to glare over his spectacles at Dan. "I think not. The necessity of our seeking sustenance in this common place should not precipitate socializing with its patrons."

Dan's hopes lay dashed, but he drew some comfort from the crestfallen expression on the face of the lovely English lass. He tossed her a resigned grin and tugged out a chair at an adjacent table where, behind her companion's back, he could feast his eyes on her. Surely in such an advantageous position he would at least be able to overhear her name, if nothing else.

She gave the barest indication of a smile, then lowered her gaze as plates of steaming, succulent beef and roasted potatoes were set before them. "Why, this looks delicious. I never expected such royal fare."

The older man bent his head and sniffed suspiciously. "It will suffice. We can but pray that God will shield us from the possible ill it might cause."

Dan snickered to himself at the elaborate grace the minister offered, noticing that the lass, too, had to subdue a smile at its conclusion. When his own supper was delivered moments later, he gave a silent prayer of thanks and forked some meat into his mouth.

The girl glanced fleetingly at him from time to time, and he decided to take it as a sign that she found him at least somewhat attractive. Toward the end of the meal he became almost certain of it.

"I shall be glad when at last I reach Prince-Town," the girl said, her voice carrying clearly to his ears. "I hear I shan't be far from the college." Her cheeks flushed above the muted emerald of her fashionable traveling costume as she looked his way, then quickly averted her gaze.

"Hmmph. Just remember your upbringing, young lady. That institution is filled with *Presbyterians.*" The man made the word sound blasphemous. "Take care that you follow the proper precepts you've been taught. Attend services nowhere but at the holy English church."

"Of course." She started to lift a slice of bread to her lips, then paused. "But don't you ever wonder about the new concepts discussed in religious circles of late?"

Her question seemed sincere, and Dan listened intently, his interest piqued.

The minister's fork clattered to his plate. "Young lady! I'm aghast that you'd give such heresies even the slightest credibility. If I believed for one moment that you were not secure in your own doctrines, I should purchase your return fare to Britain at once. Do you hear? At once!"

Dan caught the renewed tinge of rose that brightened her cheeks as she answered, "You needn't trouble yourself over that, Reverend; I assure you I most certainly intend to seek out the local Anglican church. I just thought—"

A wave of the man's bony hand cut her off. "Nonsense. A young woman of your station shouldn't ponder such weighty matters as theology. Your duty is to accept without question the truths presented by the more learned ministers of the church and abide by them."

"Yes, Your Grace." Toying with the last potato on her plate, she slipped a mollified glance at Dan.

He hoped the smile he gave her indicated his understanding of that sort of insufferably rigid authority. In a bold moment, he pointed toward the minister's back with his thumb. "Prince-Town?" he mouthed.

She moistened her lips in supreme innocence. "I do hope the weather allows you a pleasant voyage to North Carolina this eve, Reverend." Her eyes sparking with mischief, she appeared about to laugh. Instead, she coughed delicately into her napkin.

Dan tried not to look at her as his spirits soared. Surely there was some hope of talking with her after the stuffed shirt left. He might learn her name. . . .

The grating voice broke into his musings. "I did not see any troublesome weather on the horizon."

"Even so, I'm sure you must have preparations to make. Please do not let me detain you. I feel quite secure here at the inn," she offered hopefully. Would the man *ever* leave?

"Quite. But I shan't depart until I've seen you safely locked inside your room for the night. Then I shall allow that I have done all that is prudent and proper to ensure your safe passage from Britain." He wiped his mouth and stood. "Come along."

The lass's fragile shoulders slumped. "But I—"

"Do not dawdle. I haven't time to waste." His dark garment billowed as he turned and strode off.

Dejectedly, the lass rose and followed, barely pausing to offer a self-conscious smile at Dan as she passed. "Good evening, Mr. Haynes," she whispered. "Thank you again for coming to my aid." Then woodenly she retrieved her cloak at the doorway and followed the minister toward the stairs.

Dan watched after her until she was gone from his sight. He felt joyful, yet defeated. She had all but invited him to call upon her in Princeton, but he still hadn't discovered her name. And by the time she awakened on the morrow, he'd be halfway to New York.

When Reverend Selkirk stopped abruptly outside the door to room 8, Susannah nearly bumped into him. "Well, Miss Harrington, I'm sure you'll agree that my duties toward you have been fulfilled to the best of my ability."

"Yes, and it has been most . . . informative, traveling under your watchcare. I certainly thank you for your efforts on my behalf. Please do not trouble yourself by worrying further about my welfare. I shall be in God's hands."

He cleared his throat. "Ah yes. Well, my ship sails at eventide for that rebellious Carolina colony, so I must hasten away. I must caution you to remain in your room until morning. You will find no necessity to wander about this establishment on your own. Remember to keep your door bolted at all times."

With a docile smile, Susannah extended her hand. "Go with God, Reverend."

He took her fingers with brief curtness. "And you likewise. I shall post a letter to your brother of your safe arrival in Philadelphia." With a nod he was gone.

Susannah could not help but feel sorry for the Anglican parishes in North Carolina, which Luther Selkirk had been ordered by the bishop to *straighten out.*

In the privacy of her room, Susannah truly relaxed for the first time since she'd boarded the *Helen Doone.* She had found the cramped quarters of the ship to be stifling and the rigid views of her chaperon even more so. With a sigh, she draped her cape over the bedpost and crossed to the fireplace against the opposite wall. Holding her hands out before the bright flames, she glanced around the sparsely furnished room. The big mahogany bed looked comfortable.

Susannah turned away from the luminous blaze and went to the commode. Pouring some cool water from the pitcher into the basin, she undressed and washed as best she could, wishing it were a huge tub filled with steaming water. That would be the first thing she would request once she reached Julia's, she decided. Removing a night shift from the satchel, she put it on and wrapped a shawl about herself, then drew a chair closer to the warmth of the fire and sat down to read Julia's chatty letter for the hundredth time. She knew it by heart and could hear in her mind her friend's expressive voice:

Oh, do hurry, dearest Susannah. We shall have ever so much fun.

Julia had never been one to sit calmly, embroidery in hand, and converse with cool reserve. The red-gold curls she had ceased trying to control years ago would dance as her hands flew in excited accompaniment to her words. Smiling at the lively images of Julia, Susannah read on:

> *Be assured we have ample room for you to stay with us. Our apartment is quite close to Nassau Hall, where Robert takes his studies. I shall introduce you to all his classmates. I am certain we shall give grand parties, so you shall have no end of handsome beaus seeking your attention. Oh, I cannot bear to be without you a moment longer. I have not as yet informed Papa of the tiny life that is to grace our home. Soon enough I must face his displeasure, but I am certain he will come to accept our new addition with love, and then, perhaps, give his blessing to our marriage.*
>
> *Oh, please, dearest friend, come with all haste. If funds are a problem, I am certain I could persuade Papa to advance the money. Even vexed at me as he is, he would never deprive me of your company. I shall admit I have some misgivings about what I must endure when my time is upon me. It will be such a comfort having you here to give of your strength and care. I am waiting most anxiously.*

"Just a little while longer, Julia. I'm almost there." Rising with a smile, Susannah folded the letter and crossed to her satchel near the bed, where she tucked it safely inside. She turned down the quilts and knelt to recite her evening prayers.

"And please bless Teddy. I miss him so," she added at the conclusion, trying not to let her thoughts dwell on the fact that she and her brother were now all that remained of her once-happy family.

The memory of their parting on the London wharf leaped into mind, and Susannah could almost feel Theodore's just-shaved cheek against hers as she fought against sudden tears. He had pushed her gently away, and she had gazed up into clear blue eyes so like her own. "Mind you don't trifle with the sailors," he had said, trying to keep the moment light. Susannah's laugh caught on a sob, and she stared hard, trying to hold the moment forever in her heart. With one last hug, they had both bid farewell to all that was familiar, to begin another life that was altogether new.

"Do please help him to settle into his studies at Oxford," she continued in her prayer. "Father would have been proud to know he decided to follow his footsteps after all." Brushing away an unbidden tear, she rose and climbed between the feather ticks.

The events of the day teased her mind, running together in a blur: the unexpected size of the bustling red-brick city called Philadelphia, the rude customs agent, the unprincipled soldiers and their violent attack on the wharf, her own near assault—and, of course, the accusations of the stiffly proper Reverend Selkirk.

So many dreadful things had befallen her since her arrival. Had she perhaps made the wrong decision in journeying to the New World after all? In all likelihood she would never again see her own beloved England. Now that her parents' home and all their worldly belongings had been sold to finance her trip and Ted's schooling, there'd be no going back—ever. The finality of that thought brought a twinge to her heart.

Nestling into her pillow, Susannah gradually became aware of the silence surrounding her. Weeks aboard ship had accustomed her to the vast array of creakings and groanings made by a great vessel as it sliced its way across the vast ocean. She'd grown used to the snap of the sails in the wind and the hum of the rigging. She'd even learned to enjoy the rocking motion, which, though it had made her queasy during the first day at sea, had afterward lulled her to sleep as though she were a babe in a cradle. Now she missed the endless motion, and sleep escaped her.

She turned over onto her side. Would tomorrow ever come?

Then her heart recalled the better side of the day. The overbearing Luther Selkirk was now on his way to North Carolina. Tomorrow night she would again embrace her dearest friend in all the world. And for the moment, she was safe in the inn. Then, as if she'd been saving the best for last, she allowed the memory of rich brown eyes to wash over her. Daniel Haynes. The warmth of his voice had allayed her fears during those distressing moments on the dock. She felt once more the strong arm that had pulled her within its protection, as if he had been a knight of the realm. Daniel Haynes. Postrider.

Suddenly Susannah bolted upright, her cheeks flaming. Why, downstairs she had acted shamelessly. Smiling at that young man as if they were true acquaintances, speaking in tones that he would be certain to hear, practically giving him directions to her future place of residence. Whatever had happened to her sense of propriety? He must think her a hussy! Certainly a well-bred maiden of the Colonies would never take such leave of her senses.

Mortified, she lay back and pulled the quilts over her head. But, she reflected momentarily as the heat in her face subsided, he had to be the most handsome young man she had ever seen.

She folded the covers back into proper order, and a smile settled softly on her lips.

3

In his dismal room overlooking Pembroke College, Theodore Harrington heard the bells of Oxford calling him to evening chapel. The tall church spire across spacious Tom Quad reflected bright moonlight against his window. Ted rose, and, as he did so, stumbled over the books on the floor. With a swift kick he sent them flying. "This place is like a cell. How will I ever last till I take my holy orders and get out of here?" Raking his dark brown hair into place, he appeased himself by imagining the possibilities of obtaining an assignment to a post in which several generous patrons resided. He gave his reflection in the mirror a half-smirk.

A knock sounded on the door.

Ted bounded across the room and opened it. "Alex. Come in." Motioning for his blond friend to be seated on the narrow cot jammed against the wall, he smoothed wrinkles from a shirt he'd discarded earlier, then pulled it on.

With a flair, Alex Fontaine lowered his lanky form onto the cot. "We're meeting Granville and Bennett for chapel. Naturally, I assumed you'd be ready."

"I am, I am. Almost. Just have to find my other boot." Ted got down on all fours and felt about under the simple furnishings. He shoved a chair piled with clothing aside in disgust. "It's around here someplace."

"Well, don't get into a lather over it, old boy. I'll go by their rooms and get them while you finish. We'll call back for you."

Rising, he strode to the door, then turned. "Oh. Nearly forgot. I've a letter for you." He pulled an envelope from an inside pocket of his maroon velvet cloak. "Postmaster says it's been lying around the college post office. Don't you ever go for your mail?"

"What's the point? Everyone who could possibly send condolences has already done so. And there's not been time for Sue to send word from America. Who's left?" He pulled his boot from beneath the cot and took a seat to tug it on.

"I'm sure I wouldn't know, old chap." Tossing the letter onto the cluttered study table, Alex opened the door and stepped out, then peered back around it. "My father and I wage a constant war by post over my allowance. He hasn't the slightest notion that 'entertainment' costs money." With a loud laugh, he closed the door behind himself. His footsteps grew faint as he walked down the hall.

Chuckling, Ted righted the fallen chair and gathered the books from all the places they'd landed. He stacked them on the table, picked up the letter, and tore it open.

"Teddy . . . ," it began. Only one childhood friend from their village and Susannah ever called him that, and the writing was not in Susannah's hand. He checked the postal stamp. Ashford, as he'd surmised. It had to be from Brent Walters. He glanced at the signature on back to be certain, then turned the creased paper over and scanned the contents:

It was most depressing watching the last of your parents' earthly goods being disposed of over the last fortnight. The town seems a different place since their untimely passing. I know they would be pleased to know you have begun studies for the ministry. I do hope you are faring well at Oxford, Teddy, and that all will go well for you there.

No doubt it will take time for us to adjust to the new people next door. I shall not look at the old place without thought of jollier times. I have only just met the young lady of the family, but I must say she is quite fetching. I must try to arrange a few accidental meetings with her. One never knows what might come of that sort of thing.

The reason I have taken pen in hand is that Sir Tinsdale came by our tavern today with the most distressing news from America. He has received notice that his daughter died on the childbed. The poor bloke is prostrate with grief. I cannot believe it myself—our own flighty Julia gone forever. We spent such glorious times together, remember? Whenever she could escape the manor. Always out for a merry time, she was. I shall miss her sorely.

When I learned from Sir Tinsdale that your sister had made plans to journey to America to be with Julia, I thought I should contact you with all haste, in the hope that her trip would not be undertaken after all. I should hate for Susannah to sail to the other side of the world for naught. I pray this reaches you before her departure. Please give Susannah my best when you see her. All of us who knew Julia share a deep sorrow.

With best regards, I remain your friend,
Brent W.

Ted's mouth dropped open, and he let the correspondence slip from his fingers to the floor as he mulled over the shocking news. Julia? Vibrant, healthy Julia, dead? How could it be? He kneaded the hollows of his cheeks absently in thought. Had Susannah arrived as yet and learned of her death? What would become of her?

Ted had been hard-pressed to spare enough of his paltry inheritance for the expense of his sister's journey. The funds that remained would scarce cover his own necessities until he was ordained, even with the added monies from Sir Tinsdale's sale of his parents' household possessions. This was one fine mess.

"Say, Ted," called Alex, with a tap on the door. "Ready yet, old boy?"

"Hm?" Ted's thoughts returned abruptly to the present.

Chapel. "Be right there." Grabbing his cloak, he tossed it around his shoulders, then picked up his prayer book and wrenched open the door. Things would work out, somehow, of course. Certainly Julia's husband would see to Susannah's welfare. He would just say an extra prayer at vespers this evening for his sister. He smiled wanly at the threesome of cheery faces in the dismal hall. "Off to chapel it is, then."

"I say, lads." Giles Bennet placed one hand on Ted's shoulder and the other on Alex's. "I've come up with a better plan. A jolly good one, too, I might add."

Against his better judgment, Ted glanced at his friend, then at Alex. He did consider the tiresome dronings of evening chapel a dreary way to end a day. He arched a quizzical eyebrow at Giles.

"'Tis a rare and glorious night. The thought of wasting it inside a stuffy church is a bit much, is it not?"

"Right," Frederick Granville said with a firm nod. His hazel eyes twinkled as a slow grin spread mischievously across his face, softening his angular jaw. "Today's post brought my allowance. Let's go the long way round. Past the King's Head." His straight tawny brows rose in question, nearly touching his sandy hair.

Alex eyed Ted and nudged him in the ribs. "You do look a bit off, old boy. Not bad news in that letter, I hope."

"I'm afraid it was, actually." Ted expelled a pent-up breath. "But there's nothing can be done about it."

"Well then," his best friend answered, "perhaps a pint or two is in order. To take your mind off it."

Ted rubbed a hand over his jaw in thought and cocked his head. "It might help at that." Leaning down, he set his prayer book on the floor before his door and gave it a brisk tap. It slid neatly under the crack and into the room.

Frederick grinned. "Lead on, then." With a flourish, he motioned for the others to precede him down the hall toward the stairs.

Within moments, Ted and Alex were warming themselves near the ornately manteled fireplace of the King's Head Inn.

Frederick pulled up a chair and motioned for Giles to follow suit.

A flaxen-haired waitress approached with a teasing smile. "Evenin', gents. What's your pleasure?" Her long mane hung loose in crinkled waves, and she twisted one wisp of it around a tapered finger as she glanced at the foursome.

Ted let his gaze wander slowly over her, missing nothing, then raised his brows as he caught her flirtatious glance. "And whom have we here?"

"Bess, sir," she answered.

"Well, then, Bess—" Granville patted the vest pocket beneath his charcoal cloak. "Your best ale. All around. We've a mighty thirst to quench."

She smiled and left, returning in a moment carrying drinks on a round tray. She set one before each of them and sauntered away, casting a saucy glance over her shoulder.

"Whew!" Alex said with a rakish grin. "Wonder where they found that one? An improvement over that cold fish, Lucy, she is."

Giles nodded. "I say. Well, fare thee well, and all that." He lifted his glass to his mouth and took several swallows, then set it back down. "We aren't, of course, supposed to take notice of such things. We've much more important matters to occupy our minds. Let's see . . . how does my old man put it whenever I'm home? Ah yes." The corners of his generous lips drooped, and he lifted his aquiline nose snootily and lowered his voice to a snobbish tone. "'We've the greatest confidence in you, my boy, knowing you will strive to become a person of logic, enlightened, quite above superstition.'"

At this, the others broke into laughter, but Giles, barely hesitating, raised a hand and continued. "'Therefore, on that day when you assume responsibility for the family estate and holdings, you shall handle them intelligently. With sound judgment. Wise investment. Remember that.'" He relaxed his features and grinned. "Isn't that a joke?"

Frederick guffawed louder than the rest and slapped a knee with his hand. "I can top that, you know. I, too, must endure having the lofty heights preached at me. And not only those you mentioned. No indeed. I must become proficient in languages as well, so that one day I shall be of benefit in the family export and trade business." He leaned forward, a dubious expression on his face. "Could it be possible, I ask, that our parents think we remain *conscious* during study hours? That we actually open those dusty tomes penned by long-dead philosophers?"

Alex pounded the table. "My, but you chaps have your lot cut out for you, to be sure. In my family, my older brother carries that burden. However, myself being the second son, I've got it easier by half. I'm to become the pious minister. And, hopefully, in some distant future, attain the exalted position of archbishop." He pressed his palms together in mock holiness, but a grin escaped. "All in good time, of course." He led the outburst of laughter.

Ted drew a long draught from his glass and set it down, motioning to Bess for refills.

She brought another round of drinks at once and removed the empty glasses.

Ted gazed down into the shining liquid and shook his head. "I never really planned to be ordained, actually," he said quietly.

"You're jesting." Alex raised his drink to his mouth.

"No. I'm quite serious. It was my parents' dream for me to enter the ministry. That's the fact of it."

"I say." Giles frowned and leaned back. "Like the rest of us, you're jolly well on your way to fulfilling *their* wishes, you know."

Ted nodded. "I know. But since I was a lad I've thought of nothing except becoming a soldier. At times I still consider chucking all this and using what remains of my measly inheritance to buy a commission. But that's far too expensive, of course. There's no hope of seeing that through."

The trio edged closer, their sober faces peering curiously at Ted as he spoke.

"Well, think of it. Instead of being clothed in somber robes, we'd have dashing uniforms, our boots polished, reflecting the glint of sunshine with every step. And, of course, we'd have no problem finding willing female companionship. They'd fall over each other vying for our attentions."

He watched Alex's eyes narrow in thought. "Instead of dreary months and years stuck in a stuffy room listening to some pompous buzzard lecturing to us about the world, we could travel to *see* it. Anywhere. India. China. All the exotic places there are. And best of all, there'd be no more prattling battles using just our minds and tongues—but real ones, with muskets and sabres. As men. Ah, that's the life, to be sure."

Alex tilted his head to one side, and a strand of straight blond hair fell across his eyes. He brushed it carelessly out of the way. "The idea isn't at all farfetched. Your parents are gone, old chap. Sad to say, of course, but true nonetheless. Your sister is off on the other side of the sea. You've no one to answer to but yourself." He paused for a few seconds and stared long and hard at Ted. "I, too, have considered the adventurous life. Perhaps it's about time we seize the chance to pursue our own dreams."

Feeling his heartbeat quicken, Ted tried to calm himself with a serious thought. "It's far beyond my means, Alex."

"But there might be a way around the expense, don't you see?" Alex said excitedly. "My mother's cousin, Wills Hill—"

"Lord Hillsborough?"

Alex nodded. "One and the same. It may take a bit of doing, but I could contact him about procuring commissions for us in one of the regiments in America. Why, it may even be possible that he could have most of the costs waived."

"But what about your father?" Frederick asked.

Giles nodded.

With a grin, Alex drained his glass. "Dear old Father isn't on speaking terms with Lord Hillsborough. Wills' swelled head is too much for my father's taste. I'm quite sure things can be arranged."

Ted sat back, propping an ankle across his opposite knee. He wondered what Sue would think if he were to abandon his sacred duty, the lifelong dream of their parents. Would she disapprove? But then, did it matter? She was off beginning a life of her own, was she not?

Then another rationale surfaced. As an officer in the Colonies, he'd be in a better position to be of assistance to her if she needed help, now that Julia was dead.

"Alex," he said suddenly. "Are you quite certain your cousin could arrange commissions for us in America?"

$$4$$

The tarp-covered stage wagon bumped and sloshed along the soggy road to Prince-Town in chilling, steady rain. Seated behind an elderly couple, Susannah dozed fitfully on the lurching bench seat. The hours had stretched out wearily, punctuated only by bits of awkward, polite conversation that by now had been exhausted.

Memories of Julia began to float through her mind in snatches, delightful dreams of younger days, when Susannah had been brought to Sir Charles and Lady Tinsdale's grand old manor house as a playmate for their pampered only child. Many a warm summer day would find the girls in the magnificent gardens of the estate, dressed in Lady Tinsdale's outdated finery. There, at the garden table with Julia's exquisite porcelain dolls, they'd enjoy fresh-baked scones and watery tea in tiny china cups, pretending they were at some grand ball. Julia always loved parties.

Susannah's imagination flitted to another party, one where she envisioned herself in a pastel lawn gown, serving tea to the dashing Mr. Haynes, himself attired in a grandly tailored satin frock coat and matching breeches. She could see that same loving warmth come into his eyes when he beheld her. But then, of course, Julia would begin tittering and embarrass her, as always. Julia could be quite maddening.

The wagon pitched violently and stopped with a jar as one of the wheels dropped into a deep rut. Susannah's head struck one of the posts supporting the canvas top. Putting a hand to the painful bump on her temple, she lifted the bottom of the tarp with the other and peered outside into the gloom.

"Everybody out," the driver ordered.

Mr. Buchanan, the pleasant old gentleman in the front seat, turned to Susannah. "Another big puddle, no doubt." Opening the door, the stout, simply dressed man climbed down and gently assisted his frail-looking wife. He then lent a hand to Susannah.

Though the rain had lessened, it still dripped in dollops from the leaves of the overhanging trees and dense foliage of the bushes beside the road.

The stocky driver tipped his worn hat, and a rivulet of water spilled from the brim and splashed into the mud. "Sorry to bother you folks again," he said. "Have to lighten the wagon. Wouldn't want to get us all stuck."

"We understand," said Mr. Buchanan. He held out an elbow for each woman. "Ladies, shall we?"

Despite the inconvenience, Susannah and Mrs. Buchanan chuckled. It was the fourth time they had been compelled to get out and walk. They were getting used to it by now.

Helping the ladies over a fallen log beside the road, the aged gentleman led them to higher ground, where they stepped along a rise to the other side. The driver maneuvered the stage carefully through the water hole. Then Susannah and the pair climbed aboard to continue the journey.

Settled once again, Susannah grimaced at the sight of her mud-caked boots and the dark stains along the hem of her traveling clothes. No doubt this day had been their ruination. She envisioned herself appearing at Julia's door in such bedraggled fashion, wearing half the soil of Pennsylvania and New Jersey on her person.

Obviously having read the distress on Susannah's face, Mrs. Buchanan smiled over her shoulder. "Surely it can't be as bad as all that, my dear. By the time we reach Princeton, perhaps the rain will have stopped."

She smiled. "You're quite right, of course. I was just imagining the mess I'll make of my friend's home when I arrive this evening. I'm hardly presentable."

"No doubt she'll be so happy to see you, miss, she'll gladly accept you, mud and all." The old gentleman ignited a flint stick and lit his clay pipe, then touched the flame to the wick of the wagon lantern. "All the way from England, no less. Incredible." He puffed a few times, and wisps of aromatic gray smoke drifted inside the dim enclosure of the conveyance.

"I shall be happy to see the end of this journey myself. My, but this has been a long day." Unable to prevent herself from yawning, Susannah covered her mouth with her hand. "I can't seem to keep awake."

"We understand exactly how you feel, my dear," said Mrs. Buchanan, a weariness evident in her kindly blue eyes. "I'm rather sleepy too." She rested her bonneted gray head against the padding of her husband's sturdy shoulder.

Susannah sighed and leaned against a rib of the boned framework. At once she found herself back with Julia, in recollections she'd always treasured. Daring Julia, in her very first real party dress, rich copper curls piled high upon her head, twirling around and around as Susannah admired the shimmering creation of layered silk.

Once Susannah had been allowed to accompany Julia to London, and Julia had flirted scandalously with all the young gentlemen along the Strand, teasing them from behind her fan of intricate French lace. Most unbelievably, she had actually chatted with them without a proper introduction. Considering her flair for adventure, it wasn't really much of a shock when Julia eloped. But with a stranger! And then to go off to America, at that! What a trial the precocious girl had been to her poor beleaguered papa.

Smiling to herself, Susannah recalled the harried look on Sir Tinsdale's face as he'd stood beside Ted at the wharf, bidding her farewell, wishing her a safe and speedy voyage. His relief had been apparent as he thanked "sensible" Susannah for going to join his naughty Julia. Sir Tinsdale, holding both her hands in his, assured her with his usual persuasive manner that her own father, the good reverend, would have approved.

The thought of her parents pricked Susannah's heart, and the smile wilted. For years her father had taken her mum across the length and breadth of Britain in search of a cure for her lingering ailment. Then, ironically, they had both died suddenly in a tragic carriage accident, leaving her and Theodore alone in the world. She swallowed hard against the pain.

The stage jostled the passengers again over another rough section of road. Susannah tried to peer beneath the canvas, but the gradually fading darkness had deepened considerably since her last peek outside. Only one small patch of light beamed in the distance. A lonely farmhouse, she presumed.

Mr. Buchanan sighed heavily. "We must be quite near Princeton by now," he said in a hopeful tone. "We're hours overdue."

A short while later, the carriage stopped, and the driver eased down. "We're here, folks. Princeton." After lifting and securing the side flap, he held his arms out toward Susannah, then swung her over a puddle and onto the landing of a three-story stone coaching inn. "Which chest is yours, missy?" he asked as the Buchanans alighted and went inside.

Susannah pointed under her seat to the one she had been permitted to bring. "Will you please make certain my remaining trunks are shipped to me posthaste? It's most important that I have them as soon as possible."

"Sure thing."

"Thank you." She pushed a dripping bonnet feather from her eyes and waited, holding her satchel with both hands.

"I'll get this for you, missy," he said, reaching for the bag. "Take yourself inside, before you catch your death. The boy who works here'll help me with your trunk."

Susannah smiled and turned, noticing as she did so a sign in the shape of a proud lion suspended from a strong chain above the wooden door. Carved raised letters announced it as the Lyons' Den. Golden light streamed from the windows and illuminated the puddled ground and the neat shrubbery beside the establishment. Opening the iron latch, Susannah stepped inside, blinking against the brightness that met her eyes.

In seconds her vision cleared, and in the dancing glow cast by candles from brass sconces lining the long common room, her gaze swept to the fireplace at the far end. She wiped her feet on the round braided mat, already muddied by other travelers, and made her way across the smooth plank floor toward the welcome heat. She passed the Buchanans, who were seated among other damp-looking patrons at one of the long pine trestle tables. They smiled, and Susannah returned the greeting. At the massive stone hearth she tugged off her ivory gloves and spread her fingers out toward the blaze. Only then did Susannah realize how cold she had become during the journey.

Someone tapped her shoulder. "Stayin' the night, missy?" the stage driver asked. He had removed the wet outerwear that covered his faded clothes, but beneath his balding head, his large nose still shone red from the cold. "I need to know what to do with your trunk."

Susannah thought for a moment, then nodded. "I suppose that would be wise. Perhaps I shouldn't disturb my friends at this late hour."

"Well, we can't do nothin' about the weather, you know. Just make do, best we can. I'll take you to Mr. Lyons so's you can book a room." Turning, he led the way.

Susannah followed him down a row of tables toward the entrance, to a huge wooden bar. Directly behind it a majestic lion's head fashioned in wood was mounted on the wall, flanked on either side by shelves full of bottles and glasses. Her gaze was drawn to the calm knowing eyes beneath the animal's carved mane.

A gruff-looking man with a wiry shock of light gray hair stood to one side of the counter working on a column of figures, his brow furrowed. His wild silver eyebrows all but met atop the bridge of his stately nose. As the driver's clomping footsteps approached, the man looked up, and a large white bird perched on his shoulder shifted its position.

"Jasper," the driver said.

The countless lines that crisscrossed the man's face crinkled in a broad grin. "Red Stoner, you old coot. See you finally made it through from Philly, eh?"

"Yep. Always do, don't I? No matter how long it takes!" He chuckled. "Gotta be here to pick up them New York passengers, ya know."

"Well, the New York stage made it through at least an hour ago. I told 'em not to worry, though. You'd be along when you got here."

Red Stoner motioned with his head toward Susannah. "The little gal here needs a room. You'll see to it, right?"

"Sure thing. We'll take good care of her, won't we, Methuselah?" he said, raising his shoulder and peering at the feathered creature. The curious-looking bird bobbed its head and stared through transparent blue eyes at Susannah.

"Guess I'll wet my whistle, then. I've worked up a powerful thirst tryin' to keep warm in that rain." The driver turned and walked to the other end of the bar, motioning to the serving girl for a drink.

"Well, now, Miss—"

"Harrington," she supplied. "I'd like a room, if you please. For one night."

"Of course, Miss Harrington. If you'll sign the register, here." He turned the book around for her. "We'll fix you up all nice an' comfortable like. I expect you're tired after your journey. Hungry, too, if I'm any judge."

Susannah replaced the writing quill and smiled. "You're quite right. I am rather exhausted, and hungry as well."

"Well, Esther—that's the wife—has made up a big kettle of real good stew. Take yourself a seat over at one of the tables, and we'll see that you get some before you go upstairs. If there's anything else you need, just let us know. The name's Lyons. Jasper Lyons."

"Thank you. And Mr. Lyons?"

"Yes, miss?"

"I shan't need to be awakened in the morning with the other passengers. I won't be traveling on. But would it be possible for me to have a bath?"

"As you wish." The innkeeper held out his hand, and Methuselah stepped onto it. He transferred the exotic bird to a wooden stand in the corner, then turned. "Kate!" he bellowed sternly to a serving girl who stood across the room laughing with two patrons.

The buxom brunette turned and pouted in her employer's direction.

"Some supper for our young guest," he said in a tone that allowed no dispute.

Choosing a solitary square window table somewhat apart from the tiresome laughter and chatter of the other customers, Susannah sat down and watched the girl sashay toward her with deliberate slowness.

Kate approached Susannah and swept one quick glance over her. Obviously unimpressed, she grimaced. "Mm-hm. Comin' right up."

The innkeeper stopped the girl mid-stride at a doorway left of the bar. "After she's done, take her up to room 3. And tell Esther to heat up more bath water."

"Not another bath!" Kate wailed.

"Mind your tongue, girl," he said sternly.

"Yes, Mr. Lyons." Casting a grim look back at Susannah, she grumbled something inaudible and disappeared into the kitchen.

Half an hour later, Susannah at last stepped into her second-floor room. Shadow patterns danced across the bright counterpane as the flame atop the copper candlestand on the commode bowed and curled. She placed her damp bonnet on the cherry four-poster bed and turned to Kate. "It's very nice. Thank you."

"Your *bath* awaits," the girl announced without an ounce of kindness in either her voice or her manner. After setting

Susannah's satchel beside the bed, she departed, pulling the door closed as she left.

Welcome to Prince-Town, Susannah thought sarcastically. *Oh well, surely one more night alone won't be the end of the world. Tomorrow I'll be with Julia for certain!* Stripping off her mud-laden shoes and clothing, she lowered her aching body slowly into the luxury of steaming water.

The chiming of a nearby chapel bell barely disturbed Susannah's slumber as brilliant rays of April sunshine streamed through the white homespun curtains and warmed her face on the down pillow. She bolted upright. *Morning! Today's the day!*

She jumped out of bed, splashed water from the basin onto her face, and dried it. Then, her fingers trembling with excitement, she hastily dressed in the new blue velvet dress she had purchased for this occasion. She must look her best today. For Julia and her new husband as well. What would he be like? Fastening the last button, she stared into the looking glass, pleased that the rich color seemed to add roses to her cheeks. She grabbed her comb and yanked it through her long soft waves before twisting them skillfully into a coil at her neck and rushing downstairs for breakfast.

The common room gleamed cheerfully as morning sunlight streamed through parted sections of the crisp ivory muslin curtains. Neatly laid pewter tableware warmed in pools of light on the spotless white linen. Susannah glanced around at the orderly tidiness. The smooth pegged floor had been swept clean of the mud that had been tracked in during the previous night. Two coarsely dressed men sat at one table conversing quietly over coffee, their empty plates pushed aside. From his perch behind the bar, flat-beaked Methuselah turned sky blue eyes to Susannah.

"You'll be Miss Harrington, no doubt," a woman said from behind her.

Susannah took pleasure in the rich-sounding rustle of the blue velvet gown as she turned. "Yes."

"I'm Esther Lyons," the short, plump woman said in a pleasant, low lilt. She wiped her hands on the linen apron, which protected a rust-colored dress, and smiled, crinkling the skin around her narrow eyes into a maze of fine lines. "Have yourself a seat, and I'll be seein' to your breakfast."

"Thank you."

The older woman hurried off, creating a slight breeze, which softly feathered loose wisps of fine salt-and-pepper hair below the ruffled white cap she wore.

Susannah chose a seat near the hearth and gazed out the window at trees that waved budding branches in the soft wind. Above them, a flotilla of great fleecy clouds sailed across the New Jersey sky.

Mrs. Lyons returned shortly with a plate and set it before Susannah. "Here you be."

"It looks lovely." Susannah admired the eggs and crisp bacon with a smile. The yellow griddle bread on the side she surmised to be what Julia had described in a letter as corn bread.

"Hope you enjoy it. I just put on a fresh pot of coffee, so I'll be bringin' you some in just a few minutes."

"If it wouldn't be too awfully much trouble, could I possibly have tea instead? I'd prefer it, if you don't mind." Susannah raised her brows hopefully.

The woman placed her hands on her plump hips and tilted her head. "Well, now, it's not that I'd be mindin' it, you understand. But it's the boycott."

"I beg your pardon?"

"The boycott, miss. Thanks to Parliament, we're becomin' a land of coffee drinkers. Course, if they ever see fit to lift the tea tax, things'll be different. Till then, we'll just be doin' without." She smiled, and her glowing cheeks rounded like apples as she leaned closer. "Well, now, I can brew you some native tea, if you're of a mind to have some of that instead, but it's a mite bitter." Her narrow hazel eyes sparkled.

Susannah smiled and shook her head. "Thank you all the same, Mrs. Lyons. But no, I shouldn't want to put you out. Actually, I'm in a bit of a hurry this morning. I shan't notice the lack of my usual tea at all."

"Then you'll have some coffee, right quick." The woman hastened toward the kitchen.

Susannah bit into the warm buttered corn bread cautiously, surprised at its delightful taste and texture. As she ate she pondered why people would rebel over a little tax. Surely they were aware it cost Britain a great deal of money to maintain the far reaches of the Empire . . . which *included* the American Colonies. Perhaps Reverend Selkirk's assumptions had been accurate after all. Perhaps the Colonies *were* little more than a land full of sinful dissenters and ruffian convicts. Had she herself not witnessed a blatant act of smuggling by two seamen while their captain looked the other way? And one might have expected that handsome Mr. Haynes, the former seminary student, to have been a more respectable sort instead of consorting with lawbreakers. She swallowed suddenly. What was happening to her? She herself had actually abetted them in their getaway. Were her values already being corrupted? And her common sense as well?

She gazed through the window at the meadow beyond the road. Edged by a dense stand of tall trees, it bore the awakening green of spring. Hardy young wildflowers lifted white faces toward the sun and swayed on an invisible breeze. This new country seemed filled with beauty, much like the placid verdant hills of her homeland. Surely if it were not a good place to be, Julia wouldn't have asked her to come.

A slender serving girl with downcast eyes and a silent, skittish manner came into the room carrying a pot of coffee. Long flaxen hair, hanging in a single braid down to the middle of her back, drew attention to the huddled slump of her shoulders. Her hand trembled slightly as she filled Susannah's cup. Then, her blonde head still bowed, she approached the two men. Finished with their meal, they waved her away.

Susannah frowned as she watched the girl scurrying back to the kitchen. With her slight build, the waif might have been a child, were she not quite so tall. Susannah had never seen anyone her age so shy, so frightened of everyone. The girl looked as if she'd been terribly mistreated.

Oh well, sad as that might be, the girl was no concern of hers. Susannah gulped the last of her coffee and set the cup down. She had better just obtain directions to Julia's house and be on her way. She rose and crossed the open space toward the kitchen to speak to Mrs. Lyons.

She saw the young girl standing with her back turned, washing dishes in a large tub. Susannah approached and tapped her on the shoulder. "Excuse me."

Startled, the servant jumped, and a soapy platter slipped from her hands and shattered on the floor, sending chunks of china in all different directions. "Oh no!" she gasped. Her eyes welled with tears as she stooped to gather the broken pieces.

Esther Lyons peeked around from beneath the stairs, her arms filled with clean folded towels. "What's that clatter, Mary Clare?"

"I'm sorry. I'm sorry," the girl whimpered, her eyes wide and tearful. She quickly stacked the pieces on the sideboard, then dropped down to wipe the wet spots on the floor with a rag.

"I'm afraid I must have frightened her, Mrs. Lyons," Susannah said. "It was most unfortunate. I came in to ask directions to my friend's house."

Setting the linens down on an empty worktable, Mrs. Lyons went to the still sniffling girl and knelt beside her, placing an arm around her huddled shoulders. "Now, don't you be frettin' over an old broken dish, love. It's of no importance a'tall."

Susannah put a hand on the girl's arm. "Truly, I must apologize—Mary Clare, is it? It was my fault for startling you. Look," she added, holding two of the larger pieces together, "I'm certain it can be glued together again, good as new."

"Do you think so?" she asked hopefully, easing out of the older woman's embrace.

Mrs. Lyons patted her gently. "Yes, love. Good as new. Now, how about washin' up the rest of the dishes, huh? And afterward, go help Christopher with the wood."

Mary Clare dried her cheeks with one hand and returned to her chore with a teary smile.

"Now then," Mrs. Lyons said, turning to Susannah. "What directions would you be needin'?"

Taking Julia's latest letter from her skirt pocket, Susannah glanced at the writing. "I must find out how to get to the Holmby House. Is it far from here?"

"Not a'tall," Mrs. Lyons answered with a smile. "It's just up this road a ways, past the houses. Then take the first turn to the right. You run upstairs for your wrap, and when you come back down, I'll point you toward it."

"Would it be terribly inconvenient if I were to leave my trunk in the room for a bit? It shouldn't be long, I'm sure."

"Don't even give it a thought. Leave it as long as you need to."

Moments later, walking in the glorious sunshine toward Julia's, Susannah loosened her white knitted shawl and glanced back toward the coaching house. The fieldstone had been washed clean by the rain, and the structure looked neat and inviting with its tidy grounds and outbuildings. Mary Clare stood at one of the windows, but as Susannah caught sight of her, she vanished.

Strange child, she thought. *But I'm most certain Mrs. Lyons is not the sort to be mistreating her. I can't be sure about that gruff husband of hers, though. I shouldn't want to be on his bad side. But Mrs. Lyons couldn't be nicer. Or more motherly.*

I wish Mum could've been like that, she thought with a twinge of melancholy as she passed the last house on the street. But her mother's asthma had come so suddenly and so frequently—the shortness of breath, the wheezing and coughing, the tremendous weakness. She became susceptible to every change of weather, every passing fever. It had been a strain on the whole family as she sought relief in first one set of new powders and herbs, then another.

Susannah sighed, shaking off the sad thoughts. She knew her mother was finally at peace.

Susannah felt her heartbeat quicken as she turned the corner and, looking down the tree-shaded street, saw the sign for Holmby House. She couldn't wait to surprise Julia. Hurriedly she neared the two-story brick structure, noticing smaller words on the sign in passing. "Rooms for Rent," she read aloud. Julia lived in a common boardinghouse? With a frown, she lifted the iron knocker and rapped.

The door opened, and an unsmiling woman with a thin face appeared. She wore a gray linen dress, and only a wisp of mousy hair showed from beneath her stiff white cap. "Yes?" she asked with a frown, as though answering the door had been an intrusion upon her day.

"I'm here to see Mrs. Julia Chandler," Susannah said hesitantly.

"Well, now, that ain't exactly possible, dearie."

"I beg your pardon? She gave me this address."

"Well, she was livin' here some time back. Up till she died, that is."

Susannah's heart plummeted, and she felt the color drain from her face. Her voice came in a near whisper. "Surely there must be some mistake." This had to be a bad dream. Any moment she would awaken and find it all had been her imagination.

"No, no mistake about it, dearie. She's been gone near two months now. Died in childbirth, she did."

Susannah swayed in stunned silence, her mouth agape. She felt her knees begin to give way and struggled to maintain her balance.

The woman stepped back and started to close the door.

"No. Wait. Please." Susannah put out a hand to prevent the door from latching. "I don't understand. It wasn't time for the baby yet. I'm most certain of it."

The woman shook her head in a huff and tapped her foot

impatiently. "It was the fall she took, you see. Made things start up early. Judgment from the Almighty, if you ask me."

Susannah flinched inwardly, as though she'd been slapped in the face. She barely restrained herself from flying at the hateful stranger. How could anyone say such dreadful things about Julia, her dearest sweetest friend? "But—the baby. What about the baby?"

"The young'un didn't make it neither. Terrible thing, it was. God's judgment for sure."

Susannah shook her head, rejecting the words that stung her ears. She couldn't listen to any more of the horrible lies. "Please, may I speak to Mr. Chandler?"

"Look, dearie. He's gone back where he come from. In fact," she spouted, one hand going to her hip, "if I would 'a knowed those two was here without the blessing, or even knowledge, of their parents, I woulda never rented 'em a room."

"Why, what ever do you mean?"

"Wasn't till the missus died that he broke down and told me they got married secretly and came here on a lark, livin' off his allowance. Not even the good reverend, President Witherspoon, knew about the two of 'em. Or he woulda sent 'em both packin', you can be sure of that."

Numbed by the startling revelation of Julia's death, Susannah pressed her fingers to her throbbing temples and moistened her lips. Suddenly cold in this harsh, foreign land, she shivered despite the warmth of the sunshine. "Please," she said, pulling her shawl tighter. "I've come an awfully long way. From England. I've only just arrived, and I had no knowledge of any of this. It's most difficult for me to believe it all."

Her expression softening, the woman nodded. "Well, I can see you're caught off balance by the news. Why don't you come in and sit down for a spell?"

Susannah hesitated, uncertain whether she should go inside or not. But she had nowhere else to go at the moment. Not now. Everything had changed. Dazed, she stepped through the doorway and followed the woman to a sitting room, where she sank down onto a worn upholstered settee of faded gold velvet. Her heart still wrenched painfully in her breast. Clasping her trembling hands tightly in her lap to fortify herself, she fought to keep her voice even. "Could you . . . please tell me where Mr. Chandler . . . b-buried Julia and the baby?"

"Yes, miss. He took her remains home to the family plot in North Carolina. Her and the wee one both."

Susannah sighed and closed her eyes against the sharp ache inside.

After a span of silence, the woman spoke again. "Your name wouldn't happen to be Harrington, would it?"

"Yes, it is. Susannah Harrington."

"Well, a couple of weeks ago a letter arrived here for Mrs. Chandler with your name as sender. Since I never got around to sendin' it on to her husband, you might as well have it as not, seein' as it's yours. Wait here." After leaving the room for a few seconds, she returned with the letter and handed it to Susannah. "Look, I'm real sorry about your friends, dearie. They seemed decent enough," she added grudgingly. "I'll be the first to admit they never caused me no trouble."

Susannah stared at the unbroken seal. Julia had died without ever knowing she was coming. Without knowing of the death of her parents or the anticipated joy Susannah felt at the thought of joining her friend and being a part of college life. And without knowing the rapture of holding her own babe in her arms.

Susannah rose, unable to hold her tears at bay any longer. "Sorry to have troubled you. I—must go." She groped blindly for the door and fled outside. Lifting the hem of her skirt, she escaped from Holmby House as fast as she could, neither knowing nor caring where she ran. Blinding tears streamed unchecked down her face, emptying her of all hope.

Never had she felt so alone. So lost. England was on the other side of the world, along with everything familiar to her. *You should never have come here,* a voice inside taunted through her desolation. *What will you do now? Where will you go?*

The delicate fringe of the shawl snagged on a scraggly bush, tearing it from Susannah's shoulders. Stopping to retrieve it, she gulped in great breaths of air. She brushed away her tears and surveyed the grove of white birch trees that now surrounded her. The settlement of Prince-Town, the college with its impressive Nassau Hall, lay in the distance. But she was in no hurry to go back to it . . . she could think of no reason to.

Forgetting her new velvet dress, she sank to the ground and leaned back against a tree. A new wave of sorrow washed over her, and head in her hands, she sobbed in anguish until it subsided. Her head throbbed with blinding pain. Susannah rooted in her dress pocket for a handkerchief, dabbed at her swollen eyes, and blew her nose as she tried to gather her thoughts.

She couldn't possibly have money enough to book return passage to England, of that she was certain. There might, perhaps, be enough for a return stage to Philadelphia and a packet to North Carolina. Surely the Reverend Selkirk would provide for her while he was on assignment in the Colonies. And perhaps afterward he might be able to purchase two passages back home again. But could she bear the thought of spending heaven knows how many more months in his overbearing care? She grimaced bitterly and shook her head.

She *had* no home now. The charming stone cottage that had once belonged to her parents was now owned by strangers. How could she bear to live within sight of it now, that haven where her beloved family had once shared all the joys and trials of their life together? And Ted, off at Oxford, couldn't afford the added burden of supporting her.

Susannah straightened as another thought occurred to her. Perhaps Reverend Selkirk could contact Robert Chandler and his family on her behalf. Surely they would take her in until something else could be arranged. She *had* come at Julia's request, after all. No. Impossible. How could she even consider living off the charity of people she didn't even know—and who might resent the intrusion by a stranger, at that?

Slumping forward, Susannah leaned her forehead into her

palms once more. This was simply dreadful. Horrible. Choking grief gave way to yet another torrent of sobs.

After a time, the tears subsided. Susannah took a cleansing breath and staggered to her feet. She looked about until she regained her bearings, then walked slowly back to the inn. The common room was deserted. She gravitated to the warmth of the kitchen.

Mrs. Lyons stopped stirring a pot of stew over the hearth and turned at the sound of Susannah's footsteps. She dropped the ladle. "Why, love. You've been cryin'. And you've even torn that beautiful dress." Concern etched lines into her plump face. "What's happened?"

Susannah glanced absently at her gown. Then grief overwhelmed her again, and she collapsed into a heap at the table, sobbing into her arms.

Mrs. Lyons rushed to Susannah and pulled a chair close. She placed a comforting arm about her. "Now, now," she crooned while she brushed a dried leaf from Susannah's blue velvet. "There's nothin' can be so bad as all that. Why don't you tell Auntie Esther what could bring such tears to that pretty face?"

"I—I need to take the next stage—back to Philadelphia," Susannah said between gasping sobs. "When does it leave?"

"On Tuesday, love."

At this news, Susannah wept even harder. The added expense of four more days' lodging would cut deeply into her remaining funds and would most certainly leave too little even to pay for a trip to North Carolina—or anywhere else, for that matter.

"I'm goin' to put on some coffee," Mrs. Lyons said.

Susannah moaned. Coffee. It struck her, then, that even on this, the worst day of her life, she couldn't have a comforting cup of tea in this unyielding land of America. She blotted her tears with the handkerchief and hopelessly shook her head.

"Better yet," Mrs. Lyons added, "I've been hoardin' a secret cache of tea for an emergency. I think I'll be dippin' into it right now. It'll make you feel better." Climbing onto a chair and reaching behind some items in back of one of the tall kitchen cupboards, she removed a tin of tea. She measured a sufficient amount and filled a teapot from the steaming kettle on the hearth, then set it on the table to brew near a stack of clean cups. "Now, what is it, child, that has you so upset?" She sat down next to Susannah.

Susannah raised her red-rimmed eyes, and words poured forth from her shattered heart. "I've come all this way, spent all those weeks on the high seas from England, for nothing. My friend, Julia, is dead. I've no one here, now. No one at all. She wanted me to come and live with her. Begged me for months. I spent nearly every pound I had on the journey, and now I've no place to go." She shook her head slowly. "I haven't the slightest notion what I'm to do."

Mrs. Lyons stared openmouthed until Susannah stopped speaking. "Oh, you poor dear child," she said, patting Susannah's hand. "I can't tell you how sorry I am to hear that. It's a great pity, to be sure, you coming all this way and bein' disappointed so." She reached for the teapot and filled two cups with strong tea, placing one before each of them. "You must be speakin' of Julia Chandler."

The aroma of the hot brew caressed Susannah's nostrils as she looked up. "You knew her?" Picking up her cup, she took a sip, soothed by its warmth.

Mrs. Lyons nodded. "Her and her husband both. They came by every now and then for supper, mostly with the college students. I liked the two of 'em, though I didn't approve of the secret they was tryin' to keep from the school and his family about their marriage."

Susannah managed a weak smile. "Somehow it is a comfort to me just knowing you knew Julia . . . and liked her. She was my very best friend in the world. I was the only child from our village she was allowed to play with, her being manor-born." She sighed. "Julia always had such grand dreams. Such big plans for me, too, coming here to live. I suppose I got caught up in them too and thought they'd all come true. You know."

Her breath caught on a sob. She closed her eyes for a moment, then lifted her wet lashes again.

Mrs. Lyons gave her hand a squeeze. "Well, it was a shock, truly it was, when I heard of her passin' the way she did. She shook her head. "Such suffering, being so far from her own mother and havin' no woman that was close to her to help. For weeks afterward, nary a student came through the door of the inn a'tall. And when they did, it wasn't the same as before. You know, the laughing and teasing and such. It was like a great sad gloom smothered the boys for a time. That Robert Chandler's a fine young man, though, love. And from a well-off family. I'm sure he'll not think a thing of looking after you."

Susannah barely restrained fresh tears at the thought of her friend's ordeal. Surely Julia's husband must have been crushed, losing the wife he loved. She swallowed. "Oh, but how could I ask that of him? Or of his relatives? I've not even met them."

Jasper Lyons opened the door and tromped across the room. "Esther, you seen that worthless Kate anyplace?"

"No, not today."

Muttering under his breath, he stomped out the back door, closing it with a slam.

"You be watchin' your tongue, Jasper Lyons," Mrs. Lyons called after him. Then her voice softened. "That girl will be his undoing one of these days." Turning back, the motherly woman reached around Susannah and gave her a gentle squeeze. "After you finish your tea I think what you'll be sorely needin' is a good rest."

"I can't imagine I'll ever sleep again," Susannah said in a weary whisper.

"I know, love. It's a bitter mouthful, isn't it? There's not much I can be saying to make the pain inside your heart go away. I wish there was. Life is very uncertain most of the time. But usually things have a way of working out in the end. Even those we can't understand. You must try to put it aside for a little while, if you can."

Meekly, Susannah nodded, drained her cup, and rose. "You've been most kind. Thank you ever so much for the tea—and for listening." With an effort she smiled at Mrs. Lyons. Then, leaving the room, she trudged up the stairs to her chamber.

The big bed did look inviting, but instead of crumpling onto it, she dropped to her knees beside it, as she had done every night of her life, and clasped her hands. It wasn't even noon, but today she needed strength as never before—the kind of strength her father had said came only from the Lord he served.

Almighty God, she prayed. *Whatever have I done that is so unforgivable that I must be punished so? Whatever it is, if you'll just please forgive me, I promise I'll never miss church again as long as I live. I'll give to the needy. Nurse the sick. I'll work so hard to do good. I'll be kind, I'll do my best to be charitable as much as I'm able. But please help me in this dreadful predicament. Show me what to do. I know I've not done as much service as I might have in the past. I could have been much more of a help to Mum than I actually was. I don't deserve your favor. But please remember how my father served you most faithfully all of his life. He worked so hard for you. Please help me for his sake.*

Susannah clenched her hands together, waiting for an answer. A sign. Anything.

Then in a warm rush, the memory of her father's loving voice wafted across her heart like a healing balm. *"Remember, my dear child, not even a sparrow falls to the ground without the heavenly Father's knowledge. Even the very hairs of your head are all numbered. That's how much he loves you, dear heart."* Hadn't he said those words a hundred times throughout her life?

But did God really love her that much? Could he even hear her in this faraway corner of the earth?

Pricked with doubt, she rose and removed her shoes and dress, then crawled into bed. She snuggled deep into the cloudlike softness of the feather tick. A feeling of peace began to ease through her. It filled the empty hollows, vanquishing her loneliness and despair. And she knew.

God would take care of her.

5

Susannah awakened to the sound of loud boots. Someone pounded on one of the doors down the hall.

"Kate!" Jasper Lyons' booming voice reverberated the length of the corridor.

Yawning, Susannah sat up in her bed, and at once the crushing weight of sorrow descended again upon her heart.

Julia! It hadn't been just a nightmare. A solitary tear melted softly down her cheek. With a sigh she lay back against the pillows.

"Kate!" The pounding started up again, this time closer. "Where are you, you shiftless scullion?" Mr. Lyons' footsteps paused outside Susannah's door, and he cleared his throat, then knocked.

Quickly drying her face, Susannah flung the coverlet aside and grabbed a wrap, pulling it on as she crossed the room. Opening the door, she peered out. "Yes?"

An exasperated scowl made deep crags in the innkeeper's face. "Um . . ." He shifted from one foot to the other. "Sorry to bother you, Miss Harrington. The wife told me of your misfortune, and I'm right sorry to hear of it."

Susannah nodded. "Thank you, Mr. Lyons. It was rather a shock, I daresay. But what seems to be the problem?"

"It's that worthless servin' girl, Kate. I'm tryin' to find her. Thought there was a gnat's chance she'd be cleanin' the rooms—or else with you."

"No, I've not seen her since last evening."

His expression darkened. "Hmph. Looks like she's up and gone off then. Shoulda been downstairs a couple hours ago to help. She knows our regulars are due in soon." His bushy eyebrows met as he shoved his roughened hands into the pockets of his brown breeches and shook his scraggly head. "Well, s'pose we'll have to make do somehow. Beggin' your pardon, miss. Sorry I troubled you." Turning away, he started for the stairs.

Susannah tried to compose herself. Just a short time ago, she had promised the Almighty to help and serve others whenever possible. . . .

"Mr. Lyons?"

He glanced back over his shoulder.

"Perhaps I—" She drew an unsteady breath. "Perhaps I could help out. With the customers, I mean."

"I wouldn't even consider it, miss. Imposing on a guest like that."

"But it wouldn't be an imposition, I assure you. Not at all." Susannah gained confidence from the brave words and pressed on. "Perhaps if I had something to do to occupy my time, just now. . . . You know." She searched his face hopefully.

His wild silver brows shot up, then relaxed as he kneaded his jowls. "I don't know. Don't sound right. Not after all you been through."

"But truly, I wouldn't mind. I'd like to help out, if I may."

"Well, if you're that certain," he said, doubt still evident in his voice. "I'll tell Esther."

"Thank you. I'll dress and come straightaway." Susannah closed the door and leaned against it, aware of the nervous thumping of her heart. Then she moved to the looking glass and forced herself to examine her face. Who was that stranger who stared back? Swollen eyes, pale cheeks . . . however would she make herself presentable?

Straightening her shoulders, she lifted her chin, hoping to find the strength her father had promised would be sufficient for every need. She knelt beside her trunk, searching through the clothes she had sewn expressly for the trip. The sight of them brought new sadness to her, and she swallowed hard.

Well, it most certainly wouldn't benefit her to wallow in grief. She must get busy and fill her time. Perhaps helping someone who needed her was not simply a Christian duty. Perhaps it was somehow *necessary* for her to do so, not only for salvation from her sorrow today, but also for the future, which hung in the balance.

She found nothing among her fine wardrobe really suitable to wear as a serving girl. After a moment's thought, she removed an indigo muslin dress with tiny sprigs of embroidered flowers. She tilted her head to one side. Perhaps with an apron . . . Well, it would have to suffice. Shaking it out, she laid it on the bed, gave a splash of cold water to her cheeks and eyes, and patted them dry. Hurriedly she pulled the pins from her bedraggled hair and brushed it out, tying it at the nape of her neck with a black velvet ribbon.

At last she pulled on the dress and looked at her reflection. It took several pinches to add color to her cheeks, but she was finally satisfied with her appearance and left the room.

Mrs. Lyons looked up in surprise as she entered the kitchen.

"I've come to help."

"What? Oh, now, you shouldn't be thinkin' of lowering yourself, love," the woman said kindly. "It must be the shock of being given such a burden." She rinsed two peeled potatoes and cut them in half, adding them to a large kettle boiling softly above the fire in the hearth.

"Stuff and nonsense," Susannah answered with all the bravado she could muster. "I understand you're short of help and will soon have people arriving."

"All the same—"

"Well, I'm quite capable and willing, if you'll please explain the procedure to me. It's much better than sitting alone in my room with my dreary thoughts, is it not?"

"Well, if you're sure you're feeling up to it, I won't turn you away. Heaven knows we have our hands full, Mary Clare and me." With a long wooden ladle she stirred the contents of the kettle.

Susannah forced a smile and reached for a spare apron from a hook near the sideboard. After tying it around her slender waist, she picked up a knife and began to peel the potatoes piled on the table.

At that moment the back door opened, and a skinny, freckle-faced boy of about twelve entered with a bucket of water. Catching sight of Susannah, he ducked his head and lowered his eyes in a fashion that reminded her of Mary Clare. He set the pail on the worktable and turned to Mrs. Lyons. "W-what should I d-d-do n-next?"

"The fire in the common room is needin' more wood."

The sandy-haired lad dashed past Susannah and out the door without looking at her.

Susannah frowned, staring after the boy. Then she looked toward Mary Clare. Dressed in a neat gray homespun dress, the girl stood huddled at a worktable along the wall, separating clean tableware. Were Mr. and Mrs. Lyons cruel taskmasters to their hired servants? Both Mary Clare and the young boy looked as though someone was about to strike them at any moment. Could Kate's running away have been an escape from cruelty? Troubled, she glanced at the older woman.

"Mary Clare," Mrs. Lyons said. "We'll be needin' more onions. Would you mind fetching some from the root cellar?"

With a nod, the girl picked up a basket nearby and headed out the back door.

Mrs. Lyons turned to Susannah. "I see by the look on your face you're wonderin' about those two."

Susannah felt her cheeks warm and lowered her gaze.

"Mary Clare and Christopher, you see, have had some misfortunes, too. They lost their mama a number of years ago. Their pa's a gristmill worker who took to drownin' his miseries in grog. More often than not, Silas took his anger out on the two young'uns. Oftentimes folks would hear them cryin' and cryin', and a body would have to been blind to miss the bruises and black eyes Silas passed off as caused by their clumsiness. Once or twice we threatened to summon the authorities to see what could be done, but the young'uns wouldn't say a word against their pa. After I caught him leerin' at Mary Clare once, I was afraid something far worse would start up with her, now that she's fifteen . . . if you catch my meaning."

"How perfectly horrible," Susannah said, aghast.

Mrs. Lyons nodded. "That's why when Silas finally took a notion to indenture the two of 'em so's he'd have more money for rum, we jumped at the chance to take the children in. That way, we could look after 'em."

"Oh, the poor dears. There's so much sadness in this world. But—their own father! It's hard to understand."

"I'm of the same mind. But we do what we can, all of us, when the good Lord gives us the occasion. Don't we?"

Susannah tipped her head in thought for an instant. "Well, surely their father must come by at times, to ask after them. He can't forget his own blood."

Mrs. Lyons rinsed the peeled potatoes and sliced them in two before dropping them gingerly into the bubbling kettle. "Oh, he gets to feelin' guilty at times, I suppose. He comes in when he's of a mind to, wantin' to see the young'uns. Usually when he's drunk."

"How dreadful."

Nodding, the older woman handed Susannah a large knife and indicated a pan of warm corn bread on the table. "Silas tells 'em he's sorry, and that he misses 'em. But then he gets surly and blames them for his troubles. It shames the children so. Jasper always ends up having to throw him out. Likely it's because of him that young Christopher finds it hard to talk." She sighed heavily, and her ample bosom rose and fell. "More's the pity."

The sound of voices and footsteps carried from the ordinary to the kitchen, and Susannah's own fragile courage evaporated like dewdrops in the morning sun.

"Well," Mrs. Lyons said, "looks like we have some folks who'll be wantin' to eat. Ever done any serving before?"

Eyes wide with apprehension, Susannah shook her head.

"Well, there's nothin' to be worryin' about, love. Our midday crowd is mostly just everyday folk—tradesmen from town and the like. Bachelors and widowers who don't have a body to cook for 'em."

Without so much as the rustle of her skirt, Mary Clare returned with the onions. She set the basket on the worktable and resumed her task with the utensils.

Mrs. Lyons smiled at Susannah. "You can tell the customers we're serving stew today, or beans and corn bread, whichever they be partial to. Then just try to remember who gets what. I'll be fixin' the plates here as they're needed. And Mary Clare," she added, "you'll be serving the coffee to everybody."

The girl nodded her golden head.

"And don't you forget to smile. Remember that."

Mary Clare lifted her chin with a bashful smile.

Susannah noticed the promise of beauty on the guileless face, transformed as it was by the soft upturned lips. She watched the slight girl smooth the long apron over her plain dress and check her neat braid in the reflection cast against one of the windows. Then Mary Clare picked up the coffeepot and left the room.

Susannah inhaled slowly to calm herself, then followed hesitantly to face the first customers, clenching her hands at her sides to stop them from shaking. In the doorway she passed the returning Christopher, his eyes downcast. Gathering her courage, she made her way toward a group of men seated at one of the long tables.

"Why, thank you, missy," boomed a voice from the group as Mary Clare finished filling the last cup. "I swear that gal gits comelier every day. Don't you, Hiram?"

A blush colored Mary Clare's cheeks, and she smiled shyly at the barrel-chested man who'd spoken. Ducking her head, she hurried back to the kitchen, the rapid patter of her steps echoing softly as she passed Susannah.

"That I do." The stocky man on the end chuckled as he watched Mary Clare's hasty retreat. "You sure know how to get that girl to hoppin', Asa." He wiped his bulbous nose on a grimy handkerchief and stuffed it into his pocket as Susannah approached.

"Good day, gentlemen," she said with forced brightness. "I'll be serving you today."

"Katie sick or something?" the balding man opposite the others asked.

Susannah smiled politely. "She's not here at the moment, so I'm helping out. I'm Susannah."

"Well, now, Susannah. Suppose you'll have to get used to the likes of us. We're in most ever' day. I'm Hiram Brown, and this here's Asa Appleton," he said, indicating the rotund gentleman beside him. "That one's Orin Fields." Each bowed slightly in turn.

"How do you do," she said nervously. "We have stew today, or beans and corn bread."

Just then the door opened, and two more men and a youth entered. The eldest leaned his cane against the wall while he hung his coat on a peg near the door.

"Hmph! They aren't too awful careful who they let come here, huh?" Hiram Brown said in a playful tone.

The tapping of the cane sounded as the old gentleman crossed with a decided limp to the table. "That's one thing I noticed soon as I opened the door and saw the three of *you* here," he retorted. His small blue eyes twinkled as he nodded to the trio and took a seat further down the long table, followed by his companions.

Susannah smiled to herself, and Mr. Brown grinned up at her. "Well, Miss, this here's Art Bentley, finest shoemaker in all of New Jersey, and his son, Frank. I'm not too sure about the lad."

"My nephew Ethan," Frank Bentley said. "He's one of Nellie's."

Hiram Brown nodded. "Ah. Well, welcome to our fair town, boy. Hope you like it. I *know* you'll enjoy the scenery here, starting with this right fine little lady here," he said, raising an arm. "Name's Susannah. We're supposed to tell her if we want beans or stew."

A few moments later, Susannah entered the kitchen with her head swimming. She reached for the bowls of stew Mrs. Lyons had just filled. "I'll need two more. And two with beans and corn bread."

"This plate of biscuits goes with the stew," the older woman replied with a smile. "You're doin' fine, love. Here's a big tray for the carryin'."

After loading the platter, Susannah backed out the door with it and carried it to the table.

"Well, Asa, what's the latest from across the water?" Frank Bentley asked. "I been hopin' to hear old Lord Hillsborough took a fall down a deep well."

"Or better yet," Mr. Brown added, "choked to death on a chicken bone!"

The men guffawed loudly.

Setting the bowls in place, Susannah raised her eyebrows in alarm at hearing such disrespectful remarks. Lord Hillsborough was highly respected in England. She was beginning to agree with Reverend Selkirk's assessment of the Colonies' inhabitants and, for a moment, regretted her offer to help. She hurried back to the kitchen.

"Who's Lord Hillsborough?" she heard young redheaded Ethan ask from the open door. "What's got everyone so heated up?"

"Where you been, boy?" the first voice said. "Out livin' with the Indians?"

Susannah filled the tray hastily and returned, curious in spite of herself.

"Well, well," Mr. Appleton said. "I been through that Wyoming Valley of yours once. Bit too back-woodsy for my taste. But gettin' back to your question, lad, Lord Hillsborough's the overstuffed bigwig who's head of affairs here in America. He was the blackguard who said he'd rather see every jackman in the Colonies dead than rescind the Stamp Act back in

'65. Now he's using all his power to shove those Townshend Acts down our gullets."

"And he's the one to blame," Hiram Brown added, "for all those regiments of mangy British dogs being sent to Boston and the other ports. Ain't that right, Orin?"

Orin Fields scratched his bald head and nodded. "Partly so. Partly so. But remember, he *does* have to answer to Parliament. And we *are* just as English as anyone walkin' the streets of London."

"Oh, them's right fine words. But when's the last time you or me sent a representative to Parliament?"

"Could I have more coffee, please, miss?" Old Mr. Bentley's voice brought Susannah back to the business at hand.

After the last piece of pie had been served and the coarse commoners had left, Susannah breathed with relief. She cleared the tables, gathering the dirty dishes and piling them on the tray beside the bowl of leftover biscuits.

The main door opened, and a rail-thin man strode cautiously in. Removing his hat, he patted his cropped wig with his other hand and peered back around the door as if looking for someone, then closed it. With a smirk on his face, he sauntered over to the bar where Jasper Lyons stood stacking clean pewter tankards. "Hear you was shorthanded today," he said with a snicker. "Guess that tinker that's been hangin' around finally talked Kate into movin' on with him."

Susannah saw Mr. Lyons' face redden, and he slammed his fist down hard, startling the sleeping Methuselah on his perch.

"She was our bond servant, bought and paid for! We treated her better'n she deserved. She'd no call to go running off like that. In fact, I'm gonna see the magistrate about it right now. Esther!" he shouted toward the kitchen. "I'm goin' out!"

"Well, looks like I won't be gettin' a drink out of him today," the man said, winking. With a lopsided grin, he slapped his hat on and followed Jasper out the door.

Mrs. Lyons stepped into the room. "What was that all about?"

"It seems someone knew where Kate went," Susannah answered, "and Mr. Lyons went to see the magistrate."

"I figured this was going to happen sooner or later." Mrs. Lyons placed her hands on her plump hips. "That girl's been nothin' but trouble since the day Jasper bought her papers."

Susannah carried the dirty dishes past the woman and into the kitchen, setting them on the sideboard as Mary Clare washed the pots. Then she took a clean wet rag and returned to wipe the tables.

Mrs. Lyons, finishing Jasper's chore of stacking the mugs, continued with her tale. "She was sent here from Newgate Prison, you know, that Kate."

"Oh?" Susannah looked up curiously.

"Mm-hmm. Had no respect for her betters a'tall. No decency. More's the pity, since we'll hardly get by now without her. I hate to think about the stages rollin' in on Monday night—" She reached for a broom and swept vigorously at the crumbs on the floor.

"It's quite possible that she might decide to return before then, isn't it?" Susannah asked.

Mrs. Lyons scrunched her round face thoughtfully. "I don't rightly know if I'm wantin' her to, if the truth be known. Hmph. Besides, that wanton, lazy girl won't be back unless she's dragged here by her hair. Jasper'll have to find us somebody else—and soon."

Susannah mulled over Mrs. Lyons' words as she finished the table, then walked toward the older woman. "I'd be more than happy to work for my room and board until Tuesday morning. Surely the girl will return by then—otherwise she'll be a fugitive."

"Hmph. Nothing new to that one." Mrs. Lyons' expression softened. "Thank you, love, for the kind offer. If you're certain you wouldn't be mindin' the work, we'd be grateful for your help. You did a fine job with that last bunch. You're a real godsend."

"A godsend? Me?"

Mrs. Lyons hugged her close. "Yes, you. An angel and a godsend."

The embrace reminded Susannah of Julia, and unexpected tears threatened. She quickly blinked them back.

The door opened, and three young men dressed in black robes came in on a wave of laughter.

"Right on time," Mrs. Lyons said softly, shaking her head. "My three Lords of Dunce."

Susannah laughed lightly and watched as they took seats. "Why ever would you call them that?"

"They had to be stayin' at the school over spring break," Mrs. Lyons answered. "Else they'd be dismissed. They got to havin' too much fun this year when they shoulda been at their studies. Made a real poor showin' at their orals. Come on," she said, heading in their direction. "I'll introduce you, them being some of our regulars and all."

Susannah felt three pairs of eyes scrutinize her as she and Mrs. Lyons neared the trio. She pretended not to notice one of the young men nudge his companion in the ribs. Was everyone in America so forward and disrespectful?

"Afternoon, Miz Lyons," one of the students said pleasantly. He wore a peculiar smile that curved only one corner of his mouth and barely touched his close-set gray eyes. Above a square face, his thick sandy hair looked tousled from the breeze. "Where's our girl Kate today?"

"Reckon she's taken ill or something?" the second young man asked, wrinkling his forehead in question. The window light played across the glossy brown waves of his hair, and an appealing grin softened his ruddy, boyish face.

Mrs. Lyons smiled. "No, no . . . nothin' like that a'tall. She lit out for greener pastures."

"Ha! You jest, of course!" The third young man interjected with a wave of one long arm. He narrowed his blue eyes with an exaggerated pained expression. "What greener pastures could there possibly be than right here, I ask, waiting on three of the most dashing men in the Colonies?"

Esther Lyons obviously had problems keeping a stern face, and her hazel eyes mirrored the smile on her lips. "'Tis no wonder you havin' such problems with serious studies," she teased. "Well, we do have someone helpin' out for the next few days. A real lady." She motioned for Susannah to step forward. "This is *Miss* Harrington. And I'll be expectin' you to treat her with respect—or you can be havin' your supper elsewhere. Understand?"

Three heads nodded as one.

"Susannah," she continued, indicating the young gentleman with the thick shock of sun-streaked hair. "This here is Steven Russell. He hopes to be a preacher like his daddy someday—if he can ever fit his studies in with the tomfoolery him and his friends cook up all the time."

"Master Russell," Susannah said with a nod.

He rose, maintaining an expression of seriousness, which looked at home on his square face. "How do you do?"

The half-smile appeared again as he spoke, and Susannah wondered if perhaps only one side of his mouth bore all the responsibility for indicating his responses.

"And this," Mrs. Lyons said as a sturdily built young man got up slightly without meeting Susannah's gaze, "is Jonathan Bradford." Coppery highlights glistened in his luxurious brown hair as he tightened his lips in a useless effort to look solemn. "He's come in off a farm not too far away. Hopes to leave the farming life to his brother while he goes into the ministry."

Nodding again, Susannah concentrated on keeping the names straight. These new duties she'd taken on were going to make waiting for the stage wagon seem that much longer. "Master Bradford."

"Last," Mrs. Lyons said with exasperation as the tall gangly third fellow stood in a slow casual manner that bespoke a decided lack of discipline, "is Morgan Thomas. This one I'm not sure about. Seems he's too busy funnin' and being a prankster to ever be a credit to the College of New Jersey. But leastways, he keeps us smilin'."

Susannah noticed the devilish spark in his hypnotic cobalt blue eyes and watched a mischievous grin soften his mocking expression. She had no doubt he was quite the clever character, one she must watch closely. "Master Thomas. I'm very pleased to make your acquaintance," she said politely as she swept a quick glance over them. "Please, do sit down. 'Twill be my pleasure to serve you."

"And don't forget," Mrs. Lyons added with a shake of her gnarled finger at the threesome, "I'll be expecting you to be usin' your manners."

"Yes, ma'am," they answered in unison.

Watching after Mrs. Lyons, Susannah could not help feeling a bit apprehensive. She made an effort to compose her features as she gazed back at the young men.

"I reckon we'll all have some of that fine peach pie Mrs. Lyons makes, miss—if there is any. And coffee." He sent a questioning gaze to the other pair, and they nodded.

"I'll be but a moment, then." Turning, Susannah walked toward the kitchen, the soles of her shoes making the only sound in the room. But when she returned, they were in the midst of a discussion. She crossed the room as unobtrusively as possible.

"But, Jon—" Steven Russell's blunt-tipped finger punctuated his deep voice. "If you *truly* believe Calvin's doctrine, then I see no reason a man has to be ordained in order to preach." He finished with a shake of his sandy blond head.

"You came to that conclusion all on your own, I reckon," his friend answered, leaning back as the pie was placed before them. His eyes turned up to Susannah, and his smile widened a few tiny freckles on his ruddy face.

She noticed for the first time that his eyes were mismatched—one a light blue, the other a soft green. Her lips parted in surprise, and she knocked a spoon off the edge of the table. "I beg your pardon, Master Bradford," she blurted. "I'll get you another." Stepping a few feet away, she removed a utensil from another table setting and handed it to him.

"What do you say, Morgan?" Steven turned his gaze to the prankster.

Susannah watched with amazement as Morgan Thomas's jovial countenance transformed to that of a serious thinker.

"Calvin clearly states," Steven continued, "that it's the duty of each man to interpret the Bible and then preserve the world in an orderly fashion, as God ordained."

Morgan Thomas raised his thick brown brows as if in deep concentration and put his elbows on the table, resting his chin in his palm.

Reluctant to miss anything, Susannah hurried to the kitchen and grabbed the coffeepot, returning in a few seconds to see Morgan pound a fist on the table.

"I definitely agree with Calvin." He stuffed his mouth with pie, then pointed with his empty fork. "And since we don't have to be ordained, let's quit this place and head on up to Boston. Things are getting much more exciting up there, I hear tell." He burst into laughter.

"Come on, old man, be serious," Steven said, his gray eyes intense, challenging. "If you'll think about what you just said, how orderly could it be to have any and every old fool in the world out preaching?"

His friends chuckled and gulped down bites of dessert.

"And you're forgetting that if we're to take Calvin's words literally," Steven continued, cutting his eyes to Susannah for a brief second, "even *women*—who certainly don't have the capacity for such things—would be demanding the same rights. Can you imagine the faces of the tutors if some young woman were to apply for admittance to Nassau Hall?"

Susannah was hard-pressed not to pour the entire pot of steaming coffee in the young man's lap. She struggled to remain calm.

"I'd be willing to let her share my room," Morgan Thomas said, that irritating gleam returning to his eyes.

Biting the inside corner of her lip hard, to keep back an angry reply, Susannah wondered why she'd ever even thought of coming anywhere near this theological college that had played such a part in her decision to travel to America. Obviously, no one had ever informed these gentlemen that women not only had minds, but feelings as well. She filled the three cups.

Jonathan swallowed a mouthful of coffee. "If I didn't know better, Steven, I'd figure you were an Anglican minister, believing that only the most learned of men could have a pure thought. You spout freedom for all, then you put a blight on it with a string of *ifs.*"

"What do you say we get back to the part about girls coming to stay with us at Nassau Hall?" Morgan said, raising his cup.

Steven quirked his lopsided smile and cleared his throat. He looked purposefully at Susannah. "Oh, Miss—"

"Harrington," she supplied.

"Quite right," he said, his expression brightening. "Miss Harrington, Jonathan here—that is, Master Bradford—and I are having a bit of a disagreement. I wonder if you would be so good as to put an end to it for us."

"And how ever should I do that, sir?"

"Please assure him that if you were ever presented the opportunity of attending the College of New Jersey, you wouldn't in a thousand years remotely consider such a tiresome, intellectual chore."

"Do you mean," Susannah asked, "that I would be permitted to sit inside its halls and listen to the lectures concerning the Bible as given by the professors?"

"Yes."

"And ask questions?" she added.

Steven's smile spread to the other side of his face. "Exactly."

Susannah took a thoughtful breath and slowly let it out. "I cannot think of anything in this world I would consider a greater honor."

Jonathan's mismatched eyes widened in surprise. "That has got to be the daftest notion I've ever heard."

"That's what I've been told," Susannah answered wistfully.

At this, Morgan Thomas slapped the table and laughed.

"But, why," asked Steven, "would you—a woman—want to do something so unseemly?"

Susannah gazed out the window for a moment, then looked intently into the young man's perplexed face. "My father was a village preacher, you see. Before he passed away, he was kind enough to indulge my questions. Since then I've spent much time reading his Bible. And the more I read it, the more I realize there is much I do not fully understand. I believe that unless I have greater knowledge—of what to do and how to do it—I might never be truly worthy of God's love or salvation."

Morgan snorted with disdain. "You see what happens when a female is taught to read? It but confuses her simple mind, thus rendering her hapless."

His words stung. Susannah raised her chin and glared, hoping they would not guess how deeply the remark had cut into her heart, her dreams.

Jonathan Bradford studied her for a moment. A gentleness in his gaze gave his boyish face the look of wisdom. "She merely made the same mistake as does most of the Christian world."

Before Susannah could ask what he meant by the remark, Morgan Thomas interrupted.

"Don't pay these boorish friends of mine any attention," he said with a gleam in his dark eyes. "They're simpleminded and will confuse you all the more, I'm afraid. Any time you have a question *or any other little problem,* I would be most honored to be of assistance. Remember that."

The other students grinned and shook their heads.

"Yes, Miss Harrington," Steven Russell added. "The next time you read something that puzzles you, do feel free to consult *me and my learned friends.*"

Susannah eyed each of them in a swift glance. "I do wish you truly meant that."

"We do," Jonathan answered.

Seeing nothing but sincerity in the young man's countenance this time, Susannah cleared away their empty plates and returned to the kitchen. Her heart felt somewhat lighter, even hopeful. If they *had* truly meant what they'd said, quite possibly they could tell her what she might do to atone for the nameless sins that had surely put her in her present predicament. Knowing there were many more ways for one to gain knowledge than by actually attending the lectures, she wondered how many other things she might be able to learn before Tuesday.

On impulse, she opened the kitchen door a crack and peered back at the black-robed young men. What had Jonathan Bradford meant by the remark that she and most of the Christian world were making a mistake? To what mistake could these students possibly be referring?

The threesome sat laughing and gulping the last of their coffee, nudging and jabbing at one another like silly children. As Susannah studied them, she wondered what it was those Presbyterians knew that made them act as if the rest of the world remained in the dark.

A surge of enthusiasm broke through her probing thoughts, and a mischievous smile made its way across her lips. It would be more than worth finding out!

6

Rays of spring sunshine warmed Daniel's shoulders and glistened off the smooth coat of his strawberry roan as he emerged from the stand of silver birch trees at the edge of the Haynes Farm. He breathed in the fresh woodsy scents, his eyes taking in the hilly pastureland bracketed by sections of neat wood fence. The two-story white house on the far rise beckoned to his heart. From the chimney on the kitchen side, a slender wisp of smoke curled upward with the soft breeze, and Dan could almost taste his mother's fresh-baked bread.

He nudged the horse gently with his knees, urging it to a faster gait. "Sometimes I wonder how I get caught up in things that keep me away so long, Flame," he murmured.

The horse's ears perked slightly as if to catch the words.

As Dan drew near the farm, a movement beside the spacious barn off to the left caught his attention—his father, tending another of the prized Narragansett Pacers that had made the Haynes name known far beyond Pawtucket, Rhode Island. Several sorrel mares with colts frolicked inside one of the corrals, while others grazed in the distant meadow.

Smiling, Dan pulled Flame to a stop by the barn and dismounted. Wrapping the reins around a rail, he climbed the fence and headed in his father's direction.

Edmond Haynes lowered his grooming brush, turned, and pushed back his brown felt hat. "Dan!" he shouted, dropping the tool. Then he shortened the distance between them by half as he strode toward his son and enveloped him in an affectionate hug.

Daniel noticed for the first time the abundance of gray in his father's wavy hair, and it caught him by surprise. "It's good to see you, Father."

"You, too, my boy. We were wondering at breakfast when you'd be coming by again." He stepped back, as if to get a clearer view, then grabbed Daniel for a second embrace. Finally, they broke apart, grinning.

"You look splendid, sir. And still busy, I see. That couldn't be Foxfire you were brushing, could it? Wasn't he near death when I was here six weeks ago?"

"Yes, it's Fox all right." His father turned his head in the horse's direction, then looked back. "Took a bit of attention, I must say. Some of Elijah's potions, too. But you can see he came through."

"Yes. I haven't seen him looking so energetic for a long time. I'm glad we didn't lose him."

His father smiled. "And how's Flame been handling the constant travel?" Peering around Dan, he strained to catch a glimpse of the three-year-old beyond the fence.

"Come see for yourself." Dan led the way back toward the barn. "He's drawn a lot of interest along the Post Road. But you must know that already, from all the new orders for good saddle horses."

"Quite true, quite true." Nearing the animal, his father climbed the fence, with Daniel right behind. "Oh, he *is* a fine beast." He ran a hand along the sturdy roan's neck and down one foreleg. "Just fine."

Daniel patted Flame's flank as he watched his father assess the horse. "I've had no problems at all with him."

"Good." The older man leaned closer and lowered his voice to a conspiratorial tone. "How'd you make out on that last side trip, Son? Philadelphia, wasn't it?"

Daniel nodded. "It went as expected. I . . . um . . . even tried my hand at smuggling—with a couple of the Sons of Liberty."

"Smuggling?" His father's brown eyes darkened with concern. "We've enough to worry about with you delivering those inflammatory pamphlet plates. No sense riding into the teeth of the 'royal lion' as well."

"Oh, don't trouble your mind." Dan tried to keep his tone light. "A printer I know asked me to meet two sailor friends at the dock and drive them to his shop. You know one of them, in fact. Yancy Curtis. He and a shipmate were dressed up as refined ladies to smuggle some printing paper ashore." Dan chuckled softly at the memory. "Oddest-looking women this side of the ocean, I might add."

"Still," his father said, leaning back against the fence, "I'm not altogether comfortable with this *calling* of yours. Men like Sam Adams and the Reverend Sam Cooper are constantly inciting the masses with their lofty speeches and schemes. The way they keep that pot boiling in Boston, it could spill over on all of us."

Worry and concern had etched deep lines into his father's face. Dan searched the depths of the tired brown eyes and turned his gaze away, stroking Flame's mane. "Father, I thought you had been as inspired by George Whitefield as the rest of us—by his dream of one strong America for God."

"True. But don't forget how long and hard Roger Williams struggled to create a colony where a man is free to worship as he sees fit. When the others are willing to truly practice freedom of religion, then perhaps I will consider joining with them."

"It's already more than a dream, sir. It's beginning to happen. Whitefield is allowed to preach in any church now—regardless of the denomination. And the new president at Nassau Hall is striving toward religious freedom in all the middle colonies."

"So I hear. Well, all I can say is, your mother and I will be glad when these trying days have passed."

Studying his father's face, Daniel realized how deeply concerned his parents must have been all along about his safety. His heart contracted painfully, and he squeezed his father's arm. "How *is* Mother?" he asked, his gaze veering toward the clapboard house.

"Fine, just fine." He grinned. "She'll want to know you're home. Come on, we'd best head on up there."

As they approached the house, the door burst open and lanky seventeen-year-old Benjamin bounded out. He landed with practiced ease at the edge of the top step and sailed over the other four in one jump. "Fire and brimstone! I knew it was you!" He grasped Dan's hand and tugged him close in a hug. Then, releasing him, he threw a mock punch at his jaw. "Mother! Janie! Emily!" he called. "Dan's home!"

"See that Flame gets some water and feed, would you, Ben?" Dan asked.

"At your service, my lord." With another playful poke, Benjamin hastened toward the horse as the women of the family emerged in a flutter of long skirts.

Giggling, the girls dashed out first, then stood aside so their mother could have the first embrace.

Daniel's mother descended the steps regally, her carriage erect and proud—although, Dan thought briefly, her gait seemed a bit slower. Excitement sparkled in her light green eyes.

Sophia Haynes removed a trembling hand from her lips and embraced her son warmly. "My dear. What a wonderful surprise." She assessed his appearance and softly brushed a dried leaf from his hair. "You're getting much too thin. You've not been eating regularly, I'll wager."

"Mother," Dan said, kissing her velvety cheek. "It's good to be home. I've missed you."

"Don't I get a turn?" eighteen-year-old Jane asked with a coy tilt of her head.

Dan smiled over his mother's shoulder at the slender beauty with long coppery curls and wide brown eyes. He relaxed his embrace and turned toward her.

"I do believe you're next." As Dan hugged her and kissed the top of her head, he thought for the briefest instant of another slender beauty he had recently held in his arms. *What had become of her? Had she fared well in Princeton?* He swallowed. Then, catching sight of his youngest sister, he winked. "This can't be our little Emily," he teased, noticing honey blonde waves where there had always been braids before.

She wrinkled her nose. "Janie says I must stop having fun and start acting like a lady."

"Well, the change is most becoming, little sister," Dan said, picking up the willowy girl of fifteen and swinging her in a circle. "Curls, ribbons, and all."

Emily's laugh was airy and light, like the sound of her voice. "Once in a while, though, when she's not looking, I still climb the big elm out back."

Dan grinned. "And run with the horses, no doubt."

"I can see I'll have to keep a better watch on her," Jane said, frowning.

"Well, we don't have to stand outside in the chill," their mother said, drawing her light shawl tighter about her noble shoulders. "As soon as you men wash up, we can have some dinner. You must tell us, Dan, all about your travels." Nodding to the girls, she turned and preceded them up the steps to the door.

Dan waited beside the well after his father had finished cleaning up and gone inside. When Benjamin returned from the barn, Dan tossed the lye soap to him and watched as he scrubbed and dried with the towel.

"Leave it to you," Ben teased, "to come home right on time for a meal."

"I could smell Mother and Tillie's cooking when I was still five miles away. I hurried so you wouldn't devour everything before I got here."

"That so?"

"Mm-hm. Can't stand the way you're getting as tall as me, and at your tender age, yet."

Ben straightened to his full height and cast a swift glance at Dan, as if to measure the slight difference. Then he grinned, satisfied that his brother had something to worry about. "So tell me. Did you find a woman out there who interested you yet? Even *one?*" His voice squeaked on the last word.

Again the remembrance of his encounter with the beautiful young woman in Philadelphia warmed Daniel's being. But he shrugged it off as he laughed and ruffled Benjamin's hair. "What's it to you?"

"Fire and brimstone! If you'd marry and take up your responsibilities here on the farm, *I* could be a postrider. It's my turn to go out into the world."

The laughing brown eyes in the boyish face were nearly level with Dan's own. He suddenly felt as if he'd been away for years, unaware of how fast the younger siblings were growing up. Even little Emily was wearing a flowered afternoon dress styled after the fashion of the young ladies of Philadelphia. And Janie had a spark to her as if her head were full of romantic intrigues. "Come on, runt," he said. "I'm starving."

Moments later the family bowed their heads for grace, and Tillie, the old Negro servant, placed steaming bowls of food before them. "Sho' is good to see you home again, Mister Daniel," she said, offering a toothless grin. "We been prayin' for the good Lord to keep you safe and bring you back."

"My thanks, Tillie. Must be why I seem invisible to those lobsterbacks." Cackling, she returned to the kitchen.

Daniel heaped potatoes onto his plate. Then, catching Emily's expectant look, he winked. "Yes, I brought something for you," he said as he passed the bowl to Ben on his left.

"You did? Honest?" She cast a triumphant glance in Jane's direction.

Jane merely sighed and looked dreamily into the indefinable distance. Then she tossed a lock of hair over her shoulder and reached for the plate of fresh sliced bread.

Daniel speared a chunk of ham from the platter and smiled at his mother. "Heard from Caroline or Nan lately?"

"Yes, as a matter of fact." She rose and retrieved two letters from the buffet, then resumed her seat. "These arrived just last week."

"And?" he prompted. "What's the latest?"

His mother opened one set of pages and scanned them as she sipped the bitter hyperion tea. Her nose crinkled in distaste. "A poor substitute for India tea," she said, dabbing the corners of her mouth with a linen napkin. "Everything's fine with Caroline, as always. Philip is doing well as tutor, and—ah yes. Here it is. 'Be sure to tell Daniel, when he visits again, that if he does not hurry and get married, as one expects of the eldest son and heir, he will never catch up to his sisters. Our fourth little one will enter the world in the coming fall, and we are quite thrilled about it.' Caroline is right, you know." She looked pointedly in his direction.

"About what, Mother?" Daniel, though feigning innocence, knew the answer well enough. He forked a bite of meat and barely chewed it before he swallowed.

"About the eldest son being married, having children to carry on the family name." She arched a fine brow. "We certainly try to encourage you along this course every time we see you."

Emily turned to Jane and giggled, while Ben sputtered into his hand.

"And Nancy, as well, agrees with all of us," his mother continued as she looked at the second letter. "'When our second baby arrives, we shall join you for the holidays. How I wish our children and Caroline's could be growing up on the farm and could be more than just cousins with Dan's. I should wish for them to be great friends. When will Dan give up the adventurous life and settle down?'"

"Fire and—" Ben's words stopped abruptly at his mother's stern look. "I mean, you must realize that they're getting way ahead of you."

Ignoring him, Dan put on a smile. "Well. That's great news. Our Caroline with a brood of four little ones already. And little Nan with two."

"I daresay that one bit of news would be even more wonderful to this poor mother's heart. News that this home were soon to be graced with *your* children, my dear."

Shifting in his seat, Daniel cut his eyes toward his father with a silent plea for help.

"Enough said, Sophia, my love. I'm sure Daniel has the same sort of plans for his future that you have."

"But at six and twenty," she said, "it's considerably past time for him to have been married and starting a family here on the farm. After all," she continued, not heeding his signal to drop the subject, "it was a trial, having to stretch our finances to cover the services of an additional bondsman while Daniel left for that radical Presbyterian college in New Jersey. And then running off to be a postrider. How shall we manage now that the man's seven years are nearing completion? Elijah is growing far too feeble with age to be of much help."

"I know all that, Mother," Daniel said quietly. "I have already seen to it that most of my wages as postrider have been forwarded here. And the contacts I've made along the Post Road have resulted in far more orders for horses than we can deliver."

"Yes," she countered. "But something besides horses should be raised on this farm. It needs *sons* to carry on. And if you're concerned about the loss of income from postriding, surely Benjamin is now old enough to take on those duties."

Benjamin bobbed a head in complete agreement and nudged Daniel in the ribs.

"I can't see why *I'm* the only one you're anxious to marry off," Dan said pointedly. "Jane, at eighteen, is nearly an old maid already."

"I most certainly am no such thing!" Jane cried. "Mother just wants to be assured that I marry well. To someone of substance."

Dan's eyes widened in disbelief.

"The child is quite correct," his mother answered. "The older girls could have made far better matches. Why, the very thought of Caroline trying to subsist with three small children on the pittance a mere tutor earns—and Nan having to make do living with her husband's parents, without so much as a home of her own, both in the family way besides—"

"Sophia," his father interjected.

"I can't abide the possibility of the same fate befalling Jane or Emily, when with a bit more effort . . . Well, I'm determined that at least these two shall marry well so I shan't have to worry about them as I do the other girls."

Daniel exhaled slowly, knowing that his mother's convictions were as strong as his own. Lately he'd actually found himself beginning to entertain some thoughts of settling down, thoughts of home and hearth. And he knew the day was sure to come when he *would* assume his responsibilities on the farm. But not yet. There was still far too much to do for the cause, and he had to see it through. Once the troubles with England were settled, there would be plenty of time to look for someone with whom to share his life.

Unbidden, the memory of a lovely oval face graced his mind, one with trusting eyes of summery blue. He blinked it away.

Just then, Tillie returned to clear away the dishes. "Now, who's for my special apple pie?" she asked, her perceptive black eyes darting from one grim, silent face to the next. "Yessum, sho' is good to see more of this big happy family together again."

Several moments later, over dessert and fresh tea, Daniel gave a smile of encouragement to his mother.

"While you were in Philadelphia, my dear," she said, returning his smile, "did you, perchance, call on the Somerwells as I asked? To convey our warmest regards to dear Cousin Landon and his charming wife, Rose—and, *of course,* their lovely daughter, Charlotte."

This turn in the conversation sparked Jane's renewed interest. "Yes. Did you tell them we'll be coming for a visit in June? Oh, I can hardly wait to get away from this tiresome place and go to a civilized city."

"Oh yes," Emily added with theatrical sweetness. "In Philadelphia there are lots of *refined* young gentlemen who'll come calling on us. Janie says I should encourage anyone who shows the slightest bit of interest. Oh, bother." Wrinkling her nose in disgust, she turned away from Jane's glare.

Dan shook his head. "No, I'm afraid not, Mother. Colonial business is far more pressing at the moment."

His mother stiffened visibly. "Oh, Daniel. Please don't tell me you're still consorting with that dishonorable group of rabble-rousers in Boston. Why, if Cousin Landon—or any of my other friends, for that matter—ever found out that my own son had such a disloyal bent, I'd surely be mortified. I'd never be able to hold my head up again." She cast a dismal look down to the opposite end of the table. "I told you we should never have allowed him to go to that radical college."

"Please don't feel that way, Mother," Dan began. "The Bible came alive for me while I was there. The enlightenment I received will serve me for the rest of my life." When her look softened, he gulped the last of his tea and continued. "But perhaps I'll be able to stop in at the Somerwells' on my next trip through Philadelphia. I'll most certainly try, I promise. And in June, when you visit," he said, smiling at his sisters, "I'll join you for an evening or two. And Mother, I would never embarrass you by discussing politics with your family. You must know that."

"Oh?" A gleam entered her eye. "Well then, promise you will take a serious look at Charlotte, will you? A girl like that would blend so well with the rest of the family."

As his gaze swept the length of the table and back to his mother, Dan saw Emily and Ben smirk as though he'd fallen into a trap that had been waiting all along. His father had to cover a smile with his hand. Dan rolled his eyes heavenward.

That night, seated atop a fence rail, Dan watched as Benjamin, Elijah, and the other bondsman watered and fed the stock. His father's fine herd was increasing with every year. The farm *was* in need of additional help, he could see that. But could he truly give up being part of America's destiny? George Whitefield's dream of one strong country led by God was beginning to take root in hearts all over the Colonies.

Surely it could become a reality. The patriots needed him. God had opened this way for him to be of service to his country—hadn't he? Sighing, Dan bowed his head.

"Almighty God," he murmured into the night sky, "I'm sure I've been following the course you laid out for me. I've felt your hand upon this cause, have watched a new light dawning in the minds and hearts of the people. Only as we turn to you and seek your wisdom regarding the increasing tyranny of the king and his forces, will we ever again regain the freedoms they are stripping away. My desire is but to serve you and be faithful to your calling. But if this is not your will for me any longer, then please close the door and open another where I can be of use."

Swinging a leg back over the fence, Dan climbed down and went inside, up to his bedroom, his thoughts still in turmoil. *England.* Could anything possibly come from that land besides trouble and taxes? Besides tyranny and violence? Could there not be something good? Or gentle?

Dan's gaze fell upon the dark green quilt his mother had patterned years ago. The color took his mind back to a young woman clothed in velvet of the same deep shade. He blew out the candle on the stand, undressed, and slid beneath the covers. She had been from England. And never had he heard a more gentle voice than hers. Even yet, in quiet reveries, in the stillness preceding sleep, it played across his mind like soft music.

He had held her for the briefest of moments, and later had merely been able to look at her across a table, yet something . . . *something* had passed between them. He felt deeply honored to have protected her from harm—he could have defended her from every sort of drunken fool or English lout in all of America, if she'd needed him to.

Where was she now? Still in Princeton? Still "quite near the college," as she had conveyed to her escort, loudly enough for Dan to hear?

Even his mother would approve of the lovely English lass, of that he was certain. Her obvious culture and breeding would more than stand up to the closest scrutiny. Could she feel at home in Pawtucket? Could she share his life, bear his—

Shaking the pleasant but dangerously premature musings from his mind, he smiled to himself. It could be years before he'd have time to think of marriage or raising a family. In all likelihood, the young lady wasn't even free.

What had that stuffy chaperon of hers said? Ah yes. *"Theodore, who professes such a deep love for you . . ."* Whoever this Theodore was, surely he would not readily relinquish such a jewel. He might already have come to claim her love and sail back to England with her.

Dan wished he could have heard her name, at least, tucked it inside some secret corner of his heart forever, along with the sound of her glorious voice and the treasured secret smiles she had given him.

Looking out the window to the rising moon, he tried to force his thoughts to his mission on the morrow, when he would ride to Boston to meet with Sam Adams and Reverend Cooper.

But even as he closed his mind to thoughts of the emerald maiden, he could see her eyes. Eyes gentle and soft, blue-gray as the sky at dusk.

7

"Wench!" boomed the voice of a drunken customer. He motioned for Susannah to come forward. "Fetch me another grog."

Susannah's smile froze in place, and her back stiffened as she slowly turned from the customers she had just served.

"Wench!" she heard him demand a second time as a fist slammed the surface of the dark wooden table. "More grog!"

Eyes wide, Susannah clutched the handle of the great earthen pitcher and started hesitantly toward the hulking, bearded man. She swept a curious gaze over the faces of the other patrons. No one else seemed aware of his insulting tone. She stopped to pour more flip into an upheld pewter mug.

"Might's well do it m'self," came the voice once more. The swarthy man rose unsteadily and lumbered her way. Squinty bloodshot eyes glared at Susannah as a massive arm reached to snatch the vessel from her grasp.

"I—I'm—," she stammered.

"No you don't, Silas Drummond." Jasper Lyons' strong hand clamped upon the bulging forearm, stalling the man's action. Some of the brew splashed over the rim and onto the floor. "I'll not have you bein' rude to our young lady here." With a challenging shake of the poker he'd been using to heat the sweet rum at the bar, he motioned for Mr. Drummond to take his seat.

"Reckon you should do what Mr. Lyons says," added Jonathan Bradford as he and his two friends rose at the next table.

Susannah barely breathed as she watched the play of emotions upon Silas Drummond's surly face.

"Wanna see the young'uns," he grumbled, heading instead for the door. "Gotta right to."

"They don't work after supper time," the innkeeper answered. "And we won't have you bothering them when you're swill-bellied. Go on home, Silas."

With a final glare over his shoulder, Drummond muttered something, shot a glance at Susannah, then left.

Trembling, Susannah slowly let out her breath. That horrible man was the father of Mary Clare and Christopher? No wonder the poor children cowered from everyone in fear! He was not only overbearing and rude, but frightening as well.

Mr. Lyons turned with a look of concern softening his craggy face. "My apologies, Miss Harrington. I shoulda kept a closer eye on him."

"Right," Morgan Thomas added with the hint of a smile. "Most folks are more considerate. I hope the blighter hasn't upset you."

"No, I'm fine. Thank you all for coming to my aid." Despite her flushed cheeks, she flashed an uneasy smile at her rescuers. "Well, I suppose I should get back to work now, if you'll excuse me." She set the pitcher down and went to the kitchen for a rag to wipe up the puddle.

When she had finished, she heard Hiram Brown's voice calling to her. "Might we trouble you for pie and coffee, miss?"

"Most certainly." Susannah hastened to comply, returning shortly to the small group of now-familiar faces.

"Asa, what d'ya think of the trial comin' up?" Mr. Brown asked as Susannah filled their cups. "Never thought I'd see the day when a patriot would defend a pack of murderin' redcoats in court."

Asa Appleton shook his graying head. "Hear tell three fine Boston lawyers are takin' the case, one of them being John

Adams no less." He poured cream into his coffee. "But if you ask me, they're bitin' off a tough piece to chew."

"Isn't it one of them who says all *free men* deserve a fair trial," a third man asked in a scoffing tone, "even if they *are* no-good scoundrels?"

"Even so," Hiram Brown replied, "it's hard to figure. John Adams sullyin' his name like that. 'Specially with him being Sam Adams' cousin and all." With a stained handkerchief he wiped his big red nose.

As Susannah cleared vacated places at the various tables, she overheard more of their discussion.

"I just arrived from up Boston way," said a traveler at one of the square corner tables. "And we do have just cause to detest those British dogs who lord it over us, that's for certain."

Susannah cringed inwardly. It was common knowledge that only the dregs of the British Isles served as foot soldiers. But still, their duty in the Colonies lay in protecting British interests.

"But fact is," he continued, "those redcoats were sorely provoked."

"That so?" Brown's tone was dubious. He grimaced at his friends and gestured with a calloused thumb in the direction of the newcomer.

The stranger nodded. "Some hotheads with sticks and clubs cornered them and threw stones at them. The redcoats were merely defending themselves."

"Well, would we do less," Mr. Appleton asked, smoothing his wool waistcoat over his ample stomach, "if they was stationed in *our* town bullying folks, checking wagons, confiscating supplies, taking our jobs—"

"And offending our womenfolk," added old Mr. Bentley around the pipe clenched in his teeth. "Let's not forget that." With a nod of emphasis, he puffed a cloud of fragrant smoke upward.

"Right," Hiram Brown said. "No man would stand for it. If my Bessie'd lived to see such a day—" He shook his head.

"Ah, well," another stranger remarked, "the lobsterbacks

wouldn't *be* stationed in the port towns in the first place, if not for that cur, Townshend. Too bad he had to go and drop dead like that. He shoulda lived so's him and his London laws could stand trial along with his trained British dogs, if you ask me."

"Now you're talkin'," Mr. Brown said. "Devil take the fellow's carcass an' be done with it!"

Susannah finished sweeping the floor of the common room and checked to see that fresh table linens were in place on the trestle tables for morning. Then she snuffed the candles in the wall sconces. With a weary sigh she pulled at one end of her apron sash.

Mr. Lyons was wiping down the bar. "Esther and me, we sure do appreciate your help, Miss Harrington."

Susannah draped her apron over the crook of her arm and smiled. "It has certainly kept my mind off my own problems, I daresay. But I do so wish you'd call me Susannah."

The innkeeper's eyebrows rose in bushy silver arches on his forehead. "Can't think of you except as a lady, with them fine ways. Even your name sounds proper."

In the flickering glow of the small hanging lamp above his head, Susannah scrutinized the older man's face as he spoke. At first she'd almost feared him because of his gruff manner and his loud voice. But he had demonstrated himself to be a man of character. She approached the bar and rested her elbows on the smooth wood. "Mr. Lyons, would you mind terribly if I asked you something?"

Wrinkling his forehead, he lifted an inquisitive gaze. "Well, I'm not sure I can help, Miss—Susannah, but I'll do my best."

She wondered how to put her thoughts into words. The sight of Methuselah asleep on the perch had an odd calming effect on her, and she smiled. "It's about the Colonies, you see. I've not been here for very long, and there's much I cannot seem to understand about all these political problems."

"Well, womenfolk don't need much understandin' of it, to be truthful."

Susannah lifted her chin slightly. Men held such rigid views where women were concerned. "Why ever not? The conditions affect everyone who lives here, which most certainly includes women. Surely you must agree with that."

With a grudging nod, he studied her.

"Well then, if I can't ask you to help settle matters a bit for me, whom might I ask?"

Mr. Lyons shrugged. He put the rag out of sight beneath the bar and looked intently at Susannah. "What has you muddled?"

"Quite a lot, actually. Conversations I overhear while I'm working about the common room. Criticism of my country. Parliament. The soldiers. And the late Lord Townshend. Why, in Britain he was most respected. Yet here—" She lowered her eyes.

He rubbed a work-hardened hand over his jowls in thought. "Well, I suppose it all comes down to money. Whose is whose. When England's coffers started runnin' low awhile back, she decided she needed to get her hands on what precious little money *we* have to pay for *her* war with France."

"But I thought that war was fought to save the colonists from the savagery of the French and Indians."

"So they keep telling us." He chuckled to himself. "Truth is, they was fightin' the Frenchies over all the territory west of the mountains. And if they happened to save some poor frontiersman who got caught in the middle, it was just Providence. We've always had to see to ourselves. So that's how come we resent old Townshend coming up with all kinds of taxes on things we need."

Frowning, Susannah nodded. "It hardly sounds fair."

"I should say not. But England has set up some royal courts here anyway, which we also have to foot the bill for, plus the officials to enforce the tariffs. Then they shipped over a bunch of lice-infested soldiers and said it was up to us to take 'em into our homes! Let me tell you, that's where we drew the line."

"Soldiers in your homes? Why, that's dreadful. The Colonies are being treated like a conquered land. Surely Parliament must listen to your representative on this matter and hear your side of it."

He let out a huff. "We don't *have* a representative. Not a single one. That's the sting of it!" He slammed his fist down. "And lately, since the latest trouble, they won't even allow our own assemblies to meet, because we just might object to England's tyranny. So you see, the only course we *have* is the boycott—either that or open rebellion."

"I had no idea. Julia mentioned none of this in her letters. If what you say is true, I can see why there is such unrest over the matter." Susannah pondered his words for a few moments, then sighed. "Well, I do thank you for telling me all of this, Mr. Lyons. I shan't trouble you further."

"Perhaps something will be done to smooth things over before the riots get entirely out of hand. Least we can hope so," he said kindly.

"Yes. Well, I shall pray for that as well." Apron in hand, Susannah headed for the kitchen. "Good night, Mr. Lyons."

"'Night, lass."

The bell in the cupola at Nassau Hall called the Presbyterian worshipers to the morning service, and people began to converge on foot and by wagon.

Passing the college on her way to the local Anglican church, the only approved church of the king and England—and most particularly, of Reverend Selkirk—Susannah could not help but note the Presbyterian structure's splendid design. Made of uncut native stone, the building had three front doorways, each with a flat arch, stone quoin, and separate flight of stairs. Susannah's eyes lingered on the central doorway with a bust of Homer dominating its arch. Fleetingly she imagined the joy that would be hers if she could respond to the call of the bell for morning worship each day before dawn, and then engage in the lectures that followed. But that sort of life was offered to men only. To her brother. It could never be hers.

She lifted her chin and stepped up her pace, nodding to faces she recognized along the way. When she reached the Sommerville road, she turned right.

Several minutes later, she arrived at a squat, neglected-looking clapboard church, where a handful of people stood chatting as she approached.

"Good day, miss," said a tall, thin man in clerical garb and wig. He held out a hand. "I'm Reverend Miller."

"How do you do. My name is Susannah Harrington."

"I can't recall your having worshiped with us before. Are you, perhaps, new to this town?"

"Yes, I arrived only a few days past."

"Ah. It's most fortunate you chose this morning to join us. We have only one service during the month. I alternate at three additional parishes on other Sundays. Come in."

Susannah followed him inside and chose a seat near the back. A small heating stove in the boxed enclosure radiated warmth. She knelt for a quick silent prayer, then took her seat. Glancing at the dismal surroundings as she opened her prayer book, she met pleasant nods from the scattering clusters of folk in similar family-size cubicles. Then the cross was carried up the aisle with the minister walking behind it up to the platform.

The familiar structure of the formal worship that followed brought bittersweet memories of similar services presided over by her father in the ancient stone church near their home. A stab of sadness reminded Susannah that she would never again hear that beloved voice. Swallowing against the pain inside, she forced herself to repeat the responses and sing the hymns. When at last Reverend Miller read the customary prayer before his sermon and said "Amen," Susannah opened her eyes and waited expectantly for his discourse.

"This morning I wish to speak on strife," he began. "In the thirteenth chapter of the book of Genesis, we find the story of Abraham and his nephew, Lot. They were living side by side with all of their households. When the flocks and herds the two possessed began to run out of grass, it caused strife between Abraham's herdsmen and Lot's, and ill feelings arose within the families."

He looked to his text. "Abraham went to his nephew, it states in the eighth verse. And Abraham said to him, 'Let there be no strife, I pray thee, between me and thee, and between my herdmen and thy herdmen; for we be brethren.' "

The minister gazed again at the congregation. "In these trying days, strife is around us at every turn. We've been blessed here in this young land. Yet, although we are under the protection and assistance of a most generous and righteous benefactor, Great Britain, many among you have begun to stir and rise up against her." His eyes narrowed in a scathing stare. "This is a most grievous sin."

"Consider the text this morning," he continued, "and the words 'Let there be no strife . . . for we be brethren.' Lot took his possessions and moved to Sodom, which, of course, brought disastrous consequences—" A bony finger stabbed the air for emphasis. "The sort of consequences which could possibly befall the Colonies today if you turn away from the righteousness that is Britain—to the Sodom of ungodly radicals! I should hope that a suspension of ill feelings might take place now, before matters proceed too far in measures which could be ruinous to this fledgling land."

He shook his head in silence as he studied the faces before him. "And as you know, this rebellion is not merely over taxes, but over far more serious matters—our own good Church of England here in America! Many men who proclaim to be God's servants—if I may call them that—now preach heretical ideas, spawning numbers of unlearned men who go forth to preach in blasphemous ignorance. Undermining the principles of the true church, these extravagant enthusiastic endeavors to propagate some ridiculous new system of worship with their raving notion of freedom in Christ—acting under the name of religion! These lunatics are beyond description."

With a disgusted grimace, he continued. "Such madness and folly cannot possibly last long—though they *may* unhinge rational principles for a time. I entreat—no, *demand*—that you become more cautious. Do not be led into delusion by these false prophets and pretended saints. They are an offense to those of us who have studied long and hard to be of service to almighty God!" He pounded the pulpit with his fist, his face reddening in fervor.

"This must not continue! How can men who—overnight—proclaim themselves to be ministers start churches without proper credentials or rightful order? Why, they even question the right of the government to tax the people in order to ensure that properly ordained men of the Anglican Church are brought here and provided for in the manner befitting our station! Many have been duped, pulled away; my congregations have grown so small I must travel from pillar to post each Sabbath. I say, we must stand up against this sort of tyranny, and against those criminals who stir up political strife with the mother country as well!"

A fashionably dressed woman in front of Susannah nudged her husband in the ribs and nodded knowingly, the finger curls of her wig bobbing in agreement.

"Yes," the pastor continued, "strife is all around us, destroying us as it did Lot."

Susannah wanted to give credence to his words, but she found the way he had twisted the meaning of the story of Abraham and Lot to fit his own purpose most unworthy. Her mind wandered back to her talk with Jasper Lyons about the Colonies and their problems with England. At least concerning the political strife, all the fault did not lie with the settlers. England had caused many of the problems that now stirred the crowds with resentment. So Mr. Lyons had said, and he had seemed quite sincere. More so, in fact, than did the overly righteous clergyman rebuking the pitifully small number of listeners at this church.

Luther Selkirk, another supposed man of God, had also had nothing but stiff-necked criticism for this new land and the people. How was it that those who professed to belong to God were the most uncharitable? Were there no pastors left like her papa?

Susannah was so engrossed in her musings that she was unaware that the service had ended. At last she glanced around and saw that she was alone. Picking up her small handbag, she pulled her knitted shawl over her shoulders and rose, her skirt rustling softly as she walked toward the door and looked out on the rapidly dispersing group.

As she stepped off the landing, she nodded a greeting to the woman who had been seated in the row just ahead of her.

"Good day," the lady said, smoothing her gold velvet gown as her eyes assessed the rich brocade Susannah wore. Her overly sweet smile looked false, oddly out of place on her stern face. "The name's Hattie Davidson."

"Very pleased to meet you. I'm Susannah Harrington. A most interesting service, was it not?"

"Quite." Mrs. Davidson continued to study her. "I couldn't help but notice you're alone."

"Yes, I am. You see, I've only just arrived here in Prince-Town—Princeton," she corrected. "But I shan't be staying long."

The woman's husband approached just then. The almost-grown girl on his arm was a replica of her mother's demeanor and features. Susannah had no doubt she was their daughter.

The man eyed Susannah curiously. "Why, aren't you the young lady who served me last night at the Lyons' Den?"

Susannah smiled and nodded. "Yes, you're quite right."

Mrs. Davidson gasped and fanned herself with a gloved hand. "We must go now, Henry. Eleanor. At once." Turning, she grabbed the daughter's hand and all but dragged her to a waiting carriage.

Susannah tilted her head and stared after their departing backs. Apparently, working for one's daily bread lessened a person's worth considerably, even in America. Disheartened, she headed for the inn.

A large crowd of townspeople poured out of Nassau Hall as

she passed, and again Susannah looked admiringly at the well-kept building. In a few weeks classes would commence, and the number of worshipers would burgeon even more.

Daniel Haynes had been enrolled there, she recalled. She could easily picture him in flowing black robes, accompanying other young men to lectures, to worship, to an occasional supper at the coaching house. Images of him seemed to pop into her mind at the most inconvenient times—often followed by visions of smugglers dressed up to resemble ladies of high style. That disturbing thought made her frown, and Susannah longed for Julia, to talk to her, confide in her. A wave of sadness curled over her. There was no one here who truly cared about her.

"Miss Harrington!" Steven Russell skipped down the steps and raced toward her, followed closely by his fellow student, Jonathan Bradford. Breathless, they stopped upon reaching her. "We saw you walking toward Reverend Miller's little church this morning."

She nodded, trying to shake off her melancholy.

"We'll see you safely back to the inn," Jonathan said.

"Thank you all the same, but I assure you it isn't necessary."

"Well, Mrs. Lyons would wring our necks if we allowed you to return unescorted, you know," Jonathan teased, clutching his throat. "Would you want to be a party to *that* sight?"

Susannah realized she was gaping. She closed her mouth and blinked, feeling a smile spreading across her face. "Why no. Not at all."

"Good. Then it's settled." He offered an arm.

A flush warmed Susannah's cheeks. She shook her head and started walking.

"Something troubling you?" Steven's close-set gray eyes searched her face as he fell into step beside her.

"Why yes, actually." Susannah stopped and turned to gaze at both young men. "Everything is wrong. My mind is beset with a tangle of thoughts, and I can't seem to sort them out."

"Ah," Steven said. "One of those Tories at the Anglican church must have said something distressing. Am I right?"

"No. Yes. Oh, that's just a part of it." She began walking again. "I don't know. I shall be glad when Tuesday arrives and I can be gone from here."

"Where are you bound?"

She lifted a sad smile toward them. "I have no idea. No idea at all. Frightfully absurd, isn't it?"

"Reckon so," Jonathan said thoughtfully. "But then why did you come here at all? You must have had a reason."

"Yes, I did. Quite a good one, in fact. But now that all seems part of some other life." She shrugged her shoulders. "I came here to join my friend. Julia Chandler."

"Rob's Julia?" Steven asked.

Susannah nodded. "I was to live with them. I had no idea that something had . . . that she'd—" She sighed. "Now I've nowhere to go. The journey took nearly all of my funds."

Jonathan let out a low whistle. "Her passing caught all of us off guard." Gently he touched Susannah's arm. "And now you're stranded."

"Well," Steven said, "you might consider staying on right here, you know. Considering your quest for knowledge and all." He grinned impishly and cocked his head. "You could make *new* friends."

"I believe Rob is planning to return when classes start up again next month," Jonathan added. "We could easily contact him for you."

"Of course." Steven's brows rose hopefully. "He'd want to know you've come. And under the circumstances, I'm certain he'd insist on providing for you." A half-smile gentled his expression. "It's possible he'd like to have someone to talk to about Julia, you know. And until then *we'd* be most honored if you'd allow *us* to pay for your room and board. The three of us, Morgan included. We'll be your protectors, your own personal knights."

Susannah's steps faltered as tears blurred her vision. America seemed full of knights of the realm. First brown-eyed Daniel Haynes, whose strong arms had shielded her from harm, and now these young gentlemen of Princeton. She wasn't sure which was harder to fathom . . . their presumptive kindness or the 'good' Mrs. Davidson's hostility.

"Oh, I couldn't allow that. But I do thank you, both of you." She sniffed and managed a watery smile. "Can't you just imagine what people would say then? Why, I'd be put into stocks, to be scorned in the town square. Apparently I've already compromised myself by being a serving girl. . . ."

Susannah's eyes widened. "Serving girl! Merciful heavens! I'm late. Upon my soul!" Forgetting propriety, Susannah picked up her brocade skirts and ran the rest of the way.

Mrs. Lyons looked up in surprise as Susannah burst into the kitchen followed by the two young men.

"Dreadfully sorry I'm late, Mrs. Lyons," Susannah explained on her way through. "These gentlemen were bent on comforting me after I was shunned by the hostile gentry. I'll change and come down straightaway."

Susannah noticed a twinkle in Mrs. Lyons' eyes as she clucked her tongue at Jonathan and Steven. "We serve only leftovers on Sundays. But you're more than welcome to join our table."

A short time later, Susannah descended the stairs in an afternoon dress of periwinkle blue sprigged muslin and found herself greeted by Mrs. Lyons' pointed stare.

"Hostile gentry, you say? Don't suppose it might be someone I know."

Susannah reached for the coffeepot and turned to face her. "A Mrs. Davidson. Hattie, I believe."

"That old biddy. Pshaw! Don't you be payin' that one no mind. She was common folk herself till her husband's inferior furniture got popular when we boycotted British goods. 'Twould please her to no end if the action went on forever. Now that she's so uppity, she feels it's her Christian duty to remain unspotted by the world—though I don't think that's exactly how the good Lord meant it. Here," she said, reaching for a crisp, clean apron, "don't be forgettin' this, or you'll be gettin' spots of a different sort."

Susannah raised her arms while the older woman tied the

apron strings snugly around her waist. "I shall miss you awfully, you know, after Tuesday."

"Well now, there's no real need for you to be goin' someplace else, love." Mrs. Lyons picked up a platter of fried chicken. "I've been doin' some thinking. We'd be mighty pleased if you stayed right here, like part of the family. Think on it."

Susannah studied the lined face beneath the ruffled cap—the kindly eyes, the hopeful smile. Then, fighting tears one more time, she held the door to the long room open while Mrs. Lyons preceded her. She had many things to think about, to pray about. Thoughts of remaining in Princeton had been abandoned days ago upon learning of dear Julia's death. But now, with no home to go to and no money to return to England, staying seemed a rather attractive possibility.

And if she did, Susannah reminded herself, there was a chance that the dashing Daniel Haynes might pop up in town on his postriding business. Something about him seemed to keep the memory of their meeting in Philadelphia hovering very near the surface of her every waking thought. After all, he had sought her out at the inn with that hopeful light in his eyes, had chosen a table nearby . . . and even tried to speak to her despite Luther Selkirk's uncharitable conduct. If she were to leave now, she would certainly never see him again. And a part of her was counting on their paths crossing at least once more. He seemed a kindred spirit, one which drew her for reasons she could not explain.

But another part of her tried to think much more practically, to banish from her mind all dreams of a young man who would be foolish enough to dabble in questionable affairs. Such activities were most likely illegal, possibly even treasonous. Certainly it would be more prudent to forget him.

But one thing was certain. She would have to put thoughts of him aside, somehow, while she prayed for guidance. He should not sway her decision one way or the other. Not in the least.

8

Daniel tried to steel himself against his mother's pleading as he mounted his horse in the cool early morning.

With one hand holding her shawl closed over her dressing gown, she put the other on his sleeve, gently hindering his departure. "But, Daniel, you know you should not be traveling today. At the very least, you should rest and meditate upon the goodness of almighty God."

He drew a deep breath and looked off into the distance. Would she never understand his calling, his need to assist his country against the growing tyranny from across the sea? "I'm sorry, Mother, but I must go. I'm needed in Boston."

"I can't see what difference one day would make. You could leave at first light tomorrow." At his silence her expression clouded. "Well then, go if you must, but not until you've come to church with us, at least."

"Even the Lord did what was necessary on the Sabbath, Mother. Remember how he healed the lame and helped people without considering what day of the week it might be? I've committed myself to aid in the patriotic cause—which I believe is a just and righteous one. And at this crucial time before the trial of the soldiers, it cannot be set aside for even one day out of seven. Please try to understand." Bending to kiss her cheek, he coaxed a smile from her, then squeezed her shoulder. "Good-bye."

She nodded, fighting back tears, and lifted a hand as if in dismissal.

Daniel nudged Flame into motion and headed along the lane toward the dense growth of woods at the edge of the property. But even after the forest growth had closed off the last view of the farm, he had to fight to erase from his memory the pain in his mother's eyes. It remained with him for miles.

Some hours later, he reached the narrow expanse of land known as the Boston Neck, which lay between the Charles River and the harbor. Off in the distance stood the arched double gate, marking the entrance to Boston. Maneuvering his horse carefully over the hard, dry ruts from the last rain, he approached the guard post.

As he neared the rough shack, two British soldiers stepped outside and took up a stance at the horizontal pole blocking the road, their muskets drawn at waist level. Sunlight glinted off their bayonets. "Halt and dismount, in the name of His Majesty."

Daniel drew Flame to a stop, then swung a leg over the saddle and stepped down, one hand still on the horse's mane. He faced the king's men.

"State your purpose for entering the city."

"Government business," Dan said quietly. "I'm delivering mail to Boston." Seething inwardly at their arrogance, he glanced over the uniformed pair, noticing another two soldiers inside the booth. "All of which bears stamps as required by the king."

"We'll see about that," said one. The soldier stepped over to Dan's horse, tore open the pouch fastened behind the saddle, and rummaged through the contents. He withdrew a fistful of papers and scrutinized them, then stuffed them haphazardly back inside.

Dan forced himself to breathe calmly, despite his growing anger.

The man cast a knowing sneer at Daniel. He raised the spar. "Carry on, then." Turning on one heel, he stepped back beside the other smirking redcoat. They relaxed their stances and rested the butts of their rifles at their feet.

Dan gritted his teeth and retied the leather strings of the mail pouch. Then, his features calm and composed, he remounted, dipped his head to the officials, and nudged Flame's sides gently with his knees. Not until he was well past the stopping point and farther along Orange Street did he finally feel his jaw muscles relax.

The clatter of the horse's hooves over the cobblestone echoed against the brick buildings that lined the street. The sound was oddly comforting. He tensed again when another pair of soldiers strolled by with rouged women in gaudy gowns of satin and feathers, and wondered absently what his mother would think of such brazen conduct on a Sunday afternoon.

"Well now. What have we here?" A gruff voice drew his attention to the next corner.

Approaching the intersection slowly on his horse, Daniel noticed a young, well-dressed couple turning onto the street, their passage barred by three soldiers.

"Aye. Defilin' the Sabbath, are ye?" slurred a second officer as he swayed unsteadily on his feet, his tall bearskin headgear nearly toppling from his head.

"Stand aside, gentlemen," the young man said. "We're breaking no law. We've been summoned to the bedside of our aunt, who is gravely ill. Let us pass."

"Oh. Ill, you say?" the third redcoat said in a mocking tone. He leered at the lovely woman who, dressed in amber velvet, stood with her arm through that of her companion. "The devil confound me, she doesn't appear ill. Not in the least." With a grimy hand, he reached for the rich copper plume on her bonnet and fingered the feathery strands.

The woman gasped and huddled closer to the young fellow beside her, and he put a protective arm around her.

"I say," said the soldier's deep voice again. "Give *us* leave to escort the fair wench. We've much more experience with—*ladies,* shall we say?" His face widened in a sneer.

"Aye," the second said with a guffaw. "'Twill be our pleasure—and hers, to be sure."

The young man held out a restraining hand. "Now see here!"

Dan reined Flame in and jumped down. "There you are, James, Ruth."

All five heads turned in his direction, a mixture of relief and confusion apparent on the faces of the couple.

Daniel grinned disarmingly. "Everyone's asking about you. Aunt Minerva's fading fast. Do hurry, before it's too late."

"Why, of course—Cousin." The young man in gray shot an appreciative glance at Daniel as he quickly entered into the charade. Stepping around the redcoats, he drew the young woman along. "We'll come at once. Come along—Ruth." With a grateful smile at Dan, they hastened up the street.

Daniel remounted and followed the pair for several moments, conscious of the suspicious stares of the king's men on his back. Once he was certain that the soldiers had gone their way, Daniel turned his horse and continued down Orange toward Queen Street.

Unbidden visions of another young maiden in distress surfaced in his mind, and a half-smile curved his mouth at the memory of her smooth ivory complexion, her wide, soft eyes, and the hint of a cleft in her chin. He wondered how she was faring in Princeton, and if she planned to stay there for good. Then, realizing the dallying direction taken by his thoughts, he shook his head to chase them away. This was no time to be woolgathering over a woman . . . especially one he really didn't know anything about . . . even if she *did* have the most wondrous eyes he'd ever seen. . . .

Get a grip on yourself, Haynes! he scolded himself impatiently. Perhaps his mother was right. Maybe he *had* been on the road too long . . .

Turning north onto Queen Street, Daniel stopped at Sam Cooper's brick mansion house, dismounted, and strode to the door. He glanced up and down the deserted street, then lifted the knocker and let it fall.

The latch clicked, and the heavy door swung open. "Yes?" Judith Cooper asked. When she recognized Daniel, the polite smile on her face faded, and a slight frown took its place. "Come in, please. My husband's expecting you in the parlor." She gestured toward the next room.

"My thanks, Mrs. Cooper." Dan watched her hustle away toward the kitchen, muttering as she went that nothing good would come to those who conducted business on the Sabbath.

"Why, Daniel." The Reverend Sam Cooper met him with a warm handclasp at the doorway of the elegant sitting room. "Come in, lad." He motioned toward his other guest. "We've been waiting for you. I believe you know Sam Adams."

"Yes, sir, I do. Mr. Adams." Daniel nodded and shook the other man's bony hand. "Good to see you again."

The minister motioned for them to be seated.

Dan's admiring gaze wandered over the rich furnishings of the parsonage with its embossed wall coverings and heavy drapes. With his fashionable clothing, eloquent manners, and softly modulated voice, the Reverend Cooper seemed completely at ease amidst the finery. By contrast, Sam Adams—thin and pale, trembling with palsy, and clothed in a drab, outmoded style—almost flaunted his own impoverished life-style.

"Have any problems getting here?" the reverend asked, settling back against the upholstered settee and propping his feet on a leather footstool.

"None I couldn't handle." Dan gave a careless shrug. "Ran into the usual pack at the Neck, but they let me pass."

Sam Adams nodded. "And the engravings you took to Philadelphia?"

"They arrived safely, sir."

"What of the boycott? Still holding?"

"For the most part, yes. New York's been giving us some problems, though, only halfheartedly supporting us."

Mrs. Cooper entered the room just then bearing a silver tray with coffee and dainty cakes.

"Thank you, my dear." Reverend Cooper touched her hand

lightly as she set the tray on the cherry table beside him. Seeing the disapproving curve of her mouth, he gave her fingers an extra squeeze. "Oh, don't fret, love. The neighbors won't be concerned at all with our little meeting. These men are just friends, after all."

She sighed. "I can't help it, Samuel. I fear you'll bring trouble upon us with these meetings of yours." She swept a glance over Daniel and Sam Adams.

"Nonsense, my love. We're just discussing matters that concern the Colonies. No harm in that, I assure you." He winked a clear blue eye at her.

"Even so, I daresay you could as easily meet on some other day of the week," she said. With a bob of her ruffled cap, she pulled her lace shawl closer and left the room, her full skirt swishing softly with each footstep.

Reverend Cooper poured the coffee into three bone china cups. "Ah, if there's one thing I loathe in all of this, it's having to sacrifice my blessed India tea. May doom befall those who enforce the despicable Townshend Duties." He passed a cup to Sam Adams and one to Dan, adding a bit of cream to his own before removing it from the tray.

"I'm sure there are far worse things than having to drink coffee or hyperion tea."

"Hear! Hear!" Sam Adams flailed an arm in the air.

"I do have some good news for you both," Daniel said.

"And what might that be, lad?" the minister asked.

"George Whitefield may be traveling up in this direction, come summer, for another preaching tour."

"Reverend Whitefield?" Adams' voice rose even higher. "He hasn't been in the Colonies for two years. I thought perhaps he had decided to remain in Britain."

Daniel shook his head. "Quite the contrary. He did stay in England during his wife's illness. But I hear she passed away some time ago, and he's returned to Georgia."

"Lost his wife, you say?" A frown creased Reverend Cooper's brow. "Dire bit of news."

"Yes," Adams added. "Most sorrowful. Something many of

us must face at one time or another. I recall the grief we felt when my first wife passed on, may God rest her soul."

"Whitefield's not in the best of health himself," the reverend muttered softly. "And I fear the man won't last long without a good woman to care for him."

No one spoke for several moments. The grandfather clock in one corner ticked loudly, punctuating tiny phrases of silence.

"I, for one, owe a lot to that gentleman," Sam Adams said, his voice quiet for the first time. "'Twas his dream that inspired me as a youth. A dream of one great colony, strong and united, with religious freedom for all, a shining child of the mother country." His voice grew strangely low. "But now I fear we must think of breaking away from a mother who would keep us forever under her domineering thumb."

Dan's eyes widened in surprise. "Isn't that a bit radical even to think about, sir, much less say aloud? Even behind closed doors? To expect America to turn against those who've enabled us to begin the settlements . . ."

A benign smile softened Adams' pale face. "Ah yes, lad. But who among us is to say that almighty God may not have intended independence for us all along?"

A knock sounded on the door, and no one breathed until Mrs. Cooper ushered a sailor into the room.

"Beggin' your pardons." Yancy Curtis gave a quick nod of his red head.

All three men rose, and the minister extended his hand with a smile. "Seaman Curtis. Good to see you."

"Thank you." He grinned and shook Sam Adams' hand, then his grin broadened as Daniel stepped forward.

"Greetings, Yance. I'm surprised to see you in Boston already. It's only been a few days since I met you at the dock in Philadelphia."

"The dock. Aye. Well, I caught a coastal packet on its way here, and it's been a fair wind, y' know, mate."

"Right." Dan shook his head incredulously. "By the way, I

managed to pick up the latest copy of the *Ladies' Fashion Guide* in my travels—in case you're interested."

Curtis reddened slightly as the two other gentlemen exchanged puzzled looks. He tightened his lips and managed to contain his chuckle.

"Obviously Mr. Adams and I are completely in the dark about the subject of this strange conversation," said the reverend as he searched Yancy's face. "So perhaps we might uncover the nature of your visit?"

"Aye. I've something for you." Removing a rolled paper from behind the sailor's cap he held in his hands, he extended it toward Reverend Cooper.

The minister opened the missive and scanned it. "Hallelujah!" he said at last, slapping the paper with the backs of his fingers. "The Townshend Acts have been repealed! Praise be! The boycott worked. It finally brought Parliament around."

"Meanin' no disrespect, sir," Yancy interrupted. "I suggest you look closer. Not all the duties have been withdrawn. There's still the one on tea—and the maritime laws, to boot."

"Why," Sam Adams squeaked, "that means the two British regiments here in Boston and those scattered about in the other ports will not be returning to England. Am I right?"

Yancy nodded. "It appears."

Adams pounded the arm of his chair in frustration and leaped to his feet. "So they think the colonists are so ignorant that we can be mollified by the simple lifting of a few tariffs, eh? A pox on the devils!" With a scowl, he paced back and forth across the carpet.

"Well, some people just might *be* fooled by such an action, my friend," Reverend Cooper said softly, shaking his head.

"No!" Adams' voice raised to its highest pitch of the afternoon as he stopped in mid-stride and turned, wagging a bony finger in their direction. "It shows how devious they can be. Pretending to relent, while still keeping the right to impose a tax on us. No matter how small, it sets a precedent. One that will give Britain the right to strip away the rest of our freedoms one by one. We've *got* to make sure the Colonies see the truth of this!"

Dan pondered Adams' words and nodded thoughtfully. Perhaps it *would* come to separation, after all. No one would sit still for more British tyranny. But the very thought of standing against the great royal lion was frightening. Was this truly the will of God? Would he close this mighty lion's mouth as he had for the Hebrew Daniel in the lions' den?

"And you realize," Yancy cut in, "that uppity blackguard, Hillsborough, is likely burstin' his britches with glee. He still has the authority to keep us under his heel for good," Yancy said. "He's one barnacle we'll not soon scrape off our hull."

All three men stared at the sailor.

Reverend Cooper nodded solemnly and expelled a slow breath. "Well. I fear there's no recourse for us now, gentlemen. We must pray that America is brave enough to remove her allegiance from the king of England and once again put her trust in the King of kings, as our forefathers did when they first left the mother country. I can't see any other hope for us."

After several moments of silence, Daniel cleared his throat. "How'd you come to be in Boston, Yance?"

"'Tis like this. The packet I came in on is anchored just outside of port in a wee inlet. We've a bit of cargo that needs to be . . . thinned, you might say, before we dock."

"Ah," the reverend said. "Cargo not for British eyes."

Yancy grinned. "The unloading's to be tomorrow, after dark. The cove west of Segimore Farm on the Cape. Might be we could use some extra hands—many as you can spare."

"Count me in," Dan said with a grin. "I know some others who'll be more than glad to assist. We'll meet you at the cove tomorrow."

Yancy rendered a careless salute. "See you then. Gents." Dipping his head, he turned and left.

"Well now. This is one fine pot of beans," Sam Adams said. He kneaded his chin in thought before he spoke. "I think it's time we contact the Sons of Liberty and any other friends we have of like mind. And you know, Reverend, I think we've a real need for an organization ready to undertake the responsibility of relaying news like this throughout the Colonies."

Reverend Cooper nodded. "I heartily agree. Each colony should have a committee of corresponders as well. And it must be done in all haste."

Dan felt his heartbeat quicken. "I'll be glad to get right on it, sir, soon as I've helped with the unloading tomorrow. I'll spread the word to all the other postriders."

"No, lad." Adams looked straight into his eyes. "We've decided to relieve you of your duty."

"What?" Dan felt his heart plummet within his chest. He rose slowly. "I don't understand, sir. Have I not served the patriots to the best of my abilities?" He looked to the minister for an explanation.

"Nay, lad," Reverend Cooper said with a kind smile. "It isn't that, I assure you. We've been most grateful for your faithfulness and the speed with which you've carried out your assignments while riding from one post to the next."

"Therefore I'm to be relieved?" Dan's eyes searched one face, then the other.

Both men came to their feet. Sam Adams chuckled at the minister and withdrew something from an inside pocket of his own worn frock coat. "Yes, you've more than proved your worth to us, Daniel. And we have something of much more importance for you to undertake." Palsied hands shaking, he handed Daniel the folded paper.

Dan swallowed and closed his fingers over it without looking at it.

"That is a letter from the postmaster of Boston," Adams said. "It contains a list of all colony postmasters sympathetic to our cause—men who've proven their loyalties and are above reproach. Learn their names, Daniel, then destroy the list. They'll be the first link in our new expansion, and they'll be passing coded messages by post concerning shipments of our supplies from abroad, secret meetings, and the like."

"To the British," Reverend Cooper added, "you'll appear as

just one of many postriders. But your route will fluctuate according to the need. Among your other courier duties, Daniel, you'll be informed of ships that must be unloaded in secret. You'll relay word to the other patriots and arrange help for the transfer of cargo to shore." His eyes twinkled as a smile spread over his face. "Sounds a bit more 'helpful,' does it not?"

Daniel had problems hearing over the pounding of his heart. Surely it was a dream. It had to be! His laugh echoed in the quiet of the room. "When do I start?"

Adams clapped him on the back, the sound oddly muffled against the soft deerskin of his coat. "Tonight, lad. Come by my house later this evening. I'll have a number of letters written by then regarding the cursed partial appeal. And since you'll be heading south, stop at Isaiah Peak's place on the Cape. His men always help when there are goods to unload at the cove."

"And," added the reverend, "be sure to tell any postriders you may meet in your travels the truth of this latest ploy by Parliament."

"I'll do my best. Thank you. Both of you. I won't let you down."

"Daniel—" Reverend Sam Cooper squeezed the younger man's shoulder with a well-groomed hand. "Please be careful, son. The British have increased the number of patrols along the coastal roads. They arrest anyone at all whom they suspect is remotely connected with the 'conspiracy' to smuggle goods into the Colonies."

Daniel smiled and nodded his head. "I understand. I'll keep a sharp watch." Clasping each man's hand warmly, he strode out of the room.

"Godspeed," both men said just before the door closed behind him.

Susannah moaned softly and covered her head with the down pillow. Her thoughts had awakened her over and over with maddening regularity until the wee hours. And now, with the old rooster announcing the first ray of dawn, she gave up on her uneasy slumber. She had reached no decision as to whether to stay on at the inn or leave tomorrow. How ever would she sort through all the confusion and make up her mind?

The cock crowed again, and with a resigned sigh, Susannah sat up in bed. Mrs. Lyons could no doubt use her help with breakfast. Then her gaze, drifting idly around the room in the dimness, fell upon her father's Bible on the bedside table. *Of course!* She had prayed the night before, but had forgotten her evening reading.

Reaching for the volume, she opened it to the place where a ribbon marked a favorite passage and padded over near the window light. Her father had underlined several verses in the sixth chapter of Matthew and made small notations beside the various sections for sermons. But the last four verses now seemed to stand out from the others:

> Therefore take no thought, saying, What shall we eat? or, What shall we drink? or, Wherewithal shall we be clothed? (For after all these things do the Gentiles seek:) for your heavenly Father knoweth that ye have need of all these things. But seek ye first the kingdom of God, and his righteousness; and all these things shall be added unto you. Take therefore no thought for the morrow: for the morrow shall take thought for the things of itself. Sufficient unto the day is the evil thereof.

Smiling, Susannah replaced the worn ribbon and closed the Bible, hugging it to herself. *"Seek ye first the kingdom of God."* What better place to do that than close to a school that trained ministers, where she might overhear students discussing the mysteries, the deepest messages of the biblical truths? She set the book back down and dressed hurriedly, hoping with all her heart that it was God's will and not just her own that made Princeton seem the right choice.

A few minutes later, she entered the kitchen and smiled at Mrs. Lyons.

"Praise be!" the older woman cried, spreading her motherly arms open as she flew to embrace Susannah in a cushiony hug. "So you'll be stayin' then?"

Susannah kissed her soft cheek and nodded. "I think perhaps it's best, for both of us. You and Mr. Lyons do need help, after all."

"Well." She took a step backward as she shook her head in wonder. The glow on her face stripped several years of wear from among the lines and creases. "I was doing a bit of prayin' myself, love. I had a feeling the good Lord sent you to us for a better reason than a night's lodging."

"So it would seem."

"Well, sit down, child, and have a bit of breakfast before the rush." Dishing some eggs and bacon onto a plate, Mrs. Lyons set them on the table and filled a cup with steaming coffee. "I'll just check things in the long room and make sure the door's unbolted." Happily, she hurried off.

Susannah pulled up a chair with a sigh and settled onto it, bowing her head momentarily for grace. She took a sip of coffee, then bit into a crisp piece of bacon.

The outside door opened, and Mr. Lyons strode in, wiping the last traces of shaving lather from his cheek. He filled a pewter mug with coffee and sat down opposite Susannah. "The wife says you might be stayin' on."

"Yes, for the present . . . if that's acceptable, of course."

Nodding slowly, he gulped a mouthful of coffee and returned his gaze to her. "Hm. Well, that may cause some problems for us, miss. Think you and me should have a talk."

9

Susannah's appetite vanished. Had she heard him correctly? Problems?

She pushed her plate away. "Problems, Mr. Lyons?"

Jasper Lyons nodded his scraggly head. "You and me need to talk over some things." He took another gulp of coffee and set down the mug.

"What sort of things?"

"Well, I'll tell you. Unless you're here to stay, legal-like and all, we'll have to get us someone else."

A frown drew Susannah's brows together. "I don't understand."

"Didn't figure you would. It's just that we have a good business here, Esther and me, and we don't want any misunderstandings between us and Dr. Witherspoon at the college."

Susannah searched Mr. Lyons' face. "Why ever should it cause any misunderstandings for you to have me in your employ?"

"Well, Susannah, it's like this. With you being young and fetching, and unattached besides, Witherspoon just might figure this ain't the right place for the students to be coming in their free time. And we need their business, you see? That's one reason we built the inn right here, so's we'd be nearby the school."

"Oh. I hadn't considered that at all. So you think I should leave, then, when the stage comes through in the morning?"

"I'm not sayin' that." Mr. Lyons crossed to the hearth and filled his cup, then returned and took his seat again. "If you was here under legal contract, with Esther and me as your guardians, I don't see there'd be a problem with it."

"You're speaking of an indenture, am I correct?" For a fleeting moment, Susannah could hear Luther Selkirk's voice in her mind, could see once again his sneering expression. *"Indentures. Akin to selling one's soul."* She wondered how much of her soul would be required.

"Yes. We could go see my lawyer friend and have the papers drawn up today. If you're interested."

Susannah clasped her hands together in her lap and looked at them absently. "I had no idea I'd be required to indenture myself. Might I ask exactly what terms you have in mind?"

"Course. I think—"

Mrs. Lyons returned to the room and gazed from one to the other curiously.

"Ahem." Mr. Lyons shifted in his seat and continued. "I think four years of service."

Susannah exhaled slowly. *Four years?*

"During which time, you would not be free to marry, of course." Mr. Lyons scratched his chin and gave his wife a self-conscious look.

Four years. A brief thought of Daniel surfaced. What if he did happen by? *What if*— She cut off the ridiculous notion before it had even completely formed in her mind. More than likely she'd never lay eyes on him again. But four years! It seemed an eternity.

Mrs. Lyons approached Susannah and put an arm around her shoulder. "Oh, love, Jasper did mention somethin' to me about the legal side of havin' you here. We do need you, that's one thing for sure. Why don't you and him go have a talk with Lawyer Duncan and work it out? He can fix everythin' so's it benefits you as well as us."

With a resigned shrug, Susannah rose. "Very well. A lawyer. I suppose it will do no harm to discuss the matter."

Less than an hour later, Jasper Lyons escorted Susannah to the establishment of Curtis Duncan, Attorney/Printer, on a side street. Upon entering the squat brick building, she wrinkled her nose at the acrid odor of printer's ink, for most of the place seemed devoted to his latter occupation. A large printing press and several type racks filled most of the space. An enclosure off to one side housed his office. Quality carpet and well-made furnishings gave it an efficient, businesslike atmosphere.

"Well now, what might I do for you today, Jasper?" Mr. Duncan asked, motioning for them to come inside. He extended a chubby hand toward Mr. Lyons, and his intent gaze fixed upon Susannah as he nodded politely.

She lowered her lashes and straightened her posture.

"This here's Miss Harrington," the innkeeper said. "She's been helping us out over at the inn, and I thought we should have a legal arrangement, like with Kate."

"Ah yes. Kate." The lawyer glanced again at Susannah, then gestured for them to be seated. He eased his bulky frame into the wide chair behind his rich mahogany desk. Light from the window gleamed from his head, which was bald except for a ruff of gray curving from one ear to the other. "I heard she made herself a bit scarce the other day." Picking up a pipe from a brass tray at his elbow, Duncan placed it between his teeth and sat back, puffing placidly as he studied Jasper Lyons with an amused smile.

"Ahem." Mr. Lyons' face reddened. "Well, yes. She run off. But I don't expect Miss Harrington'll give us any trouble that way. If you'll just draw up the same kind of contract we had with the other one."

"I do have that paper on file, of course. I'll get it and an indenturement form. I took the liberty of printing up a supply of them for future use. I assume you want the usual term of four years, the nonmarriage clause, and so forth, as on the one Kate signed." The lawyer opened a desk drawer and withdrew a printed sheet, which he handed to Mr. Lyons to look over. "See if this meets with your approval. Miss Harrington can put her *X* at the bottom, on the line. You can show her where."

Susannah winced inwardly at his words, but her expression remained composed.

Mr. Lyons glanced over the information and nodded. "Yes. That'll do fine. Just fine. Soon as I fill in the blanks and she signs it, we'll be on our way." He handed it back.

"One moment, if you please," Susannah said, looking from one man to the other. "Might I have a look at the contract as well?"

The lawyer raised his sparse brows and lifted the monocle that hung on a cord around his neck as he flicked an astonished gaze at Susannah. He wedged the eyepiece into place and scanned the form before giving it to her.

"Thank you," she said, nibbling her lip as she read the paper. "I see the length of the term has not as yet been filled in. Nor has the amount of the wages. Would it be possible for my service to be undertaken for a different amount of time? Say, one year, perhaps?"

"Well, I see no reason why it can't," the lawyer said hesitantly.

Mr. Lyons cleared his throat abruptly. "Now wait just one minute. You know that's not done, Curtis. An indenturement's for four years."

"Well," Susannah said, eyeing him steadily, "it's only due to my temporary circumstances, Mr. Lyons, that this arrangement has been necessitated in the first place. I couldn't possibly commit myself for such a long period of time. If my brother in England should forward more funds and provide another place for me to live during the coming year, of course I should want to abide by his wishes. He is head of the family now that our parents are gone, you see."

The innkeeper expelled a huff of air and shook his head.

"However," she added quickly, "if I've not heard from him within the next six months or so, perhaps I could commit to further service at that time."

"What do you say, Jasper?" Mr. Duncan asked, setting his

curved pipe down. "The young lady isn't asking for anything unreasonable, you must admit."

"I just thought—," Mr. Lyons began. "Oh, horsefeathers! Esther's got her heart set on having Susannah. There'd be no living with her if I go back saying the girl won't be stayin' on. Fill in the fool paper with one year, then."

"And about my wages?"

"Well, seein' as how short the time's gonna be, I'd say two pounds is about fair." Mr. Lyons gave an authoritative nod.

"Two pounds?" Susannah asked incredulously. "At the auctions in Philadelphia when I arrived, an uneducated farm woman was going for not less than twenty pounds for four years. That tallies up to five pounds a year. I should hardly expect less than that."

"All we need is someone to help out with the serving at the inn," he countered.

"Well, I'm also quite good at sums," Susannah said. "I can read scales and measurements, and you might possibly find those aptitudes an asset when you need to balance your ledgers or order supplies."

Curtis Duncan leaned back in his chair and laced his fingers together over his ample girth. A smile spread across his shiny face. "Sounds like you're taking on quite a helper, if you ask me, Jasper."

The innkeeper merely glared at him. "Well, losin' Kate set us back some. And this ain't the busiest time of the year, besides. I can go three pounds, but no more." He punctuated his words with a slap on the arm of his chair.

Susannah studied him for several moments in silence. Reaching again for the contract, she glanced over it. "Well, I shall accept the three pounds, if—"

"What do you mean, *if?*" Mr. Lyons demanded. "Three pounds is more'n fair."

Susannah lifted her chin. "I shall accept the *generous* sum of three pounds, *if* one other clause is stricken."

He grabbed the paper from her hand and looked it over.

"And just what clause might you be referring to, Miss

Harrington?" Curtis Duncan asked calmly, watching the exchange with undisguised amusement.

She leveled her gaze at him. "The one that says any other monies which I might acquire during the carrying out of my duties shall be the property of the inn. I should like to keep my own gratuities."

Stomping a foot on the floor, Mr. Lyons rolled his eyes heavenward as if she'd just obtained a mortgage on the Lyons' Den.

"Which shall it be, Mr. Lyons? Five pounds, or three pounds plus whatever tips I might earn?" Susannah leaned forward in her chair and watched the innkeeper calculate the possible difference.

His first words were muttered under his breath, and he kneaded his jowls with one rough hand. Then he looked begrudgingly at Susannah. "The three."

"Plus tips?"

"Plus tips."

"Good," she breathed. "Then I shall work for you until April 25th, next year, 1771. I'll sign the paper now, gentlemen, as soon as we arrange one more thing."

Mr. Lyons groaned.

Curtis Duncan chuckled.

"It's the matter of free time. I know it would be a hardship if I were to have all day Sunday to myself. However, I should like to attend services in the morning before starting my duties, and then I shall work through the evening."

"Agreed," Mr. Lyons said, tapping his finger on his knee.

Susannah smiled. "And I should like Wednesdays off."

"Write it in, Curtis," he muttered, staring straight ahead.

Mr. Duncan filled in the necessary information and handed Susannah the contract to approve.

After making certain that the form included all her requests as specified, Susannah reached for the quill on the desk corner and wrote her name. When she was finished, she dipped the pen again and handed it to Mr. Lyons.

The attorney examined the signatures and initialed them,

then sprinkled some silver dust over the form and blew it off. He tipped his head respectfully at Susannah. "That's a mighty fine looking *X*, I must say. I wonder if you might consider coming here one or two Wednesdays a month and helping out. I'd be happy to pay you, of course."

Susannah's head jerked up. "I beg your pardon?"

"My correspondence, you see," he began, waving a hand over a stack of papers on the desk.

The innkeeper came to his feet. "Now, wait just a minute, here. She belongs to us."

Curtis Duncan chuckled softly. "Yes, except for her free time. I'm just extending an option which might benefit her if she so desires."

Susannah rose, gazing first at one man, then the other as she drew her shawl about her shoulders. "I shall consider it."

"You know, Jasper," the lawyer said as he shook Mr. Lyons' hand and grinned, "it might have been cheaper for you to have contracted for the full five pounds." He nodded pleasantly at Susannah.

"I would've, if I'd known you was gonna hire her services, too. Seems every time I come here, I end up getting the short end of things." Shaking his head, he turned to leave, mumbling something unintelligible. Once outside, he looked upward and moaned. "Figures."

She glanced at him. "I beg your pardon?"

"Blasted sky's all clouded over. Probably more rain'll be dumped on us, too."

Examining the leaden clouds overhead, Susannah smiled brightly. "Well, just think of all the lovely flowers that will follow."

"Hmph." With a last glare over his shoulder at the law office, he quickened his pace.

Esther Lyons' face was still glowing with happiness when Susannah and Mr. Lyons returned. Glancing curiously after her scowling husband as he stomped through to the back door and out, she turned her attention to Susannah. "Somethin' got his hackles up?"

A warm flush settled across Susannah's cheeks, and she lowered her lashes. "I—I think Mr. Lyons may feel he's getting less than he expected. I signed the contract for only one year."

Mrs. Lyons set the rolling pin aside and wiped her hands on her heavy baking apron. "One year, love?"

"Why yes. My brother might be inclined to send me funds from England and ask me to join him. In that event, I should want to be free within a reasonable time."

The older woman nodded kindly and resumed cutting biscuits and putting them onto a large baking sheet.

"I shall do my best to fulfill my duties while I'm here, of course."

"I'm not feelin' doubtful, child. But I was kinda hopin' you'd be staying here for good. As part of the family, you see."

"You're most kind, Mrs. Lyons." Susannah crossed the room and hugged the woman warmly. "It does feel like a family here. I'll always be grateful you took me in."

"Well, year or no year," she said, a twinkle in her hazel eyes, "we'll be gettin' the best of the bargain, love."

Susannah smiled. "There is just one thing, though. I was wondering about my room. I'm sure you'll be needing it for paying guests. Is there some other place I might sleep from now on?"

Mrs. Lyons checked the mantel clock above the big fireplace and nodded. "It's still early. Soon as Mary Clare comes in from hanging out the linens, I'll have her take you up to the attic. Her and Kate shared a room up there, and the girl's no doubt wanting more company, off by herself like she is."

"I'm sure that will do nicely."

"Christopher can help move your things, if you'd be of a mind to gathering 'em together."

"Of course. I'll go take care of that at once." Susannah turned on her heel and hastened toward the stairs.

Pouring coffee into pewter mugs at one of the tables, Susannah looked up to see Jonathan Bradford, Steven Russell, and Morgan Thomas enter the inn. Attired for once in woolen street clothes instead of their usual robes, the young men grinned knowingly at one another and elbowed their way to a side table, where they took seats.

"Good day," she said. "Coffee, gentlemen?"

Jonathan gazed up at her, a smile lighting his eyes. "Reckon so. Thank you, Miss Susannah."

"I hope there's something warm on the menu," Steven added. "It's getting chilly outside. Looks like it might rain soon."

Susannah filled their cups and smiled. "We have Mrs. Lyons' special vegetable beef soup today, with biscuits hot from the oven."

"Mmm. That'll hit the spot," Morgan said. "We're starved."

"I'll just be a moment, then." She returned shortly and served them from a large kitchen tray.

Morgan leaned back slightly while Susannah placed his soup on the table. "Thank you," he said, looking up with a smile. "Uh, Jon told me about your dire circumstances, Miss, and I must offer my sympathies."

"Why, thank you. I'm managing well enough." Susannah turned to leave, but her action was stopped when Steven cleared his throat. She glanced back.

"I—that is, we—" Inhaling, Steven continued. "We've done a bit of talking, Miss Harrington, and I believe we may have come up with a place for you to stay."

Susannah drew her brows together in a slight frown. "I don't understand, Master Russell." She scanned the room to make certain the wagon masters at the nearest table were not listening, then returned her attention to the threesome.

The three students shifted uneasily in their seats.

Jonathan leaned a trifle nearer. "We heard of a room available at the boardinghouse on Nassau Street and reckoned you might be interested." For a brief instant, his mismatched eyes seemed the same hue.

"Yes," added Steven, a half-smile softening his normally

serious face. "It's quite reasonably priced, and we thought if we all chipped in—"

Susannah laughed softly. "Oh, how very kind of you. But entirely unnecessary, I'm pleased to say."

"No. She's found a husband," Morgan interjected with mock horror. "See, I told you we'd be too late."

"But it's perfect," Jonathan said, ignoring Morgan's jest. "You'd still be close to the college, near as a cat to a milk cow. And you could join us here for supper, once in awhile, besides." He grinned disarmingly and gulped some soup from his spoon.

"I've already made other arrangements," Susannah said softly. "But I thank you, nonetheless, for your generous offer."

"Arrangements?" Steven asked, running a hand through his thick blond hair.

"Yes. Mr. and Mrs. Lyons were kind enough to provide a room for me here, and in return, I signed on to help out in the inn."

"You can't mean— It's worse than marriage." Morgan Thomas shook his head incredulously. "She's indentured herself."

The other two young men stared in openmouthed disbelief.

"Oh, don't be alarmed," she said. "It's all quite proper, and it won't last forever. I'll still be here to listen to all the wonderful new things you learn at the college lectures. And meanwhile, I'll have two guardians to ensure my reputation. So you see, things have worked out better than I'd hoped. Now, is there anything else I might get you?"

"No, thank you. We're fine," Jonathan said quietly.

"Gentlemen." Susannah nodded, then picked up her tray and headed toward the kitchen, where Mary Clare stood peeking shyly from the door. The sight of her caught at Susannah's heart, and she gave her a conspiratorial smile. "I hear we're to be roommates," she whispered as she passed. "It'll be great fun."

"Mary Clare," Mrs. Lyons called. "Finished with those potatoes yet?"

"Almost."

"Well, hurry yourself, child. I'm needin' 'em."

"Mrs. Lyons?" Susannah asked as she set the tray on the
worktable. "After we've finished with the cleaning up, would
you mind terribly if I asked your advice about something?"

The ruffled capped head turned in her direction. "What
might that be?"

"I must write a letter to my brother. Quite possibly, Theodore's heard about Julia by now, and I'm sure he must be
worried about me. I must let him know where I am."

Mrs. Lyons nodded. "He'd want to know that."

"I . . . don't know how I shall tell him about my indenturement. I'm afraid he might find it somewhat . . . upsetting."
Even as she said it, Susannah felt the crushing weight of the
dismal tidings she'd be passing on. And with it came something more distressing: A dreadful foreboding of Theodore's
reaction.

10

Holding the candlestick high to dispel the darkness, Mary Clare led Susannah up the narrow creaking stairs to the attic. "This way," she said, turning right at the top and heading toward a room at one end of the cluttered, low-browed hall.

"My," Susannah exclaimed as they passed canvas-covered furniture and stacked crates. "You're really off by yourself, aren't you? Does the other room belong to Christopher?"

Mary Clare shook her head. "The stage drivers," she said in her airy, breathless voice. "Chip has a cot in the kitchen, under the stairs." Taking a key from the pocket of her brown cotton dress, she inserted it into the lock, opened the door, and entered, stepping aside for Susannah. The girl set the candle on a table beside one of the beds.

Susannah closed the door and glanced about the cramped room. A simple dressing table separated two narrow low-post bedsteads, so close together that they shared the same hand-made rag rug. Each had a bedside table. Against the end wall stood an empty fireplace, and to one side of it sat a sturdy walnut armoire.

"There's some candle pieces in your drawer." Mary Clare nodded toward Susannah's bedside table. "Mrs. Lyons lets us have the short ones from downstairs. So's we don't be wastin' things."

Susannah nodded. Soft rainfall pattered against the sloped ceiling and cascaded down the windows on either side. Crossing to the far one, she parted a faded curtain to peer out into the dreariness. "I just love to listen to rain, don't you?" She smiled at her slender companion. "I had an attic bedroom back home in England, and on rainy days I used to lie on my bed and dream I was in a secret cave under a waterfall that no one ever knew existed except me. I suppose that was rather silly."

Mary Clare shrugged a slim shoulder and looked away.

"I do hope you don't mind sharing your room. I have a dreadful tendency to ramble on quite a lot, I'm afraid. But I shall try very hard to be quiet." Setting her satchel down near the other bed, Susannah picked up the folded linens and threw back the quilted coverlet.

"I don't mind if you talk."

"Even so, I'll try not to do it *all* the time." She shook out one of the sheets over the feather tick.

"Need help?" Mary Clare asked shyly.

Susannah nodded. "Thank you. It's much easier with two of us." As soon as the linens and wool blanket had been tucked in and the coverlet spread again over the top, Susannah turned down the upper edge and fluffed the pillow.

"There." With a deep sigh, she sank down gingerly to try it out as Mary Clare returned to her own bed. "Most adequate, I must say."

She went across to the armoire, threw open the doors, and only barely stifled her surprise. Oversized and obviously intended for two, it was empty, except for one gray homespun dress and Mary Clare's night things. Surely the child had a dress or two in the laundry. . . . Susannah set the satchel inside and closed the doors. "Well. We'd better hurry back downstairs and help with supper."

On Wednesday morning, Susannah resisted the urge to waste any of her free day by sleeping late. Her trunks had arrived from Philadelphia on the stage wagon the day before and now sat before the fireplace waiting to be unpacked. As soon as Mary Clare had hurried off to do her chores, Susannah tugged one of the chests over to the armoire. Opening the curved lid, she shook out each folded dress and hung it up, considering as she went which ones could be taken in to fit Mary Clare's barely blossoming frame. Those she put nearest the girl's half of the closet so they'd be within easy reach to alter.

The second chest contained some personal items and a few remembrances from her life in Ashford—a delicately crocheted shawl cushioning an ornate hand-held silver looking glass and a matching brush. With a sigh, Susannah put the brush and mirror on the dressing table and began smoothing out the shawl that had once graced her mother's frail shoulders.

The faint scent of dried lavender from their gardens still clung to it, and tears brimmed in Susannah's eyes as a memory of her mother surfaced. Her father had presented the warm shawl to his wife on their anniversary. . . .

Susannah buried her face in it and allowed herself to weep for a moment. Then, with a prolonged sniff, she dried her eyes and swallowed. It would do no good to grieve forever. Her parents had gone to a better place, where nothing could hurt them ever again. And in time she would join them . . . somehow she would ensure her salvation and earn the favor of almighty God.

Beneath a colorful quilt her mother had pieced years ago for Susannah's wedding day, she found a second looking glass, in a scrolled leather frame. She lifted the heavy mirror out of the padding and hung it on a bare side wall, then folded the counterpane and put it back inside the chest. After a moment's thought she removed her floral-patterned sewing case from the trunk and set to work.

When Mary Clare returned after the dinner rush, she flopped down upon her bed with a yawn and closed her eyes.

"You must have been busy."

A soft moan sounded from the still figure.

"How dreadful. I had something to show you. But if you're too tired, I suppose it can wait."

The young girl raised her head and looked curiously in Susannah's direction.

Smiling, Susannah stood up, holding a rose-colored linen dress against herself, smoothing out the rows of intricate ivory lace down the bodice and on the edges of the flounced sleeves.

Mary Clare's clear blue eyes grew wide as she tilted her head and examined it. "Right fine," she said, a wistful note in her voice.

Susannah smiled hopefully. "Do you like it? It . . . um, was a bit tight on me, you see. So I thought perhaps you might be able to use it."

Her mouth gaping, the young serving girl swung her legs over the side of the bed and sat up. "What?"

"I said that I hoped you would like it." Susannah crossed the room and held out a fold of the skirt toward her.

"Oh," Mary Clare breathed, running a lithe hand softly down the material. "I never even touched such a fine dress before. Not ever. When I was a young'un, though, Mama used to sew me some pretty things."

Susannah smiled. "Well, why don't you try this on? We must make sure it fits, you know."

Reluctantly, Mary Clare shook her head. "I couldn't be takin' your dress. Besides, I don't go noplace to be needin' it."

"Nonsense. You can come with me to church every Sunday. Would you like that?"

She shrugged. "I never been. Well, since I was little."

Susannah gasped inwardly. "Well then, it's time you started." She could understand that Mrs. Lyons could hardly leave the inn unattended even on the Sabbath, yet the children still needed guidance. Perhaps while she was here she'd see to it that Mary Clare—and her brother as well—were taken regularly to services. After all, she had promised in her prayers to do what she could to help others, especially two young indentures who had already stolen her heart. "Stand up, so we can try this on."

Mary Clare leaped to her feet and reached to unbutton her

❦ 130 ❦

gray homespun dress, sliding it off her shoulders. It fell to the floor in a faded little pool about her feet, and she shivered in her dismal underthings as she raised her arms for Susannah to slide the rose linen over her head. Once it was on, she stood with her eyes closed, as if she were afraid that by opening them she'd awaken from a dream.

"Yes." Susannah straightened the bottom flounce and tugged the bodice together in back as she leaned around to assess Mary Clare. "It's almost perfect. A tuck here and there, and it will do quite nicely." The girl opened her eyes, straining to see into the mirror. Susannah heard her sharp intake of breath as her reflection stared back in wonder.

"Susannah!" Mary Clare breathed. "I mean, Miss Harrington."

"No," Susannah corrected gently. "Please use my first name. I'd like that. In fact, I'd like you to call me Sue. That's what my brother calls me."

Tears glistening in her eyes, the young serving girl blinked rapidly and took another look at herself. "It—it's much too fine for the likes of me."

"Nonsense. I want you to have it, Mary. It looks lovely on you. Why, you'll turn every boy's head at church, you know."

"Me?"

"Of course. Once they see you walk in looking like a soft summer rose, with that pretty golden hair all brushed and shining, how could they not notice you?"

Mary Clare grimaced. "I'd be so fearful, I'd probably trip over my own feet."

Susannah pulled the girl's waist-length braid from inside the dress. Undoing the leather band at the bottom, she loosened the strands and reached for the brush. "There's a little girl back home in Ashford who has silvery gold hair like this," she said, stroking along the length of Mary Clare's tresses. "I used to pray and pray that somehow mine would turn that color. But, as you can see, it remained quite ordinary." She smiled at the reflection of Mary Clare's heart-shaped face with its delicate cheekbones and fine features.

"We could fix your hair really elegant for services. Would you like that?"

"You know how?"

Susannah nodded. "My friend Julia and I used to spend hours working on each other's hair when we were growing up. We'd get her mother's cheek and lip rouge and jewelry, and some of her splendid gowns—she kept a whole trunk full of things we were allowed to use in our play. It was ever so much fun." As she talked, Susannah gathered a section of Mary Clare's hair together in back at the crown, tied it with a black ribbon, and arranged the long streamers to cascade over the blonde waves. She stepped back. "What do you think?"

Her cheeks glowing, Mary Clare studied the young lady in the looking glass, then turned her eyes upward. "Oh, thank you, Sue!" she breathed. A smile touched the fragile features for an instant, and the girl reached out to give Susannah a brief hug.

At that moment, Susannah decided to enlist the aid of the seminary students in finding Christopher a suitable outfit for Sundays. They seemed to know many of the townsfolk, and perhaps they would assist in her mission to get the siblings some religious influence.

Yes. It was settled. Part of her promise to God would be fulfilled in helping these two young waifs. She would prove to God that she was worthy of his love.

Sweet with the scent of Japanese honeysuckle, the Sunday morning breeze stirred the limbs of the tall elm beside the Lyons' Den. The long branches scratched against the building, and a robin added its joyful song to the glorious day.

Susannah inhaled deeply and stretched. She looked over at the other bed, wondering if Mary Clare had slept at all in her eagerness for the day's arrival.

After Susannah had finished altering the dress, the girl had tried it on every evening, twirling around, watching the rose skirt billow. She had practiced walking in Susannah's kidskin slippers and had administered a hundred strokes to her golden tresses with Susannah's hairbrush. Susannah could barely contain her own happiness in watching the girl's exuberance.

Mary Clare jumped out of bed, her hurried movements betraying her excitement. Her flawless cheeks glowed even before she poured cold water from the pitcher and splashed her face. Quickly, she straightened the blankets and coverlet on her bed, then went directly for the armoire. She removed the new dress and underthings Susannah had given her and spread them out, undoing the buttons almost reverently.

Susannah rose and freshened up, amused by the younger girl's nervous fluttering. But she had to admit that she felt a bit apprehensive herself. After all, three young gentlemen from the college would be coming by to escort Susannah and her charges to the morning service at Nassau Hall. She had heard that Dr. Witherspoon was a commanding speaker, and she couldn't help wondering how his sermon would compare to the one given at the Anglican church the previous week.

As she made her bed, Susannah wondered briefly what she should wear. She didn't want to call attention to herself; this was to be Mary's first special day. At last she decided upon a lavender gown with lace bodice and funnel sleeves. It would be just the thing to set off the rose linen.

After they finished dressing, Susannah arranged Mary Clare's hair becomingly, tying the black velvet ribbon from underneath the nape into a bow at the top of her head. "Remember to walk with your head up," she reminded the girl gently. "And do try to smile. Most people are quite friendly, given the chance to show it."

"I'll do my best," she promised.

"Good. Then I suppose we're ready."

Leaving the room, they locked the door and descended the stairs to the kitchen, where the smell of freshly baked scones welcomed them.

"Ah, now don't you look a sight?" Mrs. Lyons beamed as her young serving girl stepped into the room. "All growed, lookin' like the first flower of springtime."

Mary Clare blushed softly and smiled. "Ever see such a fine dress? Susannah gave it to me. It's like a dream."

"Well, sit down, the two of you, and have somethin' to eat before it's time to go."

"Where's Christopher?" Susannah asked as they took seats at the kitchen worktable.

"Out back, showin' his new Sunday clothes to the chickens. I told him to keep himself clean. He'll be back directly."

"Oh. He's ready, then." Splitting a warm scone in two, Susannah spread butter and strawberry preserves onto one half and bit into it. "Mm. As delicious as the ones Julia's cook used to make us for our garden parties. I only wish . . ." Her attention drifted.

A knock interrupted her wistful thoughts. Susannah could see the seminary threesome through the window beside the back door. Hurriedly she gulped her coffee as Mrs. Lyons admitted them.

Mary Clare lowered her shining blonde head and ate quietly.

"Morning, Miz Lyons." Jonathan grinned, tipping his head. He smiled at Susannah as his friends stepped in behind him, but his mismatched eyes widened at the sight of Mary Clare. "Well now. Is this lovely young lady our little Miss Mary?"

A soft flush added a most alluring pink to Mary Clare's cheeks, and she managed a shy smile before casting a pleading look toward Susannah.

"Good morning, gentlemen," Susannah said, attempting to draw their attention away from her timid friend. "Won't you have some coffee with us before services?"

"Yes," Mrs. Lyons added. "Fine idea. Pull up a couple of chairs, and I'll get you some." She hurried off, returning with cups and the big coffeepot.

"Our thanks." Morgan Thomas grinned, jostling Steven Russell out of the way. He plunked his chair down right beside Susannah—for one brief second, until Mrs. Lyons raised a brow. Then he quickly scooted a respectable distance away.

Steven Russell chose Susannah's other side, and Jonathan quietly placed his seat opposite them, beside Mary Clare.

Clearing his throat, Steven turned to Susannah. "Sure is a splendid morning. We're looking forward to the pleasure of seeing you to church." He flitted a glance about the room. "Where is our young man?"

"Just outside, Master Russell," Susannah answered. "I'm sure he's eager for this new experience, having three big brothers to take him to church and all. I do thank you for your help."

"Mercy sakes, yes." Mrs. Lyons gave an emphatic nod of her head as she set mugs before each of the young men and filled them with steaming coffee. "He was so surprised and proud of them new clothes, he dressed soon as the sun come up."

"Good. I reckon every boy needs to be treated special now and then." Jonathan looked again at Mary Clare, and his gaze softened and lingered.

"I say, Miss Harrington," Morgan said, a glint lighting his blue eyes. "You've never heard our Dr. Witherspoon, have you?"

"No, not as yet."

"Well, you're in for quite a treat. Folks come from all over to listen to his sermons."

"So I've been told."

After the conclusion of the rousing morning message, a closing hymn poured from the organ, which Steven had informed Susannah was the first used in Presbyterian services in the Colonies. She and her new group of friends emerged from majestic Nassau Hall. Her heart still astir from the sermon, Susannah could well understand why the good Dr. Witherspoon had such a following. She was sure that if she were an American, she'd have cheered his biblical dissertation on freedom's worthy cause against tyranny from foreign lands—against unrighteousness in any form, for that matter.

Yet uppermost in her mind was the pastor's jovial manner, his kindliness, the lack of rigid stuffiness in his delivery. It was no wonder the college drew numbers of ministerial students from all the Colonies. The man's very nature inspired one to strive to be the best. She wished all the more that she could have had Theodore's chance to enter Oxford.

"Well, Miss Susannah," Morgan said as he took possession of her arm. "Did the meeting live up to your expectations?"

"Oh my, yes. It was ever so inspiring." She turned to Mary Clare, who was closely attended by Jonathan. "Didn't you find it so, Mary?"

The younger girl nodded shyly.

"It w-w-was l-l-long," towheaded Christopher added, rubbing his backside. "I got t-tired of s-s-sitting."

Steven chuckled. "Well, you know, Chip, my father's a preacher, so I spent most of my life on church benches."

The lad turned his skinny freckled face toward Steven in wide-eyed disbelief.

"It's true." Mussing the boy's hair playfully, he continued. "But in time, you toughen up for the sitting part, believe me. You *will* come again next week, won't you?" he asked, a hopeful note in his tone.

"I g-guess." Christopher looked admiringly at his new brown breeches and tweed coat, and his eyes glowed as he straightened his shoulders and lengthened his stride to match Steven's.

"Well now," a gruff voice sneered just behind them, "would ya lookee here."

Susannah and her companions turned to see an unshaven, unkempt Silas Drummond come into view, a feral gleam in his glassy eyes. His unwelcome presence brought a chill with it, as if a cloud had suddenly blocked the warm rays of the sun. He started toward them, chin set intently, his gaze steady and not veering from the children.

Mary Clare gave a soft cry and cowered in fear behind Susannah. Susannah stiffened, unconsciously stepping backward in revulsion as the hulking man came nearer.

Christopher ducked into the safety of Steven Russell's shadow, shut his eyes, and gave a barely audible moan.

Drummond stopped six feet away and cocked his head with a sneer. "Right fine clothes them two young'uns is wearin'." He glanced from one child to the other. "And me with my toes hangin' clean outta my shoes. Just what's goin' on over at that tavern of theirn?"

"Please, Mr. Drummond—" Susannah blurted the first thing that came to mind. "Someone gave the children the new clothing."

"Is that so?" he snapped. He shook a massive fist in the air. "What blasted blackguard's tryin' to shame me? I'll fix him up right enough."

Steven and Morgan looked at one another, then stepped forward shoulder to shoulder in front of the girls and Christopher. Leveling their stares, they faced the man.

Jonathan spoke, his normally jovial voice low and even. "Just what is it you reckon you'd want to do to someone who favored the young ones, Mr. Drummond?" His sturdy farm-toughened hands clenched at his sides, he blocked the man's vision of Mary Clare.

"Move off, now," Morgan added. He turned to Susannah. "Let us be on our way."

Eyes narrowed, Silas Drummond nodded slowly to himself as if assessing the strength of the three protectors. He shot a wary gaze over the group but continued to hold his ground.

Susannah railed inwardly at the mortification on Mary Clare's scarlet face. Tears streamed from the young girl's eyes, and her chin quivered as she struggled to keep from crying aloud. Drawing a slow breath, Susannah placed a comforting arm about her trembling shoulders.

Mary Clare crumpled against her momentarily, then wrenched herself free. Sobbing, she ran toward a stand of evergreens some distance away.

Silas Drummond whacked his sloppy hat against his leg. "Don't that beat all!" he spat. "Devil take the whining crybaby. I got better things to do than be bothered with the likes of that. And you," he added, glaring menacingly at Christopher, who ducked deeper behind Steven and put his scrawny hand inside the young man's strong one. "Get outta them rags before you dirty 'em up. I'll get me a good price for 'em. I can hear the coin jingling in my purse already."

As the three students moved forward as one, Mr. Drummond let out a huff of breath. Shoving his fists into the pockets of his ragged frock coat, he turned on his heel and stomped unsteadily away, leaving a string of curses in his wake.

Susannah turned in time to see Mary Clare vanish into the grove and took a step to follow her. But Jonathan stayed her with a hand on her arm.

"Christopher and I will go after her, Susannah. I figure she might need somebody to look out for her. Come on, Chip," he said with a friendly tap on the boy's shoulder. The two ran in the direction Mary Clare had taken.

"The cur," Morgan said, a hardness in his dark blue eyes. "That insensitive blighter had no call to embarrass the youngsters that way. It's bad enough that he sold them. He should have the decency to leave them in peace."

Susannah nodded. "Yes. He's frightful."

"Well, we'd better see you safely home, miss," Steven said, gesturing toward the inn. "Before he decides to come back."

Susannah looked over her shoulder, trying to catch a glimpse of the sweet girl who was becoming more like a little sister with each passing day. Then, comforted by the thought of Jonathan's gallant manner, her spirits lifted a bit, and she fell into step with Morgan and Steven. Despite the few unpleasant people she had come across in this young land, there were still gentlemen of honor, like Daniel Haynes and the three ministerial students who were becoming her friends. The thought did much to calm her inner turmoil. A tiny smile softened her expression as she tilted her head questioningly at Steven Russell.

"Yes?" he asked before she spoke.

"I . . . was wondering if you ever heard of a postrider I met one day in Philadelphia. A former student. He said his name was Daniel Haynes."

Steven's brow wrinkled and his gray eyes darkened.

"Haynes," Morgan Thomas repeated. "I believe I've heard the name, once or twice, in conversation at the college. But I daresay I've not met the fellow."

"Why do you ask?" Steven said.

"Oh, no reason," Susannah replied evasively. A sudden feeling of hopelessness filled her heart; she doubted she'd ever see the handsome postrider again. And even if his duties did happen to bring him to Princeton someday, he had more than likely forgotten her by now. "I just wondered if you knew him."

With one last glance backward toward the evergreens, she sighed. "I do hope Mary is all right."

11

Bunching up the long, soiled tablecloth and laying it aside, Susannah shook out the folds of a fresh one and smoothed it into place. It was time to make ready for the evening rush of customers, which consisted mostly of students who had returned recently to the College of New Jersey for the summer session. She had already forced aside the niggling disappointment that the handsome Mr. Haynes, though older than most of the other students, had not come to register with the others as she had fancied. She hadn't admitted to herself how greatly she'd counted on that possibility. Obviously, he had forgotten her completely. With a sigh, Susannah put her sable-eyed rescuer out of her mind and went on to the next table, directly adjacent to the one occupied by her three Lords of Dunce.

"Well, I for one am finding this study of Scottish church history plumb tedious," she heard Jonathan moan as he propped an elbow and leaned his head into his palm. Late afternoon light shafted across the hills and valleys of his thick wavy hair. He bit into a piece of hot corn bread soaked with honey.

Morgan grinned and nudged Steven. "I heartily agree. Especially now that we're on John Knox and that dry-as-dust *Book of Discipline.*"

"Better not let Witherspoon hear you say that." Jonathan shot a glance toward the door as if the president, robed in yards of black, might swoop in on them at any second.

Steven nodded.

"I can't figure how in the world a Scot could've drafted anything of importance two hundred years ago," Jonathan continued. "They weren't much more than savages back then."

"True." Steven picked up a stack of notes from beside him on the bench and plunked them unceremoniously under Jonathan's nose. "But we can't let those new lads outdo us again, either."

Jonathan brushed a few crumbs from his lap. "Reckon we'll have to buckle down a sight more this term. What did the good doctor say was the reasoning behind that book again?" He leaned forward intently.

The empty trestle table was already spotless, but Susannah scrubbed vigorously at it one more time as she inched her way closer to the discussion. She turned an ear in their direction, hoping her curiosity didn't appear obvious.

Morgan straightened his shoulders. "Wasn't it supposed to define the dignity of man and his equality before God?"

"Sounds about right," Steven said. He took a sip of ale and set down the glass. "And didn't it state that the church *and* the people both had to consent on whether they wanted to unite or not? And that congregations had the right to examine the fitness and character of ministers seeking election to their churches?"

"That's revolutionary even today," Jonathan said. "And weren't there even a few stipulations regarding the elders? Weren't they supposed to be elected annually, and only eligible if they had a knowledge of the Word, led a clean life, and were faithful, decent-types?" He gave a smug smile, but then his gaze wandered across the room, and his expression suddenly exploded into a grin.

Susannah followed his line of vision to the reason. Mary Clare, in pastel blue muslin, stood at the bar polishing pewter mugs, her silky hair tied back with a white kerchief. With the girl's shy answering smile, a tinge of pink colored her cheekbones. Her young roommate had progressed from timid waif to winsome maiden over the past weeks.

"Susannah!" boomed Mr. Lyons, looking up from his columns and figures.

She started.

"Leave some of the varnish on the furniture, at least. You been washin' that same table for the last ten minutes."

"Oh. Sorry, Mr. Lyons." Ducking her head to hide her own flaming cheeks, Susannah took the damp cloth to the long bar and picked up a tray of silverware. She crossed to a table near the students again and began setting places.

Morgan flashed her an amused grin, his cobalt eyes twinkling. He forked a chunk of blueberry pie into his mouth.

"But it's pages and pages. How do you figure we're supposed to remember all this?" Jonathan asked, returning to academics again. "It's too much."

Morgan arched an eyebrow. "Just concentrate on the important points. Remember, with such men of character elected by all men—no matter their stations—to head the church, it's only natural the ministers would also be expected to make just decisions in the courts, too—with the exception of capital crimes, of course."

"Yes," added Steven. "And the suggestion concerning the need for compulsory education for all was set forth in that book, as well. Now, that is a *radical idea*. And this is also where the Presbyterians abolished the sacraments."

"Except for baptism and Holy Communion, of course," Morgan stated. "Knox and his lofty ideals sure clashed with the Roman Catholic practices of Mary, Queen of Scots."

Jonathan grimaced. "Funny how even now, after two hundred years—not to mention their own revolt against said practices—Britain is still trying to cram her hierarchy, both religious and royal, down the throats of Scotland and all her other conquests. Even the Colonies, now that we've grown into a valuable asset."

The other two nodded, and Steven cocked his head. "Ah,

but that can't continue much longer. They'll have to listen to us soon. Or else."

Accustomed by now to hearing such sentiments, Susannah barely prickled at all. She picked up the remaining tableware and idly walked to the bar and set down the tray. Was Ted studying similar concepts at Oxford, or were such things as Scottish Kirk history far too inflammatory, too mutinous? She wondered if her younger brother, always so full of himself and his own importance, had gotten her letter as yet. She cringed to think what his reaction to her indenturement might be.

"Su-san-nah," Mr. Lyons said, drawing out her name pointedly with excessive patience. "A coach just got in. Think you could tend to the travelers—without me remindin' you again?"

"Yes, of—of course," she said lamely. "I shall see to them at once." What was the matter with her? She was as easily distracted as Jonathan. She needed to buckle down herself.

Half an hour later, having served the newcomers and a table of local tradesmen as well, Susannah walked the length of the room, refilling coffee cups.

"Thanks," Jonathan said, his boyish face smiling up at her as she poured his full to the rim. "This sure hits the spot." Alone now at the table with his notes, he rubbed absently at his jaw. "I wanted to tell you what a remarkable job you've done with Mary. She doesn't skulk around anymore like she used to. And even her speech seems to be improving."

Susannah nodded, watching the flaxen-haired girl wipe a recently vacated table and walk gracefully to the kitchen with the soiled dishes. "Oh, I've not done much more than you and the others have for Christopher. The dears just needed someone to show particular interest in them. Her voice softened. "I've grown quite fond of them both."

"Reckon you would," he said quietly. "I—uh . . ."

She tipped her head and arched her eyebrows in a questioning expression.

"I finally heard from Rob Chandler."

"You have?" For some unknown reason, Susannah's heartbeat quickened, and she glanced swiftly about the room to be sure she wasn't needed elsewhere.

Jonathan nodded, and the flickering candlelight reflected in his eyes. "He wrote to say he's been detained on his plantation. Seems his father's down with the smallpox."

"Oh. No wonder he didn't return with the other students. I'll certainly include his family in my prayers tonight."

"Yes. He, um, sent this for you." Reaching beneath his black robe and into a pocket of his charcoal breeches, Jonathan drew out a wrinkled letter and handed it to her.

Hastily Susannah broke the seal and unfolded the parchment. The handwritten message was accompanied by a ten-pound note. She read the correspondence silently:

My dear Susannah,

I was quite taken with surprise to learn of your recent arrival. Julia would have been so happy to have known you were coming to America as she wished. How sad that she was denied the pleasure of your company after you undertook that arduous journey. We were most unfortunate, you and I, to have had such a loss thrust upon us. I feel as though the light has gone from my life, now that my beloved wife has been taken. I am certain you suffer the same emptiness.

I regret that with my father's grave illness it has become impossible for me to return to Princeton in the foreseeable future. However, now that the threat of smallpox is almost past, we would deem it an honor if you might come to North Carolina for a visit. I enclose a small gift for you to use for traveling expenses or some other need you might have incurred since you have been in the Colonies. However, if you should be reluctant to travel alone, I shall understand.

With warmest regards, I remain your servant,
R. C.

❧ 145 ❧

"He wants me to go for a visit," she said, looking at Jonathan.

"I didn't mention in my letter to him that you were bonded."

She shook her head. "Well, I've no choice in the matter, of course. I can't even consider it."

"But, with what he sent you, you could buy back your papers and still have enough for a packet to North Carolina."

"Oh, I couldn't do that. I promised Mr. and Mrs. Lyons I'd stay the year. And besides, I couldn't go away and leave Mary and Chip. Not yet."

"Yes. Well, I'm sure Rob'll understand."

Susannah smiled wistfully. "But I do thank you for bringing it by." She folded the letter and pocketed it.

"Miss, may we have some flip?" asked a customer at the next table.

"Certainly. I'll be just a moment," she said with a smile.

Jonathan gulped down the remainder of his coffee. Rising, he placed some coins on the table. "Better get back to my studies, I reckon. Lately I've begun to see their importance." With a dip of his head, he turned and headed for the door, casting a last glance across the room before departing.

Susannah saw Mary Clare smile his way and flush slightly as the door closed behind him. Then, as the girl resumed her work, Susannah picked up Jonathan's empty glass and the money, putting his generous tip with the funds Robert had sent. She had not spent the price of her indenturement, and now with this windfall of ten pounds to add to her tips and her occasional work for Curtis Duncan, she had gathered quite a nest egg. But she intended to live up to her contract. She had made a commitment to the Lyons' Den—and one even more binding to God, concerning the youngsters. It was scant payment, after all, for the supreme joy of absorbing all the wonderful theological discussions she often overheard during her work.

She would simply write Robert Chandler and explain. Hopefully he'd understand. But most likely he'd think, as Ted quite possibly did by now, that she was daft. She inhaled and shrugged. "So be it."

A few evenings later, Susannah had just finished lighting the last candle along the walls of the common room when the door opened, admitting Steven Russell and Morgan Thomas. They took seats at one of the square side tables and waved at Susannah.

She smoothed her apron over her skirt and approached them with a smile. "Good evening. What might I fetch for you?"

"Oh," Morgan Thomas said, leveling his mischievous gaze on her, "some of that special flip, I suppose."

"Certainly." Turning, Susannah took a step away, but stopped when her apron string caught on something. She glanced back.

"Oh, sorry." Morgan grinned, letting go of the tie his long fingers had deliberately captured.

Steven Russell swatted him. "Better not let Mrs. Lyons see you disturbing the help."

"Quite right! I forgot the wrath of the lion lady." The young man's eyes widened with exaggerated fear.

Susannah laughed lightly and shook her head. She retied the bow and crossed to the bar, where her employer sat engrossed in a ledger, the white cockatoo perched on his shoulder. "Two glasses of flip, please, Mr. Lyons."

Preoccupied, he filled a pitcher with grog and plucked a hot poker from the small brazier sitting on the end of the bar. He dipped it into the liquid, which emitted a loud sizzling sound, then poured two glasses to the brim and pushed them toward Susannah.

She took them with a nod, then returned to her patrons.

"Thank you," Steven said, a lopsided grin softening the contours of his studious face. "Say, have you ever had the pleasure of hearing George Whitefield preach?"

Susannah frowned. "No, but I've heard *of* him, of course. He's the charlatan with the golden tongue who preys on unstable widows with his overemotional sermons, all the while begging for money for some orphanage he claims to have in the wilds of Georgia."

Somewhat taken aback, Morgan hiked his dark brows. "I say. If the man were anything like that, he'd have no following at all, now, would he?"

Susannah considered his words for a few seconds. "Well, I only know what I heard at home in England."

"Then you'll be delighted to discover the reality," Steven said, his half-grin spreading across to encompass his whole mouth. "He's a tireless worker who's concerned about orphans, it's true. But even more so for hungry souls who are seeking a personal encounter with God."

"How ever could people have a *personal* encounter with almighty God?" Susannah asked incredulously. "That sounds somewhat presumptuous to me."

"But it isn't." A spark glinted in Morgan's eyes. "Not at all."

Steven nodded. "Ah, the wonders yet to unfold."

Their strange smiles piqued Susannah's curiosity. "This Mr. Whitefield . . . you've actually heard him preach?"

Morgan shook his dark head ruefully. "Well, no. Not actually."

Susannah laughed softly. "Well then, you could be quite wrong."

"Ah, but we know people who've heard Reverend Whitefield, you see," he interjected. "Our own Dr. Witherspoon, for one. And he has nothing but honor and praise to heap upon the fellow."

"Yes," Steven added. "He's forever quoting statements from the man's sermons and praising his dedication. Apparently, Whitefield is immensely burdened to tell everyone about the simple but profound grace of God—and without regard to one's denomination. Why, for the past thirty years, he's ridden the length and breadth of these colonies to proclaim the message to anyone who'd listen. Even Indians."

Morgan nodded. "I say. All this with complete disregard for

bad weather, lack of roads, or his poor health. The man suffers terribly from asthma, you know."

Asthma. Susannah's throat constricted. Even still she could hear her mum gasping for breath, hear the horrible fits of coughing. "My mother, too, had that disease."

"Well then, you above anyone else should realize how Whitefield must be pushing himself," Morgan continued, his expression easing for a moment before it became impassioned once more. "There have been times when his voice was little more than a hoarse whisper and he was burning with fever. Yet rather than fail those hundreds who'd come to hear his message, Whitefield preached to them for hours."

Susannah drew in her chin in disbelief. "But how could that be possible?"

A wry smile curved Steven's mouth. "Why, by knowing his God personally, of course. He simply prays for a strong voice. *And the God he knows doth provide.*"

Before Susannah had time even to ponder that thought, Morgan's voice intruded.

"The fact of the matter is," he said, punctuating his words with jabs of his finger upon the table, "the eloquent beauty and power of Whitefield's oratory are quite legendary."

Susannah placed a hand upon one hip. It was all quite impossible to believe, and she had no idea how to respond. "Well, just the same, I should imagine that orphanage must be quite rich by now."

"Why, Miss Harrington!" Morgan Thomas's straight brows rose in friendly challenge. "You may be quite surprised about all of this when Whitefield comes to our fair town."

"He's coming to Princeton?" Before Susannah could say more, Mr. Lyons pointedly cleared his throat from behind the bar. She glanced over to see him staring her way. "I must get back to work, I'm afraid. It's been most *interesting* talking to you both. I suppose we shall have to wait and see about this Mr. Whitefield."

"That we will," they answered.

A skeptical smirk played over Susannah's lips as she cleared tables and mused on the gullibility of her new friends. She would, indeed, have to see this marvelous Mr. Whitefield for herself.

Esther Lyons' cheeks rounded with a smile when Susannah entered the kitchen and set the tray onto the worktable. "Seems a bit quieter than usual out there."

"We've not been too busy this evening. The coach from New York has yet to arrive."

"I been thinkin' on Mary Clare, and the change you've been bringing about in her and Christopher."

Susannah removed the used items from the tray and loaded it up again with clean mugs for the bar. "But you've already said you approve."

"Yes, in some ways. It's true enough that the boy doesn't seem to stutter as much anymore, except if he's upset. And our Mary Clare's turning into quite a young lady."

Smiling, Susannah nodded. "Yes. She's a dear. Why, she's even been interested in learning how to read and write, and she's asked me to help her speak properly. I thought I might begin tutoring them when we have spare time. I think they're both rather bright."

Esther's face grew serious. "Well . . . just go slow, Susannah. Don't be setting 'em up for more hurt."

"Hurt? Why, you must know I would never do that—to either of them, ever. Aside from the fact that I've pledged to make their betterment a part of my good works, I love them both. Why, it's my Christian duty to help however I'm able."

The older woman nodded gravely. "I'm sure of that, love. But remember, the children have that no-account father to reckon with, and yesterday I caught him trying to sneak upstairs. After their Sunday clothes, most likely. I heard about the threat he made that day he accosted them after church."

Susannah stared at her in shock. "Surely he wouldn't do something so horrible."

"I'm afraid he'd do all that and more. He needs to support his drinking. That's what's most important to him, you know. And them clothes has come to mean so much to the youngsters, it'll break their hearts for sure if he takes 'em away. What's worse, now that they've had better, they'd be shamed to go without again. They could end up more backward than before." She gave Susannah's arm a squeeze. "That's why I'm advisin' you to go slow, my dear. Sometimes even the best intentions have a way of turning out just the opposite."

Susannah didn't speak for a moment as she thought over Esther Lyons' words. "I'm certain that God will reward our efforts in the end," she said. Then, sincerely hoping the older woman's dire predictions would not come true, she carried the clean mugs out to the common room.

12

Theodore Harrington left the Oxford postmaster's office with Susannah's letter in hand. Glancing at it, he was pleased to see it bore the postmark of her New Jersey destination. Julia's husband must have taken her under his protection. He breathed a sigh of relief and pocketed the letter.

"Ted, old man!" Alex Fontaine caught up with his friend in no time as his long legs carried him across the stone-paved Tom Quad. A lock of sandy hair, always too long in front, fell over his forehead, and he carelessly brushed it aside. "I've splendid news."

"Oh?" Ted studied Alex's thin, aristocratic face. "And what, pray tell, might that be?"

"'Tis about our commissions, old chap. Thought we might discuss them over a pint at the King's Head."

"Wonderful. Let's make haste, or we'll miss supper."

"Oh, who needs that sort of sustenance?" Alex queried with an airy wave of the hand. "We've much more important things to occupy our stomachs and our minds, now that I've heard from Cousin Wills."

Ted's heartbeat quickened. "You've heard? Right, then. Let's be off."

The two entered the tavern and took seats at a table midway down its smoky, narrow length.

"Ye be thirsty, gents?" the sultry Bess asked as she approached.

"Aye. Your best ale," Alex answered. "For both of us."

"Right away."

Watching the sway of her generous hips occupied Ted and Alex until she returned with tall glasses of frothy brew.

"So." After a last look at the departing wench, Ted turned back to Alex. "You've actually heard from him then? Lord Hillsborough?"

"As I assured you I would." He took a long draught from his drink. "I not only heard from the man, I've *seen* him."

"I thought your lofty cousin was wrapped up in his duties."

Alex nodded. "Quite right. But he was at a family gathering on the week's end, you see. Had quite a lot to say about the state of colonial affairs, and even more about Parliament's determination to maintain absolute supremacy. He most certainly will enforce the navigational acts and the remaining duty on tea. And he fully intends to put a stop to rabble-rousing meddlers."

Ted's even brows rose, and his eyes widened with interest. "They've been having more problems?"

With a grimace, Alex took another drink.

"Thought you said you had good news, old boy." Ted drained his glass and motioned to Bess for refills, then watched again with pleasure as she sashayed across the room and replaced their empty glasses with full ones.

"I do. That's a fact." Tossing his straggly forelock back into place with a swift whip of his head, Alex leaned closer. "Old Wills has suspended their rebellious provincial assemblies from meeting and intends to send more troops to America as a show of force. So don't you see, old chap? He's more than willing to arrange commissions . . . providing we outfit ourselves."

"Splendid." Ted wouldn't be sorry to see the end of his wearisome studies. He tapped his jaw with one finger as he considered the possibilities. "So all we need is capital enough for that, then."

"And I'm certain I can scrape up a bit extra if you find you don't have enough."

"Say, that's quite generous of you, old boy. Then it's settled. Off to America for the two of us."

Across the room a round of boisterous laughter rang out, drawing their attention. But nothing seemed out of the ordinary. They returned to the drinks at hand.

"Any word from your sister yet?" Alex set down his glass. "I saw you coming from the post."

Ted smiled, suddenly recalling his mail. "I received a letter from her today, actually. But I've as yet to read it."

"You're jesting!"

"No. In fact, I've got it with me," he said, patting his vest pocket. "Perhaps when I break my news to her about leaving college, I'll let her think I did it in order to ensure her welfare." A crafty smile spread over his mouth. "Surely she can't disapprove of my *great sacrifice* then. Right, old chap?"

Alex whacked his knee with one hand. "To be sure. Say, did she mention anything about the political climate, perchance? I'd be interested in her comments on it, since she's there, after all."

"I said I've not read the thing yet, Alex. I was on my way to my room to do just that when you happened along."

"Well, what's stopping you now, old boy? I can surely keep still long enough for you to catch up on her news." He leaned back against his chair, gesturing for another round of drinks.

Ted broke the wax and unfolded the pages, scanning them silently. He smiled at her greeting.

My dearest Teddy,

It hardly seems so many weeks since I last set eyes upon your handsome face and kissed you farewell. I pray every night for you, and hope fervently that all is going well for you in your studies at Oxford. I cannot tell you how much I miss you and long for sight and scent of my England. Yet what an incredible wonder it was to cross the vast ocean and step upon new soil. The voyage was nothing like I had expected, however. It was not without considerable pleasure that I finally departed that vessel whose incessant rocking and lurching made nearly all its passengers ill for days.

I am certain you must have heard by now about Julia's untimely passing. You cannot imagine the shock it was for me to arrive in New Jersey on my own and find that there was no one here to greet me, and no place for me to live.

Ted exhaled slowly, remembering Susannah's youth and her quiet ways. There had never been a time when there was no one to provide a home for her and take care of her needs. But what of Julia's husband? Hadn't he taken her under his wing? Ted looked back at her neatly penned words:

Reverend Selkirk sailed for North Carolina the evening before I left Philadelphia, and by the time I arrived at Julia's, Robert Chandler had departed Princeton as well. I had no choice but to pay for my lodging at an inn nearby, which severely depleted my remaining funds.

I have some rather awkward news for you, Teddy, which I am at a loss to know how to explain. I can only hope you will understand that this was my only recourse, as there was no other choice I could make. But it shall not be forever. I found it necessary to sign an indenturement—

Ted's heart stopped beating for a moment as the full impact of Susannah's words hit home. Then his expression darkened and hardened, and his mouth fell open with an audible gasp. "No! It can't be!"

"What is it?"

Ted stared at his friend. "You won't believe it. *I* don't believe it. Of all the—" He let the pages dangle from his fingers as he gazed unseeing at the ceiling of the smoky room.

"Will there be anythin' else, gents?" Bess stood beside the table, one hand propped on her hip.

Grimacing, Ted waved her away. "The girl's lost all sense of decency," he said through gritted teeth.

"You mean Bess, old chap?" Alex asked incredulously,

bending his head in her direction as a leering customer pulled her onto his lap and gave her a smacking kiss. "That never was a strong point with her, I'd venture to say."

"No, no. Not her. Sue."

"Your sister? What's she done?" A perplexed frown wrinkled Alex's high forehead.

Ted glanced nervously around the room and leaned nearer. "She's demeaned our name, Alex," he whispered. "Sold herself into servitude."

Alex searched Ted's face as if expecting to hear the rest of the joke. "You can't mean that."

"It's right here." Glaring at the neatly written paper, Ted shook his head and let out a disapproving huff. "She's indentured herself." Again he scanned the room's occupants to be certain no one was listening.

"Why ever would she have done such a thing, old boy?" Alex's tone softened. "Did she give reason?"

"What reason could there be for such an unthinkable act?" he demanded. "Women are so simpleminded. And it appears my sister is even more so. Be glad you weren't cursed with one."

Alex stared at him but didn't speak as Ted grimly read the rest of the letter in silence.

"She was alone. No funds, no place to live. So she stupidly surmised that by indenturing herself she'd find a means of support. Isn't that ridiculous? And with the bishop's emissary right there in the Colonies! I have no doubt he would have stepped in to provide for her. There must be an Anglican church in this Prince-Town, after all. She could have gone to the minister there for help until Reverend Selkirk could see to her. Can you believe it? My sister—a bond servant!"

"Well, don't be too hard on the girl, old chap. Surely her term of service can't last forever. Soon enough you'll be in a position to help her out, or even buy her out."

"No doubt that's what *she's* counting on, to be sure," Ted said flatly. "Why, if word of this ever got out, I would be looked down upon as no better than a common foot soldier. My chances for advancement in the military would be nil." Wadding up the letter, he lunged to his feet and tossed it into the fading flames of the huge fireplace. Then, slapping the price of the drinks on the table, he stomped toward the exit.

Dumbfounded, Alex rose. "Ted, wait. You shouldn't have done that. How will you contact your sister once we get to the Colonies?"

Ted cast a disgusted glance over his shoulder and waited for his friend to catch up. "Hmph. That's the best part," he whispered with a sarcastic tip of his head as he opened the door for Alex. "She's sold herself to an innkeeper. Sue's a *tavern wench!*" He waved his hand in Bess's direction before striding out after his friend. "A tavern wench—like *her!*" he almost shouted, slamming the door with a resounding thud. "How hard could she be to find? All we've to do is take in all the taverns and mughouses in Prince-Town."

Alex let out a low whistle.

"I'm about ready to forget I even *have* a sister," Ted said, his voice restrained and even, in careful control. "How long did Lord Hillsborough expect it would be until he can arrange for our commissions?"

"Not long at all, actually. What do you say that since we'll be chucking this dreary place anyway, we head on up to Bath for some fun while we wait?"

Ted's expression brightened. "Why the deuce not?" A slow grin spread across his face. "Yes. Capital idea, Alex, old boy. Capital."

13

A balmy haze rose into the twilight sky. It shimmered against the liquid gold edges of clouds high above the wooded hills surrounding the town of Bath. From the second floor of the magnificent Royal Crescent Hotel, Ted gazed out into the distance. Deep in thought, he barely noticed the Avon River, which lay like a winding, bronze-tinted ribbon discarded on the floor of the valley.

"Here, old boy," said Alex, nudging him back to consciousness with a glass of mineral water. "The maid brought this by."

"Thanks." Thirsty after the grueling sixty-mile coach trip from London, Ted drained the liquid in a steady succession of gulps. "Is there any more?"

Alex nodded, gesturing to a tray on the stand near Ted's door. "What's so interesting?" Stepping up to the window, he peered below, where an enticing array of brightly dressed young ladies strolled past a steam-spewing bath house and an assortment of shops. "Oh. I see."

"Beg your pardon?" Ted asked, coming back with a half-filled glass.

Alex wagged his head slowly. "Really, old chap, if you don't climb out of those caverns of despair, we'll waste this perfectly good opportunity to have the time of our lives."

"Sorry. You're quite right. I shan't let any dreary thoughts of Susannah intrude on our time here." He glanced around the regal room with its highly polished furniture and rich tapestries. "Did you say you had an extra frock coat?"

Alex gestured toward the chair in one corner. "Of course. It should fit rather well, seeing as how we're about the same height."

"Pity I'm not as lean, though," Ted grinned.

"All in good time, old boy, once we get into our training for the military."

"Quite." With a half-smile, Ted crossed the room and tried on the coat, a fashionable dove gray with silver buttons of French plate. Alex had also provided a silk shirt with ruffled front and cuffs. "Splendid."

"I knew you'd approve," Alex said, a nod of his head displacing his forelock. He brushed it back with his long fingers. "I shall go and change, then, while you dress. We'll have supper at the club and take in the latest stage show. Shan't be a moment." With a few long strides he was gone.

Ted changed, then stood back to admire himself in the looking glass. Almost a dandy, he determined. A far cry from the somber robes of Oxford. He winked a blue eye at the even features of his reflection before walking a few doors down the hall to Alex's room.

He knocked and entered without waiting for a reply. The room was furnished in similar fashion to his own, except that Alex's was decorated in shades of gold, whereas his own was done in turquoise. "Ready, old boy?"

His lanky friend stood buttoning a ruffled shirt with deliberate slowness. He managed an elaborate yawn for Ted's benefit as he casually reached for a shoe and sat down to put it on.

Ted ignored the charade and crossed to peer out the open window. Two particularly fetching members of the gentler sex, in gowns of layered silk and the finest lace, paraded along the stone street in front of the hotel. A whiff of French perfume wafted up to him as they passed. "You'd not be wasting so much time if you'd take a look at what we're missing while you mess about."

Alex strode to the window and gazed down. "You needn't tell *me* twice, old chap. I'll finish on the way." Grabbing his frock coat, he threw it on and buttoned it as they headed out the door toward the elegant curved staircase.

Breathless, Ted emerged from the main lobby door with Alex on his heels, in search of the fair lasses. Together they stopped short as two young military officers in bright red uniforms with an abundance of braid strutted up to the young women and bent in exaggerated bows.

"Please allow us the honor of escorting the most beautiful damsels in all of Bath this eve," one of the soldiers said.

A chorus of giggles emitted as the maidens accepted the officers' arms and strolled off into the dusk.

Ted and Alex exchanged wry glances and sighed. Then, with a shrug and a grin, they continued toward the Assembly Room.

"My mouth is watering for some roast swan in sweet sauce," Alex mused. "It's a specialty here."

"Yes," Ted groaned and stepped up the pace. "And I've not had plum pudding for a fortnight."

At the door, Alex reached for the latch and opened it for his friend. "Well, my good man, that's why we've come. Partly, in any case." Sputtering into a laugh, he followed Ted inside and glanced around.

They chose a table along the far wall of the airy, spacious hall.

"Did you notice, old boy, the ease with which those army chaps made their conquests?"

"I told you the ladies always go for a dashing uniform. And soon we'll be just as irresistible." Ted let his gaze wander about the chattering crowd of patrons seated at various linen-covered tables. With a tip of his head he indicated a three-some of beguiling young ladies a few chairs away. "And there's plenty to go around, I always say."

A conciliatory smile curved Alex's mouth as he, too, caught sight of them. "I suppose even without military dress we can regale those delicious females with the fact we're about to venture into the dark wilderness of America to save the defenseless colonists from wild savages. That ought to play upon their . . . sympathies, shall we say?"

Ted chuckled. "Well, I for one cannot wait until that tailor of yours starts designing our uniforms. I want lots of gold braid to catch the ladies' eyes."

Later, after dining on Bath's finest food, the two young men strode out to the building-lined street and headed for the evening stage performance.

Alex elbowed Ted in the ribs. "Hold on, old boy."

"What is it?"

"I just noticed a couple of king's men entering that mughouse yonder." Indicating a tavern entrance not far up the block, he stopped and turned to Ted. "What say we put off the show until tomorrow and see if we can talk to the blokes about military life?"

"Why not? Who knows what we might pick up if we ask the proper questions."

Alex set the pace, and they covered the distance in seconds. He wrenched open the heavy door.

Ted entered first into the dusky room, glancing around at the assorted clusters of people. He motioned with his head toward a pair of officers seated near the door. They looked even younger than either Alex or himself and wore the obviously new garb of those of recent commission. With a careless shrug, he approached them.

Alex lightly tapped the shoulder of the nearest one. "Your pardon, but would you mind if my friend and I join you?"

The stocky, muscular young man turned coal black eyes on Ted and Alex. His gaze darted suspiciously between them, then he relaxed his wary expression and shrugged. "Not at all."

Ted grinned and took a seat near the other fellow, a lean, wiry youth with an engaging grin that made his ears stick out slightly from under his military wig. "Ted Harrington," he said with a nod. He signaled the waitress for a round of drinks.

"My friend is Alex Fontaine. You lads on official business, or holiday?"

"On holiday, my good fellow," the stocky one said. "Second Lieutenants George Bedford and Percy Smythe, at your service. Taking advantage of our last jolly days of freedom before shipping off to the Colonies."

"You don't say." Alex's smile widened. "And where, pray tell, are you headed?"

"Why, to Boston, with the Fourteenth. We sail out of Bristol tomorrow at eventide. I must say, it's been a delight observing all the fair lasses in their bathing costumes here at the baths. How they shall survive our absence, once we've gone, I can but surmise." Smythe's jovial grin encompassed his entire face as he threw back his head and laughed. "We've only escaped with our lives, mates. Ducked in here for a bit of peace, you might say."

"Aye," his companion said with a smirk. "'Tis a wonder how our bright colors draw attention the moment we step outside. Could we but stay a few more days . . ." He shot a knowing glance at Smythe, who nodded.

A plump waitress with a polite smile delivered their drinks. For a bitter second, while he watched her make her way to another table, Ted envisioned a disgracefully flirting Susannah in her place. Blinking away the picture with an inward scowl, he looked back at Bedford and Smythe. "So you're off to Boston, then?"

George Bedford grimaced as he set down his glass and wiped the back of his hand across his mouth. "Quite right. And I assure you both, it'll be a pleasure to show those rebel colonists some real soldiers. They'll not spit in *my* eye as they do the Empire's, with their illegal courts and actions."

"Aye." Percy Smythe smoothed his wig absently. "I hear tell they even think they're going to try to hang a commissioned officer, if you can believe that. And for just stopping a riot, no less! 'Tis high time we put those rebel pigs in their place."

Alex raised his mug of ale and grinned at Ted. "Hear, hear! You know, gents," he said with a sideways glance at Bedford, "my cousin, Lord Hillsborough, informed me several days past that smuggling has increased alarmingly along the entire coast of the Colonies. And the settlers care not a whit."

Bedford cocked his eyebrows. "Lord Hillsborough, eh? Well, you can inform your esteemed cousin we'll soon put that to rights." He struck his fist on the table to emphasize his words.

"As you should," Ted said, taking up the banter. "He says they're a sorry lot. Mostly debtors, criminals out of Newgate, and religious deviates. It's quite commonplace for their ministers to preach sedition from their very pulpits!"

"Ah," Percy Smythe said with a doubtful shake of his head, "be assured they're not *all* like Hill says, now. My own father has naught but respect for old Ben Franklin. As does the rest of Parliament, for that matter."

Bedford huffed loudly. "Well now, a clever clown never lacks an audience. But the bloke is little more than a commoner himself, behind all those fine words of his." He checked the pocket watch in a fold of his uniform. "Well, we'd best be off. We've an early day of it on the morrow." Finishing the remainder of his ale, he rose.

Lieutenant Smythe did likewise. "Pleasure talking to you lads."

Ted grinned. "Perhaps we'll meet again sometime. We, too, are seeking commissions in America. They've already been arranged, in fact."

"You don't say, now." Bedford guffawed at his companion. "Where might you be heading? Which regiment?"

With a dip of his head, Alex laughed sheepishly. "Can't recall at the moment, I'm afraid. But we'll be stationed in Philadelphia."

14

Daniel Haynes whistled softly in the twilight as he rode south from Perth Amboy toward the Toms River. The waning moon had already peeked over the tops of the far hills, and a rich chorus of peepers and tree toads filled the evening air. Here and there a cricket broke into song, and a barn owl hooted nearby. Dan smiled to himself and drew a deep breath. It would be a fine evening.

But a nagging thought made its way into his head, stealing his pleasure. He shifted in his saddle and sighed. *Lord, what is it about this woman that I cannot escape the memory of her face, the sound of her voice?* he prayed, disturbed at the direction his thoughts once again had taken.

It had been months since he had met the lovely young lady in green on the Philadelphia docks. Sam Adams had kept him so busy up north that this was the first time he had been able to set foot in New Jersey since he'd come upon the lovely lass. Surely by now her *Theodore* had joined her, as he should have done in the first place. Dan frowned and shook his head. It was hardly likely that she could possibly still be unattended.

Then his breath caught. *But what if she were?* He was positive he hadn't imagined the light of promise in her eyes that night at supper. But what exactly had he to offer her, anyway? A solitary existence at home with a child or two while he was sent to—only Adams knew where—consorting with smugglers and rebels, dodging soldiers, constantly flirting with the possibility of arrest? Some fine existence that would be!

He chuckled at the preposterous idea. It might be years before he could even consider such a luxury as settling down. When the proper time came for marriage, if ever, he'd know. But for now, all he could do was dream.

An easy smile drew up the corners of his mouth, and his earlier concern eased. *Surely, Lord, dreaming can do no harm.* His thoughts drifted to a vision with golden brown hair and gray-blue eyes, tucked under his arm in a cloak of rich emerald velvet. He could still see her trusting face and hear her soft British accent.

Flame's ears pricked forward, and the hair on the back of Dan's neck bristled as the sound of hoofbeats broke into his musings.

A mounted patrol emerged from the grove off to the right.

"Halt!" said the one obviously in charge. The soldiers circled Daniel, cutting off his path.

Dan's pacer shied with a nervous whinny.

"Easy, boy." Dan gave the horse a comforting pat on the neck as he looked warily at the king's men. His heartbeat quickened at the thought of the messages in his saddlebags. Careful to maintain a composed expression, he wondered exactly how coded they'd appear to a suspicious officer of the king.

"What business have you on the roads this time of night?" the leader asked in his caustic voice. "The *good* townspeople are home and abed by dark." His steely eyes glinted in the pale light, and shadows hid among the lines of his long aristocratic face.

Dan cast what he hoped appeared to be a casual glance around at the other men, and smiled thinly. "I'm a postrider." He rested a hand on one of the pouches.

"Are you, now? At this hour?"

One of the men lit a torch and handed it to the officer. When he took it, the light revealed a long scar from one ear to his nose.

"Of course," Dan said evenly. "Why, Benjamin Franklin, the esteemed postmaster general of the northern colonies, has come up with a system we've found to be most efficient."

The steely eyes narrowed.

"We travel by day *and* night," Daniel continued, trying to sound a touch pompous himself. "And for the first time in history the postal service is sending a hefty profit to England every year."

"Efficient, is it?" the man countered. "We'll just have a look for ourselves." Handing the torch to the nearest soldier, the officer dismounted and rummaged through one of the saddlebags. He withdrew a handful of letters and scrutinized the names, carelessly allowing several pieces of mail to slip to the ground. His boot imprinted one of them as he reached into the bag for more. A satisfied smile spread across his face as his eyes scanned one of the names. "Hugh McAfee," he said, gazing up at Daniel. "Could it be the same Hugh McAfee, now, suspected of aiding the biggest smuggling ring in all the Colonies?" He ripped open the seal.

"Wait!" Dan said without thinking as he reached to take the correspondence from the soldier. "You can't do that. It's against the law to interfere with the mail."

"Not when we come across something suspicious, it isn't." The soldier deflected Dan's hand with one shoulder as he turned and took a step away to read the missive. Then he glared at one of his men. "An invitation!" he said incredulously. "To an insidious poetry reading, no less!"

With a huff he threw the letter into the air and remounted, casting a last unbelieving glance at Daniel. "Carry on. But if we meet again, and I find something to link you to those smuggling scoundrels, your mum will have to lay you out in two pieces, lad. Be most assured of that." Motioning for his men to follow, he cantered off.

Daniel watched after them with profound relief until they disappeared into the darkness of the birch grove once again. He listened in the stillness for several moments to be certain they'd gone, the pounding of his heart slowing to a reasonable pace. Then he dismounted and picked up the discarded torch. Making a wide circle around his horse to gather up all the scattered mail, he looked closely at the torn message with its smudged words. It truly was an invitation, as the officer had said—from the Colonial Poetical Society, for a reading at the Tidewater Tavern on the sixteenth of July.

Dan almost laughed aloud at the stupidity of the king's men. Anyone who knew big, blustery Hugh McAfee would know the man wouldn't be caught dead attending anything so refined as a reading of someone's collection of poems. But there *would* be a secret meeting of the Sons of Liberty at the Tidewater that night. With a chuckle of amusement, he put out the torch and climbed into the saddle, then continued on his way.

Two nights later, the air seemed eerily quiet as the dark water of the Toms River licked the pilings of a rough-hewn dock. A heavy bank of clouds veiled the half moon as Daniel and Hugh McAfee answered the tiny speck of light across the bay with a lantern signal. A handful of black-clothed men waited mutely with them. Only an occasional lonely hoot of an owl and the whirring of bat wings broke the silence.

In a matter of moments several small craft approached, the oars making barely audible slaps with each stroke.

Dan and McAfee caught the first two ropes and secured the boats. The men beside them stood and assisted the others, speaking in low hushed tones or not at all.

"Ahoy, mate," came a familiar voice. Yancy Curtis climbed out of a longboat near Dan's elbow. His grin gleamed in the soft glow of the lantern. "Seems we meet in the strangest places."

Dan shook his hand warmly, then reached for a lumpy sack of coffee beans already being passed along the line of men. "How've things been going?"

"Slimier all the time, that's the short of it. Coastal patrols are gettin' thicker any place within reach of the ports." Hefting a crate onto one shoulder, Yancy carried it to a waiting wagon and carefully set it down, then returned. "To be truthful, I thought better of comin' into Barnegat Bay. 'Tis so narrow. It would only take one frigate to block our escape."

Dan nodded. "Word has it that's why we're fool enough to *be* here," he muttered. "The British think we've got more brains."

Yancy chuckled. "Aye. Well, if those preachin' friends of yours have taught you any good prayers, you'd better set 'em aloft, lad. We'll be needin' 'em."

"I agree," Dan said, his tone almost a whisper as he cast a glance toward the dark trees behind the dock.

Yancy nudged him softly. "Say, lad. Ever get things goin' with that little damsel in distress you set off to rescue in Philadelphia?"

With a sideways glance at Yancy, Dan shook his head. "Wish I could say otherwise, but no. And she's not in Philadelphia. She was on her way to Princeton."

"That so?"

Dan nodded. "I've been running so many messages for Sam Adams, I haven't been to Princeton for months. For all I know, she's been and gone."

"Aye. Rotten luck, mate." Yancy chuckled. "But I've got a little somethin' that might just change that."

Dan felt his pulse increase. Curious, he turned and looked at the sailor silhouetted against the dim light.

"My captain has a message for Dr. Witherspoon. He's the bloke at Princeton, right?"

"Yes," Dan answered. What did Yancy have in mind?

"We were to take it as far as Trenton and pass it on. But seein' as how you're here, no reason why we shouldn't speed it on its way." A slow grin spread across Yancy's face. "Nothin's too good for a mate. Come on. I'll row you out to see the captain." Turning, he grabbed the nearest mooring rope and jumped with ease down into the boat.

Just a step behind, Daniel quietly followed suit.

"Besides," the sailor said with a grin as he sat down and maneuvered the oars over the side, "the way I figure it, we'll never get outta this trap alive anyway." He pushed away from the dock.

"Why, Yancy," Dan teased under his breath, "a moment ago you were about to trust the power of prayer. Ready to give up so soon?"

Some moments later, Daniel returned from the vessel, the letter for Witherspoon tucked next to his heart for safekeeping. He tried to contain his eagerness to set off at once for Princeton. Would he be able to find the enchanting English lass? Would she be as beautiful as he remembered?

Suddenly Yancy stiffened and stopped rowing. "Down!" he whispered.

Instantly Dan slid down below the rim of the longboat and peered toward the shore. "Why?"

Charging horses burst from the woods toward the men still at work. "Halt where you are," an officer challenged, "or we'll run you through."

Sacks of goods fell to the ground as hands went up among the lot. But on the end, one man bolted for the trees.

"Stop, in the name of the king!" the officer yelled after him. "Carver, Jenkins—run the blackguard down."

Two of the mounted soldiers wheeled in pursuit as the fellow vanished from sight into the wooded darkness.

Yancy tugged Dan's sleeve. "Can you swim, mate?"

"Some."

"Better make a dash before they spot us. Take that side. And try not to rock the boat." Without further comment, the seaman slipped over his side of the craft.

Stealthily Dan eased himself into the cold black river and set out noiselessly after Yancy, who was already heading downstream. His mind flashed to the coveted letter beneath his shirt and doeskin coat, and he resorted to using only one arm as he pressed the other tightly over the letter. Maybe it would stay dry—if he didn't drown first. Some fifty yards beyond the soldiers, he slithered, panting, onto the ground his friend had gained moments before.

Yancy nudged him. "We'd best not stay in the open."

With a nod, Dan rose to a hunched position and kept close behind him as they sought cover among the trees.

Once inside the nearest grove, Yancy's smug grin glinted in a shaft of moonlight. "'Tis such a lark, bestin' the king's own, eh?" he muttered under his breath. "Such a sorry lot." He turned, inadvertently stepping on a fallen branch. It broke with a loud snap.

An owl screeched and flapped off in a flurry of wings.

"What was that?"

Dan and Yancy froze.

"Find out," came an unmistakably British command from a dozen yards away. "Coates, Hadley—go investigate." At once the night quiet shattered as horses' hooves crashed over the old leaves and deadfall.

Grabbing Yancy's arm, Dan took off, leading in the opposite direction. But in seconds he realized the mounted pair had split up, and the horses were closing in. "In here," he whispered, tugging his friend down among a thick stand of rhododendron. Soggy and shivering, they crouched low amid the growth. Their lungs burned as they tried to still their breathing.

Outlined against the glow of the night sky, the riders passed within a few feet of the dark leafy bushes where Dan and Yancy hid motionless. The horses stopped.

"See anything?" one voice asked.

"Naw. Hiding, I'll wager. But I've a swift remedy for that." He slid his saber out of its scabbard. "Let's skewer us a couple of snipes."

The other soldier gave a snort and drew out his sword, and the pair began circling the area. Leaning down, they stabbed their long blades into every bush they passed.

Dan swallowed in alarm as Yancy's eyes grew wide. Would the sailor give away their position? Should they surrender before a blade found its mark?

Yancy tensed and inched backward slightly, but made no move to flee or stand.

Dan finally remembered to pray. *Lord, help us!*

One of the soldiers neared the clump of rhododendron and gave a savage thrust.

Dan stiffened and held his breath as the edge of the blade shaved a sliver off the heel of his boot.

The rider nudged the horse a step closer for a second jab.

Bracing himself for the sharp cold blade that was poised to bury itself in his chest, Dan closed his eyes. *Father, into thy hands. . . .*

"Hadley! Coates!" came a distant cry.

The soldier straightened in the saddle. "Here, sir. We lost track of 'em. We're backtracking."

"Cease and desist. I've something more pressing here."

Turning his horse, the man rode away.

Yancy released a long slow whoosh of breath and started to get up.

"Stay down!" Dan whispered, his pulse still hammering. "The Lord saved us this time. Let's not tempt Providence."

Princeton had never looked lovelier to Dan as he nudged Flame up Nassau Street toward the college. Bright azaleas and roses in shades of red, pink, and white bloomed in profusion, and the trees and shrubs were in full leaf. He knew the college was in session once again, which accounted for the lack of pedestrians in sight. But he could not prevent his gaze from searching past the shop windows for one special face.

With a sigh, he looped the pacer's reins over a hitching post at Nassau Hall. Then, removing a package from his saddlebag, he walked up the steps and entered the arched center doorway. He strolled down the wide hall until he reached the president's office, then knocked softly on the door.

"Come in," called a deep voice.

Daniel lifted the latch and stepped inside, where he saw a heavyset man behind a desk. "Dr. Witherspoon?"

The friendly smile on the distinguished man's face answered even before he spoke, and inquisitive blue eyes brightened his otherwise dour features. "Aye. What might I do for ye, now?"

"I'm Daniel Haynes. I have a message for you from Mr. Lee of Virginia." He handed the letter to Dr. Witherspoon.

"Good, good," Dr. Witherspoon boomed. Rising in his tutorial robes, he crossed the carpeted floor of the book-lined room and extended a welcoming hand. "Come in, laddie. I've heard a lot about ye."

Dan smiled and shook his hand warmly. "And I of you, sir. Your reputation for integrity and good works preceded you from Edinburgh. You've more than proven them correct in the two years since your arrival. I'm most honored to meet you."

"Well, come sit down, Daniel." Turning, the man led the way back to his oak desk, where he took his customary seat and indicated one for Dan. "I came across your name some days ago . . . on a past college roster, to be precise."

With a grin at the sound of the *r*'s that rolled off the Scotsman's tongue, Dan nodded and lowered himself into the chair, placing the parcel on the floor beside him. "Yes. I completed two terms. But that was a few years ago. Family matters took precedence over my studies, and my training had to be put aside."

"Ye're na' interested, then, in pursuing the vocation any further?" The friendly eyes twinkled as a concerned expression settled upon Witherspoon's kind face.

"Oh, it's not a lack of interest, sir. I'm twenty-six, now. Too old to be attending theology classes. Most of my classmates have long since graduated and gone on to churches of their own. And, as you can see, I'm otherwise occupied at the moment."

"Aye. The patriots. Reverend Cooper up in Boston wrote me aboot ye, laddie. He says ye've done a splendid job for the cause. He's quite appreciative of your efforts."

"We do what we can." Dan inclined his head. "All of us."

Dr. Witherspoon nodded. "Please be kind enough to allow me a moment to read this," he said, tearing open the envelope. "It may call for a reply." After a quick scan of the letter, he returned his piercing gaze to Dan. "Nay, 'tis aboot a meeting at the Indian King Tavern in Haddonfield with Elias Boudinot and the Philadelphia patriots."

"Sounds like an occasion you wouldn't want to miss."

"Certainly not." The older man leaned forward slightly and placed his elbows on the desk, steepling his fingertips as he studied Daniel. "Ye know, laddie, this political situation betwixt the Colonies and the mother country canna' go on forever. Ye might consider continuing your studies on your own, for that time when things've settled. I'm sure we could arrange to give ye some orals whenever ye might be passing through . . . should ye feel again that your calling lies in serving the Lord."

Daniel considered his words thoughtfully. "I've never doubted my calling, sir. But once I found myself caught up in freedom's cause, I put my studies aside. I appreciate your kind offer most sincerely. And I can cover the expense. On my next trip home, I shall pick up some of my books and get to it. I do thank you, Dr. Witherspoon."

Smiling, the man rose and removed a book from his own shelves. "Dinna' be putting it off, lad. I'd be happy if ye'd study this one in the meantime."

Dan stared openmouthed at the man's generosity. He stood and accepted reverently the treasured copy of *Foxe's Book of Martyrs*. "I don't know how to thank you, sir. I'll guard it with my life; you can be assured of that."

Clapping a big hand stoutly on Dan's shoulder, the president nodded. "I'm sure ye will, Daniel. But remember—" The r's sang again. "It's na' the book that's most important, but the effect its pages have upon him who reads it."

"I'm sure you're right," Dan said. Then, glancing down beside his chair, he picked up the parcel he'd brought along. "And I have a gift for you, Dr. Witherspoon. Some South American coffee beans I . . . sort of *acquired* from some sailors I know."

"Well, lad. Thank ye most kindly," the older man said, accepting the package. "I shall enjoy it immensely. I bid ye Godspeed, Daniel. My prayers go with ye."

"Thank you, sir. I . . . thought perhaps I might tarry a bit and visit with some of the students. Do they still congregate at the Lyons' Den?"

Before Dr. Witherspoon could answer, the sound of thundering hooves carried in through the open window. "Whitefield's riding into town!" called a voice. "George Whitefield's coming!"

Daniel and Dr. Witherspoon stared at one another in surprise. "*Whitefield?*"

Both men bolted for the door.

15

Susannah was coming up out of the root cellar when she heard a commotion from the open attic window above.

"Lemme have it!" a gravelly voice yelled.

"No! You can't!" Mary Clare shrieked. "Stop it! Stop!"

Dumping the potatoes bunched in her apron, Susannah ran into the ordinary and up the attic stairs. Sounds of a scuffle grew louder with each step.

"Ow!" Susannah heard Mary's muffled cry, followed by a thud.

The bedroom door stood ajar, and Susannah barged in. To her horror, she saw the younger girl huddled on the floor, one arm upraised as if to ward off another blow. The tender skin around Mary's eye was red and puffy with a bluish tinge. "What have you done?" she gasped, flying to Mary's side.

Silas Drummond looked up, his face contorted in a sneer.

Mary Clare, in that unguarded instant, wrenched from her father's grasp her best Sunday gown, which had been stretched tautly between them.

"I'll take that." Silas clutched a handful of rose linen and yanked it back, the gleam in his black eyes cold.

"Pa! No!" Tears streamed down Mary's face as her precious dress ripped.

Ignoring her own terror, Susannah stepped between them, her hands on her hips. "You stop this at once!"

"And just who's gonna—"

With a pitiful sob, one hand cupped over her eye, Mary Clare dashed around Susannah to the hall and down the steps.

Her heart in her throat, Susannah remained rooted in place, her eyes pinning Silas Drummond as she sent a silent plea heavenward. She dared not appear frightened. "I shall summon the sheriff, unless you unhand that gown and leave immediately."

The threat had little effect on the man. Slowly advancing on Susannah with the voluminous frock bunched in his arms, he stopped within inches of her face. The stench of rum and his own foul odor permeated the small room. He raised a fist.

It took as much strength as Susannah possessed to stand her ground and glare back without flinching.

Emitting a roar of rage, Drummond lowered his arm and barreled past her.

A sick feeling clenched Susannah's stomach. Her knees gave way, and she sank to the cot beside her. Then, remembering Mary's gown, she jumped to her feet and dashed after him. Just as she reached the landing, she heard the door slam closed.

Susannah's thoughts turned at once to Mary Clare. She went quickly to the kitchen, where Mrs. Lyons was busy preparing the evening meal. "I . . . um . . . don't suppose Mary passed this way in the last little while."

"No, why?"

Susannah flicked her tongue nervously over her lips. "I'm afraid there's been a bit of a problem. Between Mary and her father."

Mrs. Lyons dropped the paring knife she held, and her face went pale. "What? When?"

"I found them upstairs," Susannah admitted miserably. "You were right. He came for her Sunday dress."

"Oh no. I feared it would come to that sooner or later. That no-good wretch is forever tormentin' them kids. Where is the child now?"

"She ran downstairs while I was trying to get her father to leave her alone."

"Oh, my poor little Mary Clare. What'll we do? This is just plain awful." Going to the back door, she stepped out and scanned the immediate area, but in vain.

Susannah, at her side, put an arm around the woman's plump shoulders, pushing back her own guilt and fear in an effort to keep her employer calm. "Well, do go back inside and try not to worry. I'll get Chip, and the two of us will look for Mary."

Mrs. Lyons nodded. She twisted a corner of her apron nervously as she searched the distance once more, then hesitantly turned and went back inside. "I pray you'll find her."

Forcing herself to smile, Susannah breathed a prayer of her own. Then, gathering her skirts in her hands, she ran toward the woodshed and the sound of chopping.

Standing beside a pile of firewood, Christopher split a log with the stroke of an axe.

"Chip!"

He looked up, straightening as Susannah approached. He had grown during the past two months and was beginning to fill out. He barely resembled the skinny, timid boy she'd first met. His even brows drew together above his straight nose. "W-what's wrong?"

"It's Mary. She's run off crying. Could you help me find her?"

A look of rage darkened the lad's eyes. "Pa again?"

Susannah nodded. "She can't have gone far, but I've no idea where to start looking. I hoped perhaps you might."

Teeth clenched, he gave a swing to the axe, embedding its sharp edge in the chopping block. "I w-wish this w-was him," he stuttered in a choked voice. "I hate him."

His words sent a chill through Susannah. She had never heard a child speak so disparagingly of a parent. She brushed a lock of hair behind his ear with her fingers. "You can't mean that."

His pain-filled gaze assured her he was quite serious. Turning on his heel he gestured with his head for her to follow. "Come on. I th-think I know wh-where she is. There's a place w-we used to hide."

Susannah followed as he headed away from the grounds toward a thickly wooded grove not too far beyond the settlement. "You know, Chip," she began in a placating tone, grappling for the right thing to say, "those ill feelings you bear for your father are not proper. No matter what he may have done to you or to your sister, you must respect him as your elder." Susannah paused. The words sounded empty and hollow, even to her.

Christopher shot her a bitter glance as he picked up the pace. "Jon and Steve have been t-teachin' me to w-wrestle and fight. And I'm gettin' strong. They said so." As they entered the woods, he flexed an arm and studied the bulging muscle evident beneath his cotton shirtsleeve.

"Please don't do anything rash, Chip. It could cause even worse problems for you and Mary—and for Mr. and Mrs. Lyons as well." He didn't respond, so she continued. "Remember Dr. Witherspoon's sermon last Sunday? 'Vengeance is mine, said the Lord.' I'm sure God will deal with your father, in time."

"Maybe. But I'm p-planning to t-take care of him myself soon enough."

She wished there were some way to dissuade him from seeking retribution. There had to be some other apt Scripture she could quote in an instance such as this, but as she followed him into the denser growth, none came to mind. And she had to admit that she had no respectful feelings toward the unsavory Silas Drummond herself. How could she hope to quiet the rage stemming from this boy's need to protect his sister? Her own brother, Ted, had defended her honor on several occasions in their neighborhood when they were growing up.

The path turned toward a small clearing. Christopher held the heavy lower branches of an evergreen aside while Susannah stepped through the tangled underbrush into a narrow glen. Coin-sized spots of sunlight sparkled over the swirls of a bubbling stream and made bright amber designs on the packed earth. Under different circumstances, the place would have been quite charming. Lush green boughs over-head danced in the whispering breeze, while the water played over pebbles and stones in the creekbed. Not until Susannah followed the boy's gaze did she notice Mary Clare lying next to a large buttonbush. Silent sobs shook the girl's body.

In a moment Susannah was kneeling at her side. "Mary?"

Eyes glazed, she started violently and scrambled to get away.

Susannah caught her waist and held her firmly. "It's all right, honey. Chip and I are here. You're safe."

Turning her tear-stained face, Mary Clare looked at Susannah and grabbed her in a fierce hug. "I thought he—he—"

"No," Susannah said soothingly, stroking her hair. "It's just us."

"W-what happened, Mare?" Chip asked. Lines of concern rippled his forehead.

Mary Clare eased away from Susannah and sniffed. In an effort to dry her face with her fingers, she streaked dirt across her puffy cheeks. Her battered eye was swollen shut, the other red from crying. "I . . . was so frightened."

Susannah struggled against tears of her own at the pitiful sight of her friend's childlike face. Her heart constricted, outraged that someone could be so cruel. Susannah drew her close again and held her tight.

"I'll kill him," Christopher spat. "Wh-when I find him, I'm g-gonna kill him."

Susannah felt nearly as strongly herself, but knew such feelings would only make matters worse. "Please, Chip. You mustn't say things like that. Don't even think it. Mary needs us now."

He turned with a huff and stomped his foot. Bending, he picked up a dead branch and whacked the ground savagely. "It's n-not f-fair."

"I know," Susannah said, her tone even. "There's much in life that's not fair. But we must try to overcome the hard things and go on." She watched him storm away, hands in his pockets. Angrily, he kicked a stone, and it plopped in the water with a splash. With a last hug, she gently inched out of Mary Clare's grasp. "Come sit by the stream, honey. Let me wash your face."

Woodenly the girl obeyed. She sank to the ground without expression.

Susannah removed a handkerchief from her pocket and soaked it in the cool flow. Then she dabbed gently at Mary's eyes and cheeks. Rinsing out the cloth again, she repeated her ministrations, then dried Mary's face with the corner of her apron and washed the girl's hands. Swishing the handkerchief once more in the water, she folded it and handed it to Mary. "This will help your eye."

Mary Clare stared straight ahead without blinking. She took the cloth and held it over the swelling. Gradually her breathing returned to normal, and some of the puffiness of her face began to subside as she sat quietly for a while.

"Tell me about Pa," Christopher said as Susannah went to sit beside her.

Mary lowered the handkerchief, and her good eye narrowed with a pain-clouded grimace. She didn't speak for several minutes, and when she did, her voice sounded flat. "He . . . found me, in my room."

Christopher edged nearer and dropped down on her other side, his expression grim.

"He lost his job . . . again." She shook her head slowly and lowered her gaze. "He needed drinkin' money. Said my fine dress—the one Sue gave me—would . . . fetch a good price." Her breath caught on a sob as she bowed her head.

Susannah swallowed a great lump in her throat, still struggling with the idea that anyone—much less a parent—would stoop to such despicable conduct. She shuddered inwardly. Someone should inform the authorities.

"I tried . . . I tried to stop him," Mary Clare continued. "I grabbed the dress, but he hit me. It happened so fast. I barely saw the blow comin'."

Christopher snapped a twig in half. He flexed his fists open and closed, muttering something under his breath.

"I'm afraid he did take your dress," Susannah said.

Mary closed her eyes for a second, and when she opened them, a tear streamed downward as she looked at Susannah. "Then I . . . have nothin' pretty . . . for church. Jonathan wouldn't want to be seen with me in my old faded clothes. And I'm sure to have a black eye."

Susannah managed a smile. "Oh, it might not be so bad. Just keep putting cold water on it." Placing an arm around Mary's shoulder, she gave a squeeze. "And how can you think that of Jon, honey? He likes you for who you are, not for the way you dress."

"That's easy for you to say," Mary flared. "You've never had to wear rags. You aren't the daughter of . . . the town drunk. You never had to be ashamed of your father."

"That's quite true," Susannah admitted. "But there's still hope. We've nearly finished the new gown we started last week, remember? We still have a few days before Sunday. If we hurry, I'm certain it'll be ready by then." She rose and brushed off her skirt.

Mary Clare's face brightened considerably.

"You won't have to worry about being the daughter of the town drunk much longer." Chip stood still clenching his fists. "I'm gonna fix him good. I p-promise." His expression was hard, unwavering.

"No you're not, young man," Susannah said, helping Mary to her feet. Planting her knuckles on her hip, she faced him squarely. "I'll have no such talk. Why, if you should ever—"

"Susannah!" came a faint but urgent cry in the distance.

"Someone's calling," she said. "Come. We must hurry."

Mary Clare placed a hand on her arm. "You two go on. I can't come out like this," she said, indicating her swollen eye. "I'll come along in a little while. And please don't tell Jonathan about my pa."

"Susannah!" The voice sounded nearer this time.

She searched Mary's face. "Are you sure you'll be all right?"

The girl nodded.

"I really hate to leave you right now. But perhaps I should see what's so pressing." She turned. "Chip?"

Christopher shrugged reluctantly, and with a glance back at his sister, led the way out of the thicket.

Emerging into the open, Susannah heard her name again and recognized Steven Russell's voice. "Over here," she called, waving her arms at him and his two friends.

In moments the black-robed threesome rushed to meet Susannah and Christopher. "You'll never believe it," Steven said, panting, his face flushed with excitement.

"What?"

"George Whitefield has come to town!"

"He's going to preach here, now," Morgan added. "We wanted you to come with us and hear him."

Susannah cast a rueful gaze at her attire. "Well, that sounds quite tempting, but I'm hardly dressed suitably for the occasion. I must go to the inn and change."

"There isn't time," Steven said.

"We've been looking for you for ages already," Jonathan added. His eyes searched beyond Susannah and Christopher. "Where's Mary? Mrs. Lyons said if we found you we could take you with us."

"She . . . um . . . needs some time alone, right now." Unable to prevent herself from trying to peer through the dense trees for a glimpse of her young friend, Susannah tried to push aside her feelings of concern. Perhaps a bit of solitude would help the girl, after all. She'd come directly back after the meeting to check on her.

Jonathan grimaced in disappointment, then shrugged. "Well, you look fine to me the way you are. I figure we can just about make the meeting, if we go right now."

"I th-think I'll stay with Mary," Chip said.

"Oh, come on, Chip," Steven coaxed. "We shouldn't be too long."

The lad's resolve weakened, and hesitantly, he nodded.

"But—," Susannah protested, casting one more look into the wooded growth.

Morgan grabbed one hand, and Steven took the other, and they took off at a trot, escorting her at nearly twice her own pace. Jonathan and Chip easily kept up beside them, and they joined the bustling crowd already hastening toward the college.

The nearer they got to Nassau Hall, the more the crowd grew. More than three hundred people had already gathered, pressing close to the steps of the building. More were arriving constantly, stirring a huge cloud of dust into the air. Perhaps this wasn't such a good idea. Mr. Lyons would be livid if she didn't show up on time to help with the supper crowd. But just as she opened her mouth to protest, a hush fell over the audience.

"I believe this is about as close as we're going to get," Steven whispered. He turned toward the front, and his expression took on a look of joy.

Standing solemnly beside Jonathan, Christopher looked back over his shoulder into the distance again, then turned with a scowl.

"Good afternoon, dear friends," a powerful voice boomed.

Susannah rose on tiptoe and stretched to see over the people in front of her, but it was no use.

Chip jumped twice and gave up. "We can't even see."

"Here, I can fix that," Jon said, hoisting the lad up to sit on his shoulders. "Better?"

"Great."

Susannah smiled to herself. When she was a child, her father had often lifted her up that same way. The smile faded, and she faced the unyielding field of heads and backs before her eyes as the speaker continued. She cast a glance at Morgan, just catching a wink he sent in Steven's direction.

The pair linked arms, sweeping her upward and supporting her weight between them at shoulder height.

"Oh!" She gasped. She grabbed onto their heads to keep

from tumbling backward. "Whatever are you doing? You must put me down at once." But they just chuckled.

So this is what comes from being so familiar with young men rather than maintaining proper conduct. She had brought it upon herself. Her cheeks flamed with guilt. What would Reverend Selkirk say if he saw her on display like this? "Please," she coaxed. "This is dreadful."

"Ssh." Several people nearby frowned.

"And sit still," Morgan hissed in mock seriousness.

Frustrated, Susannah pressed her lips tightly together and raised her gaze toward Nassau Hall, where a man in a flowing black robe stood with outstretched arms as he spoke to the crowd.

He gestured with one hand. "First, what is meant by an *Almost Christian?*"

The thought caught Susannah by surprise. She had never heard such an idea. She struggled to gather her thoughts and listen, then caught sight of President Witherspoon standing near the preacher. She looked down at Steven and Morgan. Would they get in trouble for such conduct? Perhaps even be expelled? And would her reputation, already less than flawless because of her indenturement, be forever stained because of this? She squirmed on her unladylike perch as the Reverend Whitefield continued.

"Second, what are the chief reasons so many are no more than Almost Christians?"

His provocative words stirred her curiosity. She noted with wonder how well his rich voice carried even to the farthest person in attendance. The power and melody of his modulations were quite captivating. Surely that was no man with asthma. His face glowed like a burning light as he surveyed the listeners. No wonder people flocked to hear his messages, charlatan or no. But she was certain that she'd be able to hear equally well standing on the ground.

"Please, put me down," she begged one more time.

"Quiet," Morgan ordered. "We want to hear what he says."

Susannah sighed and forced her attention back to Reverend Whitefield.

"Third, I shall consider the ineffectualness, danger, absurdity, and uneasiness which attends those who are but Almost Christians."

Her thoughts halted on that repeated phrase. Frowning, she pondered it for several seconds. Could being a Christian entail some sort of requirement a person might fail to reach? Could it be possible for one to miss the mark and be unacceptable to God? She needed to hear more.

As he spoke, Susannah looked again at President Witherspoon, who seemed as absorbed as everyone else in the thoughts expressed by the orator. At least the students were safe, she decided. He hadn't noticed them. Her gaze drifted to the president's side, where a young man stood, tall and vaguely familiar.

A gust of wind whipped a tendril of long hair free of her coil and across her eyes. Catching it, Susannah brushed it aside for a clearer look.

Daniel Haynes! She had seen that face so often in her dreams that his every feature was engraved upon her mind.

Susannah couldn't breathe. A wave of dizziness washed over her. She glanced down at her dress, at the smudges of flour from the morning's biscuits, at the dust from the root cellar, at her soiled apron, which bore streaks of dirt from Mary Clare's face.

Of all the days for him to finally appear, why, oh why, did he have to choose this one in particular? What ever would he think of the ever-so-refined English lass he had rescued in Philadelphia, now seated so brazenly on the shoulders of two fine seminary students?

At that moment he turned from the speaker and slowly looked across the audience. His dark eyes locked on hers.

Susannah wished the earth would open up and swallow her, scarlet face and all.

16

When Daniel caught sight of the lovely English girl he had met in Philadelphia, his heart soared. Her beauty had grown even beyond what he'd remembered. He let his eyes drink in the vision of her. But then he noticed her inglorious position, perched like a common tavern wench upon the shoulders of two students, her hair uncovered, with the wind tangling long tawny strands about her head. Was *this* the delicate English flower whose perfume had sweetened his dreams during the past months? The fair, innocent maiden he had considered as pure as the first feathery snowflakes of winter?

His spirit plummeted. He had actually fantasized about bringing her home to his family, believing that even his mother would bestow unquestioning approval on such a finely bred young lady. He had envisioned sharing a life with her, complete with two or three tiny daughters with golden curls and faces like miniatures of hers. . . .

He ground his teeth as he stared at her incredulously. Even the joy of hearing the renowned George Whitefield preach disappeared. His dream vanished before his very eyes.

As Susannah felt the utter disillusionment emanating from Daniel Haynes's piercing look, all her beautiful imaginings crumbled into ashes. She had pictured a thousand different ways their paths would cross again when his travels brought him at last to Princeton . . . but never one that remotely resembled the stark reality of this moment.

Other spectators on the outer edges of the congregation had taken similar positions on the shoulders of their acquaintances, but the awareness brought no consolation. She felt brazen, exposed, like a flag waving at the top of a pole, as though every eye had turned her way. How could she have allowed herself to be put in such a position? However it had happened, it could not be undone. She had to endure it and pay whatever price would be required.

She lifted her chin and willed her attention to return to Reverend Whitefield. Within seconds the childlike joy radiating from his face and his wondrous elocution poured a calmness over her being. Once again she felt amazed that the unbelievably clear, resonant voice belonged to a man suffering from the same disease that had plagued her mum.

"The Almost Christian is fond of form," he said, gesturing dramatically with one arm, "but never experiences the power of godliness in his heart." Clasping his hands together, he pressed them to his chest.

Susannah frowned at the disturbing thought. What did he mean? No one had ever before hinted that an individual such as herself could ever hope to experience godly power. Wasn't life one constant struggle toward earning favor with almighty God so he would hear the humble prayers of one's heart and deign to answer? Curious, she concentrated harder on the minister's message.

"So many set out with false notions of religion." He shook his head slowly. "Though they live in a Christian country, yet they know not what Christianity is."

Susannah leaned forward to catch his every word. Surely Christianity lay in decent living, in respecting authority, in—

Reverend Whitefield scanned the audience. "Some people place Christianity in being part of one certain communion. Others think it lies in morality."

A frown tightened Susannah's forehead. Most certainly

Christianity was that. Why, she'd heard as much since child-hood.

"But very few acknowledge it to be what it really is," he said with a sad nod of his head, "a thorough inward change of nature . . . a divine life . . . a vital participation with Jesus Christ." He spoke slowly, leaving a distinct pause between phrases, as if to give the listeners time to absorb them. Then his voice lowered a measure. "A union of the soul with God, which the apostle expresses by saying, 'We are joined to the Lord by his spirit.' "

The silence of the crowd seemed to intensify as everyone stood in solemn respect and awe. Not so much as a cough or a whisper interrupted the flow of words from the steps of Nassau Hall.

Joined to the Lord? thought Susannah. *By his spirit? What does that mean?*

"Sad to say," he continued, "even the most knowing profes-sors confess themselves ignorant of the matter. I speak of the essence, the life, the *soul* of religion . . . our new birth in Jesus Christ."

Susannah's mind whirled in wonder. Christianity—more than morality or good works! A union of the soul with God, being joined by the Holy Spirit! A verse she had learned in childhood popped into her memory:

Except a man be born of water and of the Spirit, he cannot enter into the kingdom of God.

Susannah knew her father had seen to her baptism with water. But had she been born of the Spirit? Judging from Reverend Whitefield's sermon, she seriously doubted she had.

The pastor's voice rang out once more. "'How can this thing be?' they cry with Nicodemus. No wonder so many are only Almost Christians, when they know not what Christianity is! It's no marvel that so many take up with the form—when they are strangers to the power of godliness! They content themselves with the shadow . . . when they know so little about the substance of it!"

As she sorted through her confusion, snatches of verses from John's Gospel flooded her thoughts, and as if a veil had been lifted from her understanding, they now came alive: *For God so loved the world, that he gave his only begotten Son. He that believeth on the Son hath everlasting life. . . .* She studied George Whitefield's face once more and saw the glorious Spirit of the Lord in his countenance. He spoke the truth. She saw herself, saw her life, saw the well-meaning promise she'd made to God after learning of Julia's death. To be good. To serve. To *earn* favor. To *merit* salvation. She had spent so many years trying to win righteousness by her own efforts.

Her heart pounded within her, sending pulses of guilt throughout her being as she thought of the sheer hopelessness of it all. What God had required was the sacrifice of his Son, the blood of Jesus Christ, which had purchased her salvation. Passages her father had quoted so often from Ephesians echoed within her like a tolling bell, and she understood them at last: *For by grace are ye saved through faith . . . it is the gift of God: Not of works. . . .*

That was it! Tears of wonder filled her eyes and overflowed. Salvation was not something to be earned! It had been purchased with blood to be given *freely* to those who believe! Such a precious thought! Indescribable freedom swelled within her as a lifetime of misunderstandings fell away like broken shackles. *Dear God,* she prayed, *I cannot but thank you with all my heart for sending your Son to be my Savior, for his blood, which cleanses away my sin.*

For the very first time in her life, Susannah felt completely whole. Free. She could see herself as described in Ephesians, walking as a child of the light. Peace unlike anything she'd ever known flowed through her, filling her with love, with joy, with light. She looked about her and saw in everyone, in every single person, someone she could love. She had so much to give, so much she needed to share before she burst with the glory of it!

The buzz of voices broke through her consciousness as Morgan and Steven lowered her from their shoulders. She had been so absorbed in her own thoughts she had completely missed the end of the sermon . . . yet she had heard all that she needed. "Did you ever hear anything so beautiful?" she whispered, smiling through her tears.

"We thought you might find a few answers here," Morgan said gently. He removed a handkerchief from his pocket and handed it to her.

"I believe we all have been similarly moved," Steven added.

Susannah stood on tiptoe and glanced toward the front again. Although most of the crowd had dispersed, a large cluster remained before the steps of the hall, waiting to speak personally with the great man. She was glad that so many other people seeking peace with God had found it.

Her heart in her throat, she ventured a gaze to one side of the preacher and Dr. Witherspoon as they conversed with those who lingered after the meeting. Her spirit sank.

Daniel Haynes was gone.

Trudging aimlessly away from the gathering, Dan shoved his hands into his pockets and watched fine dust from his footsteps dull the sheen of his boots. It had been an incredible experience seeing the great George Whitefield again and standing with the masses to hear him deliver the burning message of his heart. But how frail the man had looked since the last time Dan had heard him preach! Surely his rigorous schedule exacted a heavy toll. What a loss it would be to those who knew and loved him when he was no longer able to continue his ministry. And who would ever replace him?

Dan breathed out slowly as he walked, and his thoughts drifted from Whitefield to another discomfort. *She* had been there. How ironic that instead of the boundless joy he had anticipated, the first glimpse of that glorious face he had waited months to see had brought profound disappointment instead. Obviously she had not pined away here during all that time awaiting his arrival.

And it was just as well he had seen her when he had, he assured himself. All for the best, really. Far too much of his time had already been wasted dreaming about her when his priority should have been his commitment to the cause against the king's tyranny.

His mouth tightened in a bitter grimace. He had been a fool. What ever had made him think he could trust anyone from England—much less a young woman he didn't even know?

Raising his gaze to a wooded grove just ahead, he noticed a flash of light blue amid the trees. A young girl strolled in the slanted rays of late afternoon. Even with her head bowed, he could see clearly her fine profile and the way the scattered bits of sunlight dazzled over her golden hair. *Now* that *is the kind of young woman I should be searching for. Plainly dressed, probably a simple, hardworking colonial girl.* He watched her for several moments and saw her glance up and start as a wiry, ruddy-faced young man approached. She turned as if to run.

Thinking she needed assistance, Dan took a step toward them, but stopped at the sound of the young fellow's voice.

"Please don't go," Dan overheard him say. "Chip told me where to find you." His tone didn't sound threatening, so Dan held still behind a tree, not wanting to draw any attention to himself.

"Why didn't you come with us to the meeting?" the young man asked.

She did not answer, but instead tucked her chin deeper into her chest.

"Mary Clare?" Lifting the girl's jaw with a finger, he turned her face toward the light. "Oh no," he murmured. "My poor, dear little Mary."

Focusing through the pine boughs, Dan could see the discolored swelling surrounding her eye. It looked especially cruel against her otherwise fragile features. He wondered what sort of man would hurt a pretty little thing like her. There was no justification for that, ever.

When the young fellow gently touched the bruise, the lass

whimpered and swayed into him. He kissed her eye and wrapped his arms around her, holding her for several moments. "Wish I'd been there to stop the brute." Then letting out a deep breath, he lowered one arm to her slight waist. "Come on. Reckon I'd better see you back to the inn."

Watching the tender exchange, Dan felt as never before the oppressive weight of his own loneliness. He waited in the stillness until the pair had gone, allowing himself to remember for the briefest second the joy he'd felt when his eyes had searched the vast sea of faces at the college and seen the one he had so longed to find.

Then the bitter half of the recollection forced its way into his mind. Pulling off his hat, he raked his fingers through his hair, then slammed the hat back on. She had been surrounded by young men from the college, no doubt had developed some relationship with them that allowed a familiarity he had only dreamed of. After all, she'd been sitting quite pertly on the shoulders of a pair of them, hadn't she? Perhaps one was even her Theodore, back to watch over her.

Obviously, too much time had elapsed since that chance meeting in Philadelphia more than two months ago. How could he even hope she'd remember him? She probably hadn't given him so much as a thought. No point now in wasting any more time in Princeton. He had more important things to do. He'd leave right away . . . just as soon as he satisfied his curiosity by asking a few questions about her.

Perhaps the two students who had held his fallen angel would still be about. On a wild impulse, he hurried back toward the college. Upon reaching the building, he swung the heavy door wide and entered the hall, where he could hear a lesson in progress in one of the classrooms.

A few heads turned his way as he strode into the room. With an apologetic smile at the professor, Dan sought an unobtrusive position along one of the side walls to listen.

Professor Barton, a former teacher of his, gave a nod of recognition. Clearing his throat pointedly, he continued on with the obvious topic of the day. "But, gentlemen, take a closer look at this passage. Don't you think Paul's use of the example of a race, of persistence, of pressing on toward the goal, was simplistic? Even elemental? Often the deepest truths can be made absurdly clear by using something commonplace for an illustration, something to which everyone might relate. Why, even George Whitefield uses the method, as you most certainly must have noted."

An underlying buzz of conversation became audible during the professor's pause. Dan observed the restless shifting of positions on the hard seats and repeated glances in the direction of the door. Among them he spotted a face that he was sure belonged to one of the two he wanted to find. Dan scanned the others for the second young man and found him.

Professor Barton coughed. "Well, I had hoped, gentlemen, that the stirring message we heard today would inspire you to further study. But I see I made an error in judgment. I see no recourse but to dismiss for the day—"

Immediately, several shot up from their seats.

"However," the instructor said tersely above the hubbub, "I shall expect each of you to write an observation on Reverend Whitefield's sermon for our next class."

Dan smiled to himself at the subdued groans, recalling similar assignments from his own college days. Pressing closer to the wall to let the students by, he waited until the pair he had sought approached, then fell into step behind them. "Um, excuse me, lads. I wonder if you could help me."

Inquisitive gray eyes glanced over the shoulder of the studious-looking one as he reached for the door and held it open for them. "Certainly. Steven Russell is my name. This," he said, indicating with his head, "is Morgan Thomas."

Relief flickered through Dan that neither of them was named Theodore. "I'm Daniel Haynes." Smiling, he shook hands with them, and the three descended the steps, stopping at the bottom.

Steven's straight brows rose a fraction, and he cut a glance at Morgan. "Haynes, you say?"

Dan frowned. Why the odd reaction to his name? With a

nod, he continued, averting his eyes self-consciously to a brilliant azalea bush in full pink bloom. Forcing himself to get on with it, he met their gazes again. "It's rather complicated, you see. But I'd appreciate it if you could tell me something."

Steven stared. His lanky friend cocked his head as if waiting for the question.

Dan drew a breath to fortify himself. "I . . . noticed you were—in the company of a certain young woman this afternoon. In fact, you must know her quite well, seeing as how she sat on your shoulders at the meeting."

A quick glance passed between them. "Well, you mustn't judge her too harshly, old man," Morgan said. "We held her up, true. But under protest, I assure you."

Dan shrugged, feeling the complete opposite of the nonchalance he was hoping to put forth. "It's of no consequence. It's just that she looked very much like someone I met recently in Philadelphia. I wouldn't want to embarrass her if I'm mistaken. I promised to look her up when I came to town, but I can't remember where she said she'd be staying." He searched their faces hopefully.

"You wouldn't have found her anyway, my good fellow," Morgan added. "She isn't staying with anyone."

"Not staying with anyone?" Dan echoed. How could that be?

"Well," Steven said hesitantly, "she's . . . at the coaching inn."

Dan tilted his head. "Hm. At the inn. She must be quite wealthy, to be staying there all this time."

Morgan cast a swift glance in Steven's direction, then turned back to Dan. "Not really."

Daniel looked in confusion from one to the other. He had the distinct impression they were keeping something from him.

"Actually," Morgan continued, rubbing his jaw almost guiltily with a thumb and finger, "she's . . . well, she's bonded there. To the owners."

Dan's heart sank like a millstone. How could that be? The

woman with the fine clothes and snooty guardian, indentured? That was the last thing he would have expected. With an effort not to appear surprised, Dan forced his expression to remain relaxed. "Oh. I see. She works for the Lyonses."

Steven narrowed his eyes. "But if the truth were told, she's practically as much a student of the college as the two of us—only Witherspoon doesn't know it. She's more interested in our studies than we are!"

His friend chuckled at the amazement apparent on Dan's face. "That's right. She hangs on our every word at supper, when we discuss the day's lectures. Sometimes she even asks questions while she's serving, which brings down old Jasper's wrath. We've quite grown used to it."

Dan considered their words for a moment. His thoughts went back to the young lady in the woods, who had also appeared to be a serving girl. He frowned, wondering if the workers of the coaching inn were being treated in some abusive manner. "Has Mr. Lyons grown to be a hard taskmaster these days? Seems I remember him as being a fair man, if a bit gruff."

Morgan laughed. "Oh no. Not at all. The man's fair all right. But he does expect the inn to run smoothly. He keeps his bond servants hopping."

"Considering that fact," Steven added thoughtfully, "soon as I pass my orals I'm thinking of saving that particular bond servant from her thankless life there."

With a blink of surprise, Dan shifted his weight. What had happened to her Theodore? How could this young lad voice such a thought?

"After me, that is," Morgan said with a good-natured nudge, "since I'll no doubt pass mine long before you. Besides, I'm more suited to her, you know, with my family being from England, and all. We've more in common."

Dan eyed the pair. From their mischievous grins he concluded that they were less than serious, and for some reason, it brought him a measure of comfort. Up till now, the lads had been quite obliging in answering his questions. He might as well find out a bit more.

He looked directly at Steven. "Since she's British and all, I find it quite amazing she'd concern herself with Presbyterian theology."

"Ah yes," Morgan interjected. "It is, rather."

Steven smothered the beginnings of a smile. "But she's quite close to abandoning the lifeless dronings to become a 'new light,' if she hasn't already. Whitefield's sermon moved her tremendously."

"She only went in the first place because she thought him to be a sham," Morgan added. "Now she's quite the ardent supporter."

"Yes, quite a fetching young lady, our Susannah Harrington," Steven said, grinning.

Susannah Harrington! Susannah. The sound of her name sang to him like soft night winds. He glanced in the direction of the Lyons' Den.

Morgan interrupted his thoughts. "But hopefully her last name won't remain Harrington for long. Not if I have my way, that is."

"Oh?" Steven said, raising a wry brow. "If you ask me, Susannah *Russell* would suit her infinitely better than Susannah *Thomas.*"

Listening to the bantering argument, Dan frowned in exasperation. After all, neither name could compete with the sound of Susannah *Haynes.*

Dan blinked in surprise. Now where had *that* thought come from . . . ? Removing his tricorn, he blotted his forehead with a sleeve. He was becoming as ridiculous as this pair. Yet he had to see her at least once more, this Susannah Harrington, who would care so little about her reputation that she'd bond herself out to an innkeeper and consort with a college full of impressionable young lads—and then forsake her proper womanly station by pursuing the study of theological concepts.

That sort of nonsense could only lead to her being stubborn-headed in the end, he was sure. But he'd have to see her again, just to judge for himself. *Lord, I need to know for sure that I was wrong. Then maybe I can forget her . . .*

He looked again toward the inn, then back to his companions. "Say, before you two come to blows over her, why don't you let me buy you supper at the Lyons' Den? You can explain a few more things on the way."

Feeling airy, as if her feet had wings, Susannah flitted from table to table, preparing for the supper customers. All but the remnants of the afternoon crowd had left some time ago. She shook out a crisp linen cloth with a snap and smoothed it in place over a trestle table. Never had she waited on such a horde in one day, yet she wasn't the least tired.

The knowledge that her salvation was secure, now and forever, purchased and given freely by almighty God, filled her with peace and rest. There was nothing to be earned, nothing to merit, only something she had reached out and accepted, like any other gift. How utterly precious! Just believe in Jesus and the salvation he provided . . . as simple as that! Why had it taken so long for her to see it?

The white cockatoo gave a startled squawk as a second tablecloth snapped. Susannah giggled, glancing at its perch behind the bar. "Sorry, Methuselah. I could almost kiss even you, you cantankerous bird."

The melody of a favorite hymn drifted through her mind, and she hummed as she worked. Had there ever been a more glorious day? With joy she recalled the warm breeze on her face at the meeting, and she felt like one of the kites she and Teddy had flown back home. She envisioned herself soaring high above the crowd on the summer wind, halfway to heaven, hearing the glorious message of God. But a slight tug reminded her she was still tied to earth. She glanced down.

Daniel Haynes held the string . . . and unsmiling, he was winding it onto the spool, reeling her back.

Susannah blinked and swallowed. What a silly daydream. Well, she wouldn't let it put a damper on *her* joy. It couldn't.

With a squeak, the door swung open.

Susannah turned sharply . . . and met the cool, steady eyes of Daniel Haynes. The rest of the song vanished from her memory.

17

Susannah struggled for breath as Daniel Haynes strode to one of the side tables with, of all people, Morgan and Steven. How ever had Providence brought *him* to the inn—the one man to whom she'd felt instinctively drawn from that first moment on the Philadelphia wharf? The one who'd seen her in the most compromising, embarrassing circumstance of her entire life. She had been sure he'd left town in disgust, but now she would have to face him! For a fleeting moment she wished she might trade places with Mrs. Lyons in the kitchen and submerge herself in the endless stack of dishes from the rush of Whitefield followers.

Trying to ignore the good-natured chatter coming from the three young men, Susannah made her way in the opposite direction, to the last soiled table across the room. She wiped it down and gazed out the window, hoping to find something to distract her for even a few more minutes. She smiled when she noticed Jonathan and Mary Clare beside one of the sheds, holding hands, absorbed in one another. The sight of Mary's happy face tugged at Susannah's heart as Jonathan bent his head closer in conversation. He was so good for Mary. And she deserved some happiness, after all she'd been through.

The sting of tears brought Susannah back to reality. Quickly she blinked them away and, on suddenly leaden feet, walked to the bar. Depositing the cloth, she took a fortifying breath and plastered on what she hoped was a bright smile.

She approached the threesome without meeting their eyes. "Good day, gentlemen."

"Yes, it is, rather," Morgan chided in a tone ripe with mischief. "We've brought along a new chap . . . but, of course, you two have already met, I believe."

Susannah's heart pounded in her ears, and she felt her cheeks flame. She fought a strong urge to kick Morgan in the shin. Instead, she glared at him.

Steven flashed an annoying grin. "Don't you recognize him? It's Daniel Haynes, remember? The fellow you were asking about not too long ago. And you know our Susannah Harrington, don't you?" he asked, transferring his attention to Dan.

This couldn't be happening! Susannah had had nightmares before. She'd wake up soon. But as she slid her gaze to the young man across from Steven and Morgan and met his deep brown eyes, she knew he was really there. She swallowed nervously. "Uh . . . M-Mr. Haynes. Nice to see you again."

"The pleasure's mine, Miss Harrington."

Had it been night, the glow from her face would have illuminated the entire room, of that Susannah had no doubt.

Morgan nudged Steven with a chuckle and leaned forward on his elbows, his fingertips lightly interlaced. "Well now, to be fair, Mr. Haynes was quite inquisitive concerning you, too. Isn't that so?" He eyed Daniel.

Dan shifted in his seat with the grim realization that the two lads were attempting to liven up their humdrum existence at his and Susannah Harrington's expense. "Well, I did tell them I had promised to look you up," he admitted to Susannah with a guilty quirk of his mouth. "Needless to say, they were quite eager to help." Elevating an eyebrow, he shot them a shrewd glance.

Expressionless, Susannah stared at him for an instant before turning a scathing look toward the two students. Dan couldn't help but notice how her rich, thick lashes veiled her eyes . . . or the way anger turned the dusky blue to ice.

"I can imagine," she said, her tone cool. She tapped a foot impatiently. "Will you be having supper?"

Morgan gave a knowing laugh. "Aren't you interested in hearing about today's lecture?"

Dan watched her expression harden.

"Not in the least." She planted a fist on either side of her waist. "Now, will you be having supper, or not?"

Jasper Lyons strode in the back door at that moment and tossed them a pointed glance as he took his place behind the bar and reached for his ledgers.

"We've chicken and dumplings this evening," she continued.

"That will do just fine, Miss Harrington," Dan said.

"Same here," the other two chimed in.

"As you wish." Susannah sent a gaze heavenward and hurried to the kitchen, where she leaned her back against the wall just inside the door and buried her face in her hands. *Dear God, how shall I ever get through this? I wanted him to come to Princeton, but—*

"Are you all right, love?" Mrs. Lyons asked.

Susannah's eyes shot open to see the older woman peering at her and drying her hands on a flour sack towel. "Oh, y-yes, of course." She pressed icy fingers to her warm face. "Everything's fine."

With a hesitant nod, Mrs. Lyons returned to her chore. "Think I heard a stage drivin' up. And with the stragglers still here from today's crowd, too. Give a holler if you need help with the servin'."

"Thank you," Susannah breathed. More customers were precisely what she required at the moment to keep her occupied. "Right now I need three supper portions. I'll get them, since you're so busy."

When she returned to the common room, she noticed a few new clusters of patrons seated at the trestle tables. Several individuals stood at the bar with tankards of frothy ale. "I'll be right with you," she assured them with a smile as she passed by. Swiftly she set the heaping plates before Daniel and the two students, barely giving them time to request coffee before she left to tend the others.

Another wagon arrived, bringing more hungry folks, and Susannah thanked the Lord. At least she wouldn't have time to dwell on Daniel's presence in the room. But her pulse still throbbed in her throat. What must he think of her after her conduct this afternoon? And what about the matter of her indenturement? Would that be a black mark against her in his mind, too? If so, she had better banish all thought of him forever.

Dan watched Susannah as she waited on the other customers. She looked quite fetching in an ivory waist and violet skirt protected by a starched white apron. Her hair, pulled back and tied at the nape of her neck with a black velvet ribbon, had a wispy side curl by each ear. But it seemed she went out of her way to maintain her distance from him and the lads he'd met that day. A rosy tint ever present on her cheekbones, she avoided even his most persistent stare.

"So how'd you come to be a postrider?" Steven asked, sincerity replacing the mischievous spark in his slate-gray eyes.

"Some influential men I know presented me with a most interesting proposition," Dan said. "I could do nothing but accept. And I have access to excellent horseflesh, which was a real asset."

"You say your father raises Narragansett Pacers?" Morgan inquired. "I've heard nothing but good things about that breed."

Dan nodded. "They're reliable, sturdy horses. And riding one in my duties has tripled my family's business."

"How did you find the atmosphere up Boston way while on your travels?" Steven asked, changing the subject as he sipped his coffee.

"Not to mention in Philadelphia," Morgan added. "Are things truly settling down there and in New York as we're hearing?"

Dan looked at them both. "To a certain extent. Only two merchants in New York—Isaac Sears, a sloop captain, and John Lamb, a wine importer—are still pushing to convince the others to continue the boycott. But no one's paying them much mind." He met Susannah's eyes briefly across the room, but she looked away.

"Well," Steven said, "isn't the crisis about over, now that most of the Townshend Acts have been repealed?"

Dan chuckled. "Looks that way to most folks. But America's a pretty plump chicken. King George and Parliament will find some way to pluck it soon enough."

Absently brushing a few crumbs from the tablecloth, Morgan straightened on his chair and turned to Dan. "How do you feel the trial in Boston will go?"

Dan furrowed his forehead in thought. "Well, the defendants have some pretty prominent names behind them—Adams, and the like. At least we'll give the accused a chance to be heard. That's a lot more than the colony gets when it comes to dealing with Parliament."

"True," Steven said with a wry smile. Drawing a watch from his pocket, he checked it and clicked the lid shut. "Well, old man, it's been a pleasure talking with you. Hope you didn't mind us giving you a bit of a hard time with—" He cut his eyes sheepishly in Susannah's direction, then glanced at Morgan. "We've barely time to make it back for evening prayer. Let's be off."

Morgan grinned and stood, extending his hand to Dan. "Godspeed in your travels. We'll be sure to look after Susannah, won't we?" he said, with a wink at Steven.

"You do that," Dan said, rising to shake their hands. "Thanks for the company."

Susannah watched with some relief as the two students left the inn. They had dawdled an inordinately long time over their meal, but she hadn't once gone near their table, except to refill their cups. She wasn't sure she'd ever forgive them for causing her such embarrassment. Until now, she'd thought they were her friends. They'd been so considerate of her a scant few hours ago.

Of their own volition, her eyes sought Daniel Haynes and watched him drain his mug and set it down. She let herself linger on his straight posture, his strong, appealing profile. He looked a reasonable sort. She gathered up the courage to try out one of the explanations she'd come up with for her unseemly behavior. Tightening her grip on the handle of the coffeepot, she took several steps in his direction.

The door opened just then, and two local men entered.

One of them emitted a loud belch. "Who b'longs to that good-lookin' pacer at the rail?" he asked, fiddling with the buttons on his worn waistcoat. "Understand he's for sale."

Dan rose. "I do."

"Then ye're jus' the man we need to see," slurred his mangy-haired friend with thick spectacles, his eyes roaming until they landed on Susannah. "'Less we kin talk to the purty lass for awhile firsht." He curled a finger, gesturing for her to come over.

Susannah's glance swung from the besotted fellow to Dan.

A look of utter shock came over his face. In the blink of an eye, he dropped some coins on the table. Plucking his hat from a peg, he ushered the pair swiftly out the door with a disapproving frown.

Unable to stay the blush that heated her face from his glance, Susannah picked up a tray and walked over to clear the table he'd just vacated.

Now that he had seen what sort of men she attracted, she thought with dreadful finality, he would never come back to Princeton again. She had seen Daniel Haynes for the last time.

With a grimace, she stacked the dirty dishes on the tray and set it on the next table while she shook out the linen and turned it to the clean side. So much for wanting to defend herself. He couldn't possibly be interested in anything she had to say. Now or ever.

Dan smoothed on his fawn-colored frock coat and stretched with an elaborate yawn as dim morning light filtered into the livery stable. Every muscle in his body protested the hard cot upon which he'd slept. He needed some good strong coffee after that restless night. And one of Esther Lyons' sumptuous breakfasts. Stepping over to Flame, he saw to it the horse had plenty of water and feed, then washed up and headed for the Lyons' Den.

He had not been able to get Susannah Harrington off his mind. There was too much he did not understand about her. Steven and Morgan had explained a bit about her predicament to him the night before, had told him of Robert Chandler's forwarding a sum of money to her. Why had she not left? Why had she chosen to remain a bondwoman instead? It made no sense.

Passing Nassau Hall, he glanced absently at the imposing stone building. And her strong interest in theological studies—now, really, was that normal for a woman? Could her curiosity possibly run so deep that it outweighed the opportunity to live in luxury and respectability, while she chose instead a life of servitude?

He let out a huff. No man in search of a wife would look among servants to choose one, that was for sure. He could just imagine the expression on his mother's face if he were to bring home a bond servant for a wife.

Dan hurried his pace. He had to see Susannah Harrington once more. If the two drunks had not occupied so much of his time the night before, he might have gotten back to the inn before the hour had grown so late. But at least he had received a deposit on a horse, that was one consolation. It would please his father.

Arriving at the Lyons' Den, Dan noticed a bevy of empty carts and stage wagons outside. Wouldn't yesterday's throng ever leave? Through the windows he could see Susannah scurrying about among them. Perhaps he should go and give Flame a good brushing then return to the inn later. With all the traveling, the horse could use some grooming. He turned and retraced his steps.

"Haynes? Dan Haynes?" a voice called as he neared the college.

Dan stopped and peered toward the school, catching sight of Professor Barton. "Yes?" he said, approaching him at the main door.

"Dr. Witherspoon asked me to keep an eye out for you. He has a letter to be delivered to Charles Thomson in Philadelphia, with all haste."

Dan recognized the name. Thomson was the most outspoken of the Philadelphia merchants who favored the boycott. "Sure. I'll take care of it." Dan sent a fleeting glance over his shoulder at the Lyons' Den and followed the instructor up the steps and inside.

Right after the morning rush, Susannah led Mary Clare and Chip out back for another lesson. Though she no longer felt the need to merit favor with God, she now felt compelled to tutor the siblings out of this new love that filled her heart. Mrs. Lyons allowed them an hour or more every day, unless the arrival of unexpected travelers required their time and assistance.

Leaning her slate against the furrowed gray bark of an elm tree, Susannah handed the younger pair slates of their own, plus a bit of chalk. They sat down in the shade.

The swelling in Mary's eye had subsided and was no longer so pronounced, especially with her hair parted to fall on that side. Susannah glanced at Christopher, who sat with a grim expression, muttering to himself about their father. "Really, Chip," she said, trying to brighten his mood. "It's such a lovely day. Let's not spoil it with ugly thoughts."

With a grudging nod he straightened his shoulders.

"Good. I was thinking . . . if you promise to concentrate on today's lesson, I'd like to take you both down to Mr. Bentley's shop to be fitted for some good Sunday shoes. You can even pick out the buckles. How's that?"

Christopher cheered up a bit, and Mary Clare's smile rivaled even the morning sun.

Susannah breathed a sigh of relief. "Then let's begin. I've chosen the Beatitudes in the fifth chapter of Matthew. Remember we've been practicing the words I wrote on your slates for you to study? While I read each verse, draw a line from the list of the ones the Lord calls blessed, to their reward. First, 'Blessed are the poor in spirit: for theirs is the kingdom of heaven.'" She watched as her charges painstakingly followed her instructions.

The emptiness of the Lyons' Den caught Dan by surprise when he finally made it over for breakfast. He nodded to Mr. Lyons and quietly chose a window table on the far side of the deserted room.

"Be right with you," the innkeeper said, drying pewter mugs and stacking them one by one.

"Take your time. I'm in no hurry." Glancing outside, Dan blinked at the sight of Susannah and the two young people. With their backs to him, they seemed absorbed in something. Curious, Dan edged the window open a few inches and strained to hear some of their conversation.

"You read this one, Chip," he heard Susannah say. "I'm sure you know all these words."

The boy took the Bible she held out to him. "'B-blessed are the mer-merciful,'" the lad read, "'for they shall ob-obtain mercy.'" He slammed the book shut. "I don't want to hear any more of these. You only p-picked them because you know I'm p-planning to get back at P-Pa for what he did to Mary."

"That's not true," Susannah said quietly, "and you know it."

"Then why aren't we r-reading the p-part that says an eye for an eye, or s-something good, instead?"

Susannah opened to the passage again. "Let's just go on to the next verse, all right? We've nearly finished."

Dan heard footsteps on the plank floor and casually slid the window back down. He looked up to see Jasper Lyons. "What can I get you, lad? Haynes, isn't it?"

He nodded. "I'm surprised you remember me, Mr. Lyons. It's been quite some time since I've been in Princeton."

"We try to remember most of our regulars. How 'bout some eggs and corn bread?"

Dan hesitated. "Sounds good. But I have to step outside for a minute, if you don't mind. I'll be back shortly." He left the innkeeper gaping after him.

Circling the inn, Dan moved to the corner of the building nearest the big elm shading the young people. He remained just out of sight, listening.

"This one isn't hard, Mary. You try it," Susannah said.

"'Blessed are the . . . pure in heart,'" the younger girl's airy voice read, "'for they shall see God.'"

"Isn't that a lovely promise?" Susannah said brightly. "Think of it. One day all who are pure in heart will see almighty God."

Warmed by Susannah Harrington's obvious efforts to help the youngsters, Dan realized that many of his previous impressions of her had been unkind, unjust. He should have been far more open when Morgan Thomas and Steven Russell had praised her character to no end. He moved a few feet closer, just within view.

The boy held the Bible. "'B-blessed are the p-peacemakers,'" he spat with disdain, "'for they shall be c-called the children of God.'" He shoved the book back at Susannah. "That d-does it!" He clamped his mouth together, jumped to his feet, and whirled around. At the sight of Dan, he stopped and stared.

Susannah and the younger girl followed his gaze.

Dan smiled. "Couldn't help hearing your fine lesson," he said, looking expressly at Susannah, who lowered her eyes. Then he turned to the boy. "But you seem to be having a problem believing what you're reading, young man. What's wrong with trusting God enough to let him deal with whoever it is that has wronged you—and letting God decide whether his mercy fits best or his wrath?"

The lad frowned and looked away.

Dan squatted beside them. "Don't you remember the story of young David, son?" he said, coaxing the boy's reluctant attention. "There was a time when he was more popular with the Israelites than King Saul was. This really got the king's dander up, because David was just a youth. Saul thought the Israelites were being disloyal. So he decided to get the problem over with—by getting rid of that kid. He got a bunch of his best men together, and they hunted David day and night. Went to all the places they figured he might try to hide."

The lad's expression eased, and he allowed a tiny smile as he listened with obvious interest.

"Well, son, God gave David a kind heart. A loyal one, too. David loved King Saul, because he was his best friend's father and had been nice to him for so many years. And he knew the king had been anointed by God. If there was one thing he didn't want to do, it was lay a finger on God's man."

"Hmph," the boy snorted. "Only th-thing that ever anointed my p-pa is l-l-liquor." He jumped to his feet. "I l-like the story where David k-killed the giant much b-better!" With that, he turned and ran off.

Dan grimaced apologetically at Susannah. "Forgive me for butting in. I guess I should have left it to you."

She reached out and laid her hand on his arm, then instantly drew it back as her cheeks flushed.

Susannah struggled to find her voice. "Please don't apologize, Mr. Haynes, for trying. Christopher has a great deal of hatred inside."

Beside Susannah, the younger girl smiled shyly, and Dan recognized her as the girl he'd seen in the woods the day before. She looked much younger up close. She nodded. "Yes. It was nice of you to try to help," she said. "I'd better go after him. Perhaps he'll listen to me." Gathering her skirts, she hurried in the same direction the lad had taken.

Susannah stared after her in dismay. *No, wait,* she wanted to call. *Please don't leave us alone here. I don't know what to do, what to say.* She swallowed, hearing in the heavy stillness only her own breathing. And his. She shot a nervous glance at the handsome young gentleman beside her.

Dan met Susannah's eyes for a brief instant before she averted her gaze. As if he had seen her uneasiness, he smiled gently. "Sorry I wasn't able to return to the inn last evening. I really wanted to talk to you."

Lifting her lashes, she searched his face. "I-I'm surprised you remembered me," she whispered.

"How could I forget you . . . Susannah. May I call you that?"

She gave an almost imperceptible nod and moistened her lips.

"After all," he said with a reminiscent smile, "you kept me from being caught by the redcoats the first day I saw you."

Susannah recalled the sight of him with the 'lady' smugglers. The ridiculous image fortified her. She laughed lightly. "I still wonder if I should perhaps have summoned the officials."

"Does that mean you give me a thought from time to time too?" he asked softly, "as your eyes promised over supper that evening in Philadelphia?"

She lowered her gaze to her shoes. He was most perceptive. Had she thought of anything else? The heat in her cheeks heightened with the increase of her pulse. Unsuccessfully, she tried to hide the smile which tugged at the corners of her lips.

Daniel watched as the mysterious play of emotions tinted Susannah's face every delicate pink he'd ever seen. He felt an unexpected ache inside. From what the two students had told him, her venture from England had taken many twists and turns, leaving her to fend for herself in a strange new land. He marveled at her strength and courage, and felt once again the strong attraction he'd been fighting for months. This time, however, he didn't fight it. *It is time to find out who you are, and why you draw me the way you do . . .*

Gently he took her hand, surprised by his own daring. Susannah tried to withdraw from his grasp, but he tightened his hold. Her gaze seemed to be drawn to his of its own will.

"I came to tell you I've been called to Philadelphia."

"So soon?" Did he hear disappointment in her voice? Inadvertently, he drew in a sharp breath.

He covered her hand with his other one and tilted his head. "I'll be bringing back a return message. I should be back by the Sabbath. Would you . . . that is, I'd deem it an honor if you'd allow me to escort you to church."

Susannah put her hand to her heart but could not look away. "I'd be . . . happy to accompany you," she murmured, attempting a smile.

"Dan," he finished.

"Dan."

Bending over her hand, Dan brushed it softly with his lips. "I shall count the hours . . . Susannah."

Her breath caught in her throat. The way he made her name sound, as if it were written in heaven's own music, filled her with wonder.

He smiled warmly into her eyes. Then he walked away, pausing with a disarming grin just before he rounded the corner of the inn.

Susannah pressed the hand he had kissed to her own lips and melted slowly to the ground.

18

It's Sunday. Sunday! Susannah's heart sang as she hurried up the stairs to the attic with a pitcher of fresh water.

When she opened the bedroom door, Mary Clare's dreamy smile met her from across the room. "What do you think?" she asked, spreading her arms wide as she took a few wobbly steps. "Do my new shoes show when I walk?"

Susannah set the container on the washstand, struggling to keep her expression serious. "Yes, but I rather doubt anyone will see them with you teetering about that way."

Instantly a frown darkened the younger girl's face. She relaxed her arms. "But I want them to show. I never had such slippers in my whole life . . . soft and light, and with silver buckles. I feel like a fine lady."

"They do look quite pretty on you."

An idea sparked in Mary's eyes. "Well, what if I hold my skirt up just a little?" She gathered a handful of cornflower blue muslin, took a few exaggerated steps, then stopped and turned. The billowing skirts settled around her feet as she peered at Susannah.

Susannah crossed the cramped room and took hold of the younger girl's upper arms. "Mary," she said gently, "you don't want people only to see your feet, do you? That would be like trying to draw attention to one blossom, when all together you're a bouquet. Do you understand?"

"I suppose." She gave a hesitant shrug. "Well, does my dress look all right? I just finished puttin' in the hem."

"Quite saucy. With your new bonnet and lacy shawl, Jonathan won't be able to keep his eyes off you. Now come sit down, and I'll fix your hair." She guided Mary Clare to the stool in front of the dressing table.

Obediently Mary Clare sank to the seat, then raised her lashes shyly. "You think he'll . . . I mean, will he think I'm . . . pretty?"

Susannah tried to still her own heart. She'd been wondering the same thing about Daniel and herself. She smiled at her roommate's reflection in the glass. "How could he not? You're becoming quite the young lady, you know." Taking the silver-handled brush, she drew it down the shiny curled hair, then gathered the crown section to one side. "I think I've just the ribbon for you to wear. Hold this." She took Mary's hand and placed the strands into her grasp, then stepped to the wardrobe, where she rummaged through a handbag on the floor.

"Ah yes. Here it is. It's perfect." Returning to the dressing table, she tied the blue satin bow and arranged the streamers, then used the brush to shape soft ringlets around her fingers all across the back of Mary's hair. At last she stepped away to admire her handiwork.

Susannah noticed a faint yellowish-purple tinge still evident high on Mary Clare's cheekbone. "Perhaps if we use a tiny bit of rice powder right below your eye, no one will ever know anything happened. Do you think?" Taking a small tin from the drawer, Susannah dipped a fingertip gingerly into the contents and bent to apply the barest touch of powder to the discoloration. "Not even Jonathan will remember now," she said with a light smile as she straightened.

Mary Clare tilted her head and studied her image for a few seconds. "Do you think he . . . likes me? Really?" She turned sideways on the stool toward Susannah.

"I'm sure of it, honey. I saw you two together out by the shed the other day." Mary blushed, and Susannah tweaked the girl's chin. "I don't think you should doubt his feelings toward you any longer."

A tiny smile curved the girl's lips. "Never figured anybody'd give me a second glance." She looked directly at Susannah. "Not like Steven and Morgan moon over you when you're not lookin' . . . looking," she corrected herself.

Susannah's eyes grew round. "Whatever do you mean? I'm sure you must be imagining things."

"No, I'm not. They're always tryin' to best each other and win you before somebody else beats them to it."

"Why, that's ridiculous." The outlandish suggestion disturbed Susannah. She didn't want even to think of anything so preposterous. She noticed her rumpled bedclothes and felt thankful for even that small diversion. After smoothing the linens and counterpane, she picked up her feather pillow and plumped it with more fervor than necessary.

Mary Clare stood and turned. "When Jon told them you'd be goin' to church with somebody else today, they got real sulky. Almost . . . jealous, Jon said."

An unexpected flush warmed Susannah's face, and she dropped the pillow in place with a muffled thump. "Morgan and Steven do enjoy teasing me. Young lads like to see a maiden blush. But mostly they're just indulging my questions and strutting the fact that they're men of learning." She giggled. "But they're both just boys."

"I wouldn't be so quick to say that." Mary's expression barely hid her glee. "They're about the same age as you. Steven's eighteen, and Morgan's nineteen."

Exasperated, Susannah placed her hands on either side of her waist. "Well, they certainly *seem* younger."

"Younger than your Mr. Haynes, you mean?" Mary asked with mock sweetness. "Funny you never mentioned him before. Now all of a sudden you're all taken up with him."

Susannah grimaced and stepped to the wardrobe to take out her own Sunday gown. Draping it on the bed, she began undoing the buttons of her everyday frock with trembling fingers as she looked at the one she'd been saving for a special occasion. In whisper-soft white batiste, it was embroidered all around with sprays of multicolored flowers and trimmed with shimmery white lace. Her heart fluttered. Would Dan like it?

The rustle of petticoats drew her out of her musings, and she looked up to see the younger girl peering out the window. "Actually, it isn't all that sudden," Susannah said. "I met him the day I arrived from England, when he came to my rescue on the Philadelphia docks. I just didn't know for certain when, or if, I'd see him again." She sent a quick glance Mary's way, then continued in a rush. "And I've been daydreaming about him ever since. He's ever so handsome, don't you think?" Holding out the gown, she stepped into the circle of skirts and put her arms into the full sleeves, drawing them up.

"Not as handsome as Jon," Mary said lightly over her shoulder. The teasing glint in her eyes faded with her next words. "I daydream, too. But I can't imagine Jon wantin' to make a life with a girl like me, the daughter of the town drunk." She flopped dejectedly onto her bed.

"Don't say that, honey," Susannah objected. But she was only too aware that Mary could be right. Jonathan didn't appear to hold Mary's background against her, but he had never mentioned having told his family about her. "Well, you're both still young. Perhaps by the time he finishes his studies, his love will grow so strong that he'll marry you no matter what anyone thinks."

"I don't know." Mary went to the window again and pushed aside the unbleached muslin curtain. "At least the rain stopped yesterday. There's hardly any mud now."

Susannah moved to stand beside her, trying not to appear overly anxious as she searched for a glimpse of Daniel. It had taken forever for Sunday to arrive. He might have arranged for a room at the inn for last night, even though he hadn't expected to get back to town before the Sabbath. She sighed.

Mary Clare's sky-colored eyes turned her way.

"I'm afraid we're both getting ourselves into a state," Susannah said with a guilty smile. "I could use some help with my lacings. Would you mind? And perhaps you could try to see if you've any skills at dressing hair. I seem to be all thumbs."

Dan left his horse at the livery and strode up the packed dirt street toward the Lyons' Den. The stone inn looked freshly washed from the rainstorm that had slowed his trip from Philadelphia, and sunshine glinted off the shrubbery and trees. Reaching the building, he headed for the back door and gave a few light taps.

Mrs. Lyons' little round face appeared in the window as she peeked through the curtains, and her expression brightened. She threw open the door.

"Morning, Mrs. Lyons," he said, removing his hat.

"Dan Haynes, as I live and breathe. Jasper said you was by the other day, but I was so busy scrubbin' dishes I never got out to greet you myself."

"Could you spare a cup of coffee for a weary traveler?"

"Why, sure enough. You come right in and have yourself a seat." She stepped aside. "I wondered if you'd ever be coming this way again. It's been such a spell." Her button eyes twinkled with merriment as she bustled about getting a cup of fresh coffee.

Dan watched her take an opposite chair and take a sip from her own half-filled cup. "Why, if I didn't know better," he said with a sly smile, "I'd say that's India tea you're having."

Mrs. Lyons' cheeks reddened. "And you'd be right. I've a tiny stash. Every once in a while I brew just a wee cup. But it's nearly gone."

With a flourish, Dan removed a packet from inside his dark blue frock coat and handed it to her. "And once in a while, some falls off a boat, right into my pocket! I thought you might be needing some."

"Oh, Daniel, Daniel," she beamed, holding the prize to her bosom. "You always was the thoughtful one of all my boys . . . even if you did take that notion to nail the outhouse door shut on one of the professors."

Dan laughed at the memory. "Well, I have other things to occupy me now. I'll leave the pranks to the new fellows."

"And there's some who took right up with them carryin's on." A gracious smile plumped her cheeks, and she patted the treasure on the table before her. "I truly appreciate this." She leaned closer. "There's a little English lass here who's been through some hard things since she come to America. She's a real sweetheart, and such a help to us. Every now and then the two of us have a nice cup of tea between chores."

"You must mean Susannah Harrington," he said evenly. "I've come to escort her to the morning service today."

Mrs. Lyons' sparse brows rose. "You know Susannah? She mentioned a 'Daniel' would be takin' her to church, but I assumed she meant one of the students."

"I certainly hope not," he said sheepishly, "since I invited her to go with me. I met her in Philadelphia when her ship arrived from England."

"You mean you're the one who rescued her on the docks? Why, she's done nothin' but sing your praises ever since."

His heart leaped. "That's good to know. I haven't been able to get her off my mind either." Grinning, he took a gulp of coffee and put his cup back down.

The ruffle on Mrs. Lyons' cap stirred as she tipped her head and studied Dan. "Well, I just hope your intentions toward her are proper and honorable. The lass's been through more'n her share of troubles."

Dan's grin faded as he met her fixed gaze. "Most honorable, I can assure you. I've nothing but the highest regard for the young lady."

"Well, I want you to know we love her, just like she's our own. If any harm came to her because of your tomfoolery, I'd track you all the way to Rhode Island myself. She's quality, a lady to be sure, and I plan to see she marries up with some fine gentleman who'll appreciate her." With that, she drained her tea.

"Far be it from me to bring more pain into her life. It must have been a terrible day that forced her into servitude."

Mrs. Lyons stiffened slightly. "She's bein' looked after right and proper, be sure of that. And the things she's learnin' here'll help her once she's married off." Rising, she took her cup to the dish tub.

Dan felt warmth around his ears and shifted in his chair. If colony matters weren't so pressing, he'd consider courting Susannah Harrington in earnest. But it *was* possible the difficulties with Great Britain could be resolved soon. After all, the striking down of most of the Townshend Acts had been a victory of sorts. Talk was mellowing out, despite all of Sam Adams' efforts to keep feelings at a high pitch. The trouble could just about be nearing an end.

And besides, he'd never forgive himself if he let her slip away . . . especially in the direction of some randy student like the two he'd met the other day. He'd better make his intentions known. It was the sensible thing to do.

He cleared his throat. "Say," he said, trying to sound casual, "did I ever tell you that besides being a postrider, I'll inherit a prosperous horse farm one day?"

Reaching for the coffeepot, Mrs. Lyons turned with a smile that spelled conspiracy. "No. I never knowed." She stepped over to refill his cup, then replaced the pot.

Dan smiled as she sat down again. "Thank you. This is delicious." He paused. "Since I left school I've earned a fair salary from the government and drawn some good horse trade my father's way in the bargain."

"That so?"

He nodded. "I'll be needing a wife . . . when the proper time comes." Watching the older woman's expression soften considerably, he decided to push on. "Suppose it could be arranged for me to . . . take Susannah on a picnic today after the service?"

Mrs. Lyons pressed her lips together, then relaxed them. "Well, she's been workin' real hard, what with all the extra serving during Whitefield's visit. She deserves an afternoon junket."

"Then could I impose upon you to fix a basket for us,

perhaps?" Drawing on his reserve charm, Dan grinned disarmingly. No woman could resist that combination, but just in case . . .

He took out a second packet, the one he'd planned to give Susannah. "For some extra tea?" He tossed it onto the table, along with several coins to cover the expense of the food.

Mrs. Lyons' hazel eyes sparkled with mirth as they slowly met his. "Well now, I suppose I could. You can pick it up right after church."

"Splendid. I won't forget this, Mrs. Lyons."

"Just see that you treat her proper, Daniel Haynes. I'll go tell her you're here."

Trying to calm his pounding pulse, Dan inhaled slowly as he stood. He straightened his coat and adjusted the lace cuffs of his shirt to show properly below the edges of his dark sleeves.

During the worship service, Susannah cringed, no longer able to ignore the dozens of eyes on her and Dan. She wondered if her face would ever stop flaming. Stealing a self-conscious glance his way, she noticed with some chagrin that his neck seemed unusually red. A muscle twitched in his jaw.

"Yet we *must* discipline our minds," came Dr. Witherspoon's booming voice, "and live our lives in such fashion as to—"

At his abrupt pause, a heavy hush fell upon the congregation. A slight flutter of robes sounded as the students in the immediate vicinity of Susannah and Dan stopped their gawking and turned sheepishly to face the front again.

For several moments, the president glared pointedly at them. Then he continued his sentence without diminishing his gaze. "In such fashion as to radiate the glory of the Lord to those around us." He blinked and returned to the text. "The Lord calls us the salt of the earth. . . ."

Susannah clasped her trembling fingers together in her lap and tried to concentrate on the message. She was extremely uncomfortable with the idea that she and Daniel were the center of attention. The students seated in front of them had at last stopped their rude leering and whispering, but she still felt a multitude of eyes boring holes into her back. She couldn't wait for the service to end.

When at last it did, she stood beside Daniel in the line of those waiting to greet the president. With some trepidation she wished the moment could be avoided completely—or at the very least, delayed. But all too soon their turn arrived.

The minister's stern expression, somber as his clerical robes, seemed even more severe as they drew near, but he held out a polite hand.

"Fine service, Dr. Witherspoon," Daniel said, pumping the man's arm quite exuberantly.

"Daniel," the president said. "The Lord bless you. And you, lass." He pinned Susannah with a piercing look that made her forget her name.

"G-good day," she managed. Dan's gentle tug on her arm unglued her feet from the floor, and grateful, she followed his lead outside into the summer sunshine. She blinked and tipped her head slightly, ducking into the welcome shade of her flower-trimmed bonnet brim.

The congregation still milled about the grounds, and at the foot of the steps Susannah could see the three Lords of Dunce, along with Mary and Christopher. Their expressions, too, seemed to emit mocking amusement. She gathered the remains of her dignity and thrust out her chin as she and Dan descended the steps.

"Splendid sermon," Morgan said, a devilish gleam in his eyes. "Don't you agree?"

"From what I was able to hear of it," Susannah said icily, adding a scathing look for good measure.

Morgan snickered. Hands in his pockets, he rocked back onto his heels.

"So. Haynes." Steven moved stiffly from Morgan's other side. "I see you're back again already."

With a nod, Dan grinned. "I had a personal message to

deliver to Dr. Witherspoon. I made fairly good time, once the storm blew over."

Jonathan shifted his weight and smiled pleasantly. "I've heard about you, but I don't believe we've met. I'm Jon Bradford." He held out his hand.

The young man's warm clasp held a measure of reassurance, and Dan felt himself begin to relax. "Dan Haynes."

"Glad to have you in town," Jonathan continued. "Will you be joining us for dinner?" He swept an appreciative glance over Mary Clare, who blushed daintily. "Mrs. Lyons has come to expect us after services."

"Thanks for the invitation," Dan answered, taking note of Morgan and Steven's cool reserve. "But we'll have to make it some time in the future. Susannah and I have other plans this afternoon."

"We have?"

He met her startled look with his most charming grin. "Oh, didn't I mention it? Mrs. Lyons said you've been working very hard lately. She's made up a picnic basket for us."

Susannah gaped at him as if she couldn't believe what she was hearing.

Morgan nudged Steven in the ribs and frowned. "I say, that does sound inviting. We'd be happy to—"

Dan stopped him with a hand. "Thanks, but no. We'll manage quite well on our own."

"Just the two of you?" Steven shot in.

"I'm afraid so. And we wouldn't want to keep the dear lady waiting, after all her trouble. Excuse us, lads." With a nod, Dan nudged his three-cornered hat and drew Susannah away from the others.

As they strolled back toward the inn, he couldn't help but notice the rude behavior of the womenfolk they passed. They smiled beguilingly at him, yet without exception every one of them ignored Susannah completely. His heart wrenched at the price her indenturement had cost her with the fine ladies of Princeton. There had to be some way to save her from her predicament. But for now, he'd savor this day alone with her.

He smiled down into her dusky blue eyes. "Hope you didn't mind my getting us away from the college in a hurry."

"Not at all. I must say, I'm dreadfully sorry about the conduct of my supposed *friends.*"

He chuckled.

"I'd no idea they'd derive any sort of pleasure from humiliating us so during the service."

"I suppose it's to be expected," he said gallantly. "After all, I have the loveliest young woman in the Colonies on my arm."

A glow settled over Susannah's face that seemed to fill her whole being. Daniel's heart swelled. She was, indeed, the loveliest lady he had ever seen. And for this one afternoon, he had her all to himself.

Rays of afternoon sunshine gleamed through the tall elms and wove strands of pure gold among Susannah's tawny curls. Through almost-closed eyelids, Dan watched her from his relaxed position against the trunk of an elm as she puttered about, putting away the remainder of their lunch and covering the basket with a cloth. Her bonnet lay beside her on the blanket, its ribbon ties in pretty disarray. Her skin looked as creamy as alabaster against the pristine dress.

". . . Then your two unmarried sisters are quite different from one another," she said, favoring him with a smile.

"Well, they have different views of living on a horse farm." He sank down on one elbow, his long legs stretched out to the side, grateful that most of their initial awkwardness had vanished while they had talked over their food. "Janie thinks life revolves around the latest fashion trends from Paris. She barely exists from one party to the next, and she is forever pleading to go to Philadelphia."

"Yet you said Emily prefers being outdoors with the horses. I should like very much to meet her. She sounds sweet."

"Perhaps you shall." His gaze found hers and held it until Susannah broke the spell.

"Oh, look," she breathed, pointing over his shoulder toward the brook a few yards away. "We've got company."

Dan shot a glance behind himself, expecting to see a familiar male student or two out to spoil their day. But instead he saw a little gray bird.

After a harsh-sounding *chack chack,* the feathered creature dipped its bill into the brook, then spread its white-tipped wings and splashed delicately in the shimmering ripples.

They watched in silence as it fluttered to a low branch nearby and began to sing.

"Why, what a bright song," Susannah whispered. "It rivals even that of the nightingale."

"It's a mockingbird. It mimics the sounds of other birds around it."

"How very curious. Well, it must have enjoyed the water, to want to sing about it."

Dan chuckled. "Probably found it refreshing. In fact, so would we. Would you like to go wading?" Without waiting for a reply, he yanked off his boots and socks.

"You must be daft," she said with a light laugh as he got up and bent to help her. "Why, I've not gone since Teddy and I were children."

"Teddy?"

"My brother, Theodore. We had a small creek quite near our home."

Theodore . . . her *brother!* That possibility had never entered Dan's mind. He felt a slow grin spread across his face. "Then I'm sure you must remember what fun it was," he said on a teasing note. "Come on. How often do you have a chance like this?"

Susannah tried unsuccessfully to steel herself against his enormous smile. What was it about this young postrider that made her forget all proprieties? Whatever it was, she felt her resolve melt like candle wax. "Why ever not?" she said, matching his mood. "But you must turn around while I take off my stockings."

"Anything for a lady," he quipped good-naturedly, locking his thumbs behind his back while he waited.

"I'm ready."

He turned, and with a bow, held his arm out to her.

Placing her hand in his, Susannah felt his strong grip as he pulled her effortlessly to her feet. Her fingers tingled from his touch, and she felt her heart flutter so that she could barely breathe.

At the edge of the brook Dan released her. "Looks wonderful," he said, testing the water with a toe. Without further hesitation, he took two steps into it.

"Is it cold?"

He just smiled, gesturing for her to come in.

Grasping her skirts with both hands, Susannah stepped gingerly into the ankle-deep water. "Upon my soul!" she shrieked, hopping out. "I thought you said it wasn't cold."

"Did I?" he asked innocently, a humorous twinkle in his brown-black eyes. "You hardly gave it much chance."

With a light laugh, Susannah inched her skirts a little bit higher. "You're right, of course." Eyes wide, she reentered cautiously, then gradually relaxed her hunched shoulders. Smiling, she lifted her lashes.

Daniel watched her, beguiled by her loveliness. For a moment his breath caught in his chest and he couldn't speak. At last he found his voice.

"Did you and Theodore go wading often?"

"Oh yes. Every summer. We had great fun." Her expression grew serious, and a frown pulled her slender eyebrows downward. "I've not heard from him since I left England. I posted a letter informing him of my indenturement. . . . I'm sure the very thought of it upset him."

"Ah." Dan gave an understanding nod. He tried to imagine how he'd take that kind of news if he'd heard it from Jane or Emily. Even in circumstances similar to Susannah's, he doubted he'd welcome it. In fact, he'd probably be furious! With great effort, he bit back the first remark that came to mind. He didn't want to mar their first time alone together with a difference of opinion. Nothing should ruin this day. He wanted to just look at her, to bask in her lilting, musical accent . . . to touch her. The intensity of his thoughts astounded him.

Yet somehow it felt so right, being with her. As if he'd known her always.

"Teddy is studying for the ministry, you know," Susannah said, looking into the water. She moved one foot from side to side in an arc, making little sparkly waves. "At Oxford. I often wonder how he'd fare at Princeton, with all the political discussions which sometimes take precedence over theology. He'd be aghast at the lack of support for King George, I'm afraid."

Dan studied her as she took a few tentative steps away. "He doesn't agree with the Whigs and their liberal thinking."

With a shake of her head, Susannah turned back. "Oh no. Our family has always embraced the old traditions . . . most of all those of the church. But since I've been here I see things quite differently. Especially since I've found such peace and freedom in Christ." She searched his face.

"Oh?"

She averted her eyes to some distant point. "I'm beginning to see that too many rules and regulations in religion get in the way of the close relationship Christ wants to share with us." She paused and looked again at him. "And it must be the same with government."

"How is that?"

"Well, acts of Parliament and new laws only get in the way of the good, profitable relationship we could have with Britain. Do you know what I mean?"

"*We?* You're beginning to sound like an American."

"Yes. It's strange, isn't it? But I've grown accustomed to hearing the Colonies' side of things, and it all makes perfect sense. All except—"

"Except what?" A light breeze whispered through the trees about them, scattering a lock of Dan's hair forward. He raked it back into place with his fingers as he watched Susannah. Her thoughts ran far deeper than those of any of his own sisters. And despite the fact that most women didn't bother to concern themselves with political affairs, he felt compelled to hear her views.

With a final swish of her foot in the shallows, Susannah stepped onto the dry ground and looked intently at him. "Well, Americans aren't willing to help pay the expense for their own protection. The French and Indian War—whether or not Mr. Lyons thinks so—was fought, after all, to keep the frontier safe from the savages led by the French. It's common knowledge in England."

Dan bent down, plucked a pair of shiny stones from those near his feet, and rolled them in his fingers. He really didn't want to argue with her, but she stood waiting, expecting a response. He skipped a flat pebble over the water. "The English were fighting over disputed territory, not to save the settlers from the Indians. We've always had to look out for ourselves."

Susannah's countenance remained doubtful.

With another smooth toss, he sent the second stone hopping over the surface. It vanished into the ripples. "European countries squabble constantly, and that time they stirred up a heap of trouble trying to best each other. It cost a lot of lives, Indian and white. Now there may never be true peace between the two races."

Dan looked at the lithe beauty beside the brook and read her belief in his words, her trust. Unlike the narrow-minded Anglican escort who'd accompanied her across the vast ocean, she seemed eager to hear about what concerned the Colonies, even sympathetic to the patriots' cause. Surely she was a treasure. Then he noticed her attention drift to something across the creek.

A smile glowed in her eyes. "Violets," she whispered. "The sun just lit upon them. How very lovely."

Dan strode to her side and, without so much as a single rational thought, scooped her up in his arms and grinned. "Anything you desire is yours, m'lady."

Susannah gasped. Her first impulse—to demand he put her down and behave in a more gentlemanly fashion—lost out to her enjoyment of the moment. She clasped her arms around his shoulders and laughed as he splashed through the water.

On the other side of the stream, he lowered her ever so slowly to her feet beside the mass of fragile blue violets.

Their eyes met and lingered for the space of a heartbeat. And Susannah forgot that the flowers were even there.

19

Susannah floated through the next several days like down on the wind. Memories of the picnic she and Daniel Haynes had shared rose in her mind, bringing smiles she fought to control. It wasn't proper—surely it wasn't—to let idle thoughts of that handsome postrider distract her from her duties at the inn. But during the last quiet moments before sleep, when only Mary's faint, even breathing stirred in the darkness of their room, all her good intentions could not dim the picture of his face. The sound of his rich voice echoed in her mind. He had spoken of his love for America, about his family and the sprawling horse farm of which his father was so proud. She remembered his strong shoulders and felt again the power of his muscled arms when he had set her onto her feet amid the violets—gently, as though she were made of priceless porcelain.

But since that glorious afternoon, a fortnight had elapsed, during which Susannah had not heard a word from him. And when two weeks stretched out to several more, a niggling concern began to prod at her heart. Perhaps she had acted in an unladylike manner in his presence, or had been too familiar. After all, she was only a bond servant. If he truly were the slightest bit as interested as he had appeared to be during their time together, surely he'd at least have kept in touch. And besides, he seemed to think nothing of consorting with lawbreakers. She had been foolish even to entertain fantasies of having any sort of permanent relationship with him.

With a deep sigh, Susannah sprinkled flour onto the table and began pummeling the bread dough before her. She gave it a swift punch, then another; finally she picked up the mass and slammed it with a resounding thud onto the work surface, sending a floury cloud in all directions. Sheepishly she shot a glance about the kitchen to be certain Mrs. Lyons had not returned from the butcher's. She rounded the mixture and covered it with a clean cloth to rest while she stepped out for a breath of air and a drink of water.

Susannah's hand was still on the outside latch when she heard the murmur of voices and light laughter coming from the direction of the well. She stepped cautiously to the corner of the building and peered around it, just in time to see Jonathan assisting Mary Clare with a pail of water. Tenderly the young man brushed a golden curl away from Mary's eyes and brushed her rose petal lips with his.

Susannah drew back and returned to the kitchen, struggling to subdue the jealousy that squeezed its cold fingers around her heart.

Moments later, footsteps sounded outside the door, and the pair entered. Jonathan set the water onto the sideboard.

Mary stepped around him and tilted her head. "Well, you could've failed your orals, you know, like you did last spring, so you wouldn't have to go home for the harvest."

The young man's chest rose and fell as he cast a quick look at Susannah, who quickly buried her attention in the yeasty dough again. "Come on, Mare. I had to work hard to get through all my studies this term. My folks would never stand for another poor showing. They'd plant me so deep on the farm I'd never see Princeton again."

Mary Clare flopped dejectedly onto a chair.

"Besides, I figured you'd want me to take my courses seriously," he continued. "My whole future will depend on them." He paused. "Anyway, Hunterdon's not that far away, and a month isn't all that long. You won't have time to start missing me. Right, Susannah?"

Susannah met his eager gaze with a smile. "Yes. I've only just heard how well you did at school. I must say, I'm awfully proud of you."

He grinned. "Reckon I owe a good chunk of my success to you, now that you mention it."

"Why, whatever do you mean?"

"All those questions you asked made us study harder so we'd sound like we knew what we were talking about."

Susannah felt Mary's stare and gave her a teasing wink. "Well, I'm glad they served some purpose for all of us, then." With a sharp knife she sliced a portion of dough and shaped it into a loaf, then continued with the remainder until several more were lined beside it. "When will you be leaving?" she asked, breaking the heavy silence.

Jonathan thrust his hands into the pockets of his breeches. "Within the hour. Soon as my pa's wagon gets here. I just came to say good-bye."

Susannah saw tears glistening in the corners of Mary's eyes and watched her blink them away.

"Suppose it'd be all right if Mary walked with me back to Nassau Hall?" he asked.

With a shrug of one shoulder, Susannah smiled. "I'm quite certain Mrs. Lyons wouldn't mind. Try not to be long, though." She turned and covered the loaves with a clean cloth.

Susannah gazed after them as they walked hand in hand toward the college, wishing for a fleeting second that it were Daniel Haynes clutching her own hand so tightly, looking so longingly into her own eyes. She turned away, her own spirits as gray as the clouding sky.

She wiped her fingers on her apron, crossed to the hearth, and poured herself a cup of Mrs. Lyons' strong coffee. The first sip tasted as bitter as the thoughts now edging their way into her heart. Dan obviously had considered her, flirted a bit for a day, and then rejected her. No doubt his ever-so-proper family would frown upon his courting a mere bond servant.

Susannah took another gulp and winced. *Coffee.* It would never be as comforting as tea. Leaving the remainder untouched, she rose and lifted a corner of the cloth to peek at the rising bread. It would be ready to bake soon. She gathered the bowls and mixing utensils and set them to soak, then wiped down the table. Rejection of one sort or another was beginning to turn up in every corner of her life. It was more than obvious that Ted would never speak to her again. Her brother had had ample time to answer any one of the letters she'd posted to Oxford. He had made his displeasure abundantly clear by choosing to ignore them.

The only one she could turn to now was God. Now that she knew his peace and comfort, she knew she'd find the strength to go on somehow. *Dear Father,* she prayed silently, *forgive me for dwelling upon my disappointments. Thank you for all your precious gifts, and for the knowledge that you will never leave me or forsake me.* A warm peacefulness settled over her.

At that moment the door opened, and a weeping Mary Clare came in. "He's . . . he's gone." She buried her face in her hands and sobbed.

Susannah put the cloth aside and went to hug the younger girl, gently patting her back. "Now, now, you know October is not far away. He'll be back before you know it."

"No he won't."

"Don't be silly. Of course he will."

"No one comes back. Not Mama, not Papa the way he used to love us. Jon won't, either, I just know it. I'll never see him again."

Blotting Mary's tears with the corner of her apron, Susannah tried to coax a little smile from her. "How can he not, when you've completely stolen his heart? He'll have to come back for it. Besides, he still has two more years of study before he can be ordained."

A stubborn pout hardened the girl's countenance. "Why are you so hopeful, when you're just the same as me? The people you loved have all left you, too. How can you bear it? Your parents died, your brother won't write—even your precious Mr. Haynes has all but disappeared."

With a huff she shoved her hand into the pocket of her dress, and a strange expression settled upon her tear-streaked face. "Oh. President Witherspoon gave Jon a letter to bring you. We got to talkin', and I forgot." She held it out.

Susannah's pulse went wild, and she took the letter reverently, noting that it was addressed to her in care of the college.

"Dr. Witherspoon apologized," Mary said. "It got lost among his other papers. He just found it a little while ago."

A little while ago? Susannah's heart sang as she broke the seal and unfolded the parchment, noting it was dated two weeks earlier.

> *My dear Susannah,*
>
> *My duties will keep me rather busy for the next several weeks between Boston, Providence, and New York, so I fear I will not get to see you in the immediate future. I shall draw comfort from thoughts of our picnic at the brook and the memory of your enchanting smile. I leave you in God's care until I find another free day and can come to Princeton.*
>
> > *Until then, I remain, affectionately,*
> > *Dan*

With a joyous smile, Susannah crushed the letter to her bosom, beaming at Mary Clare. "You see? All this time, when I was despondent and without word from Dan, God knew Dan had written. I should have had more faith. It'll be the same for you, too. Trust God. Our heavenly Father wants only the best for his children." With an impulsive hug, she planted a kiss on Mary's cheek. "Would you be a dear and watch the bread for me? I'd like to be alone with my letter for a few minutes."

As he rode toward Purchase Street and Sam Adams' house in Boston, Daniel noticed a familiar shabby figure heading on foot from that direction. "Mr. Adams," he called, drawing Flame to a halt and dismounting.

"Why, Daniel. Back from the west country already?"

Dan gripped the man's hand and shook it warmly. "Yes. I was on my way to tell you all about it."

"Good. Good. But let's make haste, lad." His high-pitched voice squeaked as the words came out in a rush, and his palsied hands fluttered in the air. "I'm afraid I'm late for a meeting. Walk with me and tell me your news."

Dan knew that despite his poor health, the influential gentleman rarely missed a meeting with the patriots. With a nod, he took the reins and led the horse at a pace that matched that of the frail man.

"I was sent to Albany, by way of Brookfield and Northampton," Dan said, "and had a chance to talk to quite a few people along the way."

"And what did you hear in the churches and taverns, my boy? Will we have any support after we convict those soldiers for massacring our local folk?"

Dan shrugged. "Well, there's some pretty strong sentiment for the Bostonians, I have to say that. As long as the Crown keeps soldiers here for the sole purpose of policing the colonists, the people will resent it and resist. But since Reverend Whitefield came through Massachusetts last month preaching—"

His words were drowned out as a gap-toothed man rushed up to them. "Corky Jenkins, the Cambridge gunsmith, just rode in with some news! Preacher Whitefield is comin' our way!"

Mr. Adams frowned and waved a threadbare arm in a helpless gesture. "How can that be? He was on his way to Canada."

"All's I know is, Jenkins says the man's comin' back," the fellow said, stroking his curly black beard with a thumb and forefinger. "And that's good enough for me, I says."

"Did Mr. Jenkins mention anything about his musket business?"

"Well, sir," the newcomer continued, "he was up Exeter way yesterday delivering a passel of muskets. Says he's busier than ever, what with the trial coming up. Says folks are takin' a real interest in hunting nowadays and are *partial to red squirrel*. Says they're practicing up for anything else what's wearin' red. That's all I know. Good day to you, now. I hafta be tellin' Reverend Cooper and the other preachers that Whitefield's coming." With a mock salute, he grinned and turned away.

Adams stood rooted, shaking his head. He lifted his gaze to Dan, then started walking a bit more slowly. "Well, getting back to our subject, lad, it seems quite a number of people are becoming downright charitable over the plight of the soldiers. They're saying the lobsterbacks were merely defending themselves, that they don't have a choice about where they're posted, that sort of thing. And even if that's true, it's quite beside the point. Whether an unwieldy tree limb chooses to fall or not, the person who gets crushed when it hits the ground is no less dead. The prudent thing would be to keep wayward branches pruned in the first place. Do you get my meaning?"

"Yes sir, I believe I do."

"I fear our good Reverend Whitefield does not see the realities of life, Daniel." The older man turned a probing glance toward Dan. "He has incredibly childish and romantic ideas that are totally impractical. He seems to look at *this* world 'through a glass darkly,' as Paul says in First Corinthians."

Dan didn't fully understand the moody conversation, but he remained silent out of respect for the esteemed councilman as they turned onto King Street. Adams' squeaky voice continued.

"A practical, reasoning man can easily see the impossibility of ever uniting all churches into one body. Why, the differences between them are insurmountable. And as for us all becoming one big happy colony," he said, stabbing a bony finger into the air, "I refuse absolutely to give up what we've built for ourselves here in Massachusetts. Could you even imagine us joining with those bowing, scraping colonists to the south, I ask?"

Dan smiled and said nothing.

"Or even your own Rhode Island joining with them?" Mr. Adams asked. "Impossible. Utterly impossible."

"It would give Roger Williams cause to turn a few times, coffin or no," Dan said wryly.

"We're losing too many of our freedoms already, lad. Too many of our rights. We shouldn't have had that heinous traitor, Thomas Hutchinson, shoved down our throats, either. Parliament had no business taking away our charter right to elect our own governor."

As the two men turned onto tree-lined Cornhill Avenue, pounding hoofbeats and yelling reverberated over the cobbled surface of the street. Sam Adams stepped into the middle of the road and raised a hand as the horse and rider approached. "What is it, my good man?"

He drew the reins sharply. "Whitefield is dead!"

"What's that?" Mr. Adams asked, aghast.

"Died last night in Newburyport, he did. I must be on, to spread the word." Nudging his sturdy mount with his knees, the man galloped off as swiftly as he'd come.

Dan watched the color drain from his companion's face, and an odd weight pressed upon his own chest. He swallowed hard. Adams began to tremble visibly. He ignored the heaviness of his own grief and put an arm around the man's shoulders. "Why don't we head into the Bunch of Grapes for some cider?" he asked. "It's just around the corner from here."

Within moments they took seats at a secluded corner table inside the dark, smoke-filled establishment. After a few gulps of his cider, Sam Adams sagged against the back of the chair. He stared pensively into the cloudy amber liquid in his glass.

Dan allowed his thoughts to drift to America's tremendous loss in the death of the great evangelist. The dreadful news would undoubtedly come as a shock to Susannah, since she had so recently been affected by Whitefield's message. He wished he were there to comfort her.

The door burst open and a man leaned inside. "George Whitefield is dead! He died yesterday in Newburyport!"

An audible gasp rose in the tavern as the door squeaked closed again. Then the room fell silent.

Adams took another gulp of cider. His weary eyes glistened as he drew his mouth into a tight circle, then he sighed heavily. "I first heard him many years ago," he said, his voice unnaturally soft, "when I was a young man myself. The message he preached changed the course of my life." He raised his gaze and searched Dan's face. "Made me look outside myself and my own affairs to the world around me, to the people and their plight. Why, I even planned to become a minister. Went to Harvard." He shook his head sadly. "But there was too much unrest. I switched my course and got a Master of Arts degree."

Dan drained his glass and signaled for refills. His own experience had been similar. Inspired by Whitefield to study for the ministry, he'd diverted toward the revolutionary cause. Had he made the right choice? He opened his mouth to voice his thoughts.

But Adams rambled on in a flat tone. "Never been anyone like Whitefield, not since the apostles themselves. He had the zeal and determination of Paul, the gentle love of John. Preached the grace of God on two continents. He quite literally turned the Anglican hierarchy on its ear. Why, a hundred years from now, Daniel, my boy, our grandchildren—and theirs—will extol him as the most influential man of the eighteenth century. He was the first man to ride horseback from Georgia to New Hampshire. He preached to everyone, even slaves and Indians."

"He was truly amazing."

"Whitefield hated any lines that separate—charter, race, or color. He wanted to eliminate them and have everyone love God and neighbor. Would that I could have shared that enthusiasm with the same gentleness he had. He seemed always to see heaven just around the corner."

Adams inhaled slowly and expelled the breath. "But alas, the heaven on earth he dreamed about will probably never come to pass before the return of the Lord."

He shook his hand. "A pity his preaching in England didn't have more of an impact on Parliament and those other pompous hoity-toities. If only he could have made them understand that in Christ we're all equal in the sight of God. Perhaps we wouldn't be in the sorry state we are in now, if they had listened. But now I fear we may yet have to resort to open conflict. Mark my words."

Dan took another drink in the ensuing silence and pondered the disastrous consequences that would unquestionably befall the Colonies unless God intervened.

As Sam Adams settled deeper into his seat, his lips twitched, curving into a strange smile. "Ah, but wouldn't it have been wonderful?" he asked wistfully.

"What's that, sir?"

"All of us becoming loving, caring brothers—the way Whitefield so fervently wanted us to be."

"Well, perhaps I, too, am naive, but I'd like to see a measure of that brotherly peace and freedom for us in this lifetime. That's why I'm so dedicated to our cause."

Adams reached over a trembling hand and gave Dan's a pat. "And we will, my boy, if I have anything to say about it. But I fear the Colonies must first be tested by fire." He took another sip of cider. "Perhaps it's just as well that God, in his providence, called Whitefield home at this time. It would have broken the man's heart to witness the children of his two precious flocks shedding one another's blood."

20

As Dan traveled toward Pawtucket, silver shards of light from the three-quarter moon sliced through the dense woodlands edging the road. A profound emptiness in his chest brought a weary sag to his shoulders. Not even the twoscore miles he'd traveled since learning earlier that day of George Whitefield's passing had eased the heaviness of his heart.

Giving little thought to the letters Sam Adams had given him to deliver to Providence, New York, and Philadelphia, Dan expended only minimal effort dodging patrols as he pressed on, eager for the solace of his own home. He hoped someone in the family would still be up. Anyone.

At last he emerged from the forest onto the rolling fenced land surrounding the Haynes Farm. Moonglow frosted the large enclosed pasture that separated him from the darkened two-story house on the far hill. Several sturdy Narragansetts stirred and pranced off into the distance at the sound of his approach. A beam of amber light spilled from the open barn door, silhouetting his father and Elijah, the freed Negro who worked for him. Dan gave a gentle nudge to Flame's sides and guided the horse toward the weathered building.

Both heads turned his way as Flame's hoofbeats echoed in the night.

"Son!" called his father. A broad grin spread across his face as he and the hired man strode to meet him.

Dan met their smiles halfheartedly. "Father," he said with a nod. "Elijah. You're looking well." Dismounting, he shook their hands.

His father put an arm around Dan. "It's a real treat to have you home, my boy. Will you be staying long?"

"No," Dan answered, meeting his father's eyes. "Not long."

"Well, we're always glad to see you come, anyway, and know the good Lord's been looking out for you." He tightened his grip for an instant, then lowered his arm. "Looks like we made it through another crisis with the mare's infected hoof," he said to Elijah. "No reason you can't turn in."

"Yessuh. I'll be goin' directly. I'll just be seein' to your horse, Dan'l."

"Thanks." With a grateful tip of his head, Dan watched as Flame plodded obediently after the dark-skinned man. He swept a wide glance over the grounds and smiled as he and his father strode toward the house. "It's good to be home again. But I wouldn't want to get anyone out of bed. It must be ten o'clock."

"Nonsense, lad. That's one thing we all agree on. Whenever you find time to be with us, we want to enjoy it. We can sleep anytime. I'm just glad I happened to be out in the barn when you got here, so I was able to greet you. Come on, let's go wake your mother." Bounding up the steps, he crossed the porch and threw open the door. "Hey, everybody!" he bellowed. "Wake up! Company's come." Fastening the latch behind them, he set about lighting oil lamps.

A hinge or two squeaked on the second floor as bedroom doors opened, and Dan saw his lanky younger brother lean over the banister with a yawn. "What's going on?"

"Benjamin," came his mother's voice from the top of the stairs as she held a candle high. "Mind your manners. Your father said we have company." Straightening her spine, she made a majestic descent, the hem of her dressing gown trailing the edge of each step after her.

Clattering down behind their mother, curls flying, Emily and Jane tied the sashes of their wraps and tugged at their nightcaps.

"Oh, it's Dan!" squealed Emily in delight. She barely allowed her mother the customary first embrace before she flung herself into her brother's arms.

Right behind her, Benjamin motioned for Jane to be next, then grabbed Dan in a hug, giving his shoulder blades a few enthusiastic whacks.

"Well," Dan said with a grin, "this is sure a great welcome."

"You've never ridden in quite so late before," his mother said. "Is everything all right?"

He nodded. "I've just come from Boston. I have some urgent post to deliver to New York and Philadelphia, so I thought I'd better squeeze in a visit while I had the chance."

"Philadelphia," Jane sighed dreamily. "Mother's promised us we'll go there to Cousin Landon's for the Christmas parties, no matter what. I can't wait."

"Oh?" Dan hid an inward smile at the sparkle in Jane's wide brown eyes. He wondered if Philadelphia would be ready for his romantic eighteen-year-old sister.

"Yes," she continued, casting a sideways glare at Emily. "It'll make up for this little scamp's catching the chicken pox this summer when we *should* have gone."

"Yeah," Ben interjected. "And just when Johnny Franks, the blacksmith's apprentice, started comin' around, too. One look at her all festered up, and we never saw him again!"

"Oh, bother," the younger girl said with a pout. "I *told* him to go. I have better things to do than sit in the parlor with some freckle-faced boy who's making moon eyes at me."

"Now, come on, settle down," their father said. "In fact, now that it's been brought up, let's go sit in the parlor and catch up on Dan's news." He led the way. "Have you had supper, lad?"

"Not really. I wasn't very hungry."

About to settle onto one of the overstuffed parlor chairs, his mother straightened instead. "Nonsense." She flailed a hand toward Emily. "Go get your brother some of that nice ham from supper, dear, and a cold sweet potato." Then, watching the girl comply, she relaxed into the wing-backed chair nearest the luminous embers in the hearth. She drew her dressing gown close and brushed back the trailing ribbon that tied her auburn hair.

While everyone found seats, their father circled the spacious room, lighting the remaining lamps. The soft glow illuminated rich mahogany furnishings upholstered in wine reds and soft grays. Tossing the lighting stick into the ashes, he added a few logs and coaxed the flames to life again, then sat across from his wife.

Jane tucked her bare feet under herself on the settee and smoothed the folds of her flannel wrap in place. "Well," she said, arching a slender eyebrow, "I for one intend to draw lots of attention from young men while we're in the city."

"Is that a fact?" Dan teased.

His sister's expressive face softened with a dreamy smile. "Mother's having some new party frocks made for us. The taffeta I chose is the prettiest ever, and the design is the very latest fashion." She toyed with a long silken curl as she spoke, twisting it in her fingers. The fire's glow danced brightly in her dark eyes.

"Then you'll surely turn a few heads," he conceded. He transferred his attention to his mother, noticing the way her ivory silk wrapper draped elegantly over her chair, and his gaze lingered on her soft hands. Even without the fine rings she normally wore, her skin was smooth, flawless. He blinked and looked away.

"So, big brother." Ben leaned forward on the sofa and cocked his head at a jaunty angle. "What about those slimy lobsterbacks? Any more incidents?" A lively grin flared across his boyish features.

"No, actually—"

"Really, Benjamin," their mother interrupted. "I'm quite beside myself at your disloyal attitude toward our own mother country. You must learn to curb that tongue of yours before we go to the city, or you shall spend the holidays here. Alone."

She turned to Dan. "You *will* try to make arrangements to

be with us for Christmas, won't you, dear? And you'll remember your promise to conduct yourself in proper fashion."

"I'll do my best, Mother." A tantalizing picture of Susannah flashed into his mind, all ruffles and curls and lace, and he smiled. Perhaps he might be able to convince her to join him and his family for the holidays.

Across the room, Jane flashed a coy smile. "I'm sure Cousin Charlotte will be pleased if you're there. She asks after you whenever she writes."

Trying not to appear annoyed while he thought of a suitable reply, Dan recalled the memory of his plain third cousin and her incessant giggles. On every visit to the Somerwell mansion, Charlotte stuck to him like a tattoo.

"Hey, that'd be great," Ben added with an eager nod. "If you keep good old Charlotte entertained, *I* can survey the rest of the fair young maidens."

"Only if you're there, of course," his mother reminded Ben. "You're quite close to remaining behind."

With a grimace, he rolled his eyes.

Normally the banter would have amused Dan, but on this occasion he found it oddly tiring instead. He shifted his position. Then, feeling his father's stare, he looked up.

"What is it that's brought you home, Son? So late, I mean."

Emily returned just then with a plate of food and a glass of cider.

Dan accepted them with a smile, setting the drink beside the porcelain figurine on the end table at his elbow. Then as his little sister plopped down onto the braided rug at his feet, he gave a playful flick to one of her blonde curls. He managed a mouthful of ham, despite his lack of appetite, and chewed slowly.

"You were about to tell us what brought you our way," his father prodded.

"Well, actually, I . . . came bearing bad news."

"Oh?"

Dan nodded. "George Whitefield died yesterday. In Newburyport."

For several moments only the crackling and hiss of the burning wood broke the silence. Dan watched his mother look away as the others stared at various parts of the room.

Emily's soft green eyes glistened with tears, and she leaned her head against his knee. "Oh, how sad."

Finally his father stood and crossed the space between them. He put a hand on Dan's shoulder and gave a comforting squeeze. "He was a good man. We're blessed to have known him."

"That's for sure," Ben added. "Whenever he came to town, it was better than having two fairs in one year."

"Oh, I wouldn't say that," Jane said with a toss of russet curls. "I always thought all the sensation he caused was—I don't know—too enthusiastic. Too *common*. I mean, all the commotion, the yelling and screaming, women swooning. I couldn't abide it. Don't you agree, Mother?"

Dan looked at his sister in disbelief.

"Now, that'll be quite enough, young lady," their father said, his quiet voice laced with uncharacteristic sternness. "A great man has died. Untold multitudes have found peace with God precisely *because* of his untiring enthusiasm for preaching the gospel. Why, it was because of him that Dan chose to go to seminary. Baptists, like myself, Anglicans—" he looked at his wife. "Even people of other denominations will feel the loss deeply. Just like Dan." He gave another encouraging squeeze. "I think we should bow our heads and thank God for sending that gentle, loving servant our way—and ask him to send others to fill the great hole left by Whitefield's passing."

Susannah placed some new candles in the wall sconces and lit them as the darkness brought increasing gloom to the common room. Glancing over her shoulder at Mary Clare, she couldn't help but notice the girl's forced smile as she poured a glass of flip for one of the few remaining customers. Picking up a stack of dirty dishes, Susannah made her way to the kitchen and pushed at the door.

Mrs. Lyons barely got out of the way in time.

"Oh, how clumsy of me," Susannah said, her cheeks flaming. "I'm dreadfully sorry. I didn't know you were there." She set down the dishes and turned to face her.

With a wry grimace, Mrs. Lyons shrugged. "Don't be worryin' yourself over it, love. 'Twasn't your fault. I was so busy peekin' out at Mary Clare, I wasn't watchin' for you."

"So you're concerned about her, too."

She nodded. "And I don't mind sayin' so." While Susannah stacked the pewter plates onto the sideboard, the older woman stepped to the hearth and removed the kettle of hot water, pouring some into the dish tub.

Susannah began washing the dishes.

"Oh, now, let me do that, child. No sense in spoilin' those pretty hands with lye soap before you catch yourself a good husband."

Susannah giggled. "Stuff and nonsense. It's quite late, and you've worked hard all day. Off to bed with you, I'll finish up." Vigorously she lifted a plate from the sudsy water and scrubbed at some dried-on food.

Mrs. Lyons wiped her brow with the back of a hand. "Well now, aren't you the dear one? But—" The white dust cap stirred as she gestured with her head. "My worrying over *her* will plague me till I know she's tucked away safe. I'll see to the dishes. You sweep out the ordinary."

"Mary's one step ahead of us both. She's flitting about the room one minute with the broom, the next with the pitcher of flip—and that before anyone's glass is even empty. I've not seen anything like it."

"Nor I." Mrs. Lyons picked up a linen dish towel and started drying the growing stack of dishes. "Classes started up yesterday. That young Jonathan better be gettin' here pretty quick."

Susannah stopped working and looked into Mrs. Lyons' concerned face. "Wouldn't it be horrible if he didn't? You don't suppose his family would stand in the way of his schooling?"

"I hope not. But still—" She shot a glance toward the

common room. "It's not somethin' new for a boy to start at the college and never come back to finish his studies."

"Well, perhaps there's been a poor harvest. Or it could be that prices are down and the tuition would pose a financial problem. It's quite possible he could be forced to skip a term." Even as she spoke, Susannah realized how hollow the words sounded.

Mrs. Lyons shook her head in dismal resignation. She crossed to the door, peeked through the crack, then quietly returned to the sink. "Or," she whispered, "his ma and pa heard he was courtin' a bond servant."

"Surely you don't mean that." Susannah ran her tongue absently over her lips. "But he has been courting her, hasn't he?"

Untying the soiled apron that covered her faded cotton work dress, Mrs. Lyons rolled it up in her lap and lowered her plump frame onto one of the wooden chairs. She tucked some stray wisps inside her ruffled cap, which now sat askew on her graying hair. "He did talk some to me about winding up with Mary Clare after graduation. Never once tried to hide it."

"And, of course, you approved."

She nodded. "Saw no reason not to. At the time, anyway. Never said nothin' about his family to make me think they'd cause trouble for them. But now that I think about it, if they heard she's bonded out with nothing to bring to a marriage . . . who knows? They might have stopped him from returning. Kept him out of harm's way, so to speak."

"Oh, I pray that's not so." Susannah cushioned her back with her hands and leaned against the sink as she faced Mrs. Lyons. "Mary and Jon are so much in love."

"I know. I know. It purely breaks my heart to see her takin' on so."

With a glance toward the door, Susannah straightened her shoulders. "Well, I'm not content to give up hope. Jonathan's just been delayed, that's all. It has to be that. He's not the sort to abandon Mary without a word. He'd have written, at least."

Mrs. Lyons tilted her head. "Well, you never can be sure about a young whippersnapper like him. Maybe he was too ashamed to let her know he's spineless as a snake."

Susannah forced a smile. "No. He'll write if he's not coming. He must."

"I'm glad you can still find some faith in that boy." She swatted her apron halfheartedly at Susannah. "But in the meantime, you'd best be spending less energy on them dishes and more on convincin' poor Mary Clare of that."

From outside came the sound of hoofbeats as wagon wheels crunched over the gravel drive in front of the inn.

Mrs. Lyons heaved a sigh. "Must be that stage from New York, finally. You'd best see to the travelers—and then steer Mary Clare off to bed."

"Yes ma'am." Leaving the kitchen, Susannah strode directly to the front door and opened it for the customers. "Good evening," she said with a smile, noting that the first two patrons carried valises. "Please allow me to escort you to the proprietor."

They nodded pleasantly as they entered the inn, followed moments later by the remaining passengers.

At the bar, Susannah gestured toward Mr. Lyons. "This gentleman will assist you in arranging rooms for the night. Will you be having supper before you retire?"

"Yes, miss. Thanks for your help." The older of the two, a wiry, ruddy-faced man with a full beard, bowed his head politely.

His companion, a short, rotund fellow whose buttons strained over his girth, smiled as well. In one puffy hand he clutched a letter, which he held out to Mr. Lyons. "We were asked to deliver this to the inn."

The proprietor scanned the name on the parchment. Tossing a glance in Mary Clare's direction, he passed the folded paper to Susannah. "Seat these folks and see to their supper, then give this to the girl. Maybe now she'll go upstairs and quit tormentin' us all with her stargazing an' jumping everytime the door opens."

Susannah's heartbeat doubled as she put the letter into her skirt pocket. It seemed to take an extra long time before the new customers appeared settled and content. But when they finally had all their requests, she breathed more easily. Mary Clare stood across the room fussing with the hearth. "I have something for you," Susannah said, approaching her. "It arrived on the stage." She held out the letter.

At the sight of it, the color drained from Mary's face. She swallowed. Then, hesitantly she took it and stared at the writing. Her eyes brimmed. She blinked quickly and ducked her head.

Susannah put a hand on the girl's arm. "If you need help reading any of the words, I'll be up shortly."

With an almost imperceptible nod, Mary scurried away.

Please, Father, let it be good news, Susannah prayed silently. *Please, for Mary's sake.* Then she checked the customers' cups and hurried to the kitchen for the coffeepot.

Mrs. Lyons looked up as she entered.

"I . . . I need the coffee," she said, trying to still the pulse pounding within her ears. "A letter came for Mary."

"Oh no." Mrs. Lyons eased herself slowly onto a chair. "I was fearin' it would come to that."

"Well, he might have written to say he's been delayed a few days," Susannah heard her own voice say. The words sounded distant, unreal. She grabbed the enamel pot and made for the other room, trying to beat the older woman's response.

"No."

Even with her hand about to push against the door, she stopped.

"Ever since he left I've had a bad feeling about him not coming back. Even been prayin' it's not so. My little Mary's been through so much in her life already. I hoped the good Lord would see fit to work a miracle for her. Just this once."

Susannah's heart plummeted. "Well, we've got to trust him, then, instead of letting our imaginations run away with us. After all, neither of us knows what's in that letter, now, do we?"

"That's a fact. No sense giving up hope just yet. You might be right."

With an encouraging nod, Susannah gripped the pot tighter and went into the ordinary, where she began filling mugs with the rich steaming brew. Her mind set on Mary Clare, she glanced toward the stairs, barely catching the name *Whitefield* in the conversation at her elbow. "I beg your pardon," she said to the traveler, a well-dressed gentleman in a fine wool greatcoat. "I couldn't help but overhear you mention the Reverend Whitefield. Is he perhaps coming this way again soon?"

"Oh my, lass," said the stout woman next to him. "You haven't heard, then. The dear man passed away just last week. In Newburyport. Isn't that right, sweetheart?" She brushed a few crumbs from her husband's sleeve.

Susannah's knees crumpled. She sank to the bench beside the customers.

The lady took Susannah's hand and searched her face, concern evident in her eyes. "Are you all right, my dear?"

"It—it can't be," Susannah said, staring unseeing in her confusion.

"Yes, it's a great loss," said the lady's husband. "A great loss indeed."

"He preached mere hours before he passed on," the kindly woman said. "Never stopped long enough to give his ailing body a rest, just kept on toiling for the Lord. Yet, who could have known? He said, 'Works? Works? A man get to heaven by works? I would as soon think of climbing to the moon on a rope of sand.' I'll never forget it."

"You saw him just before he . . . died?" Susannah whispered.

The woman's cheeks plumped with a sad smile. "Well, not exactly. A few weeks ago. We got the sorrowful news just yesterday, while we were waiting to cross the ferry at New York. A young man—a postrider, I believe—told us the news."

Susannah's mind flashed to Dan, and she wished with all her heart that he were with her now, to offer the comfort and strength of his arms. She forced her loneliness aside as the voice of the woman's husband drifted into her consciousness.

"Yes. The young man said no one was surprised that the reverend died that night. He looked so frail as he preached, but his countenance shone—so the young fellow said—like an unclouded sun."

"And," the woman continued, "as he was helped off the platform, he cried, 'I go! I go to rest prepared!' What a wondrous life that man lived."

The devastating reality hit Susannah all at once. That magnificent voice, which had so faithfully proclaimed the incredible grace of God and had broken through her own spiritual blindness, was now forever stilled. Would death always lay such swift claim to those who'd had the most profound effect upon her? First her parents, then her dearest friend, and now this man from God who had brought with him the peace from heaven that she had sought all her years. She tasted the tang of salt on her lips and realized that tears were streaming down her face. She wanted nothing more than to fling herself across her bed and give in to her grief.

She looked despairingly toward the staircase leading to the attic.

Then she remembered Mary Clare. How ever could she offer the girl any comfort now? She had none to give.

Rising, she walked blindly to the back door, laid her head against the doorpost, and wept.

$$21$$

Nearing its zenith, the sun intensified the warmth of Indian summer as Dan nudged Flame to a faster pace. He unbuttoned his coat, feeling a twinge of guilt at the sight of the glistening sheen that covered the horse. "Sorry to make you work so hard, boy," he said with a pat on the animal's neck. "But I've got to get to the Lyons' Den before the noon rush. I'll make it up to you, I promise."

The pacer flicked its ears and snorted, then cantered on, panting heavily as it covered the rutted road toward Princeton.

Already the hills and mountains were taking on hues of gold and rust among the evergreens; soon the brilliant reds and oranges of the maples would add a riot of color to the landscape. Even the flatter lands around Princeton showed the dormant shades of fall and winter, and Dan had noticed several flocks of Canada geese honking their way south in scraggly arrowhead formation. The nights were growing too cool for using his bedroll along his route, and he had begun seeking indoor lodging.

Reaching the town, Dan slowed Flame to a trot. At the front entrance of the Lyons' Den he reined to a stop and saw towheaded Christopher Drummond bounding around the corner of the inn.

"Chip!"

"D-did you w-want me?"

"Yeah." Dan dismounted and flipped a coin in the lad's direction. "Would you mind giving my horse some water and feed? I'm in a bit of a hurry."

Chip eyed the money gleaming in his palm and closed his fingers over it. His expression brightened. "Sure thing! I'll s-see to him."

Nodding his thanks, Dan strode inside.

The sight of the dozen or more patrons already seated and being attended by Susannah sent his hopes into a downward spiral. Too late. He hung his hat on a peg by the door.

From across the room, Susannah caught his eye, and a surprised smile spread across her face. The generous folds of her dark blue skirt billowed as she hurried toward him. "Good day, Dan," she said breathlessly. "Have you come for dinner?"

He grinned. "That depends, actually."

"What ever do you mean?"

He swept a glance around the roomful of jovial customers who were eating the noon meal and engaging in good-natured chatter. "I wanted to talk to you. I thought perhaps we could take a walk down by the brook. Is Mary on duty today?"

Susannah looked crestfallen. "Normally she would be, but I'm afraid she's not feeling well. She's lying down."

"Well, guess I'll just have dinner, then." Trying to hide his disappointment at having to forgo his intended plan, he winked.

A soft blush accompanied her smile. "Of course. Just be seated. I'll bring your stew at once." With a swirl of indigo, she headed toward the kitchen, returning in a moment with his food in one hand and the coffeepot in the other. She set down his steaming bowl and made her way around to the other customers, filling their cups before returning to Dan. Pouring his coffee, she took a spare cup from the next table and, to his surprise, filled it for herself and sat down across from him. "It's lovely to see you again."

"Funny, I was about to say the same thing." He chewed a

chunk of biscuit slowly, studying her glowing face, her incredible eyes.

She took a small sip and set down her cup. "Thank you for the letter. I wanted to send a return post, but didn't know where it should go."

Her words set his spirit aloft. He nodded. "You can write to me in care of the post office in Boston, if you like. I work mostly in Massachusetts . . . much to my dismay," he added, spooning up some stew. His gaze feasted on her, fastening on the loose spiral curls feathering her face. He wished he could thread his fingers into them and draw her close for a kiss. Swallowing too quickly, he nearly choked. He cleared his throat to help himself recover. "I'm on my way to Philadelphia right now. I'm late, in fact. I'm off as soon as I'm finished."

"Oh." Susannah's lashes lowered. "I thought . . ."

Dan smiled gently. Fairly sure he wasn't the only one wishing he could stay longer, he put a hand over hers where it lay on the table.

Slowly she met his gaze.

"I'll be coming directly back to Princeton after that," he said. "Perhaps it will be more convenient, and we can talk then."

Conscious of the warmth of Dan's hand still covering her own, Susannah gently drew hers away. "Convenient or not, I'll try to arrange some time. I'm sure Mary will be feeling better by then."

"What seems to be the problem?" Dan dunked another biscuit into the remains of his stew.

She raised her eyebrows. "Do you recall Jonathan Bradford, the student who escorted her to church when you were last here?"

Dan nodded.

"Well, he hasn't returned from the harvest recess, and classes have already begun. He sent a letter saying he wouldn't come back this term, but it was quite vague. We have no idea what's kept him."

"Hm. Could be any number of logical reasons, you know."

"That's what I've been hoping. But Mrs. Lyons feels certain that his family learned of his interest in a penniless bond servant."

She stopped abruptly. Did Dan share the biased attitude so common among the more prominent class? Susannah waited, watching him, trying unsuccessfully to gauge the effect of her words on him.

"I've tried to convince Mary that perhaps money is lacking for the tuition," she went on at last. "But she says his family is quite prosperous. Not only do they own a large farm, but the local mill and cooperage as well. She is certain he has no intention of returning, ever. And his closing, 'with fondest regards' was no comfort to her whatsoever. She's taken to bed."

"That's too bad. The young man seemed quite smitten with her." Dan rubbed his jaw. "I'd tell Mary not to give up hope. Even if his family is a problem, in time he may convince them to allow him to return and resume his studies."

"I pray that is true."

"Speaking of returning," Dan began, "I—"

The door banged open as a group of laughing students clattered in, their robes askew as they jabbed one another and tried to avoid stumbling over their awkward feet. Making a beeline for Susannah, they surrounded her.

Dan attempted a friendly grin at the boisterous group, but it froze half-formed when Morgan Thomas unceremoniously picked Susannah up and swung her in a wide circle.

"Ah, but it's good to be back," he said, setting her down. "And to know you're here to brighten our day after those tedious classes."

Right at Morgan's elbow, Steven Russell grabbed both Susannah's hands in his. "You should've seen the way we bamboozled old 'Long Nose Barton' this morning with that *little question* you asked us last night. Things got so stirred up, he never did get back to his dreary lecture on Calvin's *Institutes of Christian Religion.*"

Feeling the outsider in this familiar group, Dan rose and began fastening the buttons of his coat.

Susannah cast him a helpless look, then transferred her attention to the students again. "Oh? You mean the one about two Christian states at war both assuming their position to be the correct one? How can God answer one's prayer for victory over the other?"

"Precisely," Morgan said, his dark eyes twinkling. "'Twas as if we'd tossed a hornet's nest into the room!"

"I'll say," Steven concurred. "Almost started a war of our own, then and there."

"You should have heard it!"

Watching the exuberant exchange, Dan released a pent-up breath and decided to make his exit. He wondered if Susannah would even notice. Turning, he shot a last glance over his shoulder as he crossed the room.

"Well, find yourself some seats, gentlemen," he heard Susannah say. "I'll be with you in just a moment."

Dan took his hat from the peg. Behind him he heard her light footsteps, then felt her touch on his arm. He turned and met her eyes.

"I'm terribly sorry about that," she said. "They get so caught up sometimes."

"I know. I remember feeling the same at their age." Suddenly that seemed a hundred years ago. And now, caught up as *he* was in the cause to regain the freedoms Britain had snatched away, he felt a nagging fear that these young students had a far greater advantage than he—that of being near Susannah every day. He let his gaze linger on her face, committing it to memory so he could call it up in the lonely nights ahead. "I expect to be back in two or three days, unless something unforeseen comes up."

"God be with you," she said softly.

With a tip of his head, he left, wondering how in the world he expected Susannah to wait around for him, with all those eager students at her beck and call. His shoulders slumped, and he kicked at a rock in his path.

Susannah hummed as she finished sweeping the floor of the ordinary. The reality of Dan's surprise visit—and even better, his expected return within two or three days—still sent tingles through her. Even the normally dismal chore of sweeping couldn't dim the smile on her face. If only she could share her happiness with Mary Clare! But such news would merely add bitterness and jealousy to her young friend's downheartedness.

Even as the thought lingered in Susannah's mind, Mary's footsteps sounded on the stairs. Susannah closed her eyes. *Please help me, heavenly Father. Give me something comforting to say to her that will help raise her spirits. It hurts so to see her in such melancholy—*

Suddenly the front door slammed, rattling the sconces on the long wall.

Rubbing a filthy hand over his splotched gray face, Silas Drummond staggered into the room. In worn and wrinkled clothes, his hair matted and wild, he quivered like an old man in his dotage. He stood in the entryway and gulped great breaths of air.

From the corner of her eye, Susannah saw Mary Clare shrink back against the stairwell. Then the girl's expression shifted. It became resigned, even disinterested, as though the person approaching her were a mere stranger.

Drummond's black eyes flitted from one to the other like a frightened animal's as he advanced toward his daughter.

Susannah regretted not having followed through with her threat to summon the sheriff during the last confrontation with Silas. She watched his face crumple miserably.

"Aw, gal," he whined to Mary Clare, "you can see I can't help m'self. Ain't had money for a drink in nigh three days, an' I'm powerful thirsty. Gotta have one, gal." His voice lowered to a groan. "Gotta have one now. I'll die if I don't." He flicked a glance toward the bar, then back at her.

Mary Clare stared at him evenly, with no apparent emotion, as he took a step closer.

Blocking Drummond with the broom, Susannah glowered

at him. "Go away, Mr. Drummond. You've sold your right to call this child your daughter. There's nothing more for you here."

A flinch of remorse brought a tear to his bloodshot eyes, but Susannah was more concerned with Mary Clare's fragile state of mind at the moment. She watched the man's grimace turn the girl's way.

"Please, gal, I'm beggin' ya. I need money. I'm dyin' for a drink. Just one's all. Take pity on your pa."

Lifting her chin, Mary whirled around and ran up the stairs.

Drummond started after her.

"No!" Susannah stopped his progress with the handle of the broom. "Don't even think of bothering her again. I insist that you leave. At once."

Silas shoved the broom aside and lashed at her with his arms. "Lemme alone! Get outta my way."

His useless flailing was easily dodged, but Susannah feared he'd resort to using some of the brute force she knew he possessed. "Go! Go away!" she yelled, her pulse beating erratically. She half expected him to strike her.

"Hey, what's all the hollerin' about?" Jasper said, clomping in from the kitchen. "I mighta knowed." Gesturing for Susannah to finish her work, Jasper took the man by the arm. "It appears like you need a swig real bad."

"Yeah. Hurt all over, I do. Nigh unto death."

"Well, come on over to the bar. I'll give you a jug, if you'll go nice and quiet like."

Drummond's dark eyes brimmed as he accepted the rum. His hands shaking, he tugged the cork out of the way, then lifted the jug for a long, slow drink. "You saved my life, Jasper. Bless ya." He replaced the cork.

"Just don't make me regret it. It does no good for the youngsters to see you in such a sorry state, you know. I wouldn't want to bring the sheriff down on you, but if you keep comin' back, you'd face up to thirty days without so much as one swallow of liquor. Keep that in mind."

Silas stiffened and gave a nod as he turned to leave.

Just then Mary Clare burst into the room, her arms filled with a tangle of voluminous skirts and ruffles and lace. Crossing the room with clipped steps, she faced her father. "Here! You want dresses? I'll give you dresses!"

Her eyes blazing, she flung all three of her Sunday gowns at his feet. "I have no use for them anyhow, thanks to you." Two bright circles flared high on her cheeks. "That is everything I own. Now get out and leave me alone. I never want to set eyes on you again. Ever!" Clamping her lips together, she turned and ran back up the staircase.

Susannah and Mr. Lyons stood gawking after Mary Clare in shock. Silas Drummond bent to scoop up the bounty.

"You're going to let him do it?" Susannah asked Mr. Lyons. "Let him actually take Mary's things like this?" Even as she spoke, she was making her way toward the despicable drunkard. "Well, I most certainly will not." Dropping the broom with a clatter, she grabbed at the clothes. "Unhand those gowns, you wretched man."

"She give 'em to me."

Susannah gasped in disbelief and tugged against his superior strength. "No!"

At last, just as Mr. Lyons started to come to her aid, Susannah saw Christopher come in the front door.

At once the lad charged over and threw himself on his pa's back, pounding him with both fists. "P-put them down. I hate you! I hate you! I'm g-gonna make you p-pay for this. I swear."

Reaching the scuffle, Mr. Lyons managed to separate the two. He held them at arm's length. "Silas, you'd best take your leave, before I turn the lad loose on you."

Drummond scowled at his son and the innkeeper, then, still clutching the dresses, grabbed the jug of rum he'd dropped in the struggle.

Susannah refused to let go. Yanking with all her might, the frocks gave way, catching her off balance. She landed on her backside with two of the gowns heaped over her as Silas bounded out the door with the third.

"Stop!" She scrambled to her feet to pursue.

Mr. Lyons stayed her with one arm, the other still trapping a squirming, wiggling Chip. "Let him go. Poor bedeviled fool needs it far more than Mary Clare does right now."

Dan watched Seth Parker unwrap the latest packet he'd just brought to the man's print shop.

Nodding his balding head slowly in silence, Parker eagerly assessed the items. "Good, good, Daniel, my lad. I'm glad to see you've brought more open letters from 'Vindex' and 'Determinatus.' Your Mr. Adams' essays are the only thing stirring up folks here in Philadelphia these days."

Dan grinned. "He's determined not to let the Colonies settle for those crumbs offered by Parliament through partial withdrawal of the Townshend Acts. He feels that if we accept one of their oppressions, it's the same as accepting the lot. After all, the Lord came to set us free, and civil liberty should be part and parcel."

With another nod of his head, Parker drew his lips together momentarily. "That last letter of his, though, was like opening a can of worms. It had to be passed around in an anonymous pamphlet so the shop wouldn't be implicated. I'll tell you, Daniel, the closer we get to the day of that trial over the Boston Massacre, the more aggressive those lobsterbacks become around here."

Dan straightened in his chair and peered outside. "I thought it was my imagination that there were more of them than usual loitering across the way."

"Not at all, my boy. Hardly a week passes when they're not in here to riffle through all my papers and make a holy mess of things. I'm sure they're hoping to catch me in the middle of printing something disloyal."

"Whew. I wouldn't want to be in your shoes. I've enough problems just carrying the mail, especially in or out of Boston. How do you manage?"

"Well, thanks to their own regimentation, I do have a wee chance to print the hot sheets. When they have reveille I put the time to good use, you might say. Then I dispose of the evidence—like I'd better do with these right now." Slipping Adams' letters into a narrow shelf attached to the bottom of the desk, he grinned and dusted his hands. "The redcoat dogs search all the drawers and look for secret compartments, but so far they haven't suspected a false bottom."

With a chuckle at the man's ingenuity, Dan stood and retrieved his leather pouch from the floor beside his feet. "Well, sir, I'd best be on my way."

Just as he turned, the door banged open, setting the bell above into motion. The noise rang through the cluttered room as four unkempt soldiers strode toward Dan.

"I'll take charge of this," a burly officer said, jerking the pouch from Dan's grasp. Flipping the cover open, he spilled the contents over the piled-up desktop.

"Knew it was him," said the second soldier. A gap-toothed sneer split his unshaven face as he slammed Dan up against the wall. "Ever since you rode into the city yesterday we've been watchin' for you to come here."

Out of the corner of his eye, Dan saw the other two sift through the letters from his bag. Knowing they were all innocent decoys, he maintained a composed expression. But only with great effort did he keep himself from voicing his opinion of the king's puppets.

The heavy officer nudged his cohort aside and grabbed Dan, turning him around. He leaned close, spewing his foul breath into Dan's face. "When you came flying into town as if you had rumors hot for the spreading, I found your flimsy excuses beyond belief. And I don't believe them now. You're lying sure as you're standing in front of me."

"What do you mean, my good man?" Dan asked innocently.

"Just this, lad. No regular postrider's ever so backlogged he can't tote all his mail. And *you* claimed to be in haste to deliver what was in your pack. Yet we find you here, with all the *same important letters,* all still waiting delivery. And besides that, consorting with this known rebel, here." He glared at Seth Parker. "What'd you bring him?"

Mr. Parker stepped forward. "My good sirs," he said evenly. "The lad brought me some advertising orders that had to go into the next edition of the paper, that's all." Crossing to the desk, he removed two forms from one of the cubbyholes and held them out. "Just some orders. These, in fact."

The gap-toothed soldier eyed Parker and the papers with suspicion. "And how does that explain the fact that our young man here's not been near the post office yet?"

The two pair cocked their heads with knowing grins. One shoved Dan hard against the wall again. "Aye. What d'ya say about that, laddie?"

Struggling for breath, Dan gritted his teeth. "I had to go by my cousin's house to deliver a message from my family. We got to talking. Had some wine. I lost track of time."

"Oh, is that so?" the stocky officer asked, a note of disdain in his tone. "And who, pray tell, would that illustrious 'cousin' be, if I might ask?"

"Somerwell," he stated. "Mr. Landon Somerwell."

The redcoat's bulging eyes flared with surprise. "Release him," he ordered, then cleared his throat and adjusted the collar of his uniform. "We meant you no disrespect, lad. Just doing our job, you understand." Then, resuming his authoritative stance, he leveled his stare at Dan again. "You'd do well to remember that as long as you frequent questionable establishments, you'll be under suspicion as well." He shot a pointed glance at Parker. With a nod toward his soldiers, he led the way outside.

Dan released an unsteady breath and relaxed as his pulse gradually returned to normal.

Parker picked up his clay pipe from the desktop and began filling it from a tobacco pouch in his pocket. "Looks like they've got the word out on you, too, lad."

"So it appears. Well, let's hope they keep it only to that. No telling what kind of retaliation might await us if those soldiers in Boston are convicted." Gathering the scattered letters and replacing them in his bag, he flipped the top closed. "Guess I'll be off."

"Keep watch, Daniel. Use every caution."

With a nod, Dan left the office and untied his horse at the rail. Who would have expected that kind of encounter? If the king's men had arrived a moment sooner, they would have had Adams' inflammatory letters in their hands, and Daniel himself might have been imprisoned for years, possibly even sent to the gallows. Attaching the pouch behind the saddle, he mounted Flame and headed up Fourth Street.

Then a horrible thought struck him. What if he *had* been caught? He would never again set eyes on his beautiful Susannah. . . .

An enticing vision surfaced of her dressed in a draped hoop gown, dancing gaily with him at the Christmas parties, her tawny hair piled in curls atop her head. His troubled thoughts churned within him as he tried to figure out some way to make that dream happen. Did she share his longings? If so, surely she'd agree to let him buy her papers and send her to his family, where she'd have someone to look after her. And they'd bring her with them to Cousin Landon's. It would all be quite proper, quite respectable.

But if he were to send her to his parents, the only possible reason would be that she was to be his wife. Yet how could he ask her to share his life, when he was in constant peril? That was more evident than ever, after today.

He groaned. Perhaps marriage would even be a hindrance to his mission right now; adding a wife would be like trying to serve two masters. The very thought wrenched his insides.

But if the soldiers on trial in Boston were found not guilty—which was entirely feasible, considering they were being attacked by a mob when they opened fire—things could begin to settle down. Parliament seemed to be getting more reasonable, of late. An amicable resolution to the tensions was quite possible.

And in his heart, Dan was more than convinced that Susannah Harrington was the mate God intended Dan to have. But did *she* share that same conviction? He had to be careful how he approached her, swarmed as she was every day by moonstruck fellows from the college. All too easily one of them could become a force to be reckoned with.

The thought sank in his gut like a rock. He'd have to go slowly, be businesslike. Yes, indeed. Slow and easy, the way a good horseman would approach a nervous filly.

Susannah walked briskly along the street from Curtis Duncan's office, admiring the colors on the tree-lined route back toward the inn. Already the elms had turned a glorious yellow, and with a light gust of autumn wind, a dozen or so leaves swirled lazily to the ground. It hadn't taken much of her day off to help the lawyer catch up on his backlog of correspondence, but she had left the Lyons' Den with some reluctance, considering Mary's state of mind—and, of course, the fact that Dan might arrive at any time.

As the thought of him came to the fore, she heard approaching hoofbeats, and her eyes focused on the familiar roan carrying Daniel Haynes. Happily she waved.

He drew Flame to a stop and jumped down, brushing the traveling dust from his coat and breeches. Removing his hat, he bowed with a flourish. "Good day, m'lady."

Conscious of her pinking cheeks, Susannah smiled. She was glad she had donned her rich sapphire velvet frock that morning. Seldom had Dan seen her in anything but her working clothes.

"Out for a stroll on this grand day?"

She shook her head. "Actually, I've just finished writing some letters for Attorney Duncan. He requested my assistance."

"So you're working for him, too?"

Noting the odd expression on Dan's face, Susannah wondered if he disapproved. "Only on occasion. I'm on my way back to the coaching house now."

His eyebrows rose in question. "Dare I assume you have a free afternoon?"

Susannah answered with a smile and a nod.

"A chance to have you to myself? Splendid." Letting the

horse's reins drop, Dan tipped his head. "I've something important for you to consider." Taking her elbow, he guided her to a low stone wall edging the road and gestured for her to have a seat.

Willing herself not to imagine what important news Dan wished to impart, Susannah tried to still her pounding heart. But her mind ran ahead of her will. What could be of greater import than marriage? Even in her dearest dreams she doubted that Daniel Haynes, the most handsome man she'd ever met, and who most certainly knew every marriageable maiden in all the northern colonies, would ever truly propose to her. Of course, there *was* the matter of her indenturement, but she had already served half the allotted time. In just a matter of months she would be free. She clasped her hands together in her lap to keep them from shaking.

Dan eased down beside her, moving a fold of her skirt aside as he turned to face her. His neck took on a mottled shade of rose. "I've been very concerned about you."

"Oh?"

"Since that day last spring when I sent those drunken louts on the Philadelphia wharf packing, I've thought of little else than your predicament."

Susannah studied his face, trying not to lose herself in the liquid depths of his eyes as she waited breathlessly for him to continue.

"Then after I learned of your . . . circumstance, that a gentle lady such as yourself had fallen victim to problems beyond her control, I found myself even more concerned. Since I was one of the first Americans you met upon your arrival in the Colonies, you must know I feel a certain . . . responsibility toward you."

"You've been most kind. I appreciate that."

He nodded. "And now my conscience will no longer allow me to ride off and leave you in this compromised state—especially since you've told me about young Mary Clare, and how being indentured has been a severe hindrance to her dreams of future happiness."

"What ever are you trying to say? I don't understand." Susannah twisted a section of blue velvet in her fingers as she searched Dan's eyes.

He turned his tricornered hat nervously in his hands. Then he raised his gaze. "I intend to approach Mr. Lyons this very day and purchase your papers. I've already arranged passage for you from Philadelphia to Rhode Island, where you'll stay at my family's horse farm. They're fine people. They'll treat you well."

He'll buy my papers? she thought with disdain. *They'll treat me well?* Disappointment, bordering on rage, brought Susannah instantly to her feet. Why, it was not marriage at all that this pompous postrider was proposing! He merely wanted to send her into servitude someplace else. How very noble! And how very stupid she had been ever to have dreamed someone like him could possibly have true feelings for her.

She noticed absently that Daniel had also risen and appeared to be awaiting her response. Susannah raised her chin, and with every ounce of inner strength she possessed, she forced herself to look at his face, but not directly into his eyes. Calling up whatever dignity she could muster, she managed to control her tone. "Why, that is most kind of you, Mr. Haynes." It amazed even her to hear how composed she sounded. "I'm sure I shall never forget your *generous* offer. But let me assure you, I am quite content to serve my time out where I am. In fact, I am exactly where I want to be."

Not even the sight of his eyes widening in disbelief stemmed her words, and she gave them free rein. "I am blessed with many good Christian friends. And I deem my reputation a very small sacrifice for the incredibly great rewards of the new and stimulating theology I hear discussed at the inn. Now, if you'll be so kind as to excuse me, I've not been feeling quite myself this afternoon." Straightening her spine, she turned and walked with clipped precision the remaining yards to the inn.

Her pulse thundered in her ears. Susannah barely heard Dan call softly to his horse, which had wandered off in its grazing, and then heard him run after it. Without looking back, she grabbed for the latch and yanked the door open.

Inside, Susannah saw Mary Clare folding napkins at the bar. New sympathy for her young charge flooded her as she realized her own pain could not match Mary's. Squaring her shoulders, Susannah rushed past the girl and approached the staircase. "I'm afraid I'm feeling rather ill," she said. "I don't wish to be disturbed. By anyone." With a last pained glance toward the door, she hurried up to the attic.

Dan stepped cautiously into the common room and found it virtually empty for the first time since his recent travels had brought him back to Princeton. Except for Mary, working at some task all alone, no one else was present. Hope faded as he scanned all the corners in a fruitless search for Susannah. He drew a fortifying breath and took a step toward the bar.

"I wouldn't bother comin' any further." Her words fell like chunks of ice into Dan's heart and sent a chill through the ordinary.

The brittle hardness in Mary Clare's face and manner stunned him. He cast a fleeting glance in the direction of the stairs. *What the devil happened?* What had he said that could have killed Susannah's good favor so completely? Heavy of heart, he turned and left. He marched resolutely toward the hitching post, untied Flame, and mounted, nudging him forward.

What a fool he had been, to assume that Susannah felt the same intense feelings that burned inside him! If she so completely rejected his offer to secure her papers, there was no telling with what finality she might have refused an offer of marriage. That would have been the ultimate humiliation. Perhaps this was God's way of letting him know he should keep his mind and his purpose focused on the more important task of helping freedom's cause. After all, it wasn't as if there were a lack of eligible bachelors in this town. For all he knew, Susannah Harrington could have gone wading with every boy at the college by now!

22

The next endless days and weeks passed in a blur of sameness for Susannah as the short days of mid-December crept upon her. Her gloom matched Mary Clare's. Not even the glorious covering of new snow that brightened the landscape outside could bolster her spirits. In two weeks she would experience her first Christmas alone, with no family at all. Julia was dead, her parents were dead—and Ted might as well be, she thought with a sigh. He hadn't answered a single one of her letters.

"Deck the halls with boughs of holly . . ." The cheery holiday chorus rose up as Susannah carried a tray of food to a group of early evening revelers caught up in the spirit of the season. A crackling fire blazed in the huge fireplace, and the candles and oil lamps cast a flickering bronze glow throughout the ordinary.

"And what might ol' Father Christmas be bringin' you this year, lass?" a new arrival asked. Unbuttoning his black wool greatcoat, he grinned, then accepted the plate Susannah set before him.

She forced a semblance of a smile. "Why, I've no idea."

"Well, well," the patron continued, "he knows just what you'll be needin'. Be sure of that."

With a nod, she turned away, and her smile faded. What she *needed* was the knowledge that somebody on this earth still cared about her. One Christmas ago she had been blissfully unaware that life would turn the tables on her. Now every carol brought home to her all the sadness that filled her being. This year there would be no church pageant reenacting the holy birth, no nights gathered around the organ singing of the glad tidings, no hushed whisperings about secret gifts. She had expected that her new faith would provide peace and joy, as she had felt upon finding salvation, but even her Bible offered little comfort.

The squeak of the door hinge brought her out of her reverie as Ralph Nelson, the newest driver of the Philadelphia-Princeton route, followed his passengers in on a gust of cold air. Susannah watched him stomp snow off his big boots and hang his heavy coat and hat on a peg before making his way toward a side table where Mary Clare sat sipping hot cider.

"Hi, sweets," he said with a huge smile as he raked a hand through his curly rust-colored hair. "I brought you somethin'."

Susannah frowned as she watched Mary's expression brighten. The younger girl returned the man's smile and reached for the package he held out toward her. His large hand covered Mary's on the table and lingered.

Susannah clenched her teeth and slammed the dirty dishes onto a tray. Although he was attractive in a rough sort of way, with his freckled face and jovial disposition, the man was much too old for an impressionable girl like Mary Clare.

Blushing shyly, Mary ducked her head, then raised it boldly as she tore off the wrapping with eager fingers. "Ohh," she breathed.

Susannah picked up the dishes and headed for the kitchen. If she thought for a moment that Mary would listen to her, she would lecture her on the proper behavior of a young maiden. But since Jonathan's letter, Mary Clare had withdrawn into her own bitterness, blaming Susannah and God for holding out that ray of hope to her and then just as quickly snatching it away. Neither Mary nor Chip had been to church in weeks. Mary couldn't abide having people looking at her with pity, and Chip wasn't about to listen to any more sermons on forgiveness—not even from the students he had so admired. His hatred of his father seemed to grow more fierce with each passing day.

Returning from the kitchen, Susannah noticed a man wave from the other side of the room. "Some flip, please, miss?"

She nodded in acknowledgment and stepped to the bar.

Mr. Lyons rubbed his jowls, then filled an earthen pitcher with the amber liquid. With Methuselah riding on his shoulder, he reached for the hot poker at the brazier and dipped it into the brew.

The sizzling sound took Susannah back a hundred nights. Perhaps she *was* to blame for Mary Clare and Chip's unhappiness. Hadn't Mrs. Lyons warned her in the beginning that even the best of intentions could go awry? She shrugged off the thought. Surely God wouldn't allow more hurt to be heaped upon those unfortunate children—would he? Or was she deluding herself that her prayers were even heard, let alone answered? After all, she had been so certain that God's plan had brought Daniel Haynes into her life. . . .

Mr. Lyons bent to replace the glowing rod, then straightened. "You'd best sleep with one eye open," he said quietly as he flicked a glance toward Mary. "That no-account driver's been stalking Mary Clare for weeks. Wouldn't be surprised if he tried to bed her, with the drivers' room just across the attic. And her droopin' in the mouth like she is, she'd fall for any smooth talker. We sure don't need a child like her comin' up sullied, and with a big belly besides."

Susannah blushed at his crude words. "Why, I'm most certain nothing like that has happened, Mr. Lyons."

"Just see that it doesn't, is all I'm sayin'. Keep her in that room—even if you have to tie her to the bed. I'll have me a talk with the bounder first chance I get."

With a nod, Susannah turned. Out of the corner of her eye she saw Mary rise, and with a shy smile at Ralph Nelson, she made her way up to the attic.

"Just finish serving these drinks," Mr. Lyons said. "Then go on upstairs. I'll be takin' care of the rest of things tonight."

Susannah felt someone's hand shaking her arm. She sat up with a start. Was it morning already? She felt as if she had just closed her eyes.

Still in her nightgown, Mary Clare stood over her. A candle burned on the night table between their cots, casting wavy shadows in the early morning darkness.

Susannah wondered how long Mary had been awake.

"I think I must be comin' down with somethin'," the younger girl said. "I have a real bad headache, and I feel hot. Could you take my place and serve breakfast?"

"Of course." Flipping the blankets aside, Susannah swung her feet to the floor. Despite the small rag rug between the two beds, the cold made her toes curl. She rose and put a hand to Mary's forehead. "I don't think you've got a fever, but perhaps it would be best if you stay in bed." She crossed to the armoire and took out a work dress. After donning it and brushing her hair, she gave Mary a comforting pat. "I shall come up later and check on you."

"You don't have to. No sense wearin' yourself out goin' up and down the stairs all day."

"Nonsense. I'll be worried about you, you know."

"Suit yourself, then." Giving a toss of blonde hair, Mary Clare climbed into her bed and turned her back.

Susannah's mind kept returning to her young roommate all morning. It seemed that there were twice as many customers as usual, but when the last of them had finally departed, she piled the dishes to one side and mounted the stairs to the attic. Quietly she lifted the latch so as not to disturb the sleeping girl.

The room was silent. Empty. Both beds were neatly made.

Susannah's heart lurched, and she struggled to breathe around the foreboding dread that clogged her throat. Swallowing hard, she walked to the armoire and threw open

Mary's side. Everything belonging to the younger girl was gone. And Susannah's own satchel was nowhere to be seen.

Barely closing the door behind her, Susannah raced downstairs to the kitchen. "Mrs. Lyons!"

The older woman was scraping fresh vegetables from the cutting board into the kettle of stew. "What is it, child?"

Susannah ran her tongue nervously over her lips as her mind groped for words.

"You look a sight. What on earth is the matter?"

"It—it's Mary. She's . . . gone."

Mrs. Lyons put a hand to her bosom. "What?"

"She's gone. There was that stage driver, last night, and she must have . . . Oh, it's too horrible even to imagine."

"Merciful heavens!" Mrs. Lyons sank onto a chair, clutching at handfuls of her work apron. Her small round eyes glistened with tears. "Merciful heavens."

"Where is Mr. Lyons?" Susannah asked. "Perhaps he can go after them before . . . before something bad happens."

"Yes," the woman said, coming to her feet. "Yes, you're right. Jasper can go after her. Where is he?" Shaking her head in confusion, she put a hand to her temples. "What day is it?"

"Saturday."

"Oh yes. We needed flour. He had to go to the miller's. We'll have to send Christopher to get him."

"But that's almost two miles away. He's sure to be well on his way back by now."

"Well, we can't just sit and do nothin', now, can we?" Rushing to the back door, she wrenched it open.

"Christopher! Come quick! Hurry!"

Within moments the boy came in, his face glowing from the cold air. "What's wrong?"

"I need you to run to the grist mill and fetch Jasper, quick as you can."

"Why? What happened?"

"There's no time for talkin'. Just go. Now!"

With a shrug, Christopher took off at a run, casting a puzzled glance backward.

Mrs. Lyons began pacing the length of the kitchen, wadding her apron in her gnarled hands. "I knowed somethin' like this was going to happen. I just knowed it. Nothin' anyone's said to her since Jonathan didn't come back has made the slightest difference. It's like she's given up on herself completely and doesn't care anymore."

"I know," Susannah said softly. "She's stopped all her lessons. Chip has, too."

Mrs. Lyons wagged her head sadly. "I just don't know what to do about them. They was doin' so well, acting like regular kids. I just don't know." After a moment she got up again. Grabbing a shawl from the back of a chair, she threw it on and walked quickly through the common room and out the front door, heading down the drive to the post road.

Susannah whipped a tablecloth from one of the side tables and wrapped it around her shoulders as she followed Mrs. Lyons, ignoring the cold. Their breath made little clouds of mist that blended together as they stood staring down the road. "This is all my fault," Susannah whispered.

"Now, don't you be sayin' that, love," Mrs. Lyons said, turning her concerned gaze toward Susannah. "Don't even be thinkin' it. There's no blame to be put on anybody. Mary and Christopher were headed down this sad road long before you ever came along. Why, before you, there was nobody except Jasper and me who cared a whit about either of 'em. And you tried your best. Nobody can fault you for that."

Shivering, Susannah attempted a weak smile and hugged herself for warmth.

"None of us can stop what's already set in motion anymore'n you can stop the sun from rising."

"None of *us,* perhaps," Susannah said. "But God could have stopped it. Why didn't he stop it? I prayed and p-prayed." Her voice quivered on the last word, and the tears she had kept at bay finally brimmed and broke over her lashes.

Mrs. Lyons put a comforting arm around Susannah's slim form. "I don't know what's the matter with me, dragging you outside in this freezing weather with nary a shawl to keep you warm. We'd best go wait inside, before both of us catch our death."

She gave Susannah a loving squeeze as they walked back. "We've all been doing our share of prayin', love. We can't always see the reasons why things happen in this life. But we mustn't lose faith. The good Lord gave us free choice, and he doesn't interfere with that, even if sometimes we wish he would."

"But it hurts so."

"I know." She stopped suddenly. "Oh, I think I hear the wagon comin'. Dry your tears. I don't want the boy to see you so upset."

Lifting a corner of her apron, Susannah wiped her face and did her best to compose herself.

Mr. Lyons' one-horse wagon approached at a fast clip, the runners making a swishing sound on the packed snow. He drew back on the reins as he and Christopher neared the inn. "What is it, woman?"

"It's Mary," Mrs. Lyons answered. "She's gone off with that brigand stage driver, just like you figured she would. You gotta go after her right now."

"Mary's run off?" Christopher asked, his eyes wide with disbelief. "Without t-telling me? She w-w-wouldn't."

Mr. Lyons sat immobile. Only his eyes moved as he stared first at his wife, then at Susannah.

"Come on, Jasper," Mrs. Lyons urged. "We'll help unload the flour. There's not a minute to waste."

"It's already too late," he said. "They've been gone for what—three hours? Four? This old nag of ours is no prime stage horse. No hope of us catchin' 'em."

Susannah's lips parted. "You can't mean that. We can't just let that man take Mary and—and have his way with her."

He turned his craggy face toward her, and the sag of his shoulders added years to his age. "Look, the die's been cast. All we can do is hope she sees the error of her ways herself and comes back on the next stage."

"And if she doesn't?" Susannah whispered. The thought chilled her more than the freezing temperature.

His expression turned grim. "If she doesn't, I'll have the driver arrested next time he comes through. Either he'll return her to us, or buy me out and marry her. If the scoundrel doesn't already have a wife, that is."

Two nights had passed since Mary's disappearance, and the return stage was due in at any moment.

Susannah couldn't find it in herself to join in the merriment at the hilarious comment Morgan made to his two friends as they pored over a textbook near the hearth. Oblivious to their laughter, she wiped down a table near the door.

The jingle of a harness carried from outside as a team of horses neared the inn.

Susannah dropped her cloth and ran out, hoping against hope that Mary Clare had come to her senses and returned. A movement behind a bush next to the inn caught her eye, and she turned to see Chip hiding there, gripping a stout club. She leaned over and grabbed him by the arm, yanking him upright. "Just what do you think you're doing, young man?"

He tried to jerk free, but she held fast. "I'm gonna k-kill that r-r-rotten lecher," he spat. "N-nobody's gonna stop me."

Expelling a breath of frustration, Susannah glanced up at the driver, his face illuminated by the dim stage lanterns. He was not the culprit. She shot a look of exasperation at Chip.

He relaxed and dropped the weapon, and the instant she let go, he trudged off around the corner. Susannah heard his muffled sob, sounding as if it tore from his heart.

She ached for the lad, knowing he was at the end of his endurance. "Excuse me," she said, returning her gaze to the wagon. "This is the stage from Philadelphia, is it not?"

"That it is." The lean, muscular man jumped down from the seat and prepared to assist the passengers.

"But where is the regular driver?" she asked.

"Him? Oh, he up and quit t'other day, right out of the blue.

It was my lucky day, I'd say." With a loud laugh, he gave a hand to the first lady to step out of the conveyance, then reached for the second. "Been prayin' for steady work for two months, now. Fact is, I was sittin' at the table with the wife and kids— poor meal it was, too—prayin' to the Almighty about a job, and there comes a knock at the door. And who was standin' there but the owner of the line. I'd been there twice askin'—"

"Why, that's wonderful," Susannah said, breaking in. "Truly. But where is Mr. Nelson?"

"Can't say. And he didn't have no friends I could ask, far as I know."

"Oh." Dejected, Susannah whirled around to step inside, missing one of the passengers by mere inches. With a wan smile of apology, she followed the group in.

Morgan Thomas was leaning against the doorjamb, a strange grin playing over his mouth as she closed the door behind herself. "I take it Mary's not back, and neither is the ne'er-do-well."

Susannah's shoulders drooped, and she gave him a weary look. "Right on both counts. I feel so helpless. Mr. Lyons is threatening to have the man arrested on sight, but all I can think about is our poor little Mary. Dragged off to the big city without a soul to turn to, with no money of her own."

Morgan cocked his head to one side, and the typical devilish spark in his dark blue eyes disappeared. "Perhaps it'll be all right. Perhaps the fellow really cares about her and will look after her. It's not impossible, you know. She's quite the sweet girl."

"I do hope you're right. But the man was such a blatant flirt. He made passes at anyone in a skirt, including me. I doubt he could suddenly have become enamored with just our dear Mary."

Morgan shrugged.

"And now he's quit his job," Susannah continued. "Even if he knew there'd be the piper to pay if he ever showed his face around here again, it still was irresponsible, to say the least."

"Quite right. If old man Lyons didn't shoot the bounder

outright with that pistol he keeps behind the bar, he'd use it to march him down to Sheriff Banks' place."

"I know," Susannah moaned with despair. "But I've just got to do something to help poor Mary."

"Tell you what," Morgan said, his tone barely serious. "Get out your fanciest ball gowns, and—"

"My ball gowns?" Susannah planted her fists on either side of her waist and glared. "Why, Morgan Thomas, you've not been listening to a single word I've said."

"Oh, but I have. And now it's your turn to listen. I've a proposition to make. Sit down and hear me out."

Susannah swept a glance around the room, then back to Morgan. "I've got a roomful of passengers to tend to just now. Mr. Lyons will have my head if I don't get busy."

"So I'll wait here until you take care of them." He grinned disarmingly and gestured with his head for her to be off.

Curious to find out what Morgan had to say, Susannah worked swiftly until the travelers ran out of orders. At last, blowing a wisp of hair out of her eyes, she returned to the table where Morgan sat watching her.

He rose and pulled out the chair for her, then took his own seat again.

"You were saying something about ball gowns?"

A wide grin spread across his face for an instant and then transformed into an expression of sincerity. "I'm just as worried about Mary Clare as you are. And so is Jonathan, whether you believe it or not."

Susannah's eyebrows rose. "Oh? I must say, he's got a strange way of showing his concern, considering we've not had a word from him for over two months."

"Well, I've had word. Just last week, in fact. He wants to come back. Desperately. He specifically asked Steven and me to look after Mary until he can persuade his family to allow him to return."

"They kept him home because of her, didn't they?"

He nodded. "He didn't want her to know. The bloke's far too trusting, too naive. He never once thought his family would be so narrow-minded. He's not nearly so mature as I am." At her scornful look, he grinned and shrugged. "Speaking of that, I've a proposition for you."

Susannah crossed her arms. "I can't wait to hear it."

"No, no. Nothing like that. Honestly, Susannah, I'm crushed that you'd think me a person of ungentlemanly tendencies."

She laughed lightly. "Do forgive my rash judgment, then."

"Done. But I've an idea which could solve both our problems."

"You, the carefree son of a prominent Philadelphia merchant, have problems? I find that incredibly hard to believe."

His intent expression did not waver. "I'm booked to leave here Wednesday on the next stage. I must go home for the holidays, you see. My mother and three sisters have graciously chosen my future bride for me, and my father is in agreement with them."

"And you're not?"

"I've not even met the girl. But Father says it would be good for business—that's the deciding factor where he is concerned. He also feels I should quit this school, especially since Witherspoon is turning all the students into a bunch of disloyal rebels. He wants me to come home and take up my responsibilities at the warehouse, where I'm needed. Now that the Boston trial is ending so amicably—as he puts it— with the British soldiers up in Boston being found innocent, the boycott is all but over. Orders are pouring in for goods from abroad."

"I don't understand what all of this has to do with Mary."

"I'm getting to that." He paused for a moment, then looked directly at Susannah. "If you will accompany me to Philadelphia, I swear I'll not rest until we find Mary Clare."

Forgetting propriety, Susannah grabbed his hands. "You're quite serious? You would do that?"

"Absolutely. But, in return—"

She let go and leaned back. Apparently, everything had a price.

"Once we rescue the girl, you must agree to accompany me to the round of holiday parties. You know, keep me safe from that simpering ninny they've picked for me."

Susannah's relief came out in a whoosh of breath. Despite her own inner turmoil, she could see the humor in Morgan's predicament. "How can you be so unchivalrous?"

"I prefer to choose my own wife." He gave the barest flicker of a wink.

Warmth rose slowly into Susannah's cheeks. "If I do agree to go with you—and I do mean *if*—it will be for the sole purpose of finding Mary. I wouldn't want you to read anything further into it."

"As you wish. For now, being saved from the females in my family will suffice. And believe me, with them constantly flitting about, your honor will have absolutely no chance of being compromised." He snorted in disgust. "None at all."

"Well, tempting as the offer sounds, I can't see how I could go." Susannah glanced around the common room. "I'm indentured here, you know. And with Mary gone, we're more shorthanded than we've ever been. How could I possibly even consider leaving just now?"

Morgan leaned forward on his elbows. "What if I were able to find someone to fill in for you?"

23

The sharp December wind rattled the branches of barren trees along the city street, driving holiday customers inside the shops—as much to seek shelter as to purchase gifts for the season.

Ted huddled down into the warmth of his military cape and stepped over an icy spot in the walkway. He gave a brief nod to a couple approaching a waiting phaeton, their arms laden with brightly wrapped packages. Once out of earshot, he turned to Alex. "I say, old man. Doesn't it seem to you that we could as easily be in London at this instant as here in Philadelphia?"

"What do you mean?"

Ted gestured with his head toward the people they had just passed. "The residents of the city seem to afford us all due respect. Takes a good deal away from our purpose for being here—teaching the ungrateful colonists that the Crown is still in control. We've yet to encounter a single hostile individual since our arrival a week past. I can't help wishing your illustrious cousin had seen to it that we were stationed in Boston. Surely there's much more action there."

Alex chuckled. "Sorry to disillusion you, old chap, but I doubt that a post at Boston would have made much difference. From what I've been told, once the truth was brought to light at the trial over that so-called massacre, even the subjects up in Massachusetts have quieted down."

"More's the pity." Coming upon an arrangement of shiny knives and tools displayed in a store window, Ted stopped for a moment to look at them, then turned back to Alex. "Still, if only we had known before our departure from Britain that things here would settle down so quickly, we could have requested a post in some more exotic place. India. The Orient. 'Twould have been far more adventurous."

A group of young colonials came out just then, full of laughter and jovial banter. They nodded politely to Ted and Alex, and the last young man lifted a hand and waved as they walked on down the row of gaily decorated stores and businesses.

As Ted began walking again, Alex fell into step. "Actually, it isn't out of the question for us to find a taste of the exotic here, if we give it a chance. Even in a provincial town like this there's sure to be an enchanting maiden or two. And with everyone milling about in preparation for the holidays, we've a great opportunity to view the assortment, don't you think?"

"I suppose." Ted's hopes rose a notch. "Have there been many invitations requesting our presence at the Christmas parties as yet?"

"Five, so far. And from some very influential merchants, I understand."

"All desiring to associate with the Lord Hillsborough's relative, no doubt."

"Quite." Alex hiked his brows and snickered. "But so long as I am permitted to become acquainted with their lovely daughters, it's fine with me. Speaking of which—" He made a grand sweep with one arm as they turned the corner.

Ted followed Alex's gaze to where clusters of people stood looking into the windows of various clothing, millinery, and specialty shops. At once his eyes picked out a dozen fair young lasses attired in fur-trimmed pelisses or rich velvet cloaks over their gowns. "Yes. I'm beginning to see what you mean."

Alex brushed off his uniform and straightened his hat. "What do you say we investigate, old chap?"

"Capital idea. We might even ask the loveliest ones to save us dances at the upcoming balls."

They crossed the cobbled street, dodging a pair of middle-aged women coming from the opposite direction.

Ted bestowed a benign smile on them as they passed, then turned his attention forward again. His eyes, as if drawn by some invisible magnet, came to rest on an enticing maiden several paces ahead, laughing and chatting with two younger girls as they came toward the next shop. The copper-haired lass with her huge brown eyes and skin flawless as an English rose could not have been more perfect had he been dreaming. He halted abruptly and stared in shock. Here was the epitome of all his fantasies.

Alex stopped as well. "Is something amiss?"

Realizing he was gaping, Ted closed his mouth. But he didn't even try to stop the smile that spread across his face of its own volition. The vision looked his way just then, and after a brief eternity, lowered her gaze demurely. Ted swallowed. "Alex, old man, the rest of the street is yours for the taking. I've made my choice."

"You jest." Alex searched the faces in sight.

"No. She's the one I've been looking for. The one with the magnificent red hair." As he spoke, she lifted her eyes once more and curved the edges of her lips enticingly.

Ted had to go to her. Not once looking away, he walked toward her as if no other people existed in the world except for the two of them. Reaching the maiden, he captured her gloved hand in his in a bold move that surprised even him. And even more incredibly, as her two companions gasped in shock, he heard his own voice whisper his deepest, most secret thought. "I thought I would never find you."

Her eyes grew wide, and she moistened her lips.

Ted suddenly remembered himself. "Your pardon, miss. I'm Lieutenant Theodore Harrington, recently arrived from England. I would be most honored if you would call me Ted."

"Of course," she said in the throaty voice he knew she would have. "But only if you will call me Jane."

With his mouth set in a grim line, Dan descended the elaborate staircase leading to the main floor of the Somerwell mansion. The polished walnut handrail gleamed, reflecting glints of light from the tall foyer windows. He was careful not to mar the dark shining wood with a fingerprint, instead occupying his hands with smoothing the frilly lace front of his new shirt. Why his mother had insisted upon commissioning a new wardrobe for him for the holidays was a mystery, not to mention a needless expense. He had plenty of clothes at home. He reached the first landing, made a turn, and continued down.

His mother and her cousin Rose, looking like two more flower clusters against the floral rug, stood conversing in their bright draped gowns before the hall mirror. Cousin Rose stood half a head taller than his mother, though they had similar bearing. Her wide-set blue eyes sat above a rather prominent nose, but her well-shaped mouth drew attention away from it. At his approach, the two women looked up.

"Yes," his mother said. "You can see for yourself the fine workmanship our new tailor put into Daniel's ensemble. I was somewhat hesitant to try a new craftsman, but I found the quality more than worth the expense. Turn around, dear, so Rose can see you."

"Really, Mother," he began. But at the disappointed look on her face he rolled his eyes and followed orders.

"Oh yes," Cousin Rose said, tipping her head to one side as she spoke, a mannerism typical of her. Her sharp voice had a decidedly irritating quality to it, but she managed to minimize it unless she was agitated. Arms folded across her bosom, she tapped a finger against one side of her mouth as she surveyed Dan's appearance. "Most exquisite. And you say the tailor works out of Providence, yet. How fortunate. Lottie must see this. Charlotte!" she called.

Dan held his breath, wishing for all the world that he were somewhere else running messages for Sam Adams.

His cousin appeared at once in the doorway of the dining room, thin as six o'clock in her green silk gown. Her bouncy strawberry blonde curls did not quite offset the prominence of her nose, which was a replica of her mother's and stuck out in solitary splendor on her gaunt face. "Yes, Mama," she said, stopping abruptly as she caught sight of Dan. "Oh." She tried to hide her amusement behind a painfully thin white hand.

"What do you think of your handsome cousin Dan, my dear?" her mother prodded. "Is he not far above the mark in his new attire?"

Charlotte giggled.

Dan groaned inwardly, but managed a polite smile. Would that girl ever open her mouth without emitting that annoying snicker? He watched her swallow another laugh, and he braced himself for her high-pitched voice, not as controlled as her mother's.

"Oh yes. He's quite the catch of the season. For some lucky girl, of course." Averting her gaze, she snickered again.

Dan felt his smile growing brittle. In his tight aqua velvet breeches he felt like a peacock, ready to be plucked and served up on a silver platter. He released a sigh. "Well, ladies, shall we join the others?"

At that moment, several voices echoed from the parlor as Dan's father and his mother's cousin Landon stepped into the entry hall, followed by Benjamin, looking tall and filled-out in his rust velvet breeches. On either arm were Jane and Emily in gowns of rustling taffeta.

Even Dan noticed how splendid everyone looked in evening attire, and he felt less awkward. "Good evening, Cousin Landon," he said with a nod.

"Why, Daniel," the tall, impeccably dressed man boomed. His broad smile emphasized the laugh lines beside his mouth. The deep set of his eyes emphasized the receding of his gray hair above a high, wide forehead. "So glad you were able to join us for the occasion. It's been some time." He extended a hand and grasped Dan's warmly.

"Thank you, sir. Good to be here."

"Well, then, since everyone is present, let's go in to supper. Cook's getting irritated."

"And you know," Cousin Rose said, tilting her head, "how difficult it is for one to find someone on this primitive continent who is competent enough to prepare pheasant amandine." She took her husband's arm, and they led the way to the dining room.

Resplendent in café-au-lait satin, Dan's father ushered his mother in next, followed by Ben and his two sisters in an extremely smooth move that left only Charlotte unescorted. Dan swept a glance her way and reminded himself to be nice. The poor girl probably had little opportunity to enjoy male company.

She gave a snorting little laugh and fidgeted, a rosy blush brightening her cheeks.

Drawing a breath for composure, he grinned and cocked an elbow. "Shall we?" He barely caught Ben's wink and Emily's understanding smile over their shoulders.

It came as no surprise to Dan that the first ones into the room chose the prime seats around the rectangular mahogany table, with Cousin Landon and Cousin Rose at opposite ends. Dan casually pulled out one of the two remaining empty chairs for Charlotte and seated her, then took the last position, between her and his mother.

Immediately, their host rang a small silver bell at his place.

Servants in black coats and starched white shirts carried in the platters of food, set them along the table, then left quietly.

"Well," Cousin Landon said, beaming over the gathering, "it has been a ghastly long time since the whole family has come together under our roof. Let us give thanks for our blessings." He bowed his head. "Almighty God, we thank thee for this wonderful feast and for these days of growing peace that allow us to enjoy this opportunity to share our bounty with those we love. We ask thy blessing upon us all. Amen." Looking up again, he gazed at everyone. "It's a great pity that Christmas comes but once each year."

Everyone nodded and smiled.

"And rest assured," he continued, smoothing his dark mustache absently with a finger, "my dear wife has every moment planned, right up to Christmas Eve. We've all been given our marching orders." Picking up the bowl of mashed potatoes, he helped himself and passed them to Dan's mother, on his right.

Charlotte made a futile attempt to appear serious.

Emily moaned softly and shifted in her chair as her father nudged her in the ribs and passed the cranberries.

"Why, Landon," Cousin Rose scoffed, putting a slice of succulent pheasant on her plate. "You make me sound like one of those sergeants down on the wharf." She shook her head in mock disgust.

Unsummoned, a memory of Susannah Harrington surfaced in Dan's mind as he filled his plate. He saw her as he had upon first sight, dressed in emerald velvet, with seagulls soaring overhead against a billowy backdrop of blue and white. He barely heard the end of his uncle's patronizing apology.

Jane inclined her head, spilling her curls forward across her shoulder. "Oh, speaking of soldiers, Charlotte, Emily, and I met two of the most handsome and charming officers today while we were out at the shops." Her rich brown eyes sparkled as she cast a conspiratorial look across the table at Charlotte, then glanced at Dan.

Charlotte tittered into her napkin.

Obviously this conversation was a ploy to make Cousin Charlotte seem somewhat desirable. But the girl was barely sixteen. Dan hoped that the coming years would show her some kindness, fill her out a bit, perhaps. Compared to her, even Emily's newly blossoming frame seemed quite appealing. And next to effervescent Jane, Charlotte would be all but invisible. Oh well, he consoled himself, at least the food served this evening was good. He would live with whatever else transpired . . . somehow.

Dan's mother smoothed her pompadour and raised an eyebrow. "Why, Jane, I find it most disconcerting to learn that you speak to strange men. Don't you, Edmond?"

"Yes, my dear, I do." Her father drilled her with a stare as anxious lines rippled his forehead. "Young lady, I sincerely hope you are not forgetting to conduct yourself in ladylike fashion."

Jane gave a toss of her head. "Oh, you two dears mustn't concern yourselves. The officers we met come with the most impeccable credentials. Why, one of them is actually related to Lord Hillsborough."

Charlotte nodded eagerly. "And when Jane mentioned a few of the holiday parties we'd be attending, they said that our paths would definitely cross during the holiday festivities."

"Yes," Jane added in a triumphant tone. "As you know, only the very best people are invited."

"And they were ever so handsome." Charlotte peered quickly at Dan, and her shoulders shook with mirth. "In a way, I mean."

"That depends on your point of view," Emily interjected. "Unless, of course, lobster red happens to be your favorite color." Wrinkling her nose at Jane, she took a drink and set down her glass.

A delighted grin spread across Ben's boyish face, and he sat back as if giving free rein to this sudden turn in the conversation.

Dan scowled at Emily, hoping to silence her before the dinner-table banter became a political discussion.

"And what, exactly, does that mean, Emily?" Jane asked, leaning forward to see past Ben.

"Now, girls," their mother broke in. "Remember your manners. Since the soldiers on trial in Boston have been acquitted and that awful business put to rest, it's time our English brothers were again treated with more congeniality. I, for one, will be most pleased to meet the young officers." She directed a stern look at Jane. "But I insist that proper introductions be forthcoming."

"Oh, Mother," Jane gushed. "Just wait till you see them. Tall and splendid, and one especially is quite handsome. He had an air of obvious quality about him."

Dan watched his father for a reaction, then glanced at

Cousin Landon. Neither seemed to act as though anything were amiss with his sister keeping company with a soldier. Now that most of the taxes had been lifted, the other colonies cared not a whit that regiments of king's men still overran Boston. He doubted there would ever be a cause great enough to unite the colonists for very long. It had all been for naught, his giving up the seminary for the cause of freedom.

And what of Susannah? Her face rose once more in his memory. But she was never really his to give up, was she? As the image of her faded, he remembered his manners and expelled a long, slow breath. Beside him, his cousin sat dressed in a poor imitation of Susannah's rich emerald. He smiled at her. "You look lovely this evening, Charlotte."

She blushed and broke into another giggle.

Chip wound his wool scarf an extra time around his neck and snuggled his nose into its warmth to ward off the predawn cold. From within the shadows alongside the Lyons' Den, he watched as Morgan and Susannah boarded the stage for Philadelphia.

He heard the driver give a whistle and snap the reins, and the team of horses started up, the wagon wheels crunching over the snow-packed gravel of the drive.

Straightening up tall, Chip watched until the stagecoach was out of sight, then breathed easier as a hopeful smile curved his mouth. Susannah wouldn't let him down. She'd look for Mary until she found her, and she'd bring her back.

He blew some warm breath into his hands and rubbed them together. He wondered where Mary was, and how long it would take to find her. The thought of his sister running off cut like a knife at his insides. It would never have happened if Jonathan had come back. How could someone who'd seemed so friendly and nice have let Mary down? Chip ground his teeth. It was all because of Pa. If he wasn't such a disgrace, Mary wouldn't have become indentured. And Jonathan would have been loyal to her. It was all because of Pa.

He remembered Mary Clare's blackened eye, the pitiful

way she had cried and hidden in the grove. And the memory brought the same sharp pain. Mary had been so shamed she hadn't wanted Jonathan to know about it. And when Pa had tried to make off with all her Sunday frocks, he had finally crushed her already bruised spirit.

Now Susannah had gone to find his sister one more time and bring her back where she belonged. And when she got here, he'd see to it that Mary never again had reason to cry or run away. Pa would never hurt her again.

24

Chip jammed his hands into the pockets of his heavy coat and felt the cold steel of Mr. Lyons' big pistol. It was all up to him now.

Chip grimaced at the foul odor that permeated the very air surrounding Pa's ramshackle cabin. Since he and Mary had left, Pa had no doubt been too lazy to dispose of a single shred of refuse. He could only imagine what it must smell like inside. Chip grunted with indignation. Anyone who stayed so besotted that he'd wallow in his own filth doubly deserved what was coming to him—as if there wasn't already just cause to carry out this deed.

He lifted the latch on the door. The rusty hinges squeaked, but Christopher felt no fear. His father was certain to be falling-down drunk, if not unconscious.

As a stench of rum, sweat, human waste, and rotten food assaulted his nostrils, Chip held his breath and scanned the dark room. The muted reddish glow given off by the embers of the dying fire revealed that the only furniture remaining was a worktable and a rough bed. The rest had probably been sold to buy rum. He cast a scathing glance at the soiled clothes haphazardly strewn about and the few dirty dishes and utensils that must have been of too little value to provide additional money.

Pa was nowhere in sight. He must have found some other hole to crawl into tonight.

Just as Christopher turned to leave, a disgruntled snore startled him. The wretch *was* here after all!

Chip swung back and moved toward the sound. Pa lay sideways behind the footboard of the rickety bed, bundled in some old quilts. The very sight of him, drunk and despicable, made Chip's rage rise up in him once more.

Nervously he fingered the cold steel of the gun. Mr. Lyons kept only one shell in the long-barreled pistol.

He had to hit his mark on the first shot. Chip lifted the weapon carefully from his coat and crept closer. A trembling began inside his gut, but he fought to subdue it. Mary didn't deserve to be tormented anymore, and neither did he.

But as Chip circled the foot of the bed, his foot tangled in a corner of a blanket. He stumbled and fell, landing half atop his father.

Pa groaned as Chip scrambled to his feet. "Who's that? What d'ya want?"

If not for the thought of Mary's suffering driving him on, Chip probably would have run away. But as his pa pushed himself up to a sitting position, Christopher felt anger returning with its full force.

"That you, Chris?"

Narrowing his eyes, Chip straightened to his full height and held the pistol with both hands. He leveled it at his father. "It-it's me. And I'm h-here to k-k-kill you."

"What? No, boy!" His father lunged forward until his chest met the end of the gun barrel. He peered down at it, then up at Christopher with astonishment. "I don't—what the—? Give me that gun." Visibly trembling, he reached for it.

Christopher took a few steps back. "I'm g-glad you woke up. It w-wouldn't be fitting for you to d-die all sleeping and peaceful after the w-way you've shamed us."

Pa's features twisted. "I'm your pa. You got no right to be talkin' to me like that. I've a good mind to take my belt and tan your hide." Slowly he eased himself to his feet and started forward.

The loud click of the hammer echoed off the stark surfaces of the room as Chip gripped the weapon tighter.

For the first time, his father's fear became evident. The man reared back and raised his hands as if to ward off the shot. "Chris, me lad. I'm your pa. You can't shoot your own pa."

Chip moved his finger over the trigger. "Mary's r-run off with a stage driver, and it's all y-your f-fault. No decent m-man wants to marry up w-with the p-p-penniless daughter of the town d-drunk. I c-can't get m-money for a dowry for her, s-since you s-sold us into bondage, b-but I can make sure y-you never hurt her again."

"No! Don't shoot me. You can't." Pa cowered on the floor, his hands covering his head. "I know I'm worthless and no-good. But—but I can change. See if I can't." He lifted his head a fraction. "I will. Promise. I'll quit drinkin' and go ask for my old job back."

"No you won't. W-we've heard all that b-before. S-soon as you get the sh-shakes you'll lie or steal or hurt s-somebody to get a jug. Y-you know it, and s-so do I."

His father sat up and slumped back against the bed. "You're right. There's naught but truth in the words. I ain't been worth spit since your ma died. I deserve whatever you want to do."

Defeated, he scrunched up his unshaven face, and tears made paths through the filth on his cheeks as he rolled his eyes upward to the ceiling. "God almighty, up in heaven, it's been more'n a long time since the last time I done any prayin'. And bein' the lowest sinner crawlin' on this cold earth, I know I ain't got the right to expect you to listen to the likes of me. But I need forgivin' for the awful things I've did to my kids, all just to get my filthy hands on another swig. Let the blood I be sheddin' here and now cleanse my soul of my sins. Take me home now, home to my Jenny."

With a resigned breath, he lowered his gaze at Christopher. "Get on with it. I'm ready."

A flicker of satisfaction curled the edge of Chip's mouth

upward in a sneer. This was the moment he'd been waiting for. Sweat slickened his grip on the gun, and his fingers began to shake. Gritting his teeth, he transferred its weight to his left hand while he wiped his right palm on his coat. He took a firm grip on the pistol and raised it.

"Well, what you waitin' for, Son? You don't have to worry, I cain't blame you for killin' me. I more'n drove you to it."

Chip's heart thundered against his chest. It was all he could do to breathe. Squeezing his eyes closed, he took a deep breath and pulled the trigger.

Great feathery flakes of white filled the sky and floated silently down over the cobbled streets of the red brick city. Sparkling and glistening, it drifted through shafts of light from the street lamps and the glow from brightly lit homes, transforming Philadelphia into a fairyland. Susannah gazed past the parted curtains of the stage wagon to the festive street decorations. If only she had come to share in the joys of the Christmas season, instead of undertaking such a distressing mission. Morgan had long since ceased trying to draw her out of her morbid imaginings. Worry for Mary Clare had cast a pall upon even his most hilarious story.

The stage slowed to a stop, and Morgan alighted, then helped Susannah down. She filled her lungs with the fresh cold air before the urgency of the trip gripped her. "We must find Mary. Quickly."

He helped the driver unload Susannah's trunk and his own satchel, then glanced around the stage stop. "Well, I see our carriage, but the driver doesn't seem to be with it. I'll just settle you inside while I track him down."

"No, that isn't necessary. I've got to question the stable man and find out about that driver who absconded with Mary Clare."

Forcibly taking hold of Susannah's elbow, Morgan steered her to the carriage and all but pushed her inside. "Do me a favor for once, will you? Indulge my ego. I'm the man. I'll see to everything. Now you stay here and wait for me."

Amazed at the sudden change in Morgan, Susannah acquiesced. She clasped her hands together in her lap and relaxed against the plush seat as he closed the door. The prankster-student had vanished, and a capable young man had stepped into Morgan's shoes. Something indefinable had shone from his eyes when he'd taken control. But for the moment she had to concentrate on finding Mary. After that, perhaps, Susannah could examine more closely this new rescuer who had come to offer his aid in time of need.

Breathing another prayer for her young friend, Susannah peered out the carriage window. White covered the empty street, muffling the harsh sounds of the city. Surely it was getting late. She wished Morgan would come back.

In a moment or two, some footsteps stomped near, and she heard the thump of luggage being heaved into the back.

Susannah heard Morgan give the driver an order, then the coach tilted on its springs as the man climbed up onto the front seat. Morgan opened the door and stepped inside, and the conveyance jolted forward.

"You've found out where she is?"

"Not exactly."

"What ever do you mean? What exactly *did* you learn?"

"Only that Nelson frequents a common tavern down in the wharf area. I'll send Geoffrey around in the morning to make further inquiries."

Susannah found herself fighting back tears. "Morgan, don't you understand? We must go there now. Tomorrow may be too late."

He raked his fingers through his dark hair, and his expression eased. "That area is extremely dangerous at this hour, Susannah. I made a solemn vow to Mrs. Lyons that I'd not let anything happen to you. And one to myself as well," he added almost as an afterthought.

"Then just think how much more we should be concerned for Mary's safety. Can't you see that? If you won't escort me there, then I'll jump out at once and ask the stable man myself."

Morgan took a deep breath. "You're quite serious, aren't you?"

Susannah didn't answer.

"Oh, very well." He turned in his seat and knocked on the front of the coach. "Geoffrey, we'll be going down to Woody's Tavern this evening after all."

"You're sure of that, sir?"

"Quite." Morgan straightened in his seat again as the horse's muffled hoofbeats thumped over the snow-packed street.

The wind picked up as they neared the wharf. Through the window, Susannah noticed how eerie the tall ship masts appeared in the dark snowy sky, rocking in the force of the wind. She felt again the terror she had known when the two drunks had approached her. But that day Daniel had come, like a knight of the realm, to give aid to a maiden in distress.

Closing her mind to memories of things never meant to be, she forced her thoughts back to the present. Mary Clare was the one in distress, in the clutches of that dastardly man. Susannah whispered a quick prayer that she and Morgan would be able to rescue the girl. Her pulse pounded in her veins.

The carriage drew to a stop before a dreary brick building with badly peeling sashes. Above the door a sign creaked on chains, bearing a painted tankard with the words *Woody's Tavern.*

"Wait here," Morgan ordered as he stepped out.

Susannah didn't need a second command. The sight of the disreputable establishment evoked strong memories of her last experience in this area. She shrank back against the seat. "Godspeed," she whispered.

"Stay with her, Geoff," came Morgan's voice again. Then his footfalls grew faint, and the squeak of rusty hinges rent the night air as he went inside.

As the door swung shut behind him, a girl screamed.

Susannah's breath stopped.

The second cry was muted. "Help me! Please help!"

Positive that the voice belonged to Mary Clare, Susannah jumped out of the carriage.

"Wait, miss!" Geoffrey said from his perch.

The words barely made an impression on Susannah. Forgetting about her own safety, she ran to the tavern door, with the driver only a step behind. She clutched the latch in both hands and tugged it open.

It took only a few seconds for her vision to adjust to the dark, smoke-filled room. The dank stench of stale cheap rum assaulted her nostrils as she searched through the haze for Mary Clare.

Then a scuffle on the stairs across the room caught her eye. Mary was struggling to extract herself from the grip of a grizzled redcoat as he fought to drag her up the steps.

"Stop!" Susannah yelled. "Let her go!"

"Not a chance, lady," he gritted around the stub of a fat cigar.

Every eye turned in Susannah's direction, and a chorus of raucous laughter erupted.

Morgan, flat on his face in the midst of it all, scrambled up from the floor and delivered a swift punch to a bearded jaw. Another soldier grabbed him from behind.

Geoffrey unfastened the man's arms, swung him around, and gave a resounding jab to his nose. Blood trickling, the would-be attacker fell in a heap.

Morgan and Geoffrey crouched back to back and circled slowly to check for any other interference.

"Let me go!" Writhing in her abductor's grip, Mary Clare thrust an elbow into the soldier's ribs, but he pulled her up another few steps.

Susannah stomped over to the barkeeper and shook her finger in his face. "You make that lout release my servant this instant, or I'll have the authorities close down this establishment."

The man's pockmarked countenance took on a look of astonishment. "Don't see what I can do. He's not one of my reg'lars."

"I shall bring charges if she is not released. Make no mistake about that." Her gaze did not waver, although her stomach felt a quivering mass. She was amazed that her voice didn't tremble. From the corner of her eye she saw Morgan and Geoffrey race up the stairs, where the whimpering Mary Clare was being pulled into a bedroom.

The echoing thud of punches resounded. The open door slammed into the wall. A body hit the floor, and for a few tense, silent seconds, all was quiet.

Susannah caught her lower lip between her teeth as she stared beyond the upstairs railing.

After what seemed an eternity, Mary Clare appeared in the doorway and flew down the steps into Susannah's arms. "God answered my prayers!" she sobbed. "You came!"

Brushing themselves off and straightening their coats, Morgan and Geoffrey followed triumphantly.

Susannah leveled a scathing glare at the barman and marched out the door. The others followed in single file.

Outside in the snowy winter night, Susannah pulled Mary Clare into a fierce hug, thankful beyond words that her friend was safe once more. Their tears of relief mingled as Susannah kissed the younger girl's cheek, then hugged her again.

Morgan and the driver ushered them gently to the carriage and helped them inside. Then they sputtered into howls of laughter.

25

Morgan placed a thick wool lap robe around Mary Clare's shivering shoulders. She clung to Susannah as the carriage sped homeward.

"How can I ever thank you?" Mary sobbed. "How can I ever thank God for sending you when he did?"

"Wasn't our Susannah a sight," Morgan asked with a grin, "her arm raised in unwavering authority as she dared the barkeeper to hinder your release?" He chuckled and shook his head. "Pity the British army let their best commander get away. If she had been in charge of things up there in Boston, we'd all be bowing the knee to old King George by now."

Holding Mary in her arms, Susannah patted the younger girl's back. Now that she thought about it, her courage during the ordeal had come from beyond herself. She blushed as she thought of the tone of voice she'd used in her demand. "Well, it's over, thank heaven," she whispered, giving Mary Clare a comforting squeeze. "You're safe once more—and we'll never let you out of our sight again."

Mary lifted her tear-streaked face and straightened, relaxing back against the seat as she dabbed at her nose with Susannah's silk handkerchief. "I'll never doubt God again," she declared, setting her jaw. "Not after this. When Jonathan went home, I hated God for taking him away from me. But now I see that God loves me. He does care. Only he could have sent you to save me just when I needed you most!"

Susannah patted her friend's arm. "Surely you must know it was Jon's family, not God, who kept him at home. And he's trying very hard to work things out with them so he can come back."

With a sniff, Mary raised her lashes. "I understand that now. Or, at least, I'm trying to. I never truly trusted the Lord before . . . not on my own. I believed in you—and Mrs. Lyons, and Jon. All of you trusted God. And I relied on your faith. But now I see I must find my own faith, and that it is God who will help me to do that."

Susannah blinked tears away as she embraced the younger girl. "I'm so thankful to hear that. Why, do you realize it was nothing short of a miracle that we found you, when we'd only just arrived in Philadelphia ourselves?"

Mary drew the blanket closer and relaxed into its warmth as the coach lurched through a snowdrift. After a few quiet moments, when they were once again riding smoothly, her eyes took on a faraway look. "There's been quite a string of miracles . . . ever since I got here," she said softly, then looked again at Susannah and Morgan. "When Ralph first brought me here, he wanted to stop at the tavern and have a drink before we went to his place. So that's what we did. Only he didn't drink just flip, and it wasn't only one drink. He started right out with rum. One after the other, until he couldn't even talk straight."

"How dreadful," Susannah murmured.

With a nod, the girl continued. "All of a sudden it came to me. I escaped Pa—to run off with another sot! And I regretted ever believing his fine words. He started leerin' at me, and saying that after he had one more drink he'd take me home and show me—" She grimaced and shrugged one shoulder. "You know."

Susannah swallowed. She could only imagine how frightening the experience must have been. But she kept silent, feeling Mary's need to talk, to put the whole thing behind her.

"I was afraid of him then. And I kept watching the door, wondering if Mr. Lyons would be coming after me. Ralph got mad that every time the door opened I'd jump. That's when I said my first real prayer," Mary said. "I asked the Lord to save me somehow. Then it came to me to tell Ralph I was indentured. I told him I still had years left on my indenturement, and he became furious. Said if the 'old man' did come, he'd take care of him right enough. But then he realized the sheriff would be *with* Mr. Lyons. He jumped up so fast he knocked his drink over."

Susannah shuddered as Mary's voice droned on.

"'You're bonded?' he shouted at my face. 'I'm ruined. I'll have no job. They'll throw me in jail.' He looked at me with real hate then and yelled even louder. 'I don't need no skinny kid like you, anyway. I never saw you before in my life.' And just like that, he stomped out of the tavern, leaving me sitting there at that table, with rum dripping all over the floor."

Morgan gave a low whistle. "The bounder wasn't a man at all. But if that was your first night here, what happened after that? How'd you manage?"

Mary's lips tightened into a thin smile. "The owner of the tavern told me I could sleep upstairs if I'd help out. And I could keep whatever tips I made until I saved up my fare to go back home."

"That man I screamed at?" Susannah gasped. "He was *helping* you?"

She nodded. "He kept me safe from the dockworkers. But when the soldiers came in tonight, they weren't about to take orders from him. So I started praying again. At first it didn't seem to help at all. Things got scary. And when that soldier picked me up and—" She cringed. "I started to think this time God couldn't help. I was never so scared in my whole life! But then you came, Sue. And you, Morgan. Chargin' in like an army of angels. God answered my prayers one more time. I know I belong to him now." A bright tear glistened in the glow of the coach lantern, crested Mary's cheekbone, and traced a silver path down her face.

Both Morgan and Susannah reached for Mary's hands, and the three of them ended up in one big joyful embrace.

"I'm afraid you'll have to lace it up tighter," Susannah panted. "I didn't realize the price I'd pay for Mrs. Lyons' delicious cooking." She took a deep breath and held on to a spindle of the massive four-poster. She squinted as she braced herself for the worst, and the watercolor green pattern on the wallpaper ran together before her eyes.

Mary Clare laughed and tugged the corset strings with all her might.

"Stop! Another quarter inch, and I'll never breathe again. Isn't it frightful, what we do to ourselves in the name of beauty? Well, this has gone beyond even that. It is vanity, pure and simple."

"If you'd stop talking so much it wouldn't *be* so hard," Mary chided good-naturedly. "Let's try the dress again."

"I can't even bend. You'll have to do it."

Mary collected the satin ties of the triple-hooped pannier circling Susannah's feet and drew it up, tying a neat bow. Then, gathering armfuls of the embroidered silk gown, she adjusted the bountiful skirt evenly over the framework.

Sliding her arms into the elbow-length sleeves edged with lace, Susannah eased into the bodice and straightened her spine. "There are cords inside for drawing up the sections," she said in a tight voice.

"Yes, I see." In moments, the pale pink silk skirt draped in three panels above the accordion-pleated white lace under-skirt, revealing a silver rose at each point. Mary Clare laced up the back closure, then stepped away. "That is the most beautiful gown I've ever seen," she whispered.

Susannah moved to the looking glass and studied her reflection, smiling as she examined the skirt and her silver kid slippers. The smile faded as her eyes traveled upward. Having grown used to her modest working clothes, the fashionable gown now seemed daring. "There's so much skin showing," she moaned. "I'll surely catch my death—if I don't spill out of it first, that is."

Mary Clare couldn't stop her giggle. "I wouldn't worry.

You'll only fall out of it if you breathe, and it's far too tight for that."

The younger girl's mirth was contagious, and Susannah laughed with her. Then she gave a resigned tilt of her head. "Well, I suppose it's no worse than the others will be wearing. Will you help with my wig?"

Within moments she left the bedroom. Stepping out onto the wide U-shaped balcony overlooking the elegant reception hall, she felt Mary's quick squeeze.

"It'll be like a dream," the girl said softly from beside her. "You'll have so much fun."

"I hope so. If I had brought another ball gown, you could be attending, too. I should have had more faith that we'd find you right off as we did."

"Oh, I don't mind. I wouldn't know how to act. I'll be more comfortable up here, watchin' with Evelyn and Frances."

Susannah smiled at her. Mary would fit right in with Morgan's two younger sisters. Indeed, the girl looked like a child again . . . and only days ago she'd run away with an older man. How wonderful of God to bring dear Mary back!

They walked slowly to the staircase at the far end of the balcony, stopping now and then to peer down at the activity below, where servants flitted about setting out huge arrangements of pine boughs and holly.

"It was so good of Morgan's family to take us in so unexpectedly," Mary Clare said.

Susannah shot her a glance from the corner of her eye. "Yes. But I do wish he hadn't exaggerated our circumstances quite beyond belief. If the truth comes to light, we'll be worse off than before."

"Oh, it'll be all right," Mary announced. "I'll pray about it."

"Just don't expect the Lord to condone Morgan's deception. Lies are still that . . . just lies. Imagine his family believing we're the daughters of a high church official!"

"But Morgan sure sounded important, didn't he—bein' given the great honor of escorting us."

"I only hope this lofty new position in his family doesn't crumble at his feet."

Reaching the end of the landing, Susannah cast a last smile over her shoulder. "Pray me through this, will you? I'm ever so nervous. The last grand ball I attended was at Julia's. Do I . . . look presentable?"

"No one will look so fine. Morgan's going to love you."

Susannah frowned. "I pray *that* isn't true. He has been acting quite possessive since I've accepted his help. But I hope he's not seeing that as any sort of sign of encouragement. I don't need a serious suitor right now. What I do need is his friendship." She sighed, twisting a delicate lace handkerchief in her fingers, then descended the first step.

Mary placed a hand on her arm. "Don't be throwin' away any keys. You might want to walk through this door again someday. Morgan's smitten with you but good, and his family must be one of the richest in Philadelphia. You could live with him in grand style."

Searching Mary's face, Susannah realized the younger girl had a point. Daniel Haynes might have looked down upon her because of her indenturement, but Morgan Thomas held her in high esteem. He made certain his family welcomed her as an honored guest in their home, not a purchased servant— even if it was a lie. In time she might possibly grow fond of her new rescuer.

But even as she thought this, she knew it would never happen. For her heart had given itself—seemingly of its own volition—to a man with warm sable eyes . . . a man she probably would never see again. Besides, it was not fitting to be thinking of the future. She had the present—and a very real one at that—to live through first. And that included impressing Mr. and Mrs. Waldon Griffith Thomas with her most gracious behavior. She took a steadying breath. "Wish me luck."

Mary nodded, then turned to greet Evelyn and Frances, Morgan's nine- and eleven-year-old sisters, who were bouncing out of their bedroom across the hall in their frilly nightclothes and caps. Miniatures of Morgan, with their sparkling eyes and dark braids, they hushed one another. Then with muffled giggles, the three girls sank to their knees within sight of the ballroom to survey the festivities.

Sweet with the rich fragrance of evergreen and holly, the expansive entry lay in marbled glory at Susannah's feet. As she made her way down, her hand brushed one of the huge red velvet bows placed at intervals among the pine branches adorning the gilt-trimmed stair rail. At the halfway point she caught sight of Morgan standing with his father at the door, greeting arriving guests beneath a huge glowing chandelier.

Morgan turned and his eyes widened. Excusing himself with a bow, he crossed to the bottom of the staircase, where he waited silently. He wore a sapphire brocade frock coat and velvet breeches, and his dark hair was tied at the nape of his neck with a bow as pristine white as the lace front of his shirt.

"You look magnificent," he said, extending a hand to Susannah. "You quite take my breath away."

"Thank you. I might say the same about you," she murmured.

"I'm afraid I must play the gracious host for a while yet," he said with a wink. "But allow me to escort you to the library. I believe Mother is in there."

"Thank you." Susannah allowed her eyes to roam beyond the arched double doorway of the ballroom, flanked by heavy marble urns bearing festive holiday arrangements. Formal portraits of the Thomas ancestors glared down at her from both sides of the wall as she passed.

Ushering her into the wood-paneled library across the hall, Morgan bowed. "I shall return shortly, my dear Miss Harrington. Please make yourself comfortable."

She nodded and watched him stride confidently away. But once he was out of sight, she sighed. There wasn't one familiar face among the guests who conversed in clusters about the library and the dining room beyond. At last Morgan's mother and his sister Melinda, a willowy fifteen-year-old with dark curls, moved into sight, visiting with people a short distance away. Hesitantly she gravitated in their direction.

A few words drifted to her ears as she waited for a group of middle-aged men blocking her path to move aside.

"Will it never end?" one of them asked. "Just when things begin to settle after that trial affair in Boston, the assembly in Maryland has to start trouble."

"I fear," said another, "that this will be far worse for trade than that tea tax business."

"Ah yes," a third piped in. "It's one thing to cease importing a few taxed items. But tobacco—now *that's* the lifeblood of the middle colonies. We'll all feel the pinch if the growers refuse to have it inspected for shipping."

"Trade will absolutely suffer. Mark my words. And just when business was getting back to normal, too. Pity, that."

"Well, I don't understand," came the first voice again. "They've always paid the inspection tax in the past. It isn't as if it were just now being foisted upon them. Besides, if it were abolished, there'd just have to be another tax to replace it. From what I understand, the money is used to support their clergy and to pay the inspecting officials."

"If they don't come to their senses rather quickly, they may find themselves playing host to a regiment just like in Boston. And we've more than enough soldiers nosing around down this way as it is."

"Bad for business," muttered another. "Bad for business."

As the group walked away toward the spacious dining room, Susannah stared after them. Was there anyplace she could go in the Colonies where the men did not talk politics? She doubted it. But why was there such a difference in attitude between these city merchants and the people in Princeton? Perhaps it was as the last man had said . . . in a port such as Philadelphia, it was bad for business. That must account for the difference.

Approaching the lavishly spread tables at the far side of the dining room, Susannah gave a fleeting thought to similar gatherings at Julia's mansion in Ashford. There, as here, servants moved efficiently among the crowd of important guests, managing to avoid knocking over priceless treasures as they carried food and drinks back and forth.

But unless she wanted to spoil the evening, she had to dismiss the sad recollections of Julia . . . and her death. Susannah lifted her chin and accepted a glass of punch from a serving girl. She felt like a stranger, overhearing a group of ladies clad in the latest Paris vogue discuss a recent shipment of fabric that had arrived too late for holiday use. She hoped Morgan would join her soon.

The first musical notes drifted from the ballroom across the hall as a string quartet tuned their instruments, and a group of chattering young people rushed past Susannah in that direction. After they had gone, Susannah followed.

Morgan's broad smile was most welcome as he hurried into view. "Thank goodness that tiresome duty is over," he said, making a wide gesture with one arm. "Forgive me for having left you unattended so long."

Susannah returned his smile.

"I managed to escape just as I saw Charlotte Somerwell, the young lady I mentioned before, arriving with her family. I am so glad I could inform Father that I had you to look after." The characteristic devilish spark glinted in his cobalt eyes.

"Surely she can't be all that unattractive."

"In a few years, perhaps," he said with a grimace. "But right now she hardly appears more than a child."

Susannah turned her gaze upward to meet his. "But I thought children weren't invited."

"They're not, that's true. Miss Somerwell is older than she appears. You'll understand when I introduce you later— much later, if I've anything to say about it. Let's grab a quick sip of punch before we join the others."

Dan stood on the sidelines of the mirrored ballroom with its flocked wallpaper, observing the young men and fair maidens out on the polished hardwood dance floor. He wished he could remember the fancy patterns and steps he hadn't practiced since the previous Christmas ball. Frowning, he rubbed his jaw and tried to memorize the movements again.

Off to one side stood Jane, her eyes sparkling with excitement. A rosy flush heightened her coloring as she swayed to the music in her apricot frock. Beside her, Charlotte's face radiated supreme happiness.

Emily pulled on Dan's sleeve. "Oh, I do hope no clumsy boy asks me to dance." She wrinkled her nose in distaste.

He smiled into her green eyes, then brushed the backs of his fingers lightly over her sun-kissed cheek. Even in winter, Emily carried the freshness of the outdoors. In her peach taffeta, she looked like a fragile blossom waiting to be picked. It wouldn't be long before some young man began to take serious notice of his impish little sister . . . and her of him. "If I can remember all the steps, I'll take you out for a few turns. How does that sound?"

"Wonderful. Mama," she said, turning to her other side, "Dan's going to dance with me."

"Not just yet, though, dear," their mother said. "He's promised Charlotte his first dance this evening."

The music stopped for a few seconds, then the slow three-beat pattern of a minuet started up.

Dan felt his mother's stare and turned dutifully to his cousin. "Would you care to dance, Charlotte?"

With a soft giggle, she took his arm, and they joined the line.

The reed-thin Charlotte seemed little heavier than a feather in her lavender gauze frock. Dan was surprised that the breeze created by all the swirling skirts didn't whisk her up and about in the air at will. The lights from the crystal chandeliers overhead reflected in her wide eyes, and he smiled at her excitement as he managed to keep from stepping on her feet. As they danced he watched his mother and Cousin Rose chatting with the hostess, Mrs. Thomas, and a handful of other older women dressed in the rich brocades and silks of the season. When at last the music ended, Dan led Charlotte back to the sidelines.

"My turn," Emily teased when he reached her.

"As you wish." With a smile at his cousin, he bowed gallantly at his youngest sister. "May I have the honor of the next dance, miss?"

Emily's light laugh bubbled over him as the beginning notes sang forth from the instruments. She curtsied, then tucked her hand into the crook of his elbow, and they walked to the floor.

Dan stopped short. "I don't believe I know this one."

"I don't either."

"Let's watch and see how it goes, and I'll take you out on the next minuet."

She nodded, gave a sigh, and relaxed on his arm.

With a nudge, Dan pointed to Ben, dancing his heart out in the thick of things with a petite brunette in ivory satin.

After watching his younger brother with some amusement, Dan's gaze drifted idly over the other dancers. One couple seemed especially graceful and adept, and he watched their intricate movements and turns. The tall young man with dark hair seemed oddly familiar, and from his attire—by far the richest in the room—Dan was sure the fellow must be the son of Mr. and Mrs. Thomas that his mother had mentioned, home from school for the holidays.

His attention drifted to the young man's partner, who also seemed familiar. In the soft pink of a winter sunset, her back was to Dan. He admired her softly feminine arms and creamy skin, the enchanting tilt of her head in its elaborately curled wig. Then she turned, bestowing a sweet smile upon her partner.

Dan's heart stopped. *Susannah Harrington!*

In all of his dreams he'd never seen her so stunningly beautiful, moving with the refined grace of a lady of quality. He stared at her in wonder. Then her partner's identity dawned on him. This family's last name was Thomas. He was *Morgan* Thomas, from Princeton . . . and obviously the reason Susannah had rejected Dan so resoundingly. His fists tightened. "I'll be right back, Emily."

Striding over to the cluster of women around the hostess, he turned on his most charming smile and inclined his head. "Ladies. My, it would be hard to choose the loveliest one among you this evening."

"Why, dear," his mother gushed, placing a hand on her bosom. Her silk gloves matched the butternut shade of her gown. "How sweet."

"Yes," Mrs. Thomas agreed. "Most gallant, I must say." Her refined features made her a strikingly attractive woman. She nodded beneath her elaborate wig and smiled graciously.

"It's a wonderful party, Mrs. Thomas," he said. "Excellent string quartet."

The hostess laid a jeweled hand upon his satin sleeve. "Thank you, Daniel," she said in her well-modulated voice. "Your mother's been telling us of your travels. You must find your occupation most interesting."

"I do. But it's quite rewarding to forget about business and enjoy a wonderful holiday get-together such as this. It must be a special treat for you to have your son here to enjoy it as well."

"Why yes. He studies so hard at college. I told him he should take a rest from the dreary classes and spend some time with the family."

"And his lovely partner? She looks familiar, somehow, but I've not been able to place her."

"It's the most amazing thing, now that you mention it. Morgan brought the dear girl and her sister here late last night. They're the daughters of a high church official, straight from the archbishop. The man was called away on some emergency, and Morgan, the dear boy, agreed to look after them until the good reverend can join them."

Puzzled, Dan turned to study Susannah. So that was how the young man managed to palm a bond servant off on his family without so much as a suspicion. Were the Lyonses part of this ruse as well? He watched Susannah smile at Morgan and curtsy. The fine creation she wore would more than have paid for her return to England . . . unless, as she had said, there was nothing left for her back there. "A sister, you say?"

"Yes," Mrs. Thomas continued. "A shy slip of a thing, the little girl is. She's barely uttered a word since their arrival last night. She preferred to stay upstairs with our Evelyn and Frances. But as you can see, her sister is quite accomplished in all the arts of gentle society."

"She is quite lovely," Dan's mother admitted. "Her father is associated with the archbishop of Canterbury, you say? How impressive."

After a few moments Cousin Rose leaned forward and motioned for Dan to bend his ear. "Be a dear, and do me a favor," she whispered behind her gloved hand. "It would please Landon no end to see our darling Charlotte dance at least once with Morgan. At the end of this piece, would you mind taking her out onto the floor and maneuvering a change of partners?"

Reluctant at first to encounter Susannah after her stinging rejection, Dan gave in to Cousin Rose's hopeful expression and smiled. Then, taking a fortifying breath, he turned to Charlotte. "Would you care to dance? I'd like to try and speak to Morgan."

Charlotte's lips twitched. "Oh yes."

"Dan!" Emily blurted from the edge of the group.

He felt warmth on his neck. Flustered, he turned an embarrassed smile on his cousin. "Oh, I forgot. I've already promised this dance to my little sister."

"Oh no," their mother chimed in, moving to stand between the siblings. "Emily needs to be accepting dances from someone other than her brother. You go on with Charlotte."

With a nod, Dan took his cousin's arm and escorted her to the opposite side of the room, near the stage. He could see Susannah there, gazing at the musicians as other guests milled about in the quiet span between musical selections.

Fingering one of the long ringlets of her powdered wig as she waited for the next piece to begin, she turned. Her blue eyes lifted his way and stopped for a breathless moment.

At the glorious look of joy that transformed her features, Dan's heart burst into a wild tempo.

"Daniel," she whispered, taking a hesitant step forward. Her hand fluttered to her breast.

"Susannah."

26

Time stood still for Susannah, lost as she was in the warm sable depths of Dan's eyes. What miracle had brought him here? Or was the whole glorious evening just a dream? Her gaze wandered over his midnight blue satin frock coat, his coal velvet breeches, until a soft tug on her arm brought her back to reality. At once she became aware that she'd been standing in the middle of the dance floor staring at a man who was not even her partner—and who had another young woman on his arm besides. She tore her gaze from Dan and shifted it to Morgan.

"A moment with the lovely lady, if you don't mind," she heard Dan say. "I'm sure my cousin Charlotte would be gracious enough to take her place for this dance."

Susannah saw a muscle twitch in Morgan's jaw as he glared at Dan in rigid silence. Then he turned a polite smile toward the blushing redhead.

Susannah gave a slight curtsy. "Charlotte. I'm Susannah Harrington. It's very nice to meet you." She shot a glance at Morgan and moved out of his grasp. "Why, only moments ago, Morgan was reciting your charms."

"Really?" the younger girl tittered. She raised her head shyly at him as the first violin and 'cello sang out the introduction to the next piece.

Watching a mixture of volatile emotions flash across Morgan's face as he peered first at Dan and then herself, Susannah half expected him to say something unpleasant. Finally he expelled a breath and turned to Dan's partner. "Miss Somerwell. May I have the honor of this dance?"

Susannah's eyes slid to Dan's.

He smiled. Offering an arm, he guided her to the line as the rich music from the strings filled the room. Once in position, he bowed.

Susannah curtsied and rose, held to his gaze by some invisible cord. A liquid warmth flowed through her as they stepped in time with the pattern of the minuet, and whenever the dance brought them together, his touch set her afire. But she noticed something deep and indefinable in his eyes during those moments . . . something she couldn't quite read. Had he already asked about her? Had he heard Morgan's lie? She was quite certain he'd been as delighted to see her as she had been to see him. But when the music brought them close again, the mysterious glint in his gaze seemed more apparent than ever.

Off to one side, Susannah caught sight of Morgan glowering her way with obvious jealousy as he moved with Charlotte. A twinge of guilt pricked. He had been wonderful to her the past few days. She hated the knowledge that he might be suffering now because of her. She'd have to make a special effort to appease him, and somehow make this up to him.

Swinging back to Dan, her gaze locked on his. Uneasily, she realized there was more to be considered here than Morgan's hurt feelings. Much more. She had better explain about the story the young man had concocted before Dan should inadvertently happen to mention who she was to his and Morgan's families. It wouldn't be right for him to find out about the lie and believe her to be a party to Morgan's scheme.

The music slowed and stopped.

She smiled at Dan. "I'm terribly thirsty. Do you think we could possibly get a glass of punch?"

"You've read my mind." Offering a satin-clad arm, he escorted her swiftly past the crowd and across the hall.

Susannah glanced up the stairwell, where earlier she had

seen Mary Clare and the Thomas sisters being served refreshments by one of the maids. But the upstairs balcony was empty now. The girls must have finally grown tired and gone to bed.

Dan ushered her through the library and to the beverage table in the dining room. Collecting two cups, he handed one to her. After a few sips, Dan guided her to the far end of the room and on into the kitchen.

A pair of servants stopped their work and glanced up momentarily.

Dan finished his punch and waited for Susannah to do the same. Then, setting their cups down on a worktable, he steered her to the back door, where he borrowed a wool cloak from a peg and placed it around her shoulders before they stepped outside.

Susannah's breath caught at the dazzling sight of the Thomas grounds. Moonlight poured liquid silver through silhouetted branches and cast halos around the snow-topped hedges and formal shrubbery. A huge fountain—still now, and empty except for new snow—was bathed in an ivory glow, along with the curved marble benches flanking it. She filled her lungs with the cold night air as the faint melody of another minuet floated softly from within the mansion.

"I hope you'll forgive my boldness," came Dan's deep voice from beside her.

She turned toward him.

"I needed to speak to you. It seems I heard a rather odd story about the happenstance of your becoming a houseguest here—you and your . . . *sister,* if I heard correctly?"

Susannah drew the wrap closer to ward off a sudden chill. "And did you, perchance, correct the misinformation?" she whispered.

"No." A slow smile curved his mouth. "I did consider it. But I kept remembering how you remained silent for me that day on the wharf."

She returned his smile, and her deep sigh came out in a frosty cloud. "It's quite beyond belief, isn't it? I almost clouted Morgan when he told me the fable he'd spun for his family.

But he's been such a godsend I've not been able to bring myself to expose the fabrication."

"A godsend?"

"Yes." At Dan's hardened expression, Susannah hastened to explain. "You remember Mary Clare, don't you? Our young serving girl at the inn?"

He nodded.

"Well, an unscrupulous stage driver wooed her away from us and absconded with her to Philadelphia."

"How terrible. She's still bonded, is she not?"

"Yes. And she's such an innocent, I'm quite sure she had no idea just what he had planned. Anyway, Morgan was kind enough to offer to help me find her—which we did, within an hour of our own arrival. We managed to save her before her honor was taken. It was a miracle." Without thinking, she took his hands. "Truly a miracle." Suddenly aware of her boldness, Susannah tried to release her hold.

Dan's fingers wrapped around hers more strongly, and his gaze deepened.

She lowered her lashes. "But in order for me to get Morgan to assist me, he asked that I also do something for him." Looking up again, she saw Dan's brows raise. "I agreed to attend the Christmas balls with him."

"Thomas thinks there's a lack of feminine company in this big city?"

"No, not at all," Susannah assured him. "Nothing like that. But it seems his father is set on a match between him and the young lady you were escorting. Charlotte Somerwell. A merger of rich merchants, so to speak."

"Ah." He gave a slight nod of understanding. "Seems there's quite an abundance of those sort of plans in the air."

Susannah's eyebrows drew together as she tried to decipher what he meant. "Anyway," she continued, still unsure, "I've most certainly failed him, leaving him to her mercy. He looked quite disturbed about that when last I noticed. Perhaps we'd better return." She tried to draw away.

Dan's hold tightened, and he leaned his head to one side.

"Well, his father is the most successful merchant in Philadelphia. I suppose I can understand why you might choose Thomas for a husband over me."

Her lips parted at his preposterous thought. "Over you? Why, the only hand of mine you ever asked for was one of a pair that would be serving your family!"

"I beg your pardon?"

"I can't believe the buying and selling of human life means so little to you that you can't even remember." Pulling free, she turned toward the door, but felt Dan's hand close upon her shoulder.

His touch immediately gentled, and he turned her to face him. "Susannah, I don't understand."

"Well *I* most certainly did," she said, her words coming out in a misty rush. "You'd planned to save this poor unfortunate serving girl from the unsavory confines of the inn to indenture her to your more savory family."

His mouth dropped open. "Is that what you thought? And that's why you left me standing there like some sort of fool?" Daniel took a step toward her—and from the look on his face it was hard to tell whether he was going to embrace Susannah . . . or throttle her.

Ted and Alex stomped the snow off their immaculate boots and tapped the brass knocker of the Thomas mansion. The sounds of laughter and music seemed to accompany the bright shafts of light reflecting through every window onto the snowdrifts.

"Ho hum. Another boring provincial party," Alex said with a grin, slapping Ted's back.

"Quite," Ted agreed with a laugh. "Amazing how bandying your cousin's name about has enhanced our popularity with the local gentry to such heights."

Alex brushed away a few snowflakes from the military cape covering his gold-braided red coat. "And our smart uniforms also have done the work they were 'cut out' for, I might add." He whacked the knocker a bit harder.

"Well, before we go in," Ted said, leaning forward, "you're quite welcome to all the sweet young maidens you can juggle, old man. My interest lies in but one."

With a jab in the ribs, Alex gave a sly smile. "It's beyond me why you'd want to be so stingy, limiting your favors to a single lass already. What was her name, did you say?"

"Miss Haynes. And I'm serious, old boy."

"You're always serious. Far too serious, in truth." Alex shrugged. "I'll bow to your wishes . . . but if she happens to be the fairest of the fair at the ball, you'll be in my debt."

"So be it, for she's without a doubt the loveliest lady on either side of the Atlantic."

The heavy walnut door swung open. "Good evening, Lieutenants. We're honored you could join us." Mr. Thomas stepped aside as Ted and Alex entered, then shook their hands exuberantly. "Waldon Thomas, at your service."

"How do you do, sir. Ted Harrington."

"And Alex Fontaine," his friend added with a nod.

"Please," said their host, "don't hesitate to inform me if you lack anything." He gestured to a servant nearby, who took their capes and fur hats.

"Thank you, Mr. Thomas. Most kind of you." Ted shifted his weight slightly. "Actually, I'd be most grateful for a proper introduction to a certain young lady I believe to be in attendance. A Mistress Jane Haynes."

"Haynes," the man said with a nod. "She would be the Somerwells' cousin from Rhode Island. Follow me."

Ted spotted Jane the moment he and Alex stepped into the ballroom and dipped his head as she caught sight of him on their approach.

She smiled coyly and whispered something behind a gloved hand to a younger girl standing beside her.

Taking that as an encouraging sign, Ted grinned inwardly, barely managing to maintain his proper dignity through the round of introductions—the Haynes family, the Somerwells, Mr. Thomas's wife and scowling son, who barely met Ted's eyes in the introduction. Ted wondered if the young fellow was merely preoccupied with other matters or rude to soldiers of the Crown in general.

"And this lovely young lady," the host said, finally reaching her, "is Miss Jane Haynes. You met her parents first, I believe." He made a broad gesture toward them.

"Yes," Ted said with a slight nod. As his gaze settled at last upon the beauty in rustling, flounced apricot and a cascade of powdered coppery curls, he clicked his heels together and bowed to Jane.

As if on cue, the musicians began another piece, and lilting strings filled the air.

"'Tis a pleasure to meet you," he said. "Might I have the honor of this dance?"

She moistened her lips and gave him her hand. "I'd be delighted."

Alex tapped his shoulder as they passed. Nodding in the direction of an open door, through which a balcony could be seen, he lowered his voice. "I've just discovered a princess of my own."

Following his gaze, Ted stopped, immobilized by shock at the sight of his own younger sister talking with a colonial. When at last he found his voice, he dropped Jane's arm.

"Excuse me." His boots clunking against the polished hardwood, Ted tromped through the dancers and out the door, wrenching Susannah away from the man. "Just what in heaven's name do you think you're doing here?"

Susannah gasped, two circles of rose-pink flaming her cheeks as everyone near the doorway stopped dancing.

Dan grabbed the officer's elbow and swung him around. "Take your hands off—"

"It's all right, Dan." Susannah stepped between them. "He's my brother." She turned and took Ted's sleeve. "Ted, please. Let's talk in the hall."

Dan stared after Susannah and her brother for some moments before following. Should he intrude? Apprehensive, he started toward his mother and sisters on the sidelines. Now that he'd finally gotten back to his beloved Susannah, had it been all for nothing? He hadn't had a chance to explain to Susannah how she had misunderstood his proposal in Princeton. What if her brother used his authority to force her to return to Britain? What if she left, never knowing how he felt about her? He couldn't let that happen. He wouldn't.

"Excuse me, chap," came the angry voice of a second tall young officer. "Where did they go?"

"I assume you mean Mistress Harrington and her brother?"

"Brother? That enchanting young lady is Susannah?" he said incredulously. A wide grin spread across his face. "Ah, what a comely wench. I'd no idea." He pushed his military wig back a notch from his forehead.

Jane stalked up to Dan's other side, her mouth tight and dark eyes flashing. "Exactly who is that woman, Dan?"

The lanky officer gave an exaggerated bow. "Please allow me the honor of this dance, Miss Haynes, and I'll gladly enlighten you about *all* of it."

With a stiff smile, she shot him a curious glance. "Well, I do love a good piece of gossip, Lieutenant Fontaine." Her arm in his, Jane and the redcoat headed for the floor.

Catching expressions of Morgan and his mother, Dan quickly decided that he had more pressing matters than trying to satsify their curiosity. He strode to the entry hall after Susannah and her brother, stopping just beyond the doorway.

Susannah's voice carried easily from behind the stairs, where she and Ted stood partially hidden by an arrangement of evergreen boughs and holly. "How dare you leave Oxford?" Susannah cried. "We sold everything that was dear to our family, just so you could go. I came to the Colonies almost penniless for that very reason—so that Father's dream for you could be fulfilled. How could you betray him like this—betray me?"

Ted's lower tones barely concealed an intense anger. "Father might have preferred I take up his calling rather than the one I've chosen. But you! Selling yourself into servitude . . . a bondwoman . . . a serving wench in some roadside inn!

Did you actually think I could face my classmates after the shame of that came out?"

"Well, if you were so concerned about your *good name,* you needn't have told them." She put her fists on either side of her waist.

"I entrusted you to Reverend Selkirk's care. It was not your place to take matters into your own hands. I once thought that—for a girl—you possessed at least some spark of good sense. But quite obviously, I was wrong."

Dan bristled at the insult, and his hands clenched into fists.

"Oh, is that right?" Susannah continued. "Well, I've sense enough to deduce that you received my letters and chose to ignore them *and* me—your sister in need. What else was I to do, I ask? And since you've so obviously disowned me, why are we even having this conversation? Why did you create such a scene?"

"Because," he spat, "you've lied to me, and I demand to know why."

"Lied to you? About what?"

"Come off it, Sue." He took hold of her elbow. "I haven't just arrived in the Colonies, you know. Even in this primitive country the gentry frowns upon inviting serving wenches to their parties. How did you manage an invitation? Where are you living now—or should I ask *with whom?* What's the bounder's name?"

"How dare you!" Susannah wrenched free from his grasp and delivered a resounding slap to his face. "I'll have you know I'm staying *here,* with the Thomases. And if you don't mind, I'll be retiring—now that you've made an impossible mess of my evening."

Ted grabbed her shoulders. "Not until you tell me why you lied."

His action nearly caused Dan to intervene, but he saw Susannah shrug out of her brother's hold.

"*I didn't lie,*" she gritted from between her teeth. "I do work at an inn in Princeton. Morgan Thomas invited me here for the Christmas holidays."

"What, that young pup? I'll thrash him within an inch of his sniveling life."

Dan felt the beginnings of a wicked smile. That would save *him* the trouble of having to deal with young Thomas. But his conscience pricked at Susannah's retort.

"Oh, do stop acting as though we're in the midst of a Shakespearean tragedy, will you, Teddy?" Susannah shook her head and put a hand to her temples. "If you'll quiet down long enough, I'll tell you some of the wonderful things that have happened to me since I've been in the Colonies. I live with a lovely family. And you'd be surprised at how much theology I've learned from the students who frequent the inn. Most wonderful of all, I've heard George Whitefield preach. It changed my life forever."

Ted let out a huff. "So, it's even come to that, has it? Not only have you fallen in with the Presbyterians, you've sold your soul to some wild-eyed charlatan."

"It isn't like that," she said softly. "When you calm down, I'll tell you of the marvelous new light I've found in Christ, and the wondrous joy and freedom I've experienced."

"Yes. Well, by the time I've 'calmed down,' as you put it, you'll be on a ship and halfway back to England!"

No! Dan wanted to yell. He struggled to control the rage boiling within his heart at the blatant threat.

"Now get upstairs to bed," her brother ordered. "Once I've secured your passage on the morrow, I'll be back for you." Wheeling around, he charged past the ballroom and out the front door, bumping Dan on his way.

As the young officer departed, Dan caught sight of the other lobsterback standing with Jane just inside the doorway of the ballroom. How much of the exchange had they overheard?

Just then Susannah emerged from behind the stairwell. Her eyes met his, and her mouth dropped open in shock. Without a word she turned and rushed up the stairs.

He ached to follow her, to comfort her. There was no way in heaven he'd let go of her now. He would ask her to marry him at once. But surely she would misinterpret his presence in her private bedchamber. She had just started trusting him again. He couldn't risk another setback. So he turned back for the ballroom instead.

"My, my," Jane said with a malicious smile as she and the soldier exchanged amused glances. "You certainly know how to pick them, don't you, Dan? A bond servant, no less. Won't Mother be surprised?"

"Be careful, Jane," Dan said. "That's the woman I intend to marry."

27

Hours later, Dan paced in the darkness of his second-floor guestroom in the Somerwell home. If he lived to be a hundred, he'd never be able to erase from his memory the look of horror on his mother's face when Jane and her British friend had rushed back into the ballroom and informed on Susannah. Dan could still see the sneering curl of the soldier's mouth, could still hear Jane's spiteful insinuations.

"And she's indentured, Mother. *Indentured.*" Jane had spat the word out viciously, much as she might have uttered the word *snake* or *leper.* The room had gone completely silent as the vile truth imposed itself upon the hearers with unmistakable, irrevocable finality.

Dan had never believed his own sister capable of a deed so malicious. Even more unbelievable, Jane actually told them that Susannah's own brother had disowned her. He wondered if he'd ever be able to forgive Jane.

Now in the questionable solitude of his haven, Dan flexed his fists and ground his teeth in anger as he felt around in the darkness for the upholstered chaise. His toe made abrupt contact with the nearest leg, and he sank down upon the chair to clutch his throbbing foot.

It served him right for not lighting a candle. But he was not about to allow even a sliver of light under his door to announce to the rest of the family that he was still awake. They would have materialized at once to continue their ravings.

And he had already endured more of them than any one man should be expected to withstand, considering the carriage ride after their immediate departure from the Thomas mansion.

Dan had to admit that watching the flustered Morgan try to mumble and stammer his way out of the elaborate charade had been almost comical. But it wasn't nearly so funny when Dan himself had attempted to explain his own friendship with Susannah. Everything he'd said only served to add fuel to the already blazing inferno.

Well, at least Emily had been happy to leave, he recalled with a bitter smile. She hated being trotted out on the marriage block for all the available, ever-so-proper young bucks to ogle. Would the impish little tomboy ever be ready for a lasting marriage contract?

Would he? His heart pounded out the answer. *Yes. Absolutely.* His feelings for Susannah Harrington ran so deep that he still ached over the pain she had suffered that evening. And the breathtaking desire he felt in her presence set him aflame. He could not imagine living his entire life with anyone but her. Slipping off his shirt and draping it over the chair along with his waistcoat, he stood and removed his breeches and stockings.

But if he *did* marry Susannah, his mother would most emphatically disapprove. Would that last forever? He loved his family and his home. Could he give them up even for Susannah? And what sort of life could he provide for her away from the family? Could he ask her to abandon the warm, loving sanctuary of the Lyons' Den for the solitary life of a postrider's wife?

Perhaps it would be best to let her go . . . let her brother send her back to England, where no one need know of the sullied reputation she'd earned simply by being thrust into circumstances that forced her to fend for herself. That would be the logical, sensible thing to do.

Why, then, did the very thought of it send his spirit plummeting into a deep pit of despair?

Dan tried to claw his way through the damp, chilling fog that surrounded him. Somewhere in the indefinable distance the lonely wail of a ship's foghorn called out, punctuating the silence at regular intervals. The eerie blasts sent shivers of fear up his spine and made his skin crawl. It's lost, *he thought to himself.* I must find it somehow. It has to be here—it must. My life depends on it.

Trying to brush away the dense mist, he strained to focus his eyes, staring intently to see through the void. But endless grayness surrounded him, choking him. He could see nothing. Nothing. The horn blew again, piercing the stillness. Panic gripped him and, thrusting his arms ahead of his body, he started to run. Groping. Blind. Should he call out? Would anyone hear him?

He turned and stared hard. Was that a light, that faint white glow he could barely make out ahead? Reaching out with his hands again, he raced toward it. His foot thudded against something in his path, and he slammed into a rigid structure of some kind. Ignoring his pain, he explored the obstruction with his hands.

Suddenly he felt the cold iron of a door latch. He pulled down on it and pushed at the door, but it wouldn't budge. He pounded on it with his fists, then threw himself against it. It crashed open, and he found himself flooded with light. Blinking against the brightness, he raised his gaze to the source.

High above, a window in the shape of a cross emitted a shaft of light downward, downward. Following the beam with his eyes, Dan saw that it rested on his family's pew at the Baptist church in Pawtucket . . . illuminating a woman holding a small baby in her arms. He moved closer.

Susannah. Beautiful, sweet Susannah. His heart felt as though it would burst from his chest. She held the baby up to him with a smile . . . the child was his. Theirs. He reached for it, but someone spoke.

"Daniel." His mother sat on one side of Susannah, and his father on the other. "Daniel," she repeated. "Where have you been? We've been waiting for you. Take your place."

Awakening to the warmth of the morning sun shining directly on his face, Dan lay still until the beating of his pulse slowed to normal. Indescribable joy filled his being. He flung the blankets and quilts aside and dropped to his knees on the chilly rug. *Oh, Lord,* he pleaded silently, *forgive me for not praying about this last night. Because of that failure I carried the burden of my problems myself and depended upon my own wisdom to work out this whole mess. Thank you for showing me your will despite myself.*

Rising, he calculated from the brightness of the sunlight that it had been daylight for two or three hours already. He had to get to Susannah before her brother took her away. He threw on his clothes, grabbed his coat, and rushed downstairs.

As his foot struck the last step, his father emerged from the dining room, holding a cup of coffee. "Daniel," he said in his low, resonant voice. "You're up. I'd like to speak to you."

Without slowing his pace, Dan shrugged into his coat as he dashed toward the front door. "I'm in a bit of a hurry, Father."

"It's about last night, Son. The young woman."

"Could we please talk later? I have a rather urgent matter to attend." Pulling his gloves from his pockets, he thrust them on, then opened the door.

His father laid a hand on his shoulder.

Dan sighed. Turning his head, he met his father's gaze.

An understanding smile lent a twinkle to the older man's light brown eyes. "I wanted you to know that I prayed about what happened last night. About you and the young lady. And strange as it may seem, I feel completely at peace with the situation. I know that God will work it out somehow for the best."

Taking the words as a confirming sign from God, Dan looked heavenward and breathed a silent thanks. Then with a grin, he grabbed the cup from his father's hand and took a gulp, then handed it back. He wiped his mouth with the back of a glove, and his grin broadened. "That means more to me than you can possibly know, Father. And I do want to hear more about it, but I really must go now."

After an eternity of impatient rapping with the brass knocker at the Thomas home, Dan found himself admitted to the library to await Mrs. Thomas. He swept a disinterested glance over the book-lined shelves and paced the expensive carpet, watching the double doors until he heard a hand on the latch.

Still in her morning robe and ruffled sleeping cap, Mrs. Thomas entered. Her stiff smile gave evidence that she did not appreciate receiving callers before noon. "Why, Daniel. What brings you by so early?"

"I do apologize for the hour, madam. And I know this may seem presumptive of me, but I must have a word with Mistress Harrington before she leaves with her brother."

The woman's mouth tightened on one side. "Well, I'm afraid you're too late." Drawing a piece of paper from her pocket, she held it out, the white note dangling limply from her fingers. "The maid found this on the hall table a few moments ago. It's a thank-you from that imposter—and some pitiful excuse for her duplicity. As if that could ever make up for the way she involved my son in her lies and ruined my Christmas ball. I'm quite the laughingstock." She shook her head. "In any event, I must assume her brother came to fetch the upstart quite early."

Dan felt the downward plunge of his spirit. "She's already gone?"

"And good riddance, I say."

Dan started to protest, then realized that the woman's harsh words were a result of the previous evening's humiliating scene. He bowed graciously. "Well, again, my apologies for disturbing you so early, Mrs. Thomas. Thank you for your trouble." Placing his tricornered hat on his head, he tipped it, then rushed past her and out the door.

After a swift ride to the wharf, Dan drew his pacer to a stop and surveyed the sight before his eyes. At least seventy or more ships were moored along the docks, their empty masts creating a forest of tall spikes that stirred with the movements of the vessels.

Dan dismounted and looped the reins around a hitching post. Two large ships had already moved into the current of the Delaware River. He couldn't be too late, could he? He prayed he wasn't.

Then a flicker of hope rose up within him. If God really meant for him to have Susannah, she'd still be there. He'd find her. Somehow he'd find her.

At one of the nearby docks, workers were loosening mooring lines and raising the gangplank. With a cupped hand on either side of his mouth, Dan yelled to the ship's officer who stood at the railing. "Sir, did you take on a passenger this morning? A Mistress Harrington?"

The man shook his head. "No. No passengers on board. We bring them *to* America, lad, not take them *from* it. Move aside, now. We're shoving off."

Stepping back, Dan ducked as one of the dockhands tossed a heavy rope over his head. He cast a disheartened look up and down the line of ships at anchor. Where on earth should he start? He trudged on down the wharf.

Unsuccessful after the next three inquiries, Dan felt the weight of his task descending upon him. He shot a gaze toward heaven and pleaded for guidance, then, drawing a breath of sharp winter air, he approached a ship's officer heading his way, a man of medium build with a short brownish beard. "I beg your pardon, my good man."

"What can I do for ye, laddie?" Pushing back his stiff-brimmed cap with a freckled hand, he squinted, adding an abundance of wrinkles to the weathered skin surrounding hazel eyes.

"I'm trying to locate a Miss Harrington, whose passage to England was to be purchased by her brother, a British soldier. Can you help me?"

"Well now, I might just be able to." He kneaded his jaw in thought. "I believe that's the name of the young lady who'll be embarking with us. The young lieutenant hasn't brought her by, as yet, but I expect they'll be along in due course. We depart at dusk."

Grabbing the man's leathery hand, Dan pumped it exuberantly. "Thank you, sir. Thank you very much. This evening, you say." Noting the name of the vessel, Dan tipped his hat and strode back to his waiting horse, then he leaned against the rail, formulating his next step.

She's not at the Thomas house, he reminded himself, *and she hasn't arrived at the ship yet.* Could she be at her brother's lodgings at the British headquarters? A twinge of dread pricked his consciousness at the thought of making a voluntary appearance anywhere within a mile of a detachment of soldiers. He had been on the wrong end of their scrutiny more often than he cared to recall. But how else was he to find Susannah? He had to risk it.

Fighting his negative feelings, he loosened the reins from the hitching post and mounted Flame, then nudged him away from the docks and down the cobbled street.

A few moments later, he dismounted in front of a brick building beneath a frayed Union Jack. A few faces seemed uncomfortably familiar among the handful of king's men milling about the walk and steps. *What sort of fool am I,* Dan asked himself, *to walk so willingly right into the mouth of the lion?* Ducking his chin slightly in an attempt to keep his features in the shadow of his hat, he started up the steps toward the massive oak entry.

Footsteps followed from behind, and someone tapped on his shoulder.

Dan tried to ignore the interruption, but a pair of strong arms grabbed him, whirling him around.

"Now, who have we here?"

Dan's eyes met the hostile gaze of an officer who had initiated a search of his person and saddlebags a month ago on the Trenton road. Dan raised his chin.

"And who might ye be deliverin' to today?" The harsh cockney accent from a second soldier assaulted his ears. "Or is it *what?* Let's drag the bugger up on the porch and have a look-see."

"I've come to speak to—"

The lobsterbacks yanked him up the remaining steps and rammed him against the wall, knocking the breath from his lungs in a grunt. Opening his coat, half a dozen hands checked the hems and seams, then slid into his pockets, pulling the lining out into view. None too gently, they frisked his body. They found nothing of consequence, but the sergeant slammed him against the building once more.

The other two closed in. "State your business—and be quick about it."

"I need to speak to Lieutenant Harrington. He told me I'd find him here today, and if not, at his lodgings."

"Is that right? And what business could the likes of you have with a fine gentleman like the leftenant?"

Considering his reception outside headquarters, Dan was none too eager to enter the building. With an effort to keep his voice steady, he lowered it to a conspiratorial tone. "It's personal. I don't believe the lieutenant would want me to speak of it." Shooting a quick glance about, Dan leaned close. "Concerns a lady," he whispered.

The sergeant eased back. Fingering the stubble on his face, he grinned. "I see."

The other pair released Dan.

Straightening his stance, Dan smoothed his rumpled coat. "Would one of you gentlemen mind telling him I'm here?" He raised a hopeful brow and watched their furtive glances dart back and forth.

"Ain't here."

"Oh. Well, then." Dan moved slowly toward the steps. "Perhaps I can try again the next time she comes all the way from Princeton. Thanks."

"Leavin' today, is she?"

Dan nodded. "Taking the packet this afternoon."

The sergeant narrowed his eyes warily. "Well, mayhap you'd better go on over to his place, then. Helps to keep them fancy young leftenants occupied, you understand. He's taken rooms on Ninth Street—"

"Well," came a deeper voice as another officer strode up the steps. "I see our diligent postrider hasn't been quite so clever this time." He sneered. "What'd you find on him?"

"Not a blasted thing, Davis," said the first sergeant. "But how is it *you* know him? This man rides between here and New York."

"Not last week, he didn't. Stopped him on the road to Baltimore. We've been keeping watch on this one for some time. Keeps company with suspected traitors—and we're still trying to make logical sense out of his route."

Dan cringed inwardly, and his heartbeat increased, but he steeled his expression against any outward sign. He had known his business would someday bring him to a confrontation of this nature. But this was the worst possible time.

"You don't say," the officer snapped, eyeing Dan with a malevolent sneer. "Perhaps 'tis time we had ourselves a nice long chat with this one." He nodded sharply to the two privates. "Maybe a few hours with the rats will loosen his tongue. Take the guttersnipe round back and lock him in the shed."

28

Dan paced the packed dirt floor of the dim musty shed for hours, his breath coming out in puffs of white that dissipated each time he exhaled. He couldn't forget the sound of the padlock that had been snapped in place over the rusty latch. The raucous laughter of the king's puppets still rang in his ears.

Inside his thick gloves, his fingertips began to feel cold. Rubbing his hands together to generate warmth, he fought the temptation to berate himself for having allowed his own stupidity to get him into the present predicament.

No. He had been positive that God had shown him Susannah was to share his life. *Dear heavenly Father,* he prayed, *please don't desert me now. I need your help. There's got to be a way out of this. Help me to find it. I must get to Susannah's ship before it sails.*

Glancing around the dismal cell, Dan's spirits sank. He moved to the door and threw himself against it with all his weight. Once. Twice. But it wouldn't budge. Despite the decrepit condition of the outbuilding, the sturdy door seemed amazingly solid. He had no idea how long he'd been imprisoned, but it seemed forever.

The angle of the thin shafts of light that threaded between cracks in the windowless board walls added to his alarm as daylight rapidly waned. He had to get out. Had to stop Susannah. He pounded against the door with his fists. "Hey!" His gloves muffled the sound, so he tore them off and tried again. "Hey! Somebody! Help me!"

Spotting a nearby slat that appeared loose near the bottom, he tugged on it as hard as he could. It squeaked in protest and snapped out of his grasp. It had been braced from outside. The situation was hopeless.

Dan sank to the floor. How could this have happened? And why? She had been so close. Things had almost worked out for them. How could everything so suddenly have gone completely wrong? His head dropped into his hands. *Lord, you can't let this happen. It isn't right. It isn't fair. You've got to help me. You're my only hope.*

Suddenly a sharp pounding, as of a rifle butt against wood, sounded on the door. "Still in there, are ye?" a gruff voice asked.

Dan sprang to his feet. "Yes! I need help!"

"Well, I can't let ye out, but a young lass here wants to talk to ye."

"Dan?"

"Jane?" Hope rose in Dan's heart. *Thank you, Lord,* he breathed. "Is Father with you?"

"No, just Charlotte. We saw your horse tied up in front and found out you were being held back here. What have you done?"

"Nothing, I swear. Nothing at all! They threw me in here for being a postrider!"

"Stuff and nonsense. You must have done something."

"No. Jane, listen to me. There's no time. I need to get out of here. Now!"

"Then tell me what you did."

Dan let out a huff of exasperation and rolled his eyes. "I asked to see Lieutenant Harrington."

"Well, that couldn't be why they're holding you. I also asked after him—and no one arrested me."

"*Jane,*" Dan grated impatiently. "Get back to the Somerwells' and get Father for me. Now."

"Why should I?" she asked churlishly. "I don't like your

tone, Daniel Haynes. Perhaps I'll just let you sit there a while longer." She took a few steps away.

Charlotte's titter drifted through the cracks.

Hearing his sister's departing footfalls, Dan pounded the door again. "Jane! Come back here!" He struggled to control his rage as he lowered his voice. "I apologize, all right? Now, please, would you go and get Father for me?"

"Yes," she said sweetly. "Now that you've asked properly. Come on, Charlotte."

"No, wait," Dan blurted as another thought came to him. "I've changed my mind. You must do something else first. You and Charlotte go down to the wharf—but be careful. Don't dawdle along the way. Go to Pier Eighteen, where the *Bonnie Maid* is docked. Lieutenant Harrington is sending his sister back to England on it this evening."

"Oh?" she said cheerfully. "So that's where the handsome officer is. In that case, we'll go right away."

"Wait!"

"What now?"

Even through the door Dan could hear her foot tapping impatiently. "I haven't told you why."

"Oh yes. Well, I'm not so addle-brained I can't figure that out. I suppose you must have a message for the scandalous doxy. How a charming gentleman like the lieutenant could have a sister like her—"

Dan gritted his teeth. "*Jane.* There isn't time for this. Go down there and convince your *charming gentleman* friend to delay Susannah's departure until I've had a chance to speak to both of them. Please."

"Let me see, now," came her miffed voice. "You want me to ask this upstanding young officer to delay the departure of that inglorious sister of his until I'm able to arrange the release of my *jailed brother.* Do I have it right?"

Dan shook his head in exasperation and sighed. "Please, just do what you can. If nothing else, find out where she'll be staying in England. Will you do that for me?"

"Oh, very well," she said with reluctance. "But this had

better not cost me Lieutenant Harrington's friendship, I'll tell you that. Come on, Charlotte."

Another low giggle grated on his nerves.

Hours later, Dan's teeth began to chatter as he huddled in the chill darkness. It took all his reserve to relax his jaw muscles. He drew the two threadbare blankets he had found under the mattress of the rickety cot tighter about himself.

What was taking Jane so long? Had something happened to her or Charlotte? What had possessed him to have sent two defenseless young girls to the dock? *Father in heaven, what have I done?*

Susannah smiled at Mary Clare's excitement as the stage wagon drew up before the brightly lit Lyons' Den. She watched as the younger girl threw open the door and jumped out before they had stopped.

"Quick! Toss me my satchel," Mary told the driver. The instant he threw it down, she caught it and ran to the door, vanishing inside at once.

"I'll see to the rest of your things, miss," the man said, turning to Susannah. "And I'm sure glad you found your little friend all safe and sound."

"Yes." She barely managed strength enough to smile. "We were truly blessed." With a glance toward the warm, welcoming glow from the windows of the inn, Susannah paused to admire the neat three-storied building. This new home had been so very good to her, had blessed her in a hundred ways. She should be as happy as Mary was to be safely home again. But the humiliating failures of the previous evening brought a taunting restlessness to her weary mind.

She forced the memories aside and thought about the motherly comfort of Mrs. Lyons' arms. *How I wish . . . ,* her thoughts began, but she snatched them back. *Enough of that foolishness.* Drawing herself to her full height, she reached for the door latch. There'd be no more wishes . . . no more dreams.

Opening the door, she stepped inside, then wiped her feet

on the braided mat. Across the room she noted with a passing glance a slender young brunette girl waiting on a few late-night customers. But Susannah longed only to see Mrs. Lyons. Undoing the frog closure of her heavy cape, she shrugged out of the wrap, draped it over the back of a chair, and headed straight for the kitchen.

"There you are, love," came Mrs. Lyons' soothing voice. Holding Mary Clare tightly to her cushiony bosom, the plump woman beamed and held out her free arm.

Susannah went to her immediately, reveling in the warm embrace.

"An' where's that scamp, Morgan?" Mrs. Lyons asked. "He should be in on this hug, too."

The girls exchanged a quick look. "Oh," Mary Clare said, "I couldn't wait. I wanted to be here with you for Christmas."

"And what about me?" Mr. Lyons clomped into the room, running one hand through his wild silvery hair.

Mary ran to him and all but disappeared as his big arms wrapped around her. "I missed you both so much. I'm so sorry for everything. I'll never, ever, run away again."

He held her at arm's length and searched her face, then drew her close again. "We lost a lot of sleep, what with our worry," he chided, but the gruffness was missing in his tone.

"Me too. But the good Lord watched over me. I can't wait to tell you all about it." Mary eased out of his embrace, and her clear blue eyes searched around the kitchen. "But first, where's that little brother of mine? Christopher! Chip! I'm home!"

Mrs. Lyons removed her arm from Susannah and crossed to Mary Clare. "I'm afraid he's not here."

"Not here? Where else could he be?"

"Something happened while you was away," the older woman said gently. "Let's sit down." Taking Mary Clare's hand, she led her to a chair, then took the one next to her.

Susannah felt a measure of dread as she tried to imagine where the lad might be. She looked from Mr. Lyons to his wife, hoping for some clue about what was coming. She sank into the nearest seat.

"You tell 'em," Mrs. Lyons said with a pleading look to her husband.

"Well," he said, clearing his throat as he sat down on Mary's other side. "Seems the boy was more upset about your leavin' than any of us knew. He took my old pistol from under the bar and went to your pa's."

"What?" Mary gasped. "You can't mean . . . oh, this is awful. It's all my fault!" She buried her head in her hands and burst into tears.

"Now, hold on there, gal," Mr. Lyons said. "You didn't let me finish."

Mary sniffed and wiped her tears away with her fingers. With sheer determination she straightened up and clasped her hands in her lap.

"He did go there plannin' to shoot your pa," the innkeeper continued. "That's a fact."

A solitary tear rolled from the corner of Mary's eye, but she pressed her lips tightly together.

Mrs. Lyons patted her shoulder. "The way Silas tells it, the boy put the fear of God in him, all right. But, fact is, Chip couldn't do what he planned to. Instead, he shot a hole clean through the roof. No matter how much he hated your pa for how he's wronged the two of you, he couldn't kill him."

"Thank the Lord," Susannah whispered. Christopher could have ruined his whole life with one irrational act. Mary might never have seen her brother again.

"Yes," Mr. Lyons agreed. "Thank the good Lord. And I've been thinking about thanking him in person. I've a real mind to go to Christmas Eve service with you Monday night."

"Why wait till Monday?" Mrs. Lyons asked, tilting her ruffle-capped head. "If you're of a mind to do it, why not go with the children to Sunday service day after tomorrow?" Her small hazel eyes sparkled with challenge.

He stroked his jowls with a good-natured frown. "Well now," he hedged, "Christmas Eve's soon enough."

"But where's Chip, then?" Mary asked, concern apparent in her voice and features.

"Oh," Mrs. Lyons answered, "he's over to your pa's, helpin' him get his place cleaned up."

"*What?*"

Mrs. Lyons smiled. "Yes. Silas coming so close to meetin' his Maker, soaked through with sin like he was, turned him into a repentant man. Stopped his drinking, cleaned himself up—" She laughed. "Why, I wouldn't have recognized him when he walked in the door, except that I knowed him before your ma died. And before he took himself to rack and ruin."

Covering Mary Clare's tiny hand with his large weathered one, Mr. Lyons gave it a squeeze, then cleared his throat again, embarrassed. "That pa of yours hasn't had a drink in about four days, now. And the cravin' shakes haven't come on him even once. Must be the work of God, showing his forgiveness, I'm sure of that. Couldn't be nothin' else. And I'm hoping, Mary girl, you'll be able to find it in your heart to be doin' the same."

"Oh, Mr. Lyons." Mary Clare hugged him, then turned. "Mrs. Lyons." With a smile, she hugged the woman tightly. "You've made me the happiest person alive."

Susannah forced aside her morbid memories of the past few days and watched the tender exchange with wonder. Apparently God had worked out this impossible situation, too.

"Well," Mrs. Lyons said, her eyes twinkling as she drew an envelope from her pocket. "Maybe I should give this to you after a while. Too much happiness all at once might spoil you."

"What is it?" Mary asked, snatching the letter out of the woman's gnarled fingers.

"Oh, just something from Jonathan." She drew the young girl close. "He'll be here for Christmas. His folks are letting him come back to school."

"Is that really true?" Mary whispered, pulling back and staring at Mrs. Lyons.

"Yes, love. Steven told me when he brought your letter by. Jonathan wrote to him, too."

Mary Clare looked lovingly at the envelope, then pressed it to her breast. "Oh my. I . . . have to go upstairs and read it." Never taking her gaze from it, she rose and started for the steps. "Oh my."

Watching Mary Clare walk away, Susannah suddenly became aware that her own cheeks were wet with tears. She was happy for Mary, she tried to convince herself. So happy she was crying out of joy. And only out of joy.

29

Susannah watched absently from the window of the common room as the last coach of travelers pulled away, its runners shushing over the icy drive. Heavy clouds hovered barely above the skeletal trees, their sullen presence threatening more snow. Already some solitary flakes whirled about on the sharp December wind.

"Mama used to say some funny things about snow," Mary Clare said at her elbow, a cornhusk broom in one hand.

Susannah turned. "Oh?"

"Mm hmm. She said clouds were angel pillows. And when it would snow real hard—you know, with those big fluffy flakes—she told us the angels were having a pillow fight, and the snowflakes were the feathers that burst when their cloud-pillows crashed into each other."

With a smile, Susannah shifted her gaze outside again. "Well, I wouldn't be surprised if there were a bit of a pillow fight very soon, from the look of things."

"Looks like it." With renewed vigor, Mary finished sweeping the floor, collecting the dirt with a dustpan. She dumped it outside, then closed the door against a blast of cold air and went to the kitchen.

"Susannah," called old Art Bentley from one of the trestle tables, where he sat with some of his fellow tradesmen. He tipped his white head questioningly. "We'd appreciate more coffee, if it's not too much trouble."

"Of course." Hurrying to the kitchen, Susannah returned momentarily with the pot, filling their cups.

"Thank you, missy," Asa Appleton boomed. He grinned across the table at Mr. Bentley.

Hiram Brown shifted his weight on the seat while he drew out a wadded handkerchief from a back pocket and wiped his huge nose. "I swear, it's good to see you and little Mary back again. Not that we minded that quiet little Beth what filled in for you, a' course."

"Yeah," Orin Fields popped in. "Prob'ly safe to come back for a tankard of flip tonight, I'd be thinkin'." His wide belly shook with his jovial laugh.

"What ever do you mean?" Susannah asked, looking from one grinning face to the next.

Mr. Bentley set down his pipe and chuckled. "While you two were away, it seems your boss got so caught up worrying, he started living up to his name."

"Right," Mr. Appleton said with a nod. "Roared around here like some wounded old lion."

With a swift glance toward the empty bar, Susannah smiled. "Surely you can't mean our sweet, gentle Mr. Lyons."

The three men burst into laughter.

The door squeaked on its hinges, and two men in scarlet uniforms came inside. Immediately the laughter and good-natured chatter ceased, and a hostile silence took its place.

Susannah stared at Ted and the officer at his side as they removed their tall hats and held them in the crooks of their arms.

"Well, there goes my appetite," grumbled Mr. Appleton. Flipping a coin onto the table, he got up and crossed the room in half a dozen strides. He took his warm coat from a peg, pulled it on, and left.

"Yeah," Orin Fields said evenly as he and the other two rose. "The smell of lobster always turns my stomach."

Susannah saw her brother stiffen as he moved his hand to the long sword sheathed at his side. She couldn't help but notice that his military training and discipline had defined the contours of his muscled frame. But the old twinkle she had always loved was absent from his clear blue eyes, and the hard set of his jaw detracted from his otherwise handsome face. With her gaze fixed steadily on him, she walked in his direction, keeping herself between him and the exiting tradesmen. "See you this evening, gentlemen," she said. Then after the door closed, she gestured to the nearest table. "Ted, why don't you and your friend have a seat?"

The other soldier started to comply, but her brother's icy blue stare didn't waver as he stood rigidly in place.

"We're still serving breakfast," she said matter-of-factly. "Are you hungry? I'll get you some."

Ted's tall, lanky companion pulled out a chair and lowered himself onto it. "We ate in Trenton before we left early this morning. But a cup of tea would be appreciated."

Susannah slowly turned her attention to the young officer. He looked to be in his mid-twenties, as was Ted, and he had a long, narrow face and eyes gray as a rainstorm. Extremely lean, with refined features, he held himself with a distinct air of aristocracy. "Sorry, I don't believe I've had the pleasure of your acquaintance."

A quick grin spread across his face as he stood, revealing an array of straight healthy teeth. "Alex, Mistress Harrington. Alex Fontaine, at your service. Your brother and I have been chums since our Oxford days."

Slanting a glance at Ted, who remained standing in morose silence, Susannah looked back at Alex.

"You know, I was of the opinion that Ted and I had no secrets," the young man continued. "But not once did he allude to your entrancing charms or the exquisite magnificence of your beauty." Reaching for her hand, he brushed it with his lips, and a smile lit the steel gray of his eyes. "How utterly thoughtless of him, don't you agree?"

Still on her guard, Susannah gave him a cold smile. "That is most flattering, Lieutenant Fontaine," she began.

"Alex," he corrected.

She looked from him to Ted. "But if you know my brother

so well, then surely you're aware he's not here for a simple tête-à-tête. If you'll excuse me, I'll get you both some coffee. We're still boycotting tea, you know."

"Forget the blasted drinks!" Ted ordered. "Sit down."

Alex sprang to pull out a chair for Susannah, then took his own again.

She nodded her thanks, waiting for Ted to join them.

He did not. "I was seriously considering giving you a sound thrashing," he said, anger blazing in his expression.

"Thank you," she said icily. "It's such a pleasure to see you again, too."

"Now, now," Alex coaxed. "I'm sure if we can all collect ourselves, we'll be able to settle this bothersome matter and get on to more pleasant ones." As Susannah and Ted both shot him frowns of disbelief, he threw up his hands. "Oh, very well then. I'll keep silent."

Ted shifted his stance and turned to Susannah. "Surely you must know that I am *very* angry with you for running back here. Not only did you cause me great inconvenience, forcing me to go to my commanding officer for a favor so soon after having arrived at my new post, but you also caused me considerable embarrassment when I went to the Thomas home to collect you."

Grimacing, Susannah looked off into the distance.

"Most of all," he continued, "I especially did not enjoy having some uppity colonial pup refusing to tell me where my own sister had taken herself. I was ready to take measures right there and then, but his father stepped in to prevent it." His expression darkened, and he lowered his tone. "I'll not be forgetting that young upstart."

Susannah raised her eyebrows and stiffened as she peered up at him. "You mean you plan to avenge yourself on Morgan Thomas? I don't believe it. Why, you're taking up the banner of the bully boys right along with the rest of your military cohorts." She shook her head in disgust, refusing to cower even as he leaned into her face.

"And I see the time you've spent here in this traitorous

Presbyterian enclave has stolen what little sense and loyalty you once possessed."

With a gasp, Susannah stood. But before she could retort, his words cut her off.

"The traitorous attitudes at this Princeton college will not go unnoticed. Be assured of that." Shifting his weight slightly, he appeared to relax a fraction. "But 'tis all moot now. Even your running back here merely serves to expedite a final, complete removal of you and your belongings from this heretical place."

As Susannah's jaw dropped open, she heard her brother speak to his companion.

"Alex, old man, see to the hiring of a wagon, will you? My sister and I will be busy collecting her things."

"Whatever you say," Alex shot an uncomfortable glance Susannah's way. "Should take but a short—"

"Now just one minute." Susannah crossed her arms and planted her feet firmly. "You needn't bother to waste your time. I'll not be returning to my imprisoned past. Not now, not ever." Her chin raised, she glared at Ted.

He gave a hollow laugh. "You jest. You consider indenturement in some backwoods inn preferable to sojourning with relatives in England?"

"I do," she said with a defiant nod. "And I suggest you remember, *brother dear,* that I am legally indentured to Mr. Lyons. He, and he alone, has the right to say where—and when—I go. Once I tell him I don't wish to go with you, he'll not let you take me. Be assured of *that!*"

Ted sneered. "Surely you don't think you can scare me off with idle threats." He looked about the room. "Where is the miscreant? I'll have a word with him."

"Ted, old chap," Alex said nervously. "If the blighter has papers on her, he'd be within his right to send the authorities after us. It wouldn't look good, you know."

"Well, I'm not about to simply—"

"Perhaps what's needed here is time for a cooling of passions," Alex said in a somewhat stronger tone. "Then, after that, when the two of you have made your peace, we'll see about purchasing Susannah's bond." He flashed a disarming grin her way. "In fact, old man, there's no real urgency that should send your sister back to Britain if she's so set against it. We could find a small house to let in Philadelphia—and she could take care of it for us, instead of our having to board with strangers. Wouldn't you consider that a very pleasant compromise?"

Susannah raised her eyes to the ceiling. But as she considered the alternative, she felt her resolve begin to weaken. "I shall pray about it and let you know." She tightened her lips stubbornly.

"You'll *pray* about it!" Ted said in a huff. "*You* have no say in this matter!" He leveled a stare at Alex. "And as for you, my womanizing friend, I'm not so dense that I can't see through that little scheme of yours."

Alex shrugged in mock innocence. "You misjudge me."

Undaunted, Ted peered at Susannah. "I am this close," he said, holding his finger and thumb a hair's breadth apart, "to washing my hands of you for good. Only respect for our father's memory has kept me from doing that already. When you come to your senses—if ever—write to me in care of our command post in Philadelphia. Otherwise, as far as I am concerned, you shall no longer exist. I'll not jeopardize my position by admitting I have a radical-thinking bond servant for a sister." Turning on one heel, Ted stalked out the door.

Susannah fought to restrain the tears that threatened as she watched her brother's retreating back. She swallowed against the pain his words had caused, then noted absently that Lieutenant Fontaine had taken her hand in his.

"Try not to fret, my dear lady. He'll soon cool off. And when he does, I shall convince him of the practicality of your staying with us in the city. I'm sure he had no inkling that this new independent side of you even existed, and it has quite shocked him. I, on the other hand, find your spirit enchanting."

She smiled wanly. "Well, it's of some comfort to know that

he has got such a good and caring friend. I thank you in advance for anything you might be able to do to mend this breach between us."

Lifting her hand to his mouth, Alex kissed it briefly. "The gift of the lady's smile doth give wing to my purpose. I bid you adieu." With a flourish of his military cape, he swung around and strode outside.

Susannah's smile faded. The lieutenant would find out in time that Ted was now as dead to her as her parents. Everyone she loved . . . Julia, her parents, and now her only brother— all of them were gone. A crushing weight descended upon her heart, making it almost impossible to breathe.

Thoughts of Dan surfaced, bringing only a fleeting moment of hope. And what of him? She had been convinced he had come quite close to proposing in those last moments before they had been interrupted by Ted. It had been in his eyes, in his touch, in the huskiness of his voice. But how could he come for her now, when her reputation lay in scandalous ruins—witnessed by his family, at that? She'd never be able to hold any man's interest for long once the truth was told. No, Daniel Haynes was out of her life for good.

Susannah let out a deep sigh. A tear crested her cheek, then rolled down her face. This freedom, even in Christ, had a high price.

The sight that met Susannah's eyes as she carried a tray of glasses to her new family filled her with warmth. This Christmas Eve she had made them a special drink they had never tasted. The sweet, rich aroma of the eggnog teased her nostrils, and she smiled. It felt wonderful to be able to do something special for the people she had grown to love. She paused for a brief moment in the distance and surveyed the loving scene.

Chairs from the side tables had been set in a semicircle facing the fireplace, where a bright yule log snapped and popped. Low-burning candles cast a subdued golden light over that side of the common room, and delicate shadow patterns played among the arrangement of holly on the mantel. Mr. Lyons stood behind Mrs. Lyons' chair, his hands resting on her shoulders. Silas Drummond, seated next to Christopher, hugged his son close. And Mary Clare held a gift from Jonathan in her lap as she sat gazing into the young man's eyes.

Susannah felt warm in love's encompassing glow, as though someone had wrapped her in a luxuriant fur robe on this wintry night. She had lost almost everything within the past year, and she knew there would always be a measure of sadness at the memory. But God had not left her in the darkness of her sorrow. Quite the contrary. In his bountiful mercy on this gathering dawn of freedom, he'd blessed her with so much more: a loving new Christian family and a wondrous glimpse of the light and glory that beckoned her. The words from the ageless story of Christmas, of peace on earth and goodwill toward men, had never meant so much to her as they did on this eve of the holy day.

Mr. Lyons turned and motioned to Susannah. "Quit your dawdlin', lass. Bring on that tray. I worked up a fierce thirst from all that singing at church tonight."

With a soft laugh, Susannah carried the drinks to them, serving Mr. and Mrs. Lyons first before going on to the others.

Mrs. Lyons leaned over the glass and took a whiff. "My, that does smell delicious, love."

"Thank you. My mum made it for us at Christmas, back in Ashford. It would please me if you'd consider it a gift from her."

The older woman stroked Susannah's arm softly. "You must've loved her very much."

"Yes." Susannah nodded sadly. "But she was ailing for many years. I would never have burdened her with my troubles the way I do you. You have the comforting mother-arms I've always longed for."

In the bright flicker of the firelight, Mrs. Lyons' eyes glistened with the beginnings of tears. "I—I—" She pressed the tips of her crooked fingers over her lips for a second. "Well, these old arms'll always be here for you, love," she managed to say.

"I know," Susannah whispered. Bending, she bestowed a kiss on the woman's soft cheek and smiled, then sidestepped to Mr. Drummond and Chip.

The man removed his massive arm from his son's shoulders as the lad, full of Christmas excitement, grabbed one of the drinks.

"Thanks!" Chip said.

A shy toothy grin split Mr. Drummond's recently shaved face, brightening his swarthy complexion. He hesitated before taking a glass. "This don't have no rum in, does it?"

"No. It's quite harmless."

"Then I thank ye." His big hand engulfed the glass as he took it.

"And I thank *you*, too, for being here with us tonight. We're so happy to have you."

Mr. Drummond shifted his gaze to Christopher and gave an affectionate squeeze to the boy's knee.

Chip's answering grin was so like his father's that the resemblance between them quite caught Susannah by surprise. She moved to Mary Clare and Jonathan.

Caught up in each other, the pair barely dragged their eyes from one another to mumble their quick thanks.

Watching the young couple, Susannah felt a jolting ache in her own heart. She slowly filled her lungs. "You're most welcome," she uttered. Then she quickly turned away before they saw her pain, walked past them, and set the tray down on the table while she regained her composure. Nothing must spoil this lovely, precious night.

"*Now* can we open our gifts?" Chip asked.

Everyone chuckled.

"Yes, Chip," Mrs. Lyons said. "Now that Susannah's here to watch. Come on over with the rest of us," she gestured.

Just then, the front door opened, emitting a rush of cold wind from the other end of the room.

Everyone turned toward the dim entrance.

Susannah's brows shot up in wonder. Who on earth could possibly be out this late on Christmas Eve? She took a tentative step forward.

Unwinding a thick wool scarf from his neck, a bundled-up Daniel Haynes strode out of the shadows. "Merry Christmas, everyone," he said with a grin. He pulled off one glove, then the other, as he walked directly to Susannah. Taking her hands in his, he winked. "And merry Christmas to you," he said in a voice she knew was for her alone.

Her pulse raced through her body. She stared, speechless, drinking in the incredible sight of his face, glowing from the cold—and from something else as well. She felt her cheeks flush.

"Dan Haynes? That you?" Mr. Lyons said as he and the others rose. "Somethin' terrible must've happened for you to be sent out on Christmas Eve. What is it?"

Mrs. Lyons gave her husband a nudge in the ribs. "Oh, don't get all riled up. The boy's payin' a social call. Right, lad?"

He gave her a broad grin. "Yes. And I'd like a moment alone with this young lady here, if you don't mind."

"Of course," Mrs. Lyons began, but Dan had already taken her young charge halfway to the kitchen.

"But—what about our presents?" Chip asked.

"Don't wait for us," Dan said over his shoulder as he kicked the door shut behind them.

The kitchen lay in semidarkness, illuminated only by the glow from the banked fire. Dropping Susannah's hand just long enough to unbutton his coat and shrug out of it, Dan let it fall at his feet as his burning gaze rooted her to the floor. Then a slow smile spread across his face as he reached for her and drew her into his arms.

Pressed against Dan's hard chest, Susannah couldn't have taken a breath if she'd wanted to. She closed her eyes and lost herself in his strength, feeling the thundering of his heart and her own, pounding in unison against each other. She felt him release her a bit. Then his thumb and forefinger gently lifted her chin, and his warm, firm lips met hers. Susannah's knees went weak. She wanted the kiss to go on forever. Threading her arms around him, she pressed herself closer, closer, and felt his arms tighten around her.

When at last he lifted his head, Dan gave a soft laugh and hugged her again. "Oh, my dear Susannah. Do you have any idea how long I've wanted to do that?"

She raised her lashes. With his back to the fire, Dan's sable eyes were almost black. "I—"

"I'll tell you," he continued, his fingers stroking along her cheek as his warm breath feathered over her face. "Since that first day I saw you on the Philadelphia wharf."

"Oh," she breathed. For the first time in her life, she could think of nothing to say.

At her lack of response, Dan released her and moved half a step backward. "Please, forgive me. I'm rushing you. I'm sorry." He massaged his brow, then gathered her hands again. "It's just that I thought I'd lost you, you see. That you'd left for England. I was locked up in a dreary shed by some soldiers, and all I could think of was you . . . sailing farther and farther away. I sent my sister to try to stop you, but she never returned. And neither did anyone else, for two of the longest days of my life."

"Locked up?" she said inanely as his words began to dawn on her.

He nodded. "Seems my activities for the Colonies are becoming too noticeable."

"Y-you mean your smuggling?" Still feeling Dan's kiss, Susannah traced her lips with her fingertips.

"That too. If it hadn't been for your brother, I'd probably still be sitting in that stinking British cell."

Susannah's eyes came alive. "My brother? He *helped* you?"

"It seems he has a strong fondness for my sister, Jane. She convinced him to go to the captain on my behalf." He shook his head in disbelief. "Never thought I'd find myself beholden to an officer of the Crown, but since he's your brother, I'll make an effort to be more charitable in the future."

Still trying to fathom Dan's words, Susannah lowered her gaze. She fingered a fold of her violet wool skirt. Ted would never do anything for her benefit. He had disowned her. "I can't believe it," she whispered.

"My sister can be *very* persuasive, I assure you." Dan grinned disarmingly. "Besides, he didn't know I was interested in you until afterward, when I asked where I could write to you. In fact, my love, your brother told me I'd be wise to forget you. Said something about you becoming a religious radical and wholly too willful. I think those were his words."

Susannah's jumbled mind registered Dan's words at half the speed they were pouring out of him. Had he called her his love? She tried to bite back a smile. She allowed her gaze to absorb his fine wool flannel waistcoat before meeting his eyes. "I . . . see you didn't take his advice."

"No more than he'd have taken mine if I had told him what a spoiled little minx Jane is." Dan chuckled. "When I left them, the poor fool was even talking about getting a transfer to Boston so he could be within a day's ride of our farm."

With a smile, Susannah nodded. She felt chilly now that he had let go of her, and she wondered how to get back into his embrace without seeming too forward.

"Speaking of that—," he began.

"Of what?" Had she spoken her thoughts aloud? She felt her cheeks grow warm.

"The farm," Dan said, tilting his head with a puzzled look. "After I was released, my father asked me to pass on my postriding job to my younger brother, Ben, since my face has become a liability to the cause. He wants me to settle down and take up my responsibilities on the farm."

"And?" She couldn't be hearing this, the dream she thought was impossible, unattainable.

"And I'm considering it. England is beginning to take our petitions seriously. I think the trouble is all but past." Dan cleared his throat.

"That sounds wise," she said.

"I told him it would have to wait for at least a year, though."

Susannah's heart plummeted. "Oh?"

He nodded. "I'm so full of God's joy, right now, I want to share it with everyone. And you most of all. I'm coming back to finish my schooling and become ordained." With a searching look, he opened his arms. She came to him, and he enfolded her again and held her there while he breathed a prayer of thankfulness. He brought a soft curl to his face and inhaled the delicate scent of rose water.

"Do you think you could bear the sight of me day in and day out for the whole next year?"

Her nose pressed against his chest, Susannah nodded. Nothing could make her happier, she was positive of that.

"Then . . . how about night in and night out?" he asked softly.

Susannah's heart tripped over itself as she raised her eyes and met his.

"Susannah Harrington, when you are free from your contract, would you do me the very great honor of becoming my wife?"

She looked at Dan and saw the love shining from his dark eyes. A few moments ago she had been certain life held no happiness for her, and now God was casting her very dearest dream at her feet. But she could not help wondering if Dan was as confident as he appeared, or if he felt at least some small measure of the trepidation she had known so often. Something inside her wanted very much to find out. "I can't say just now. I . . . need some time to think about it."

She glanced at his face and was startled to see how pale he had gone at her words. And she could feel his hands tremble slightly as he held her.

"How much time?" he asked, his voice hoarse and uncertain.

"The time it would take," she whispered, her heart overflowing with emotion, "for one more kiss."

If you're looking for more captivating historical fiction, you'll find it in the works of these favorite fiction authors!

THE APPOMATTOX SAGA
Gilbert Morris
Intriguing, realistic stories capture the emotional and spiritual strife of the tragic Civil War era.
- #1 A Covenant of Love   0-8423-5497-2
- #2 Gate of His Enemies   0-8423-1069-X
- #3 Where Honor Dwells   0-842-6799-3
- #4 Land of the Shadow   0-8423-5742-4
- #5 Out of the Whirlwind *(New! Spring 1994)*   0-8423-1658-2

MARK OF THE LION
Francine Rivers
A Jewish Christian slave girl clings to her faith amid the forces of decadent first-century Rome.
- #1 A Voice in the Wind   0-8423-7750-6

THE SECRET OF THE ROSE
Michael Phillips
Experience the plight and steadfast faith of a noble Prussian family during World War II and its aftermath.
- #1 The Eleventh Hour   0-8423-3933-7
- #2 A Rose Remembered *(Coming Spring 1994!)*   0-8423-5929-X

THE THEYN CHRONICLES
Angela Elwell Hunt
The culture, people, and spiritual life of medieval England come alive in this rich, historical saga.
- #1 Afton of Margate Castle   0-8423-1222-6
- #2 The Troubadour's Quest *(Coming Spring 1994!)*   0-8423-1287-0